At First Flight

RENEE HARLESS

Cover design by Porcelain Paper Designs
Editor: Nicole McCurdy at Emerald Edits
Editor: Jenny Sims at Editing4Indies
Proofreader: Crystal Burnette Crystal Clear Author Services

At First Flight

RENEE HARLESS

Lila Wright never expected to flee her dress fitting covered in a cloud of lace—let alone land in a first-class seat next to the most gorgeous man she's ever seen. With mascara-streaked cheeks, a shattered heart, and no plan beyond "anywhere but here," she spills her secrets to the stranger with the sharp jawline and stormy eyes. She expects a little sympathy. She *doesn't* expect a two-week, all-expenses-paid escape on his dime.

Dean Harrington isn't just any passenger. He's a man with a heart locked up tighter than his family's luxury yacht empire. The reclusive billionaire isn't in the mood for small talk—until the runaway bride beside him turns out to be as intriguing as she is unfiltered. She's beautiful, chaotic, and clearly a flight risk. But somehow, she puts him at ease. That is, until they land—and he discovers he's now the full-time guardian of his niece and nephew.

By a twist of fate, Lila's no longer just a fleeting encounter—she's the nanny he hires from a small-town agency.
And he's her brooding, infuriatingly hot boss.

Forced under one roof in his bayside home, a temporary arrangement soon spirals into something far more complicated. Between sizzling tension and curious kids who want their uncle to be happy, Lila and Dean are on a collision course with feelings neither saw coming.

But sometimes love shows up uninvited—35,000 feet in the air.

This steamy small-town romance delivers billionaire angst, nanny sweetness, and a slow-burn love story full of heat, heart, and unexpected happily-ever-afters.

This one is for the readers who've been told they can't have it all—love, purpose, and a place to belong—and went out and proved them wrong.

Chapter One

Dean

There is something about an airport that invariably ignites my curiosity. The people rushing to get from security to the gate as the last boarding announcement is called. Or a group trying not to miss a connecting flight. Like right now, for instance.

Someone donning a bright, fire-engine-red puffy jacket with matching shoes adjusts the tiny brown-and-black purse-sized dog in their grasp, shouting and pushing their way through the crowd as they rush through the terminal. With the words spewing from their mouth, you'd think they blamed everyone else for their delay.

Or the family doing their best *not* to create their own *Home Alone* moment. The distraught-looking mom with frizzy hair fluffed around her face like a halo manically taps her small children on their heads as she counts aloud. All seven kids twirl and fight around her while the dad, or so I assume, stares down at his phone. If it wasn't for her jerking his arm as they moved on, I bet he'd have been absorbed by the other zombies controlled by the devices in their hands. No one pays any mind to their surroundings. Just going from point A to point B.

If I turn toward the squeaking barstool to my right, I see a man clad in an expensive suit, Tom Ford if I have to take a guess, with a tie loose around his neck. His jacket is precariously draped on the small back of his chair, and a pale marking on his ring finger indicates where a wedding band once rested. He sips on a cheap double whiskey and flirts with one of the two bartenders.

And if I hadn't glanced back at just the right moment, I might have missed the one woman hurrying through the terminal. Not walking, but running.

Wearing only a wedding dress.

No luggage. No bag. No jacket. This says a lot since Mother Nature glistened Connecticut with a late March flurry. Nope. The woman's only possession seems to be the small wallet, no bigger than a passport, in her hand and the white ball gown she clutches in the other. Behind her, the skirt flares like a superhero's cape. She clutches the leather wallet to her chest, weaving through the crowd with the kind of determination that makes you step aside without thinking. Even those with their focus elsewhere instinctively move out of her path.

I've yet to tear my gaze away, but just as fast as she arrives, she disappears in a bright white flash. For a second, I'm left staring at the masses as they pass, like someone frozen in time. The woman has to have been a mirage. A beautiful figment of my imagination. I didn't even see her face, but I know the vision of her will haunt me for ages. Not just the image of her in the white ensemble but also the way she frantically hurried. The wisps of her golden hair flowed like satin ribbons as they bounced against the fitted lace of her top and the subtle taking a back seat to my favorite pastime—meaningless sex.

Swirling the remains of the amber liquid in my glass, I allow my gaze to trail down her bare legs, barely encapsulated by a navy blue pencil skirt. I peg her as a CEO or business president of some sort. She has that air about her. The kind that means she's used to giving orders all day and would welcome a submissive reprieve.

I bring my glass to my mouth and watch in fascination as she licks her lips while slowly releasing the top button of her green blouse. The top of her breasts swells behind the V as if playing a game of peekaboo with me.

As the freckle-faced server rushes to fill my tawny drink again, I say, "You see that woman across the way with the red hair? Please allow her to order a drink on my tab."

"Of course, sir. Is there anything else?"

"No, just close my tab."

"Yes, sir."

A minute later, he spins back around as he sets the check in front of me. Blindly, I sign the receipt he holds out on a bill folder. The redhead tosses her clear drink in a well-practiced swallow. My silent invitation from earlier is still clearly in her eager mind.

"Thanks, Tommy," I say, reading the man's name tag. Turning my attention to the woman, I tilt my head toward the busy walkway and head toward the closest bathrooms, knowing full well that the woman will be hot on my heels.

Unlike most passengers scurrying through the airport, I travel with only my phone and wallet. In most cases, I can buy anything I need at my next stop. This time, though, I'm traveling to a five-star resort in the Scottish countryside. I'll have two weeks' worth of clothes waiting for me when I arrive, courtesy of my family's assistant. Franc is one of the hardest working men I know, especially after years of witnessing the jobs my parents put the harried man through. Yet he's never taken a vacation, even when he suffered a mild heart attack. The nurses fussed at him for being on his phone within an hour of his surgery. The man is relentless and good at his job. He's been more of a father to me than the one I share a last name with.

Thinking of my father, I rub anxiously at my chest. My family has always been significant to me, even if I haven't felt mildly important to them, but the recent news I received a couple of years ago shook me more than the volcano that took out Pompeii. Inside, my own explosion bubbles to the surface.

Walking faster than my usual saunter in an effort to clear my head, I twist my hat backward and slip open the door to an oversized companion bathroom to wait for my guest.

The moment she stumbles into the room, her luggage falls to the side, and she reaches up to cup my cheeks, sealing her lips against mine.

While I appreciate the no-nonsense greed of her kiss, I'm struck by the oddest sensation. These were not the lips I wanted to be kissing, the hips I wanted to grab, or the hair I wanted to fist. No, that all belongs to a faceless woman I saw for a split second. Someone I know nothing about and could possibly never see again but is in the forefront of my mind.

"Fuck," I say, gently pushing the woman away. My nose crinkles, and my lips sneer. "I'm sorry. I can't do this."

The room's temperature plummets until I feel like I've been transported to the southernmost tip of the planet.

"Excuse me?"

"It's not you… it's me." I recite the line, hating how it tastes in my mouth but knowing it is the most truthful explanation. I can't very well tell her that a mirage of a woman from minutes ago is the reason. Or that the moment the redhead's lips touched mine, it immediately felt wrong.

"Are you serious right now?" she asks as her cheeks redden, her sultry demeanor from earlier quickly replaced by one of anger and something akin to humiliation.

Gulping the lump in my throat, I reply, "I'm sorry. I… I need to go."

A minute later, I adjust my cap on my head as I shuffle out of the bathroom, nodding at two parents waiting for their turn in the large bathroom. Whoops. Hopefully, they don't have to deal with the angry woman still inside the room as I lose myself in the crowd.

I already know from the buzzing in my pocket and the airport intercoms that my flight is boarding. Whenever I fly commercial, I always wait until the final moment to claim my seat. The tight space makes me anxious, and even attempting to remedy my unease by purchasing the first-class seat next to mine does nothing to squash the rising agitation. What makes the situation funny is that I never had issues flying until recently.

My therapist is having a field day with the knowledge.

I go through the paces at my gate, scanning my ticket as directed, thankful that no one seems to pay me any mind. Everyone is in their own little world and doesn't notice that the sexiest billionaire heir currently boards their flight.

Fucking article.

I know Talon is having a good laugh about my new title since he had been in the number-one spot a few years ago. He met the love of his life, Aurora, and they're the perfect little family in Ashfield, Tennessee, waiting for their bundle of joy to arrive. Now I'd risen on everyone's radar.

But luckily, no one's in this airport.

"Thank you, Mr. Harrington. Enjoy your flight," the flight attendant says with an outstretched hand, guiding me toward the front of the plane to first class.

Settling in my seat, I tilt my head back as other passengers fill the cabin, using my cap to cover my face. The mindless chatter sounds like a shushing white noise, lulling me into a welcome fog.

"Here, miss, you can settle in this row here."

"Thank you so much," a wobbly voice replies. It cracks and hitches on each word.

"I'll bring you a warm towel once we get airborne. Don't you worry about a thing."

The surrounding voices slow and fall away. Or maybe I'm just too focused on hearing the rest of the conversation. I push the brim of my cap upward, and across from my seat, I see her. The woman in white—my ghost girl.

Her colossal tulle monstrosity takes over the two large seats, even as she leans toward the window. The skirt poofs out, filling every available space.

"Mr. Harrington, we'll be taking off soon. Can I get you anything before we taxi?"

I glance up at the older woman who bears the kindest of eyes. The laugh lines around the corners of her mouth put me at ease in a way that no medication ever could. The kind that reminds me of my best friend's grandmother. A woman who was closer to me than any of my immediate family.

"I'm fine, thank you. Everything okay over there?" I ask, nodding in the ghost girl's direction.

Her gray hair brushes across her shoulders as she peeks at the passenger in my row. "It will be, I'm sure."

As she walks away, I can't pull my stare from the woman. Like the sun drawing me into its orbit. Her golden strands remind me of the pale yellow rays. The kind that blinds you if you stare too long. A fluttering feeling erupts in my gut, and I wonder if it was indeed a bad idea to drink that whiskey on an empty stomach.

But all those thoughts fall away when the woman shifts in her seat, her crystal-blue stare colliding with mine. Any ability my lungs maintain to move oxygen in and out of the organ is lost. Paralyzed.

Despite my inability to do, well, anything but stare, my mouth drops open, and words rush out in a vocal cascade of embarrassment.

"Marry me?"

Her eyes widen to the size of mango pits. My favorite fruit. "What?" she whispers. I wonder if her huskiness is natural or caused by the same despair that smudged the mascara under her eyes.

I cough quickly, trying to get the oxygen moving through my system again as I register exactly what I said. Quickly, I consider retracting my words, but as her eyes move up and down my body, I'm struck silly again by her beauty.

Fuck.

She's striking in a way that doesn't ask for attention but draws it anyway, quiet and unassuming like a song you don't realize is your favorite until it's halfway through and you're holding your breath for the chorus.

Even from where I'm sitting a couple of feet away, I can see the blue color of her eyes. But they're not just any blue. Clear and piercing like a mountain lake just before dawn, the kind of blue that tells you it's seen both stillness and storms. They shine in the light, too bright to be untouched yet too shadowed not to hold stories. And the shadow is not the kind that warns you away, but the kind that dares you to lean closer and learn what caused it.

She's been crying. I can tell by the slight puff beneath those long, dark lashes and the faint shimmer that still clings to them. She blinked it all away before anyone else could notice, but not me. I notice. The delicate slope of her nose is tinged pink from where she must've wiped at it earlier.

Her cheekbones are high, sculpted to make her look like she was built from glass and grace, but they're flushed now. Not from embarrassment but something quieter. Maybe sorrow. Maybe hope. Maybe both tangled.

And God, she's soft and strong all at once. There's a bend to her spine like she's used to carrying weight that no one sees. But her shoulders are squared, chin tilted like she's daring the world to test her again.

She's the kind of woman a man doesn't just look at. She's the kind he feels. Deep down. Under the ribs. Somewhere sacred.

And before I even know her name, I want to know what it would take to put joy where that sadness lives behind her eyes.

"I said, marry me. Seems like you're dressed for the occasion, and I don't need anything fancy. Pilots aren't like ship captains, so they can't perform a ceremony. And even though I was ordained for my best friend's wedding, that was only good in Florida. But I'm certain we can figure that out when we land."

She stares as she morphs into a gasping catfish-human hybrid. Unfortunately for her, I'm not deterred in the slightest. I only find her more intriguing.

"Is this some kind of sick joke, you jerk?" Her back goes rigid against the cushioned seat. "And what gives you the right to poke fun at someone not knowing what they've been through?"

Holding my hands up in surrender, I try to crack this newly formed icy exterior on my row-mate. "I'm not poking fun. It's clear you've gone through something, and I was hoping to help lighten the mood. Make you smile."

Her eyes narrow into slits as she assesses me. A metallic taste trickles in my mouth as I bite my tongue, waiting for her to recognize me from the article this morning or any of the various gossip rags on the market. But then her gaze clears, and she huffs out a puff of air, causing the corner of my lips to tilt upward.

"I'm guessing that smirk works on most women."

"Zero fail rate," I explain as I adjust my cap, hating how it pulls at my hair.

"Well, I hate to tell you, but I'm a lost cause."

I pause to see if she elaborates, but I should know better. I can tell by the way she continues to sit with her arms crossed that she keeps her secrets close to her chest.

"Naw, no one is a lost cause."

She guffaws and nearly slaps her hand across her mouth at what is clearly an unexpected reaction.

"We really should get married. I could have everything set up by the time we land."

"Oh, my gosh." She adjusts herself in the seat, tugging her skirt closer, using it as a fluffy shield while her eyes shift up and down my body. Usually, that kind of perusal implies an invitation, but I know better than to suggest more than my marriage proposal with her.

"So since we're getting married, why don't you tell me your name?"

"I'm not telling you my name," she mumbles as I stick out my hand across the aisle.

"I'm your future husb—"

"Are you for real right now?"

A normal man would have cowered at her tone. Her frown grew with each passing second. But I'm no average man, and I've been known to poke a bear or two. But I have an end goal in mind for my ghost girl.

"One hundred percent. Ever wanted to do something spontaneous?"

"I… well… I."

"Come on," I say as I lean over the empty seat, shifting my hand back, my elbow resting on the aisle side armrest. "What have you got to lose? Marry me, ghost girl."

"You're crazy." I almost believe her. Almost let her words scathe my skin with their intention, but then the corner of her mouth tilts upward, and it all fizzles away.

Making myself seem like a lunatic is all worth it by getting her to smile.

"Certifiable," I agree.

The plane chooses that moment to lurch forward and start taxiing down the runway. The attendants go through their routine regarding safety, and the flight attendant from earlier checks on our bridal guest one last time before the engines kick into full gear.

As a kid, takeoffs sent me into a spiral of motion sickness. On our private jet, the attendants always had crackers and ginger ale ready once the plane leveled out. My motion sickness improved as I got older and utilized a plane more than the average billionaire. But as the plane surges through the sky, reaching a higher altitude with each passing second, my nausea is combated not by ginger or salty carbs but by a woman whose hands clutch the armrests as if her life depended on it. Her ivory skin has turned an ashen shade of white, matching her fingernails clawing at the metal of the support, all in stark contrast to the dark lashes fanned along her cheeks as she clenches her eyes tightly shut. The neckline of her dress moves in tandem with her short spurts of breath as she tries to pull air into her lungs. She's at a point I recognize all too well—a looming panic attack.

Peering over the headrest, I search for the flight attendants, ignoring my own wave of uneasiness as the aircraft continues to climb. When I don't locate them, I quickly unlock my seat belt and slither across the row from my seats to hers as if I were in the newest spy movie. Thankfully, no one says anything as I move.

"Hey." My voice comes out low and rough, not quite a whisper but not loud enough to startle her. "You okay?"

She doesn't answer. Her shoulders are pulled in so tight I swear she's trying to disappear inside herself. I hesitate. This isn't something I do. I don't reach across invisible lines. I don't insert myself where I'm not wanted, but something about her makes me forget all that. My body moves before my mind can catch up.

I reach over and wrap my hand around hers, easing her fingers free from the support they've welded themselves to. Her skin is warm. Soft. Too soft for how hard she's holding herself together.

Her breath hitches, and I expect her to pull away, to flinch, but she doesn't.

I keep holding her hand, cradling it in mine. Her palm is smaller than I expected. Delicate. But her grip tightens like she's been waiting for someone to anchor her.

My thumb moves in slow strokes over her clenched knuckles. A steady back and forth that feels instinctive even though nothing about this is familiar.

I've never done this before. Never offered comfort like it's mine to give. I don't know the first thing about calming panic attacks. But I don't feel out of my depth sitting here and holding her hand.

I feel steady.

Cracking one eye open, she peers over at me. And despite whatever she thought of me during our initial meeting, pink stains her cheeks as she flips her hand around and intertwines our fingers together.

For the first time in decades, I feel a sense of peace, even as the plane ascends to new heights. She must feel the same because her breath begins to slow, her skin returning to its just barely sun-kissed state.

By the time the plane levels and the seat belt light flicks off, ghost girl sports a healthy sheen of nervousness over her pale skin as our hands unclench. But not the kind related to the takeoff of the flight. More like she doesn't know what to do with me.

"So have you given it any more thought?" I ask as the attendants work their way through the aisle with their snacks and drinks. They'd serve us lunch a bit later during the almost seven-hour flight.

At first, I wonder if the bride hears me, but slowly, she grapples with her dress as she turns to face me.

"I don't even know you."

"Well, I'm hoping to change that. Dean Harrington," I say, turning to face her completely and holding a hand out. She stares wide-eyed at it as if waiting for my fingers to grow claws and score her delicate skin, clearly not recalling how she gripped my hand minutes ago. When she realizes I'm nothing more than an ordinary man with a propensity to say exactly what's on my mind, she clasps her hand within mine.

"Hello, Dean."

"Any name to go with that shake?"

She hesitates as her palm slips free and brushes away fake lent from her tulle skirt. "Lila," she says quietly, eyes cast downward. She quickly brings her gaze back up to meet mine and speaks with more strength. "My name is Lila."

"Well, Lila, we have a pretty long flight. Care to share why you're wearing a wedding dress on the way to Scotland?"

Her hand trembles as she reaches toward her hair and tucks a loose strand behind her ear. I wish I'd been the one to push the glossy strand away from her face. I bet it feels like the finest of silk. Something woven straight from the cocoon.

"It's… complicated."

With a quick flick of my wrist, my Patek Phillip watch glistens under the airline's dim overhead lighting. I make an exaggerated motion of looking at the time before I meet her eyes again.

"Well, it seems we have roughly six and a half hours to fill. Unless you want to sit in this confined tube and watch a movie or something."

"I don't have earbuds."

The attendant steps to our row and visibly jolts when she notices I've switched seats. Before she can get a word out, I explain that our guest in row 3A was suffering from a panic attack, and I attempted to calm her down. Her eyes immediately dart to Lila's, who surprisingly nods and assures the attendant everything is okay.

When she's satisfied, she moves along to the next row.

"Read a book?" I offer, smiling as Lila rolls her eyes and sinks back into her chair. The turmoil she was dealing with earlier, whatever caused her to dash onto the plane wearing a wedding dress, falls away like the bark of a birch tree.

"I haven't read a book in months."

"Want me to guess what kind of books you read?" I peg her as the kind to read smutty romances of the monster variety. Maybe paranormal. I know from my friends and their wives the kind of books that are all over social media. The steamy kind. The sex-filled kind. The kind I'd read a few of, to none of my friends' knowledge, to make sure I knew the level of expectations women held nowadays.

"No."

"I'm guessing it was a romance with dragons and fae. That sound about right?"

"Wha—how do you… I mean… no, it was a small town."

"Ah, my favorite." She probably thinks I'm joking, but the small-town trope has proven to be my favorite. Something about them reminds me of the romances from classic movies.

My ghost girl, the woman who will haunt me for life, guffaws, which only leaves me yearning to hear a full-bellied laugh rise from her chest. I'm enraptured by the woman wearing white as her laughter tinkles around the cabin. Men around us take notice as if her chuckle is a calling card for all un-mated males.

"You're the most ridiculous man I've ever met."

"Well, that's the nicest thing you've ever said to me."

"Are you normally this strange, or is it just for my benefit?"

"My only goal was to see you smile, ghost girl. Hearing you laugh was like watching the northern lights for the first time. Beautiful and fleeting."

"I… I have had little to smile about recently, but… it's been nice to laugh. Thank you."

"You're welcome. And my offer still stands."

"What offer?" she asks as she turns in her seat to fiddle with the screen attached to the back of the seat in front of her. The window cover at her side has remained closed since takeoff as if something unwelcome could peer in at any moment.

"The one where you marry me."

Lila's shoulders jerk subtly as she speaks, and I wonder if it has anything to do with the predicament she's found herself in.

"I don't think so."

"Well, we'll just have to change that, won't we?"

Chapter Two

Lila

I don't fly often, if ever. This is only the second time I've stepped foot on a plane. I much prefer driving, even across the country. Not just because I'm scared of heights and known to suffer a panic attack when I feel overwhelmed but also because flying costs money… a lot more than a measly trip in my car.

That was all until I met Prescott Hoolihan, who also didn't enjoy flying but drove us around in his family's courtesy Town Car. His family didn't believe in driving themselves anywhere, either. Of course, his detestation of flying was because he was a snooty bastard who refused to fly commercially.

Just thinking of Prescott causes a shiver of fear to ripple across my spine like I've stepped into a cave of ice.

"Cold?" the man in the now occupied seat beside me asks.

"No," I assure him, but instead of taking me at my word, he slips his jacket off his shoulders and holds it out for me to take. I'm helpless to ignore the way his shirt fits snugly around his bicep. I bet the dark maroon color brings out his eyes, which I would be able to see better if he ever removed his hat. The shadow from the cap does little to diminish his strong jawline with the hint of scruff that makes my stomach flip. His dark hair curls just slightly under the hat's confines, giving him a rugged, unruly appearance. At first glance, I take him as a cowboy or the storm chasers I binge on documentaries about when I can't sleep. Something about him gives off a wild confidence in not just his looks but also himself, and it's damn attractive. So damn enticing that I grab the jacket from his hand.

"Thanks," I mumble, slipping the warm material across my shoulders.

"You're welcome. So what are we watching?" His chin jerks toward the screen I'd brought to life a bit ago once the plane reached altitude.

"I… I don't know. To be honest, I need something to take my mind off the day."

"Well…" He smiles, and I immediately feel my pulse pick up. It's a crime for someone to be so good-looking without even trying. The man could have anyone, female or male, on this plane at his beck and call. He's that incredibly gorgeous. And I don't even notice the telltale signs of a ring wearer. No tan line. No indentation. So, either he's a playboy or not looking for a relationship.

"I have just the movie."

He starts pressing the buttons on the screen, and I even find his fingers appealing. Long and lean, with a bit of roughness around the knuckles like he isn't afraid of a fight if a situation calls for it.

"How do you feel about *The Fast and the Furious* franchise?"

I don't want to tell him it's one of my favorites, and after the morning I've had, I don't want to taint the series.

"Maybe something else?"

Dean grumbles under his breath as he searches through the movie section again.

"If you want to watch it, you can move back to your seat," I advise him, only for him to smirk in my direction.

"You're not getting rid of me so quickly, ghost girl."

He continues pressing the buttons while I ask, "Ghost girl? You've called me that a few times now."

"Yeah, well, I'd think it's pretty obvious."

Snickering, I nearly slap my hand over my mouth before saying, "Uh, clearly not."

He chuckles, and I hate the way his laugh feels like a soothing caress. "Really? I mean, with the way you were running through the airport with all that… stuff… fluffed around you, you looked like an apparition. The name came easily." Dean pins me with his stare after his explanation, and I'm almost scared to pull away, but at the same time, I'm scared to maintain it. Something is… unsettling about the way he looks at me as if he can *see* me in a way no one else can. Which is ridiculous, considering we just met minutes ago.

"Make sense?" he tacks on, and I nod before forcing my eyes from his and looking at my screen where he's requested a group watch of the movie *Runaway Bride*.

"Really? This is what you want to watch?"

"Well, I thought it was apt for the moment, and it's one of my sister's favorites."

"You have a sister?" I ask as I switch on the subtitles to read along with the movie. Sitting in first class, I know I can ask for a free set of earbuds, but I hate how those things never fit in my ear correctly.

Dean settles into his seat, his arm brushing against mine on the middle armrest. "Want to know things about me now, fiancée?"

Fiancée. Did he just say *fiancée*?

For a heartbeat, I think I misheard him or maybe the altitude is messing with my brain. Or maybe the exhaustion. Or the heartbreak. I glance over at him, fully expecting a smirk, a wink, something to tell me he's just trying to make me laugh. God knows I need it.

But he's looking at me like he means it. Like the idea of marrying a total stranger isn't the most insane thing either of us could be thinking right now. And somehow, that look, steady, amused but not mocking, unhooks something in me. I feel it in the center of my chest, like the first warm day after a brutal winter.

He's clearly a little unhinged. Or self-assured in a way only men with broad shoulders and sinfully good looks can get away with. But he's also funny, unexpectedly so. And it's the first time I've smiled all day. A real, startled, *God-I-forgot-I-could-still-feel* kind of smile.

I should brush it off and tell him I'm not in the mood for jokes, not after the day I've had. But my brain short-circuits when his eyes meet mine again. There's something behind them. Something calm and sure and just reckless enough to match the chaos inside me.

And for one crazy second, I think… maybe he *isn't* kidding. And that terrifies me almost as much as it thrills me. Because today was supposed to be the worst day of my life.

And somehow, with his rough voice and ridiculous suggestion, this stranger is making it feel like it could be the start of something else entirely.

I cross my arms, mostly to stop my hands from trembling. "We are not engaged. And I was simply making conversation," I bite out, praying my voice holds more certainty than I feel.

"*Yet*. Not engaged *yet*," he says with a smirk that should be illegal. It's too confident, too knowing, like he sees something in me I haven't dared admit out loud. And dammit, it's starting to work. My defenses fray a little more with every second I spend under that gaze.

I toss him a look, the only weapon I have left. "Do you just wake up with such a large ego, or does it progress as the day goes on?"

His smile turns wicked, eyes sparkling like he's been waiting for this exact moment. "Oh, sweetheart. This isn't ego. It's called knowing what I want. And that, ghost girl, is you."

My breath catches, and not just from the heat behind those words. *Ghost girl.* It's a tease, but it cuts too close to the truth. Because I have been a ghost lately—drifting, empty, transparent in a life I thought was mine. A woman who lost herself in someone else's story. And now here's this stranger, talking about wanting me like I'm real. Like I'm *worth* wanting.

I should laugh it off, roll my eyes, and change the subject. Instead, my heart does this ridiculous lurch, and my pulse thrums low and steady in places it has no business waking up.

Because maybe... for the first time in too long, I want to be wanted back.

The movie begins playing, and before I know it, Maggie Carpenter is riding on the back of a horse through a field, leaving the altar yet again. Thank goodness I hadn't let the sham of a relationship get to that point.

Peeking at my newly acquired companion seated next to me, I notice that his lips move subtly, and then it occurs to me that he's mouthing the words.

"How many times have you seen this movie?"

Dean smiles as he replies, "One time too many. It was my sister's favorite form of torture."

Nodding, I twist in my seat to face him more directly. "I know all about that. I have four brothers and sisters."

"Four?"

"Yep. Never a dull moment in our household."

"That sounds... amazing, actually." A wave of sadness fills our confined space. Even without saying much more, I know that his sister is a sore subject. So it surprises me when he continues. "My sister and I only got to spend a little bit of time together growing up. Holidays. The occasional family vacation. Most of our days were spent at boarding school. But when we were together, it was awesome." Dean pauses, his eyes searching mine. "But people change."

"Yeah." That is a sentiment I know all too well. Everything I knew over the last two years had changed. Not just me but also my so-called fiancé.

"You know what this is a great moment for?" he asks as he grabs a bag of chips from the attendant, who I hadn't even noticed was standing in our row again. I kindly accept the package of cookies she offers and select my lunch.

"No, I don't know what this is a great moment for," I reply, startling Dean as he shoves a few chips into his mouth.

"Huh? Oh! This is a great time for sharing. I gave you a peek at me. You give me a peek at you. And I'm sure you can guess what I'm curious about."

It didn't take a rocket scientist to figure out what Dean was referencing. The dress. The airport. The chaos.

"I'm not sure—" I say, my voice thinner than I'd like. It trembles under the weight of the words I'm not ready to say.

Dean doesn't press. Doesn't prod. He simply reaches over, his hand finding mine with quiet steadiness. His palm is warm, grounding. His thumb sweeps gently across my knuckles in the kind of motion that shouldn't feel so comforting from a stranger.

"Just tell me what you want," he says softly. "I'm not here to judge."

And it's that—his voice, his steadiness, his lack of judgment—that almost undoes me completely. My stomach coils. That familiar churn of nerves, of regret, of raw, unprocessed panic. It hasn't left me since I fled the boutique. It's still there, twisting tighter every time I breathe.

"I was…" I stop, swallowing past the lump rising fast in my throat. I glance away, out the window across the way, where clouds drift by lazily, so unaffected by the disaster unraveling inside me. My eyes focus on nothing and everything at once. A smear on the glass. The blurred outline of Dean's reflection. Anything but him.

"I was at my final dress fitting," I say eventually, voice brittle. "My wedding's in two weeks."

The words feel foreign on my tongue now. Like they don't belong to me anymore.

"My fiancé—" My chest squeezes tight around the word. "He's been handling everything. The venue, the guest list, the menu. Even the dress."

I let out a bitter breath, part laugh, part sob. "I didn't even get to pick it. His mother did. Satin and lace and… expectations. My own family wasn't involved."

The memory crashes back, vivid and unrelenting. Standing on that platform, the seamstress pinning the hem while I stared at myself in the mirror. Except I didn't recognize the woman staring back. I looked like a stranger in someone else's fantasy. A perfectly dressed mannequin in a life that wasn't mine.

My fingers twitch in Dean's grasp, fidgeting like I need to escape even now. I shift in my seat, pulse fluttering. My throat burns with the effort not to cry again. I already cried in the dressing room. In the Uber. In the airport. I'm out of tears. At least, I should be.

"And while I stood there trying to breathe in a dress I didn't choose, I got a text," I say, eyes locked on a scratch in the tray table. "From a number I didn't recognize."

I blink hard.

"She sent me a photo of my fiancé. With her. At their own wedding. Apparently, he's had another family this whole time."

My voice splinters on that last word. The truth that's been banging against the inside of my rib cage since it hit me like a freight train hours ago.

I sniff, the sound embarrassingly loud in the quiet hum of the plane.

"I didn't scream. I didn't confront him. I didn't even think. I just…" My eyes dart up to meet his, and the kindness there nearly breaks me all over again. "I ran. Grabbed my stuff and booked the next flight out. I didn't even care where it was going.

"His mom didn't even try to stop me. She just let me run out the door. Which really just left me more confused at how she was involved. How his entire family was involved."

The silence that follows isn't awkward. It's heavy and still.

I pull my hand back gently, needing space, needing air. I wrap my arms around my stomach like I'm trying to hold myself together, like I'm afraid if I don't, I'll splinter apart at the seams.

I don't tell him about the way my heart cracked open in that boutique. How it wasn't just the betrayal but also the realization that I hadn't been living my own life in months. Maybe years.

I don't tell him about the shame or the anger that gnawed at my chest the entire ride to the airport. The humiliation of realizing I was never the main character in my own story. Just a supporting actress in his.

But something in Dean's presence makes me want to. Makes the words itch beneath my skin.

"I don't usually…" My voice is smaller now. "I don't fall apart like this."

Dean nods slowly like he understands. Like he knows more is beneath the surface, and he's willing to wait me out. And somehow, that makes it easier to keep going.

"I think I've been pretending for so long, I forgot what it felt like to breathe for myself," I whisper. "To do something reckless. Or stupid. Or free."

And maybe that's what this is—freedom. Messy, terrifying, unplanned freedom.

I glance at Dean, half expecting judgment, pity, or maybe even discomfort. But there's none of that. Just quiet steadiness. Like he sees all of it, all of *me*, and he's not running.

Dean's eyes soften as he reaches for my hand again. Like he needs the tether as much as I do. The feel of his thumb brushing back and forth against my knuckle soothes the rising anger that builds as I recall what led me to this point.

"What do you think you're going to do next?"

Isn't that the most terrifying question to consider? I have no idea what I'm doing next. Pretty certain in the midst of the mayhem I caused, I won't have a job waiting for me. Or the luxury apartment I shared with my now ex.

After this spur-of-the-moment trip, I am going to be broke and homeless. And there is no way I'm crawling back to my parents' home. At least not right away.

Suddenly, a warmth spreads across my chin and jaw. Dean's strong fingers caress my skin.

"Why the frown?"

Jerking my head from his hold, I turn my attention back to the movie screen. No need to share more of my upended life with this guy who looks like he walked out of a magazine spread.

"No reason."

"Lila," he sighs.

"It's nothing you need to worry about."

Mumbling under his breath, I swear I hear him say, "Feels like I should."

My head jerks forward, hard enough to snap me out of sleep with a soft gasp. I blink, confused and momentarily lost in the muted hum of the plane and the low flicker of cabin lights. My neck aches. My body feels folded in on itself, stiff from the cramped seat and the weight of a day I haven't fully processed.

I must've dozed off. God knows how. But the panic is already creeping back in with racing thoughts, the prick of embarrassment in my cheeks.

Then I feel him. Dean.

His hand is gentle as it touches my arm, then shifts to cradle the back of my head. Nothing about the motion is invasive. It's just quiet assurance, something I wasn't expecting from a stranger. He guides me softly until my head comes to rest against his shoulder, solid and warm.

"Rest," he murmurs, low and steady like the world hasn't fallen apart today. "You can lean on me."

And somehow, I believe him.

So I do. I let go of the tension, the spinning thoughts, the part of me still waiting to shatter. His shoulder is strong beneath me, steady like he was built for moments like this. His scent wraps around me, clean and woodsy with a hint of something I can't name but already know I'll crave later. He smells like warmth. Like safety.

My muscles melt before I can stop them. The exhaustion I've been pushing down all day comes back with full force, and I let it take me. Let him hold just this one piece of me, like it's no trouble at all.

And just before the weight of sleep pulls me under again, I think, just barely, I feel the softest press of lips against the top of my head.

But maybe I'm dreaming.

God, I hope I'm not.

During the rest of the flight, we remained quiet except for some small bits of conversation and a few chuckles we shared during another movie. He tells me how he's traveling to help his friend scope out a new location for his hotels and how he's hoping to spend a few days relaxing. When the movie ends, Dean silently switches to the earlier nixed film, the corner of his mouth tilting upward when he notices my reluctant smile. Damn smug bastard.

Before long, the pilot announces the plane's upcoming descent into Edinburgh Airport. My body immediately tenses, fingers clenching around the rough material of my tulle skirt. The plane bumps mid-air as it hits a rough patch of turbulence, our first on the long flight. Just as my eyes are about to clench shut, I hear the sudden intake of air beside me. My attention diverts from our possible plummet to death to Dean's face. His tanned skin is now painted in white, and the muscles in his taut chest are frozen solid as he holds his breath.

"Dean," I whisper just as the plane rolls again, my stomach mimicking the movement. When he doesn't budge, I repeat his name. "Dean, look at me," I urge.

Finally, he turns his face toward mine as it rests against the back of the seat, tilted toward the ceiling. For the first time, I can make out his eyes from beneath the brim of his hat. They're wide, with pupils no more than tiny black dots in the center of his brown irises.

A third time, the plane rolls, and I immediately reach out to grip his hand, clutching at the denim covering his legs. His nails claw at the material, turning white at their attempt.

My fingers slip through his, and I watch in amazement as Dean's chest moves, releasing the breath he held so deeply.

He holds me the same way I had him during the takeoff—like I was his anchor.

After what feels like a lifetime, the plane jerks as the landing gear meets asphalt, and the plane's speed begins to decrease. Despite this, Dean doesn't release my fingers. Instead, his gaze drops to our clutched hands, and his fingers loosen slightly as he adjusts his grip.

"Thank you," he whispers as the plane lurches to a stop and the other passengers start to rise, something I never really understood.

Eventually, it's our turn to exit the plane, and I'm fascinated to find that Dean doesn't linger any longer than I do.

"No bags?" I ask as we travel across the passenger boarding bridge.

"Nope. I have my bags waiting for me."

I try to ignore the looks of curiosity from the other passengers as I enter the airport, but cinch Dean's jacket closer around my chest. It's only now that I realize what a state I must appear. Full-length wedding gown and a windbreaker.

"I should probably grab something from one of these stores before I go any farther."

My companion peers over his broad shoulder at the boutique across the way. The store boasts mostly scarves and jackets, but I notice a few pairs of pants over in the corner.

Together, we rifle through the racks until I find a pair of simple black pants and a graceful cashmere cardigan. I nearly choke when I glimpse the price tag.

At the register, I hand the woman my card in the tiny wallet stored in the pocket of my dress as Dean reaches into his own pocket, retrieving his cell phone. Whatever message is on the other end causes his carefree smile to drop.

"Everything okay?" I ask as the worker types a few things on her computer.

"Yeah. Just a friend sending me a stupid article."

"What's it about?" I ask as the worker holds my card toward me.

"Sorry, but this card is declined. Do you have another form of payment?"

The words hit me like a slap I should've seen coming. My throat tightens as I stare at the screen behind the counter, blinking hard, like maybe if I give it a second, the numbers will change. That the error message will vanish. But it doesn't. It's there in big, bold letters.

Declined.

Fuck.

I knew, *knew*, this was a possibility. Prescott and his family don't play fair. But I thought I'd have more time. Maybe a few days. Some sort of buffer. Something. It hasn't even been eight hours since I walked out of that boutique and left behind the life I was supposed to be grateful for.

And now here I am. In a different country, in a boisterous airport hoping for some sort of relief, clutching a now-useless credit card like it's a lifeline that's snapped right in the middle.

"I—uh, hold on a second." My voice trembles as I reach into my nearly empty wallet no bigger than my trusty passport I'd just received the day before, like there's a magic card I forgot existed. But there's nothing. Just my nearly empty checking card and a loyalty punch card for a bookstore back home. *Buy ten, get one free.*

I almost laugh. Almost.

I'm suddenly hyperaware of the woman behind the counter watching me, her expression kind but tight, like she's seen this before. The look people give someone who's unraveling quietly in public.

I mutter an apology and step aside, letting the next person in line move forward as I back away from the counter. My chest is tight, like there's a vise around my ribs. My hands won't stop shaking. And my heart, my idiot, impulsive, broken heart, is still trying to catch up.

This was supposed to be freedom.

When I booked the flight, I didn't care where it went. Scotland popped up on the list like some romantic cliché, and I clicked before I could change my mind. My fingers trembled as I typed in my information, pressing submit while still in the Uber, the boutique in the rearview mirror, my reflection in the window looking like a ghost. I didn't even look at the itinerary. I just… ran.

Now, the running has caught up with me.

I have no pounds. No working cards. No hotel reservation. No actual plan beyond escape. I don't even have toothpaste.

What the hell was I thinking?

The panic creeps in, slow and sharp, like cold air filling a cracked window. I don't cry. Not yet. But the tears are there, heavy and threatening, pressing behind my eyes like a dam that won't hold much longer.

I left because staying felt like death by slow suffocation. But now I'm here and don't know how to breathe. I'm alone in this country, this city in all its beauty, and even the air feels foreign.

What now?

What the hell do I do now?

Right now, I'm grounded, panicked, and broke. But I didn't come here to fall apart. I came here to remember who I was before all of this. Before Prescott. Before the lies and the lace and the feeling of being trapped in someone else's dream. I came here to figure out what freedom actually looks like. Even if it scares the hell out of me.

"I… I don't—I'm—" My words trip over themselves, embarrassment heating my cheeks faster than I can form a coherent thought.

Dean doesn't miss a beat. "Here," he says smoothly, sliding his card across the counter in exchange for mine, while simultaneously propping a small bag onto the counter with a recognizable mobile phone logo plastered on the front.

"No!" I protest, trying and failing to push his annoyingly solid arm back. "You don't have to do that."

His grip stays firm, steady. "I want to. We're practically married, remember? What's mine is yours." His grin is all smug charm, and it sends a ripple through my already chaotic chest.

Before I can argue further, the worker lifts the card from Dean's fingers with a small, amused smirk. "Oh, meal do naidheachd."

I blink, startled by the unfamiliar phrase. My gaze swings to her face. "Wait—what?"

"It means congratulations in Scottish, sweetheart," Dean explains as he swiftly wraps his arm around my waist and tugs me against his body. I gasp at the collision and the immediate sense of warmth that seeps through my clothes.

With a Southern drawl, Dean says, "Thank you, ma'am." I swear I see a faint redness grow on her cheeks. At least I know I'm not the only one not immune to his good looks.

Wordlessly, I take the bag and clutch it against my chest as I allow Dean to guide me out of the store with his hand on my lower back, all the while explaining that he purchased a burner phone for me with unlimited everything.

I'm so overwhelmed I barely realize that he takes us toward a bathroom across the way. It's one of the larger family-style kind, and as I shuffle inside, Dean follows suit.

"What do you think you're doing?" I screech, feeling like a bunny cornered by a fox.

"I assume you'll need help with your dress."

I did, in fact, need help unlacing the back of the dress. I was grateful during the flight that I hadn't needed his help when I used the restroom. The nice flight attendant had helped me gather the overabundant material for the much larger first-class lavatory.

"Fine, but that's it. I have to pee, and I'd like to keep what little dignity I have remaining intact."

"Of course."

Removing his jacket, I drape it over my arms as I turn my back toward him, gathering my loose hair over my shoulder. A few seconds pass, and I wonder what's holding him up. I know the laces and pearls are intricate, but nothing I didn't think he could manage. When I peer over my shoulder, my skin grows hot as I take in the tic of his jaw and his hungry eyes.

Slowly, he reaches outward toward the center of my back. Instead of touching the material, the tips of his fingers brush against the skin of my back, sliding a loose piece of hair gently across my shoulder blade to join the rest of the strands. I hold my breath through the entire contact.

Then with deft fingers that leave me considering that he must have done this before, he loosens the laces until they fall through the final loop. With my arm holding his jacket, I squeeze the top of my dress against my body as he unfastens the few buttons that grace the bottom of the bodice.

No one moves. No one speaks. And Lord knows I'm not about to peer over at the mirror to look at him again. And just when I think he's going to step away, Dean's knuckle traces each vertebra of my spine as it travels toward the base of my neck. I could do nothing to fight against the shiver that racks my body. This stranger has me ready to bend at his will, and I'm not even sure he's aware. But then again, I'm certain Dean realizes the power he holds over women.

"Dean," I moan as his finger pauses, and as if I've imagined the entire thing, his warmth slips away.

A chill settles in the room as Dean coughs and says, "You're all set. I'll wait for you outside."

Not trusting myself to look at him, I whisper that I'll be done shortly. Once I hear the door click shut, I reach out to lock it, then start pushing the white monstrosity down my body. In the mirror across the way, I stare at the pool of lace and mesh as it rests in a heap at my feet. My body is covered in nothing more than nude-colored panties and a matching cotton bra. Simple and plain, just how I'd felt this morning at the dress fitting. A pauper among all the princesses. But as my gaze catches my stare in the mirror, I'm amazed to find my cheeks flushed and my eyes shimmering. And I know, without a doubt, that the vivacity in my body comes from one person—Dean.

After relieving myself, I dig through the bag and pull out the soft black pants, grateful they're wide-leg so I don't have to wrestle with my converse in a public bathroom. The pink cardigan is just as soft as it looked, the kind that feels like borrowed comfort—safe, simple, warm. I shrug it on quickly, tugging the hem down over my hips, and glance back at the discarded wedding dress slumped in the corner like a ghost of the life I was supposed to step into.

For one reckless, wonderful second, I consider stuffing the whole damn thing into the trash can. Just bury it under the paper towels and soap wrappers.

But I don't. Unfortunately, being that I'm broke, I figure I can sell the dress to a local consignment shop. At least that may help me get enough cash to find a place to sleep for the night.

Shoving the material with all my strength into the plastic bag, I'm disappointed to find half of the skirt spilling from the sides. Gathering all my strength, I punch the material one last time and pretend the last year of my life didn't happen.

Because no matter how far I run, Prescott and his family will come looking. And not because they're worried. Because they're calculating. Because to them, everything is about appearances, and my disappearance is nothing more than a wrinkle in their perfectly curated life.

They'll try my parents first. My sweet, unsuspecting folks back in Coral Bell Cove, who have no idea how far I drifted from them in the last year. No idea that I stopped calling as often, that I missed birthdays and holidays and Sunday dinners, not because I didn't care, but because I was constantly being told I shouldn't.

Prescott never outright said, *you can't talk to them.* He was smarter than that. Smoother. A master at the subtle redirection. *Don't you want to spend that weekend at the fundraiser with my mother? Isn't it a little childish to still be so close to your family?* At first, it felt like a compromise. And then, slowly, it felt like erasure.

I thought I was imagining things when he started taking longer business trips. I told myself I was being paranoid when his texts got shorter and less frequent while he was away. I didn't have proof of anything, just the empty spaces he left behind and the gnawing feeling that I wasn't his only priority. Maybe not even his first.

Still, I tried. God, I tried. I smiled at his mother's charity galas, laughed politely at his father's off-color jokes, swallowed my discomfort and wore dresses I didn't pick, ate food I didn't like, and nodded through conversations I didn't believe in.

And the deeper I was pulled into their world, the smaller mine became.

Until today.

Until the text.

And just like that, the fragile fantasy shattered.

Now, standing in this cramped restroom in an outfit I couldn't even buy for myself, staring at the crumpled gown in the bag, it's clearer than ever: I gave up too much trying to fit into a life that never had room for me.

And whatever Prescott's family was hiding, whatever skeletons were polished up and paraded behind designer suits and practiced smiles, I sure don't know the half of it. Not yet. And I'm not even certain I want to. But what little I've learned from being around them is that truth will come soon enough.

I'm not crawling back into their world. I'm not answering their calls or explaining myself or smoothing this over with grace and pleasantries. Not this time.

I smooth down the cardigan and tighten my hands around the plastic handles of the bag, then square my shoulders.

I imagine Prescott with his superior grin when he learns I know of his wife. I think about my dream job tumbling from my grasp when I agreed to marry my ex. And then, suddenly, I imagine Dean's fingers on my back. Though I visualize his face, what I feel is irritation at myself for allowing him to let me feel temptation again. This morning, I'd sworn off men altogether, and then Dean waltzed into my airplane and threw my world for a loop.

"I'm such a fucking idiot," I mumble as I tug his jacket over my shoulders. I can't believe I even thought for a millisecond that I should let Dean do more than unlace my dress. For that small moment in time, I felt like he was unlacing a part of me that had been tightened beyond measure to fit someone's perspective of what I should be. Not who I was.

Frosty exterior back in place, I step out of the bathroom, expecting to find Dean waiting with that saucy grin of his, but he's nowhere close by. Stepping farther into the terminal, I'm jostled around as passengers rush toward their destinations. Just as my frustration builds to an explosive level, I spot Dean leaning against a large window with his phone pressed to his ear. There is no hint of the carefree man from earlier. The one before me looks battered and beaten. A level of exhaustion that I've seen only a handful of times.

"Hey," I say, the brightness in my voice forced and hollow and so at odds with the knot of nerves sitting heavy in my stomach. It doesn't sound like me, not really. But it's the only thing I can manage, and I hope it's enough to break the tension crackling in the air like a storm waiting to snap.

Dean turns toward me, slowly, like he's peeling himself out of some place dark and consuming. His eyes, once warm and teasing on the plane, are colder now—glassy and unreadable. They pass right over me like I'm invisible or, worse, like I'm interrupting something sacred. The change in him is jarring.

He ends the call with a sharp motion, slamming his fist into the metal frame of the window. The sound echoes in the quiet space, and I jump. My breath stutters in my chest.

"Fuck," he mutters, dragging the worn cap from his head and pushing his fingers through his hair. His shoulders are tense, practically vibrating with whatever emotion he's trying and failing to keep inside.

For a second, I don't move, don't speak.

And I probably should walk away. Give him space. Remind myself that I barely know this man. That just yesterday he was a stranger in first class who made me laugh when I thought I'd forgotten how. But that same man also held my hand when I couldn't breathe. Sat beside me and offered comfort without strings or questions. Just warmth and steadiness. And now, I see the cracks in him, too.

I can tell whoever was on the other end of that call rattled him and cut him in a way he wasn't prepared for. I see it in the slight tremble of his jaw. The haunted flicker behind his eyes. He looks like he's unraveling, like he's barely holding it together with frayed thread and sheer willpower.

Still, his beauty hits me like a punch to the chest. He's all hard edges and quiet fire—dark hair that curls at the ends, brows pulled together with frustration, and a jaw that could have been chiseled from stone. He looks like he belongs in a black-and-white film. Or a magazine. Or my daydreams.

"Everything okay?" I ask, my voice softer now. Gentler.

His response cuts sharp and fast.

"No," he barks, voice rough and frayed.

The sound slices right through me. Not because I'm scared. This… this is something else. This is a man pushed too far.

And then, just like that, he seems to catch himself. Like a switch being flipped, his posture changes. His shoulders dip, his hand loosens at his side, and when his eyes meet mine again, they're clear. Apologetic.

"Yes," he adds, more controlled. "Everything is fine."

The liar in me wants to nod. Accept it. Pretend I didn't see the moment his mask slipped. But I did. And it tugs at something deep inside me. The same part that's still raw from walking away from a life that was never mine to begin with. I see myself in his tension. In his unraveling. We're both running from something, even if we haven't said it out loud.

Still, I'm not just a pretty face to fill the silence with empty reassurances.

"I don't know what that call was about," I say carefully, keeping my voice low and calm. "And I won't pretend to understand. But I do know what it's like to feel like you're barely holding on. So… if you want to talk, or yell again, or throw your phone into the nearest loch—I'm here. I can take it."

He stares at me for a long moment, like he's trying to figure out how the hell I've gotten under his skin so quickly. And truthfully, I don't know either. But I can't walk away from this. From him. Not yet. Because maybe offering comfort isn't always about knowing the whole story. Sometimes it's just about standing close enough that someone knows they're not alone.

His eyes clear and fist unclenches. "Everything is fine."

"You're a terrible liar." I mimic his lean against the window and ponder what our next steps are. I have zero desire to spend my makeshift vacation slash honeymoon wallowing in self-pity, but I also don't want to interrupt whatever work trip Dean is venturing on.

"Do you have a place to stay while you're here?" Dean asks, and I lift the plastic bag straining against the contents of the wedding dress as if that explains where I'm staying. "What's that mean?"

"Well, it means I have no place to stay yet. But I'm hoping to sell the dress and get some cash. And I'm sure I can find a hostel to stay at while I'm here."

"No."

"What?"

"You're not staying in a fucking hostel where anyone could take advantage of you."

"People stay in hostels all the time. They're relatively safe. Well, except for maybe that horror movie and a few pornos," I joke.

"My wife is not staying in a hostel. Understand?"

"First off, I'm not your wife. Not now. Not ever. Second, I can do whatever I please. Thank you very much. And I don't know what's crawled up your ass all of a sudden, but you need to calm down."

Dean's frustration swells around us like a bubble ready to burst. It just feeds my anger even more. I've had someone telling me what to do for years, and I refuse to stand for it any longer. I'm a viper, ready to strike.

"Lila."

The gentleness in the way he says my name quells any fury that had been rising, taming me.

"I have to go." At my raised eyebrows, he continues, "Back to the US. I have… something going on. Someone who needs me right now."

I flinch slightly, my stomach tumbling as I ignore the disappointment swirling inside. Stupid jealousy rears her snake-covered head despite the fact that I know he was only joking about the marriage. I should be under no delusions, but then that moment in the bathroom lingers in the forefront, making that snake bare its fangs.

Seething for reasons I dare not consider, I tell him, "Okay."

"Lila, I want you to go to this address," he says, handing me a business card. "This is the hotel where I'm booked. Stay as long as you want. What's your last name so I can make sure you're able to check in?"

Stunned, I stare at him, my mouth hanging open, preparing to catch flies.

"Is this some sort of trick to get me to tell you my full name?"

"Not at all. This is me, trying to make sure you have somewhere safe to stay so I don't worry about you."

"Dean, you know the possibility of us ever running into each other again is extremely improbable, right?"

"Fine. I'll just tell them I have a guest staying with me," he says, more to himself than to me as he types away on his phone. I thought he'd started to relax, but he grows more harried with each passing second.

"Dean, I can take ca—" He interrupts me with a stern glare, one I'd only ever witnessed before from my father when I was in trouble. Only through Dean's gaze is that something dark and provocative. It makes me curious about what would happen if I defied him.

"Now, I want you to take this card. It's got no limit, so buy whatever you want."

He holds out a shiny black card between his fingers, and as if fearing it may bite, I take a quick step back.

"No."

"Damn, woman. You have no money in a foreign country. Let me do this for you, please."

"What if I max out the card?"

I'd hoped for a snicker, the briefest of chuckles, but I'm left unrewarded. His eyes hold none of the warmth from earlier. Now they're glassy with bottled-up emotions. Whatever news he's received leaves his hands shaking and breath unsteady. I wish I could make him tell me whatever, or whoever has happened, just to ease some of the pain the same way he has for me. Carry some of his burden.

"That's impossible. There's no limit."

No limit? I never really thought that was a possibility unless…

"Who are you?" I murmur.

"Someone who is just trying to do the right thing for once in my life. Please let me help you."

My gaze darts up and down between him and the card until a shrill ring sounds from his phone. He growls into the microphone that he'll be there in ten minutes, and I wonder how he is able to secure a flight so quickly.

Ending the call, he not so gracefully grabs my hand and shoves the card into my palm before forcing my fingers to close around it.

His hand lifts, still unsteady, and brushes a loose strand of hair behind my ear. The backs of his fingers trail gently down the curve of my cheek, a touch so tender it steals the breath from my lungs.

"I have to go," he murmurs, voice low and thick. "Thank you, Lila."

He steps back, and something in my chest pulls with him.

"For what?" I whisper, my breath catching, uneven and aching.

"Waking me up. Enjoy your trip."

He stares at me, eyes searching mine for a moment, before turning on his heel and joining the throngs of people.

"But how will I get this back to you?" I shout.

"Don't worry about it," he yells in return.

As he blends into the crowd, I watch and wait for him to return, only to end up disappointed. But this is what I want: a little peace and quiet to just be me. A chance to remember who I am and not who Prescott Hoolihan wanted me to be.

Unraveling my fingers, I find the black card with the name Dean J. Harrington embossed across the front. Any normal woman would feel relief at the thought of someone offering them a vacation at no expense, especially from someone as good-looking as Dean, but instead, I feel like nothing more than a charity case.

And I hate myself for it.

Reaching into the smaller plastic bag, I grab the pre-paid international phone Dean bought at the airport a few moments ago. I'd left my old phone in the boutique's fitting room. Just another thing he had control over.

Thankful I knew my best friend Ashvi's phone number by heart, I quickly type out a message letting her know I had landed and would let her know when I arrived at my hotel.

She's the only person who knows why I ran this morning, and as my best friend, she swore she'd keep it a secret until I was ready to spill the beans. And she's willing to keep my parents at bay. My poor mom must be freaking out.

Adding one more message to my mom, I let her know that I am safe and will explain everything when I'm ready. As expected, my phone begins ringing immediately, but I let it go to the voicemail box that I'll figure out how to check later.

Right now, I have a decision to make. Do I stick with my plan of winging it for the next couple of weeks, or do I take the generous hand offered to me despite how it makes me feel? I know which choice Ashvi would make.

Harnessing whatever backbone I have left, I march my way toward the transportation area and find a waiting taxi.

"Where to?" the man with graying hair and gentle eyes asks as I slide across the back seat. He doesn't speak with a strong Scottish accent like the woman in the store. He is more British than anything.

Digging into the plastic bag, I grab the business card and hand it to him.

"To this address, please."

In the reflection of the rearview mirror, I watch his eyes bulge as he reads the card, and I'm left wondering where exactly Dean was booked to stay.

"Yes, miss."

Soon, we're out of the airport, and I stare out the window, taking in every little thing as we pass.

"Are you here for business or pleasure?"

"Definitely pleasure. It's the first vacation I've taken in a long time."

"Welcome! I hope you enjoy your time in our beautiful city."

Glancing down at the overstuffed plastic bag at my feet, I tug Dean's credit card from my pants pocket where I'd stuffed it earlier.

"Thanks. It's already been one to remember."

The eight-mile journey into Edinburgh stretches ahead, but I'm not in a rush. Outside the window, the rolling green hills blur into soft watercolor streaks, dotted with sheep and the occasional stone cottage, like something out of a dream I forgot I'd been chasing. And then, just as the anxiety I've been carrying eases its grip, the city unfolds before me in understated elegance. Old, alive with character. Georgian townhouses with wrought-iron balconies, sweeping neoclassical facades, and Victorian rooftops line the streets, their grandeur softened by age and stories untold. The steady rhythm of the car matches the calm that finally settles in my chest. For the first time in what feels like years, I can breathe, really breathe. And it's not just oxygen. It's possibility. It's a flicker of something warm and weightless blooming deep in my chest. Hope. Maybe I didn't come here just to escape. Maybe… I came here to begin.

Chapter Three

Lila

The last thing I expect after discovering that my ex has an entirely separate family is kindness.

Certainly not a luxurious hotel room in Edinburgh with a view of Arthur's Seat and a crisp, linen envelope with my name on it.

I don't expect to see Dean again. Besides knowing his name, I don't really know who he is despite my best efforts. The hotel staff is polite and professional yet maddeningly tight-lipped. Whenever I ask about the man who booked the suite, who left the letters, and somehow knew exactly what I needed, they only smile and say, "He asked for privacy."

A billionaire ghost with immaculate taste and mysterious manners.

The suite is otherworldly. Floor-to-ceiling windows frame the skyline of Old Town. My bed is a cloud of down. I imagine it's what royalty would sleep on. My wardrobe, I realize, has been pre-stocked with new clothes that fit perfectly—casual sweaters, walking boots, evening dresses in colors I forgot I loved. It should feel invasive. It doesn't. It feels…thoughtful. Whomever Dean had selected to collect the clothes nailed it.

I find the first letter on the desk. Heavy paper. Ink like calligraphy. Single name.

Lila,
You don't owe anyone strength right now. Or poise. Or politeness.
You owe yourself stillness. Breath. Kindness.
Scotland is magic. Let it work on you.
I'll be here—in the ways that matter.
-Your Friend

The letter makes my throat tighten. No signature. No identifying information. Just the whisper of someone who sees me.

The next day, I walk the Royal Mile. I get lost between the closes—narrow alleys lined with stories. I visit Greyfriars Kirkyard and run my fingers over old gravestones, wondering how long grief echoes in stone.

At The Elephant House, I sip strong coffee and reread the letter. A surprise platter of biscuits arrives at my table. I ask the barista, again, about the man who arranged all this.

Another polite smile. "He said to tell you he hopes you like the lemon shortbread."

Dammit. He's everywhere and nowhere.

Lila,

Did you know I saw you running through the airport? Like a comet passing too close? Both stunningly brilliant and retina burning. You're stardust, scientifically speaking.

Go see Calton Hill today. It's touristy, but the view is worth it.

And please—eat something warm.

-Your Friend

I do what he says.

Climbing Calton Hill is like stepping into a dream. The wind slaps my face, and the city unfolds beneath me. Monuments stand tall and defiant. The sun breaks through gray clouds like a beacon in the night.

Lila,

I requested something through the concierge. A guidebook—local's notes in the margins. Circled pages. Places I thought might speak to you.

Today, take the train to North Berwick. Walk along the shore. Let the cold sea say things you can't.

You're doing better than you think.

-Your Friend

The sea smells like salt and home. I walk until my cheeks are raw and my fingers ache. I watch birds float in the sky and think about trust and love.

Each night, I come back to another letter. Slipped under my door. Nestled in my pillowcase. Tucked into the coat pocket I didn't wear until the rain started.

Lila,

This letter has no advice. No plans. Just a truth: None of this is your fault.

He was.

-Your Friend

I cry on the train back to Edinburgh. Not quietly or pretty either. But no one bothers me. It is a welcome reprieve.

Lila,

You're starting to walk straighter. I know it, even if I can't see it.

Go to Dean Village-ironic, yes. Find the café with the chipped teapot. The owner's name is Moira. Tell her you want "whatever's warm."

You're allowed to be happy.

-Your Friend

Dean Village is storybook perfect. Siobhan gives me soup and shortbread and a conspiratorial wink. When I ask about the man who sent me, she smiles and walks away.

Back at the hotel, the suite feels more like home than anywhere I've stayed. But I don't belong here, either. Nothing feels quite right.

I'm not hiding anymore. I'm healing.

I go to Stirling Castle, and then to a whiskey tasting in Oban. I talk to strangers. I buy a pair of earrings. I let myself laugh.

And each day, a letter waits. Simple. Steady. Anonymously signed. But filled with so much of him, I start to hear his voice when I read. I wish that he hadn't been called away at the airport and spent each of these days with me. A longing that overwhelms me if I think about it too long.

> *Lila,*
> *If this were a book, you'd be at the turning point.*
> *So what happens next?*
> *What do you want it to be?*
> *-Your Friend*

I sit on the floor of the suite that night, surrounded by his letters. Fourteen of them now. Each one folding open a different piece of me. I don't know who he really is. Not in the way the world defines knowing. But I know how he makes me feel. He's been a friend in all the ways I needed one when I was too embarrassed to contact home. And maybe that's enough.

The last letter is hidden in the sleeve of the coat I nearly forgot to pack. I find it just before heading to the airport.

> *Lila,*
> *You asked who I am.*
> *The truth is, I'm someone who could watch you break and do nothing. That's what the world knows me as. Cold. Heartless. Selfish.*
> *But with you, you're seeing the me I can be.*
> *I'm someone who believes in you. In the way I know you'll stand back up again and again.*
> *I hope you find your new beginning.*
> *-D*

The initial stops me.
D.

Dean. Seeing him acknowledge himself seems more personal. I sit on the edge of the bed, suitcase open, coat folded beside me. I'm not going to find him. That's not the point. The point is that I found something else: stillness, truth, and the voice I'd buried under years of being small to make someone else feel big.

I breathe in the Edinburgh air one last time, letting it fill my lungs. I'm ready to go home. Not to a person. To myself.

Chapter Four

Lila

"Honey, I'm home," I call out as I step foot in the small craftsman-style house Ashvi rents just on the outskirts of Coral Bell Cove, Virginia.

My bag drops to the floor at my feet with a thud as I slip off my tennis shoes by the front door. The new bag was a purchase in Scotland, along with my new wardrobe, courtesy of Dean's card.

It was funny how I expected the card to decline the first time I used it at the bar across the street from the hotel. My hand shook like a leaf as I handed it over, but in the end, it was all clear.

Dean had been true to his word, and over the entire two weeks, I thought more about him than my ex, which was just plain annoying, considering how we ended things in the airport.

"You're back!" my gorgeous friend shouts as she darts out of her room and nearly tackles me to the ground.

Ashvi Basu is an energetic spitfire whose energy matches her height. And with her dark features and long black hair, she turns heads wherever we go. If only they knew how much true crime she watches or her obsession with plants, they'd think differently. She is my personal Seymour Krelborn, and I may have had a nightmare or two about a real man-eating plant.

Seriously, she has at least forty succulents lining her kitchen counter, and she's named them all and has them on strict water diets.

But I love her just as much as my siblings and have since her family moved to our small coastal town in second grade. She asked to borrow my scissors to cut gum from her hair that our class bully, Ashley, put there during lunch. But instead of just cutting hers, she took the blades to the end of Ashley's braid. Her tenacity amazed me, and we've been best friends since that day.

"Oomph," I grunt as my back collides with the small table in the foyer, but instead of complaining, I wrap my arms around Ashvi and smile. Being here with her reminds me of how much I missed home over the past two years. Hell, if I'm being honest with myself, I've been missing home since I left for college ten years ago.

But I had my reasons for staying away then, just as I do now.

"Oh, how I've missed you," I murmur into her hair. I may have seen her two weeks ago, but it feels like a lifetime.

"Tell me about it," she says as she pulls back, holding me at arm's length with her graceful fingers clutching my shoulders. "And I do mean tell me. Everything."

While on my self-discovery trip, I'd spoken with Ashvi only a handful of times, just enough to keep her anxiety over my well-being at bay but clearly not enough to feed her curiosity. Especially once she learned that Prescott had canceled all my cards.

"I will…but I can't right now, Vi."

"That's okay. I'll get it all out of you with some red wine later."

"From your brother's winery?" Vi is the youngest of five, another reason we are so close, and her eldest brother owns an award-winning winery in the Napa Valley area of California. He frequently sends her boxes of his newest batches.

"You know it."

She knows how much I love his Cabernet, and like she dangles a bone in front of a dog, I nod. One glass of that red deliciousness and I turn into an open book. A fault that she loves to exploit at her whim.

Once she releases me from her grasp, I reach down for my bag and start wandering toward the guest room. Until I can find a place in town to rent, Ashvi offered to let me stay with her. She knows moving back into my family's home is the last place I want to be. Not because I don't love my parents or siblings, but because I am jobless, there are expectations to help out with my mother's business—a local nanny service. Unlike my siblings, farming doesn't come naturally to me, so on the bright side, I won't be asked to help my dad. A green thumb is not something I possess.

Setting the leather duffel on the bed, I pull the few items out, placing them in the dresser drawers. Despite the no-limit card Dean had given me, I restrained myself and only purchased a few necessities. A few pants, shirts, and undergarments.

"Oh, this is pretty," Vi says as she grabs the dark red lace lingerie I'd splurged on. When I saw it in the store, it immediately reminded me of the maroon color of Dean's shirt. Before I could blink, the sales lady was grabbing my size and packaging it up for me.

"Mm-hmm."

Holding it against her much thinner body, Ashvi twists one way, then the other, admiring the lace on her body.

"Please, for the love of all things tartan, tell me you picked this up for some sexy Scottish mystery man who helped you forget all about that prick of an ex."

Yanking it from her grasp, she cackles as I shove it into the top dresser drawer. "I just thought it was pretty, okay?"

"Sure. Sure."

Vi drapes her body dramatically on the bed as she watches me put the rest of my things away.

"So how long do you think it will take before your parents realize your home?"

"I give it two days max. The rental car isn't going to throw them off long." I sigh exasperatedly as I consider how they're going to bombard me.

"You're right. That family of yours is like fox hunters. So keen and always one step ahead of everyone. I'm pretty sure your dad knew whenever we planned to sneak out in high school before we even did."

"You are not wrong. It's even worse with my brothers. They'd call just as I was about to step out the door with Prescott, not that he ever let me answer, knowing it would probably piss him off."

"Speaking of Prescott…"

The name drops into the room like a grenade.

The pink cashmere sweater slips from my hands and pools at my feet, but I barely register it. My body stills, the breath in my lungs locking tight as if the syllables alone carry weight enough to crush me. It shouldn't hurt. He shouldn't have that kind of power anymore, but hearing his name from someone else's lips slices deeper than when I say it myself. Like it makes him real again. Like it pulls him from the shadowy corners of my past and plants him squarely in my present.

I feel like I've been yanked backward, like I'm standing in the boutique again, drowning in lace and lies. My stomach twists, and the faintest tremor runs through my hands. I blink, forcing myself to stay grounded at this moment, not the one I left behind.

Dean's name grounded me before. But Prescott's name? It splinters.

And for the first time, I realize that healing doesn't mean I'm immune. It just means I'm fighting to keep my footing every time the past tries to drag me under.

"Has he come by?" I ask in an unforgiving sense of panic.

Ashvi leans up onto her elbows and looks at me, assessing my change in demeanor. Without saying a word, she quickly rushes to my side and wraps me in her arms again.

"No, he hasn't been by," she whispers as she lovingly strokes her fingers through my mess of hair. "Is there something more I should know about, Lila? Something you're not telling me?"

Ashvi knows all about Prescott's actual family, but I've left out the part where I felt like a prisoner in my own life. I ran away from the confines of my small town, only to end up in a snow globe perched upon a shelf for my fiancé to toy with when he desired.

"No. I just…I don't want him to bother anyone here."

She leans back, reminding me so much of my mother at that moment that I also break down into the tears I'd been keeping at bay for the last two weeks.

"You're lying to me, but I'll play along this time."

Ashvi steps back, notices the soft material pooled on the floor, and reaches for it. Some unyielding force inside me stops her in her tracks, and I grab it before she can. She cocks one perfectly arched eyebrow at me as I quickly slip the cardigan on a hanger and slide it onto the closet rod.

"Explain?"

"Sorry, it's just something…special."

"Mm-hmm."

I hate lying to my best friend. At this point, I'm afraid I'm either going to spontaneously combust into a pile of ash and find my way to the deep, dark depths of hell or I'm going to tell her everything. I'm not sure which conclusion is worse. Dean was one of the few details I left out of our calls during my trip. Besides his credit card, which continues to burn a hole in my wallet, I didn't think our meeting was anything more than happenstance. A delicious moment, but a chance meeting none-the-less. And something about him wanted to keep the meeting close to the chest. That doesn't mean I didn't spill a few breadcrumbs about the hot guy who calmed me during the flight, but that was all I mentioned.

"Well, how about I entertain you for a little bit while you unpack?" She moves toward the floor-length mirror in the corner of the room and begins braiding her waist-length hair. It weaves through her fingers like strips of dark satin, and the action momentarily hypnotizes me.

"Anyway," she begins. "When I went into town over the weekend." The town she's referring to is Norfolk. One of the major cities that's a hop, skip, and a jump across our small bay. I preferred our quiet, small town, but Ashvi thrives in the hustle and bustle. Her world flourishes in the noise and bright lights. "I met the most gorgeous Navy man."

Giggling, I hang up the pink sweater and turned to face my friend. "Of course you did, Vi."

"What's that supposed to mean?" she asks with a hint of indignation in her voice.

"Oh, Ashvi. I just meant that any good-looking guy with half a brain cell would want your attention. You're beautiful. A walking Bollywood star."

Twisting her ever-present hair tie around the ends of her hair, she lets the plait fall against her back. "You're right. But this one was different."

"How so?" I ask, referencing all the armed forces men Ashvi has dated over the last few years. They go out with the tide as quickly as they come in. It was the unfortunate part about living so closely to some military bases.

"Well, for one, this guy didn't even try to buy me a drink. He asked if I wanted to be on his team during the trivia game."

My color-me-surprised look conjured up a bubble of laughter from my friend.

"I know, right?" she adds. "And the best part?"

"Is not that he's in the military?" Ashvi had a very clear and distinct type.

"Oh, he is. Engineer. The best part is that his parents are professors at Williams and Mary."

To most people, that knowledge wouldn't mean anything, but growing up in this area, we know how quickly military families and singles move in and out.

"So that means his family is local. Well, local to the area."

"Exactly," she beams, and I can't help but reciprocate her enthusiasm. Soon, she's gripped my hands, and we're spinning around my room as we screech loud enough to scare a neighborhood cat.

"Ashvi, I'm so excited for you. When are you seeing him again?"

"Tomorrow night. At first, I thought he was going to play that stupid game where they wait a week or longer to call, but I literally had a message from him right before you walked in the door."

"Wow, I'm so excited for you. This one sounds promising."

"I know, right? So now that I have shared something. It's your turn."

Ah, I knew it was too good to be true. Ashvi has always held on to the notion that one bit of personal news requires the other person to share something.

"Prescott is off the table."

Nodding, she swipes her fingers through the ends of my ponytail, draping it over my shoulder. "At least until wine."

"Um…" The blanks scroll repetitively like I'm a bill counter until nothing comes to mind.

"What about work? Any luck trying to find a research position here?"

I'd spent my life working up to getting my PhD in microbiology, researching new preventive treatments for food allergies after a close call with my first date and his undiagnosed allergy to strawberries—one of the crops harvested on my family farm. While the close call could have been tragic, it still shaped who I am. That incident set me off on the journey and I was not ready to jump off ship yet. Unfortunately, our small town didn't have opportunities for biological and immunological studies.

"I've been looking around all the research facilities and colleges in the state, but nothing with what I'd like to do specifically."

"I hate Prescott," Ashvi barks, and as I snarl at the mention of his name, she backtracks. "Sorry, your ex. I hate your ex and what he's done."

Prescott and his family were the major beneficiaries of the research facility where I worked. The center was named after them, for goodness' sake. So when he paid attention to me and my work, I assumed it was because they wanted to know what their grant money was being spent on. Little did I know it was all to groom and mold me the way they thought was best. And removing me from my position was the last phase in their arsenal.

"Well, I was naive enough to let him do it. But it's okay. I'll figure things out. I can always reach out to Wellington University and my old advisor to see if they have any leads. Mr. Shaver helped me land my internship." I'd been recruited by Stanford and Michigan to join their doctorate programs, but Wellington University had been the only to offer a full scholarship. It helped that I adored the school and campus. And their research facilities were top-notch.

"You can always work for your mom. I know it's not your dream job, but it's only until something better comes along." Just as I try to argue, Ashvi holds her perfect hand in the air. "Look, I know this isn't what you want to do for the rest of your life, but you're so great with kids, and they adore you."

It was the same argument my siblings made time and time again. Not that any of them were jumping at the chance to work with Mom and her local nanny service. We were all good with kids, brought up that way, but Mom never pressured any of us to follow in her footsteps. But unlike my siblings, I had the knack for the business that they didn't. Before we moved to Coral Bell Cove, it had been just me and my dad. My mom ran off and never looked back. He'd tried to give me a Christmas to remember when I was four, and that was the same holiday we met Claire, my mom, for all intents and purposes. She ran a nanny service and assigned herself to my dad when all her other employees were designated to other families.

It all worked out in the end, considering they fell head over heels in love during that two-week vacation, and we moved here permanently that same year.

"I know. I'm just not sure if I want to even open that Pandora's box, you know?"

"Yeah, I get it. But the money never hurts, and with the summer tourist season about to start, maybe you'll luck out and find yourself a hot single dad. Crazier things have happened."

Laughing, I push us out of the spare bedroom I'm borrowing and back into the living room. "My mom already won the jackpot with that one. I don't think it happening twice is all that probable."

"I think you should talk to her about it, anyway. When you're ready."

Reaching into the cupboard, I pull out a glass and start filling it with tap water. "I've been here for like half an hour and I feel like you're already trying to get rid of me."

Hopping onto the counter, Ashvi swings her long legs from side to side. "I'm not. I just know my best friend and how she gets bored in five seconds flat if she doesn't have a schedule or a job to keep her busy."

Swallowing the last gulp of water, I set the glass in the sink and turn to face my friend. "I hate that you know me so well."

"Duh, that's what best friends are for. And to tell you that you can't stay hidden away for long."

I flinch at her insinuation of hiding away from my problems.

"And by hiding, I mean that your mom just texted me, and we're to be at their house tonight for dinner."

Ashvi holds out her phone so I can view the series of messages from my mother to my best friend.

"Who ratted me out?" I ask under my breath.

Ashvi chuckles as she hops down from the counter and slides her phone back into the side pocket of her athletic pants.

"No one, silly. But seeing a rental car in the area in non-peak season and in a non-tourist area is going to alert the neighborhood watch. You know how Mr. Werthers is."

Mr. Werthers is a retired Naval airman who lost his wife thirty years ago. He takes it upon himself to supervise the ins and outs of all the people who reside in Coral Bell Cove. He also has a knack for spreading gossip in a way that could rival any middle schooler.

"Dang it. Did she at least say what we're having?"

Whatever is on the family table for the night is always a hint as to how many people I can expect to see seated around the custom farmhouse table. Beef stroganoff or pad Thai, I knew that it would just be Ashvi and me. If any steak or potato is involved, then one of my brothers will be present. Fish? And my sister Hadley would be making an appearance. But Italian is the call for the entire Wright family.

"Homemade lasagna."

Guess I'm getting an all-out welcome back.

As we pull up to the sprawling ranch-style home my parents bought when I was six, a strange mix of comfort and unease settles in my chest. The gravel crunches beneath the tires, familiar and jarring all at once. The wraparound porch comes into view, weathered now by sun and seasons but no less welcoming.

I take a moment to really look at the farm, at the way the early light kisses the tops of the hay bales, how the fence posts lean just a little from years of stubborn horses and busier days. The barn door is cracked open, and I know without looking that my dad has probably been working since sunrise, covered in dust and the kind of joy only this land can give him. It's his pride and joy, aside from us—his kids. He's never said it outright, but I've always felt it. Even when I disappointed him, even when I chased dreams beyond the fence line, he never made me feel like I didn't belong here.

I swallow hard.

Coming home was always supposed to be a soft place to land, but today, it feels like walking barefoot over gravel. Too many memories in the soil. Too many people who'll ask too many questions I'm not ready to answer.

But even through the dread curling at the edges of my stomach, I know this place, this home, is filled with nothing but love.

My mom will pretend not to cry when she sees me. She'll bake something absurdly sweet and fuss over how pale I look. My little sister will ask if I'm staying for good, and my brothers will act like they're too cool to care—until they throw an arm around me when no one's watching.

And I'll let them. I'll let them love me. Because for all the ways I lost myself in the past few years, this family has always been my compass. Loud, nosy, relentless, and mine.

It's not perfect. I'm not perfect. But I'm home. And maybe that's exactly what I need.

Reaching out, I grip Ashvi's hand where it rests on the gearshift as she parks the car.

"Thank you for being here."

Growing up with my clan, she knows how overwhelming they can be, especially when one of us has gone off the deep end. And running away to Scotland for two weeks after my dress fitting definitely falls into that category.

Ashvi doesn't say anything in reply. She simply squeezes my hand and lets me know she's here for me. And also to stir up her own brand of mischief if the need presents itself.

The walk to the front door feels like I'm walking toward my own death sentence. My siblings are probably standing just inside the house, peeking through the windows, and Mom is waiting at the door for my knock. But as I twist the knob and slowly open the door, I'm surprised to find the entryway empty. Not just empty, but quiet. And in the Wright household, quiet doesn't usually mean something good.

Ashvi trails behind me as I pass the stairs and head toward the back of the house, where the kitchen and den all reside under one large vaulted space.

"Mom?" I call out as we approach the threshold.

"Surprise!"

The shouts and cheers momentarily stun me, and then I'm quickly taking in the balloons and streamers.

"What's going on?" I ask and look behind me for my best friend, who has quickly moved herself closer to my siblings gathered in the den.

"Welcome home, sweetie!" Mom says as she wraps me in her arms, my stiff body still in shock from the startling greeting.

"Thanks, Mom. What…um…are we celebrating?"

I glance around the den, blinking against the bright overhead light and the soft glow of home. Something sweet bakes in the oven, the smell of cinnamon and vanilla wafting through the air like a warm hug. A banner that says "Welcome Home, Lila!" is strung haphazardly above the doorway, like they didn't have time to make it perfect but cared enough to do it anyway. A lump swells in my throat.

"Oh, just the fact that you're home, and you ended up not marrying that horrid man."

Her light voice is teasing, but I hear the layers beneath it—the relief, the quiet worry she probably carried for years and never voiced. It was no secret that my family wasn't exactly fond of Prescott. But I kept hoping they'd come around. That maybe, once they saw the version of him I thought I loved, they'd change their minds.

But the truth is, they were right. And I was too blinded by the sparkle of the life and career he promised to see what was underneath. It's amazing how love can drown out the quiet whisper of your own instincts. The ones that kept telling you something wasn't quite right. That you were shrinking to fit into a life that was never designed for you in the first place.

"I'm sorry," I murmur, voice thick.

Not just for falling for him, but for believing in the lie, for drifting away from the people who truly loved me while I tried to become someone else entirely.

My mom moves closer, wiping her hands on a dish towel before gently cupping my cheek. "Nothing to be sorry about, Lila. We're just glad to have you home."

Her words hit somewhere deep, beneath the surface calm I've tried to maintain since stepping off that plane. I nod, not trusting myself to speak. Because what do you say when your family greets you with open arms after you've disappeared into someone else's world for so long?

You say thank you. You let yourself be loved, even when you don't feel like you deserve it yet.

I blink fast, forcing down the tears that suddenly sting. I'd cried enough in Scotland. Enough to last a lifetime. But this feels different. These aren't tears of heartbreak or fear or shame. They're something softer, warmer. A beginning, not an end.

So I take a breath and force a smile, letting the air fill spaces in my chest that had been hollow for too long.

I make my way through the small crowd known as my siblings, hugging them and thanking them for being there. I'm sure they think I mean only for the impromptu party, but I mean my life in general. Ashvi is the last in that group that I hug, and I make sure to whisper that she's in for it before I release her with a smile on my face.

"Hi, Dad," I say as I wrap my arms around the best man I've ever known.

"Hey, Sugarplum." My heart immediately warms as he uses the nickname bestowed upon me when I was three and gave my first ballet recital. I wore a purple tutu, and the name stuck. "Glad you're here." I give him one last squeeze before following my siblings toward the large kitchen table, where Mom places the steaming lasagna dish.

We disperse toward the same chairs we sat in as kids. Ashvi takes the spare seat to my right, and as my father says grace, I feel a twinkle of hope that perhaps everything will turn out okay. In my perfect world, Prescott will move on and leave me be. There will be no questioning from his family about what happened. I won't suddenly find myself stalked by a crazy wife. And somewhere along the way, I'll find myself doing my part to save the world.

But as I scoop out the pasta dish and take my first bite, letting the familiar sounds of my family fill the void deep inside me, I have that all-too-familiar feeling that luck isn't on my side, and my world is about to be flipped on its axis, again.

"Oh, Lila, since you're home for a little bit, I have the perfect job for you. The poor children just lost their mother."

"I don't know, Mom. That's not really what I'm doing right now."

Mom reaches out with a gentle hand and rests it on top of mine, clenching the form with all my might. "I understand. It was just a suggestion. I thought it may help you keep your mind off everything for a while."

From my other side, Ashvi asks, "How old are the kids?"

"Poor things, five and three."

God, they're so young, and Mom is right. If anyone could relate to them, it would be me. Falling back into the nanny trap is so easy *because* I love it, but it isn't the plan I see for my life.

"That's so sad," my little sister, Hadley, says from across the table. "You don't have anyone who can fill in?"

"Unfortunately not. Everyone has their current positions, and then the summer slots are filled until a few come home from college. I suppose I'll see if I can help out instead."

"Mom," I utter sternly, head tilted in her direction. Mom's been slowly cutting back her hours until she can officially retire. Her best friend, Andrea, has been doing the same until they can leave the business to someone capable of continuing their legacy.

"It's okay," she mumbles around a piece of bread she tore from the loaf, dipping it into the tomato sauce on her plate. "It was a last-minute request, and normally, we'd turn it down, but the man seems desperate."

"Hell, I remember how desperate I was," Dad says, reminding us all how the situation was very similar to him twenty-four years ago.

The guilt gnaws away at me through the remainder of the meal, and by the time Ashvi and I are ready to head back to her house and drink that much-anticipated bottle of red wine, I feel like every ounce of me has been fed through a wire strainer.

As Mom and Dad hug me, offering to let me stay in my old room on their farm, my resolve slips away.

"Mom?"

"Yes, sweetie?"

"Maybe you could send me the information about the nanny job? I'm not promising anything, but you're right. It may be nice to keep myself occupied for a while."

"Oh, thank you, Lila."

"It's not a yes, Mom."

"Of course," she says, her thrilled smile growing with every second. "I'll send it to you once I get the kitchen cleaned up. Love you, sweet girl."

"Love you too, Mom. Dad."

We're only a few minutes into the twenty-minute drive back to Ashvi's house, nineties R&B, Ashvi's current obsession, blaring from the speakers. A girl group sings about how the man is never going to get it, and I smile, leaning my head against the window as the sun finally drifts beyond the trees. Soon, the smell of salt water will penetrate the windows, and the sun will last well into the evening. But for right now, I'm happy being in my small town, with my best friend, listening to songs far older than us.

"You did a nice thing," Ashvi says as we pass the local elementary school, suddenly reminding me that I've likely sold myself as someone's housemaid, not just a nanny, for the next six months or more.

"Yeah," I mumble, still not feeling so great about the decision, but knowing I'm helping someone who probably feels as helpless as my dad had all those years ago. "What game are we playing tonight?"

It is a tradition that wine drinking includes playing a ridiculous game together. We usually end up with Clue or Yahtzee. Scrabble and Monopoly have been banned since we were in junior high.

"Oh, without a doubt Clue. I'm hoping somewhere along the way you slip up and tell me what's really going on with you."

Groaning, I turn away so she doesn't witness my epic eye roll. The last time we played Clue, I finally got it out of Ashvi that she'd slept with her economics professor. Thankfully, it had been after she passed his class.

"You're on, but only if you agree to *two* bottles of wine. I'm going to need it."

"Deal," my best friend says with a mysterious gleam in her eye that is absolutely not from the shimmery reflection of streetlights. Instead, it came from her overzealous, competitive nature.

"Yeah. Definitely going to need two bottles tonight."

Chapter Five

Dean

Exhaustion and exhilaration duel behind my eyes as I pull into the small grocery store just within the town lines of Coral Bell Cove. Originally, I'd planned on stopping halfway during the fifteen-hour drive from Miami, Florida, to this small coastal town, but I was too keyed up to sleep as it was. Dusk turned to sunrise, and before I knew it, I was crossing the Virginia state line and headed for my new home.

Did I have reservations about packing up my entire life and moving? A bit. Do I regret the decision? Absolutely not. Not if it meant I was giving my niece and nephew their best shot at a normal life. One far more conventional than the one I'd been handed.

Thankfully, being a billionaire made purchasing a home and filling it with everything I'd need easier than snapping my finger. In less than a week, I had picked up my life and was ready for the new change.

I park the car between two faded lines, my hands still gripping the steering wheel like I'm trying to anchor myself to something solid. The leather creaks beneath my palms, the quiet tick of the engine cooling the only sound filling the cab. I stare blankly at the polished dashboard of the Lamborghini, sleek, clinical, and expensive, and feel… nothing.

The truth of it is that it still hasn't fully landed. That Genevieve is gone. That my sister. My bright, complicated, fiercely stubborn sister isn't just on the other end of a bad argument or sulking through one of our regular disagreements. She's not answering my texts because she can't. She'll never answer them again.

I grit my teeth, feel the grind of tension along my jaw and the ache behind my eyes. I'm holding on too tightly, trying not to shatter.

The worst part isn't the funeral I had to plan alone. Or the will that felt more like a slap than a farewell. It's the fact that my parents treated it all like a scheduling conflict. Something to be solved, delegated, pushed to someone else who wasn't them.

The moment the ink was dry on the death certificate, they were already boarding their private jet, bound for their summer estate in the South of France. Like grief was a bad business deal they could simply opt out of. Like Genevieve's death was a nuisance rather than the earthquake it's been in my life.

My knuckles go white as I loosen my hands from the wheel, one finger at a time.

They didn't even stay for the kids. Not that I expected them to.

Two children, confused and grieving, shuffled off to with their previous nanny while I tried to make sense of what was left behind. Evelyn and Oliver don't know yet how much has changed. They're too little to understand the permanence of loss. All they know is that their mom isn't coming back.

And somehow, I'm supposed to step in and fill the void.

The thought tightens something deep in my chest, but not in fear. In responsibility. In fury. Because I never expected to be the one holding Evelyn's hand when she cried herself to sleep, or explaining to Oliver why he won't see his mom again.

Instead, I'm the one making plans to uproot my life. To move just inside the Virginia state line where I could give the children a place to grow. Far from where Genevieve had been hiding out in the city she called home. At least I can give the kids some sort of familiarity. Stability. Something my parents seem pathologically incapable of providing.

I exhale through my nose and force the rage down. It simmers just below the surface, but I've gotten good at masking it. At least, I thought I had.

Until now.

Because for all their money and elegance and champagne-drenched indifference, they surprisingly left their daughter's legacy to me. And I'll be damned if I let them erase her memory by pretending she never mattered. I'm just waiting for the other shoe to drop. They'll want something sooner rather than later.

I close my eyes for a beat, my hand fisting once against my thigh before I climb out of the car.

Let them rot in France. I have two little hearts depending on me now. And this time—I won't fail.

"Fuck," I shout, slamming my hand against the steering wheel. The other cars in the lot start to blur, and I quickly pinch the bridge of my nose with my forefinger and thumb. Now is not the time to let my emotions get the best of me. In just a few short hours, I'll be in charge of the well-being of two little ones.

"Oh, Gen," I mumble, thinking of my sister and her death, which still didn't seem real. "I really need your help right now." This wasn't some situation I could pay my way out of. I *want* to be there for my niece and nephew, and I know I'm the best option for the kids, but it's still a lot to take on when I spend most of my days working with the companies I invest in. But Gen knew what she was doing, knew how my parents never cared for us the way we cared for each other.

Taking another deep breath, I roll my shoulders and step out of the car, heading toward the entrance to a small grocery store.

The moment I slip across the threshold of the automated doors, I immediately feel a different sense of dread. Outside of grabbing something at a convenience store, I'd never gone grocery shopping before. It was easy enough to pay someone to stock my pantry and fridge. And now it's easy enough to order what I need on an app and have it delivered.

What kind of things do a five- and three-year-old eat? Hell, I can cook, but I'm not sure the kids want to eat steak and chicken every day.

"I'm so screwed," I say to no one in particular as I grab a cart and step toward the produce. The damn front left wheel wobbles back and forth as it tries to catch the floor, reminding me of my current state of mind, fully capable but barely hanging on.

"You need any help?" a gentle voice says from behind me as I block the walkway.

"I'm sorry." Moving my cart to the side, I gesture for her to pass. "It's nothing."

"Well, I'm pretty certain a lot of nothings end up being big somethings." She smiles kindly at me, her blond hair with speckles of gray catching the fluorescent lights above us.

Suddenly, I find myself spilling my secrets as I push my wobbly cart in tandem with hers. "It's my first time grocery shopping, and I'm a little overwhelmed."

"Oh, well. What kind of things do you like to eat? Picking out your produce and meats is easy enough."

"It's not just me. I recently gained guardianship of my niece and nephew. I have no idea what I should be feeding them."

"Are you Mr. Harrington?" she asks, her eyes sparkling as she hands me a container of strawberries.

I take them hesitantly and place them in my cart as I nod.

"Oh, wonderful. You just hit the jackpot, my friend." At the tilt of my head, she continues. "Sorry, I forget you're not from here, so you have no idea who I am. I'm Claire, and I own CBC Nanny Services."

Elation courses through me. Not only is her business highly recommended with so many five-star ratings that I lost track, but she was able to accept my last-minute request.

"Wow, what a small world," I tell her with the brightest grin I could muster over the last two weeks.

"It really is. Now, if there is one thing I'm good at, not just as a nanny but as a mom to five, it's shopping for kids."

The mention of five kids immediately takes me back to the plane ride with my ghost girl. Lila had said she came from a big family, and I'd been so jealous. Even knowing that Claire is the matriarch of five kids leaves me with a bit of envy.

"I'll take any help I can get if you don't mind."

As Claire laughs and adds more fruits and vegetables to my cart, I instantly relax. Something makes me think I can actually do this. With Claire's bits of advice and an open-ended invite to her humble abode, I leave the grocery store feeling like I'd climbed Mount Everest. She answered all my questions and assured me the nanny, her daughter, coming to stay with me, was the absolute best. Who knew a mother-like figure could make everything seem okay?

As I load the items into my car, I realize I never asked for her daughter's name, not that it mattered. Truthfully, I should have asked for a lot more information, like the nanny's age and what I should expect, but I had been so overwhelmed that all those things slipped my mind. Which worries me because, with all my investments, I'm always on top of my game. But I feel like a fish out of water here in Coral Bell Cove. Hell, I hadn't even seen the house I'd purchased. I made a simple call and requested a stately home at the end of a neighborhood with a lot of land.

Following the GPS in my car, I make my way to the house that reminds me of something I'd have loved to grow up in.

As I pull into the tree-lined drive, my lips part in a grin as I take it all in. The real estate agent had truly found me a gem, and though I'd seen pictures of the large, restored Victorian Farmhouse, they were deceiving. It's the most stunning home I'd ever seen.

And I know a dock around the back leads to a small channel of Back Bay before feeding into the larger body of water. I'll have a place to fish and dock my boat—two of my favorite ways to relax.

Not that I expect to do a lot of that with the small kids.

Fuck, thinking of the dock as I park the car in the garage using the code for the automated door, I realize I'll have to call someone to install a fence in the backyard. I don't want the kids wandering back there without me.

I'm so not made for this job, but I'm their best shot right now.

As I load the grocery bags across my arms, because I spend enough time in the gym that I do not want to make more than one trip, my phone buzzes in my back pocket.

I don't have time to take in my surroundings as I slip the bags onto a bench in the attached mudroom and answer the call, recognizing the personalized ringtone I have for my best friend.

"Hey, they arrive yet?" Talon asks before I get a chance to greet him.

"No, a few more hours. Hoping I can get settled in a bit."

"When's the nanny going to arrive?"

"Not sure. The paperwork said around lunchtime."

"Think she's going to fangirl when she sees you? Rory saw more magazines with your ugly mug plastered on them in the store today."

The mention of that damn article immediately stifles any of the calm I'd been feeling before. I had no idea how one simple article naming me the world's hottest billionaire bachelor would change my life. Since the article launched, I could barely walk down the street in Miami without being recognized. At least here, no one seems to identify me outside of my name. The real estate agent had been far too happy to sell a house to a Harrington.

"I think it's going to be okay. At least I hope so. I don't have many options right now."

Talon pauses for a beat, then says, "Yeah, I know. We're here for you, man. I wish you could have brought them to Tennessee. Mom and GiGi would have been tickled to be with the kids."

"Yeah, but you know that guardianship rule. It's hard enough to navigate, with Oliver getting ready to start kindergarten and Evelyn needing a preschool. Seemed like a better choice than having to fight the state for custody right now."

The entire thing had been a mess. There I was, trying to bury my sister while the state had said the kids had no reference to a birth father. Their birth certificates had been blank. And there was no way in hell I was letting my parents take guardianship of the kids. They screwed up Gen and me enough even though they had barely been around.

"Maybe you and Rory can visit after the baby?"

"You know we will. Alright, she's asking for more pickles and ice cream, so I need to make a grocery run. I'm here, Dean, anytime."

I end the call with my best friend and send a thankful prayer to the heavens that Talon is in my life. I can't imagine how screwed up I'd be if it weren't for him and his grandma, GiGi. The spunky older woman never met a challenge she wasn't afraid to take on. That included me when I would visit during school breaks with Talon.

Putting away the groceries, I take a couple of minutes to get the lay of the kitchen and first floor.

The home had been unfurnished when I signed on the dotted line, but it didn't take long for the real estate agent to track down an interior designer to tackle the home before I arrived. Money always talks.

Once everything has been put away, I make a simple sandwich with the deli meats Claire helped me pick out, then take a quick wander through the house. The primary is on the main floor, along with my office, and the kids' rooms are upstairs. After speaking with a therapist about the kids and how I could help them while they grieve, she suggested allowing them to share a room for a while.

Popping my head into the first of the bedrooms, I find two twin beds on either side of the wall. One with a pink duvet and the other with a blue. The walls are neutral ivory, and a dresser is against the wall. The decorator lined a shelf beneath the window with books. It was nothing overwhelming, and I instantly loved it.

Happy with what I've seen so far, I take the steps to the third floor, where the designer set up a playroom. I notice the camera in the corner so I can check on them while I'm working even though I suppose that's the nanny's job.

Speaking of the nanny, the sound of a car coming down the driveway has my heart racing. I'm inviting this person into my home to help take care of the two most important people in my life.

Was I freaking nuts?

It was too late to back out, so I finished my sandwich and opened the front door to stand on the porch and hopefully greet my new nanny. Talon's call from earlier filters through my thoughts, but I toss them aside. She comes highly recommended, even if she recognizes me and my billionaire status.

The first thing I notice is the out-of-state license plate, as if the nanny is driving a rental car. I've already ordered an SUV to be delivered to the house later this week, so hopefully, I can convince this woman to return her rental and drive the larger vehicle. It has the highest safety protocols. Nothing short of perfect for my niece and nephew.

The slight glare off the windshield as the car comes to a stop in front of the house means I can't make out the person inside, but something inside my chest prickles in awareness. Something I hadn't felt since the day I hopped on a plane toward Scotland.

"Lila?" I ask as her long blond hair, the same shade of gold that I remember, comes into view.

Someone must be playing a cruel prank on me because, as she stands to her full height, her beautiful face renders me speechless.

"Is this some sort of sick joke?" she says, her feet pounding against the gravel as she makes her way toward me. "If you wanted your credit card back, you didn't have to stalk me!" she shouts as she approaches the steps.

I'm too shocked to respond. Never in a million years did I expect Lila to show up at my house as my new nanny. Hell, I didn't even care about the credit card I'd given her. She could have used it for the rest of her life, and I'd simply have paid the bills.

"I…I can't believe it's you. That you're here." My voice sounds deeper, even to my own ears.

With her hands firmly fisted on her hips, she cocks her head to the side, a wrinkle forming between her two eyebrows. Even in this fiery state, I've never seen someone so gorgeous. I'm completely entranced by her.

"Dean! That's all you're going to say?"

As she shouts at me, I can't pull my eyes away. The wind whips up, strands of her hair sticking to her lips as she speaks. Breathing deeply, hints of strawberry tickle my nose as I reach out and glide her hair behind her ear.

"Hi, Lila," I say in complete contrast to how she had just sounded. Her body sways backward, eyes growing with each passing second as I shock her. "I can promise you that this is not a trick, nor did I set this up. It's just…a fortuitous circumstance."

"What does that even mean?" she whispers as tires crunch on the driveway.

"It means that I really do need your help. My niece and nephew are here earlier than expected." My eyes dart over to the black sedan as the member of my family's security team parks next to Lila's car. Thankfully, my mother had secured a pickup at the airport for the kids since I had to scramble enough to get everything else ready.

"Oh." Lila spins on her heels, immediately forgetting I'm in her company, and focuses on the two little ones strapped in their car seats, waiting patiently to be let out.

I jump past her and make my way to the car, thanking Thomas as he pulls their luggage from the trunk. I expected more things for them, but apparently,

Genevieve preferred spending her money on herself and not the kids, one of many things we argued about.

I hurry to unbuckle them, my hands moving on autopilot, but when I lift them from the car, neither child bolts away in excitement the way they used to when I'd visit. No excited squeals. No wild, thudding footsteps across the gravel. Instead, they each cling to a leg, their tiny fingers curling tight around the fabric of my pants, stuffed animals clutched to their chests like shields.

Their silence pierces deeper than any scream could.

I glance down at them. Evelyn's wide eyes locked on the house like it might swallow her whole, and Oliver bites his lip so hard it's turning white. And I feel it like a punch to the ribs.

They used to run to me, eyes bright, voices high with excitement whenever I came to visit. Back then, I was just the fun uncle with shiny gifts and loud laughter, someone who swooped in a few times a year, whenever my sister wasn't halfway across the country chasing something new. It was easy to be the good guy when all I had to do was spoil them and then leave.

Now?

Now I'm the man left behind. The one who doesn't come and go. The one who stayed. And in their eyes, I'm no longer just Uncle Dean. I'm the reminder that their mother isn't walking through that door in front of them, if they even fully understand.

"Is this our new home?" Oliver asks, tilting his head back.

"It is. I hope you'll like it here. There is even a dock in the back for fishing."

"Oh. Cool."

I expect a similar question from Evelyn, but I'm also not surprised when her clutch on my leg tightens.

"Upstairs, there is a whole playroom just for you guys. How does that sound?"

"Really?" Oliver releases his grasp and inches toward the house, where Lila waits patiently on the porch. "Who is that?"

"That's Lila. She's going to be your new nanny. I hope."

"I don't need a nanny," Oliver demands as he stalks up the porch steps. "I start kindergarten soon."

Lila crouches down to his level and smiles. My fucking heart aches as I watch her. "Maybe I can just be your friend then. You can't ever have enough of those."

"But you're a girl."

"I am, but I have three younger brothers. One is even a cowboy. So I know all about boy stuff."

"Cool! I want to be a cowboy."

Slowly, I inch myself and Evelyn closer to the porch until we're standing at the base of the steps.

"This is Evelyn," I say, drawing Lila's attention.

"Hi, Evelyn. It's lovely to meet you." I'm fascinated as I watch Lila interact with the kids. She speaks softly but with a hint of enthusiasm. As if meeting these kids is the highlight of her day. "Who is that?" she asks, pointing toward the stuffed lamb that had seen better days.

Instead of replying, Evelyn shoves her thumb in her mouth, a habit I wasn't aware of until just now.

Crouching down, Evelyn doesn't let me get too far and nestles against my arm as I point at her lamb.

"This is Lamby, right?" She nods once but holds the stuffed toy out for Lila to inspect.

"Oh, she's very pretty. I love her little pink bow. Is that a color you like?"

Just above a whisper, Evelyn says, "Pink is my favorite."

Lila's eyes sparkle as if watching a fireworks display. "It's one of mine, too!"

Standing, Lila suggests that we show the kids their bedroom and get them some lunch as Oliver rambles on about being hungry.

The kids seem far less interested in their rooms than I expected. Each of them sets their toy on their respective beds and makes their way back toward the kitchen, Evelyn gripping my hand the entire time.

By the time we get to the kitchen, Lila has already made headway with some peanut butter sandwiches, rolled up to look like pinwheels, and sliced up peppers her mom had tossed in my cart.

I'm skeptical as she plates the meal in front of the kids at the small breakfast table in the kitchen, but they immediately dive in. Whether it be from exhaustion or pure hunger, they don't seem to mind the relatively healthy meal.

My smile catches Lila's attention as she cleans up the mess on the counter, and for a moment, I feel like everything will be alright. Especially if I can convince Lila to stay, because for every second she treats the kids like royalty, I can see that she's ready to ride off into the sunset.

Chapter Six

Lila

The house is stunning. A place I'd seen a few times when playing in the neighborhood with friends but never seen inside.

Of course, its beauty doesn't compare to the man sitting in the oversized playroom with the two kids building a tower out of Legos. While the kids ate earlier, I skimmed through the document Mom sent over the night before, listing the details of the nanny service and the terms. It already lined out a day off of my choosing every week and a salary that was frankly ridiculously high.

When I first met Dean on the plane, I hadn't given a single thought to whether he was rich or broke. He was just… kind. Someone who stepped in when I was falling apart, offering comfort without strings, a warm jacket, and a steady hand when I couldn't find my own footing.

But standing here now, in front of this sprawling estate that looks like it was ripped from a magazine spread, reality hits me square in the chest.

Dean Harrington isn't just a good guy with a charming smirk. He's someone with power. Money. Influence. The kind of man whose name probably carries weight in places I've never even stepped foot in.

And suddenly, all my carefully patched-up composure feels flimsy again.

I wrap my arms tighter around myself, unsure if the sudden chill is from the wind or the storm brewing inside me.

I'm supposed to be here to consider a job as a nanny. Live-in, no less.

But can I really work for the man who once saw me at my weakest, who offered me comfort on what was arguably the worst day of my life? Who looked at me like I was more than just a mess in a wedding dress?

The thought terrifies me.

Because I'm not sure if I'm more afraid of saying yes… or walking away.

Last night, I had been tinkering around in my notebooks and had a breakthrough regarding a chemical mixture that could combat the body's response to an allergic reaction. Almost like an epinephrine pen, but before the reaction begins. It made that urgency of finding a new research team reach a new height.

"Dean, can I speak with you for a moment?" The kids barely bat an eye in our direction as he joins me on the bench under the window, looking out to the waterway behind the house.

Of course, Dean leaves very little space between us as he sits, my body straightening as his leg brushes against mine. My reaction to him is another reason I should turn down the job and find a replacement. My sister, Hadley, is just as suited for the job as I am.

"Dean, I want to talk about the job. I'm not sure—" I begin, but he cuts me off.

"You know, when I ran into your mom at the grocery store this morning, I never would have imagined that you'd be the one showing up on my doorstep."

"I know this must be a shock to you."

"No, actually. If anything, it's a huge relief."

"How so?" I ask, twisting my body to look at him directly, but his eyes never leave the kids playing in the middle of the room. In a moment of weakness, I find myself admiring that about him. These two kids are his world, even though he never once mentioned them during our flight.

"Because I know you. It won't feel like a stranger living in this house with me."

"We only knew each other for six or seven hours, Dean. That hardly makes us friends."

Twisting his smirking face toward me, Dean says, "No, but you're going to marry me, so we're just hurrying things along a bit."

"Dean!" I reply in shock, smacking his arm playfully. The teasing reaction is one I haven't had toward a man in years, not even my ex-fiancé.

Thinking of Prescott immediately sours my mood. When I woke this morning, I had three missed calls from his number and one from his father. They all said the same thing: demands to come "home" and that I couldn't hide away forever.

The former made me laugh Ie Connecticut had never felt like home to me, but the latter left me feeling anxious. Like I was playing a stupid game of cat and mouse with a family that was all too keen to trap me again.

"What just happened? You were laughing, and suddenly, your face squished up like you'd eaten something rotten."

"Oh, it's nothing. Don't worry about it," I say, not wanting to explain the drama going on in my life.

"Hmm…" he hums just as Evelyn walks over and rests her body against Dean's leg, yawning widely.

"I think someone needs a nap. Is this around the time she normally takes one? You probably want to make sure she stays on her schedule."

"I… I don't know."

As he gently rubs a hand over her soft tuft of brown hair, I watch his entire body sag. It's immediately clear that there is more to the story than just their mother passing away recently.

"Well, we can always start a new routine, but I'm guessing she'll probably need to take a nap after lunch. That's how the preschool in town usually has their schedule."

"Yes, okay. I need to sign her up for that in the fall."

He gathers Evelyn in his arms, and together, we head down the stairs to their new room with her brother in tow. Oliver tries to mask his yawn but makes no argument when I guide him toward his own bed.

It only takes a few minutes before both kids are passed out, and I find myself alone, standing next to the door with Dean. We're close enough that I can smell his woodsy cologne and something that seems to be just him. I recognize it from our close confines two weeks ago.

"Can I help you bring in your things?" he asks, and I jump. "You can have any room you want," he adds with that smirk I am becoming way too fond of.

"I…um…didn't bring anything with me."

"You didn't?"

"I wasn't sure I was going to stay. I'm still not sure, to be honest. I'm a scientist, Dean. This is just a favor for my mom."

"Please, Lila. Those kids need you. I need you. I don't want to screw this up for them. They deserve so much more than they've been handed." Normally, I'd say someone begging and pleading like this is a great actor and really laying it on thick. But with Dean, I can't ignore the desperation in his eyes. It makes my chest ache in a way I've never experienced.

"Look…I can't promise it will be long-term, but I can help for a while. Maybe until the start of school." My voice barely sounds convincing to my own ears, but Dean's elation is electric, and as he leans forward, pressing his lips to my cheek, I find myself sparking with awareness. The kind that wants to wrap my arms around his waist and seal our lips together.

"You can't do things like that. It will confuse the kids." And my girly bits that haven't seen action in quite a while.

"Sure. Okay."

As the kids snooze, the usual hum of activity is absent, and the weight of the silence is almost suffocating. I'm not sure what I expected when we finally had a moment to talk, but this, the tension between us, certainly wasn't it.

Dean leans against the wall, arms crossed, his posture casual but his expression thoughtful. His gaze flickers to me, then to the floor, then back to my eyes. There's an air of uncertainty in him, something I hadn't expected from a guy who usually exudes such confidence.

On the other hand, I'm struggling to keep my own anxiety in check.

"Alright," Dean says, breaking the silence with a deep breath. "We need to lay down some ground rules. For both of us."

I raise an eyebrow, my arms instinctively crossing over my chest. "Ground rules?"

"Yeah," he says, his voice low, almost sheepish. "Look, I know I'm your employer here, and you're the nanny, and that's how it has to stay. But I'm also aware of how… well, how I can be. Let's just agree on some boundaries, so neither of us feels uncomfortable."

I tilt my head, watching him carefully. I can tell he's serious, but there's that same playful twinkle in his eyes, and I can't help but feel a little lighter despite the situation. I need him to clarify, though. This doesn't make sense yet.

He shifts his weight, pushing off the wall and stepping closer. "I'm allowed to flirt," he says, his lips quirking into that damn smile. "That's the deal. I mean, I can't help it. But if I do, you're allowed to roll your eyes. Or tell me to cut it out. No hard feelings. But…" He looks me straight in the eyes, his voice taking on a seriousness I'm not expecting. "But nothing goes further unless you want it to. You're in control here, Lila. You get to decide what's okay. I'll follow your lead. No pressure."

I blink, trying to process what he just said. The words hang in the air like a challenge, but there's a tenderness beneath it. I thought Dean was all about the teasing and the jokes, but now he's laying it all out by asking me for permission, for space. It catches me off guard.

"You don't have to flirt at all," I find myself saying, my voice quiet but steady. "But if you do, I'll roll my eyes and ignore you."

He laughs, the tension easing between us, though his eyes don't leave mine. "Fair enough," he says with a wink. "But in all seriousness, Lila, I'm not doing this to make you feel uncomfortable. I just want you to feel safe and… well, at ease. You deserve to feel that way here."

Something in his tone softens the knot that's been sitting in my stomach since this whole conversation started. I hadn't realized until now how much I needed someone to acknowledge how this situation might feel for me. How much I need to feel in control. And maybe, just maybe, I needed to hear that Dean understood that.

"Okay," I say, a little breathless. "I think I can handle that."

He smiles, his gaze a little too intense for my comfort, but I don't mind. "Good. We'll make this work. I'll respect the boundaries, Lila. I promise."

For a moment, we just stand there, the space between us charged with an energy that's hard to ignore. The playful banter, the teasing, the flirting—everything suddenly feels a little more real. And though I'm not entirely sure where this is going, something tells me it will change everything.

I nod, trying to steady my racing heart. "Yeah. We'll make it work."

And just like that, something shifts. There's an unspoken understanding between us, a quiet acknowledgment that what's happening here, whatever this is, feels like more than just a job. It feels like a beginning.

"I should probably go grab my things from my friend's house. I had planned to stay with her for a bit until I got back on my feet."

I slither past Dean and descend the stairs without gazing back at him.

"I'll be back before dinner."

Closing the front door, I take a deep breath, my first since arriving at the house.

What the hell have I done? I have zero desire to take this nanny job. My passion is in science. But I don't think Einstein himself could have turned down Dean and those two adorable kids.

Now I just have to figure out how to keep my heart in check around him. Because watching him step into fatherhood with such quiet strength, unwavering devotion, and a kind of fierce, selfless love? It's hands down the most dangerously attractive thing I've ever witnessed.

My grip on the steering wheel is so tight, I'm surprised it hasn't cracked under the pressure. My other hand is locked around my phone like it might fly away if I let go. I can feel my pulse in my throat, hammering against my skin as I press Ashvi's contact. The second it starts ringing, my breath catches, and when she finally picks up, my voice comes out shriller than I want. Too loud. Too desperate. But I can't help it. I'm hanging on by a thread, and she's the only one who might be able to remind me how to breathe.

"Ashvi! I'm headed to your house. I need reinforcements."

There's a beat of silence on the other end, then a rustle like she's scrambling for her other earpiece.

"Lila? What the hell happened? Are you okay?"

"No," I groan, weaving through the roads like it's personal. "Well—yes. Sort of. I mean, I haven't spontaneously combusted or driven off a cliff, so that's something. But I need your help."

"Breathe, babe. What's going on?"

I exhale, forcing the tension from my chest, but it barely budges. "I just agreed to move into a single father's place. As in, full-time. Living there. Nannying. All of it. And I have to pack up the little bits of my life before we head back over there."

Another pause, then, "Wait. Why are you freaking out right now? What aren't you telling me? Do we know him?"

"I do. Sort of. He… we met on the plane to Scotland."

"Holy shit."

"Yeah."

"You're moving in with him?"

"Yes, Ashvi. I don't have time to process all that right now. I need to pack, and I can't even remember where I left my shoes, let alone where I shoved my favorite bra. So unless you want me showing up with nothing but a duffel bag full of expired granola bars and mismatched socks—"

"I'm on it," she cuts in, voice full of motion now. "Do you want backup leggings or distraction wine?"

"Both. Obviously."

"And Lila?"

"Yeah?"

"You can do this."

Something catches in my throat. Because even though I'm spiraling and flailing and maybe making a huge mistake, there's something comforting about hearing her say that. Like I'm not completely losing it—just slightly.

"Thanks, Ashvi," I whisper.

"I'll see you in twenty. And you better spill everything while we sort your life into laundry piles."

And just like that, the chaos feels a little less loud. Because I have my best friend, a wild plan, and the tiniest flicker of hope that maybe, just maybe, this is the beginning of something real.

Wasting no time boxing up the few things I'd unpacked at Ashvi's house, I spend the next two hours trying to field all of my best friend's questions. It's not until I promise she can follow me over to his house that I get her to shut up.

The only morsel of information I give her is that I met Dean on the flight to Scotland and that he might be gorgeous.

As we arrive at his house, the lights on the main floor twinkling in the dusky sky, my nerves bubble to the surface like a volcano about to erupt.

I jump from my car, diverting Ashvi as she gleefully exits her own car.

"Ashvi, best behavior, please."

"Aw, I just want to meet the kiddos, Lila. And maybe snoop around the house."

Hitching my arm through hers, I nearly tug us to the ground as I walk up the porch. "No snooping. You're here to help me unload, and that's it, Vi."

"Aw, but the journalist in me loves to snoop. It's part of my amazing personality."

"No. Now behave."

My knock goes unanswered, the soft echo swallowed by the quiet. I hesitate only a moment before wrapping my fingers around the brushed metal knob and twisting slowly. The door creaks open on silent hinges, and I step inside, my breath catching at the stillness that greets me. The entryway is immaculate. Dark hardwood floors gleam beneath my shoes, offset by warm cream walls and crisp white trim. A narrow console table sits beneath a circular mirror, its surface bare but for a small ceramic bowl and a single, unlit candle. It's beautiful. Understated. Masculine without being cold.

But something tugs at me, subtle and hollow. There are no shoes by the door. No school bags tossed to the side. No family photos smiling back from the walls. No tiny fingerprints smudged on the glass. Just curated stillness. A house waiting to be lived in, to be claimed. To be made into something more than just square footage and good taste. It's a snapshot of someone who knows how to survive, but maybe hasn't quite figured out how to stay.

"This house is awesome," my friend mumbles, her head moving in all different directions.

Just as I'm about to force Ashvi to slip her shoes off with me, Dean comes around the corner wearing a black apron and holding a mixing bowl in his hands.

"Oh good, you're back. I thought you'd be gone longer," he says. The grin I'm learning is his signature grows by the second as our gaze's lock.

"I didn't have much to pack. Dean, this is my friend Ashvi. She's come to help."

"Oh great. Ashvi, it's nice to meet you," he says, walking forward, extending his hand in greeting. My friend stands frozen in place, mouth parted like a blow-up doll. I'm not even mad at her reaction because I know full well how enticing my new boss is.

"Ashvi." Nudging her in the side, my friend finally comes to her senses and shakes Dean's hand but remains silent.

"If you give me a minute, I can set this batter down and grab your things."

"Oh, you don't have to do that. I can grab it."

"Lila," he says forcefully. "Let me do this."

"Okay," I reply, shuffling behind him as he heads toward the kitchen. I don't check to see if Ashvi follows. "What are you making? I didn't know you could bake."

Dean glances over his shoulder at me, and I feel my core clench.

"There's a lot you don't know about me. But I thought some brownies would be a nice treat in our new home."

Our home. I hate how much I enjoy the way it sounds.

The kids are busy at the kitchen table coloring in some books Dean must have brought down for them. Ashvi and I sit with them until Dean returns fifteen minutes later.

"All you had were four boxes?" he asks as he takes some chicken breasts out of the fridge.

"Like I said, I didn't have much. If you don't mind, Ashvi and I will start putting things away and then I can prep dinner."

"I can handle dinner. You and your friend relax. There is some wine in the pantry you can help yourself to. Your mom said it was a good one."

My still speechless friend follows me dutifully as I grab the bottle and two glasses, taking in our fill of the first floor layout with a quick glance down the dock. Ashvi's on her phone the entire time while I marvel at the surroundings. Thankfully she follows as I make my way up to the second floor. I head to the bedroom next to the kids', assuming Dean will want me sleeping close to them, and luckily I'm right when I find my boxes on the floor in front of the fourposter bed.

The door swings open with a soft c"Ick,'and I step inside, stunned into stillness, thankful my boxes are already placed inside, otherwise I'd have dropped them.

This isn't a guest room.

It's a sanctuary.

The first thing I notice is the light. Golden beams filter through gauzy white curtains that billow just slightly from the open window, filling the space with a warmth that feels almost unreal. The walls are painted the softest shade of sage, fresh and calming, like something pulled straight from a high-end spa catalog. It's subtle, elegant, the kind of color that instantly settles the chaos in my chest.

A king-sized bed sits against the far wall, dressed in layers of plush white linens and an oversized tufted headboard upholstered in cream velvet. At the foot, there's a soft bench, the same neutral hue, topped with a folded knit throw in pale blush. The rug beneath my feet is thick and buttery, all texture and luxury, warming the dark wood floors with every step I take.

There's a full seating area tucked beside a built-in bookshelf, with two pale gray armchairs and a round marble-top coffee table between them. One corner boasts a writing desk, antique, by the look of it, with brass handles and a perfectly arranged tray of stationery and fountain pens I can't imagine ever using but love the thoughtfulness of.

And then there's the bathroom.

The door is slightly ajar, and I push it open like I'm afraid I'll break something. Inside, it's all cream tile and brushed gold fixtures, with a rainfall shower that could fit three people and a freestanding tub beneath a window that overlooks the backyard. A double vanity stretches along one wall, topped with granite and lit by sconces that glow like candlelight.

It smells faintly like eucalyptus and new beginnings.

There's a walk-in closet too, empty save for a few padded hangers and a full-length mirror that makes me do a double take because, for once, I don't hate what I see.

It's clear Dean spared no expense. And not just in the way that money speaks, but in the way thoughtfulness whispers. Every inch of this room feels like an invitation. A promise. A quiet reassurance that maybe… I'm not just a guest here.

"Oh my gosh. Oh my gosh. Oh my gosh," Ashvi squeals the moment she steps inside the room and closes the door behind herself. Like a hawk, she latches onto my arm with her talons and spins me to face in her direction. "Lila, do you know who that is? Do you have any idea who you're working for?"

Shrugging off her grip, I start pulling my clothes free from the boxes where I'd stuffed them earlier and laying them on the bed.

"No, but he's just a guy who got handed a tough situation, Vi." I explain as I break down one of the boxes and toss it onto the floor.

Suddenly, a phone is shoved at me and I can't look away from the screen with Dean's attractive face staring back at me.

I stare at my phone, Ashvi's words ringing in my ears. *World's Sexiest Billionaire Heir.* My brow furrows as I swipe through the article. "What kind of article is this?" I ask, skepticism lacing my voice. I can't help it, my mind is racing, trying to make sense of this. The words don't feel like they belong in the same universe as the man I know.

Ashvi's reply is immediate, the excitement practically leaping out of her screen. "Lila, your man is like the hottest guy in the world, literally, and he's heir to one of the oldest yacht and boating companies. The man makes a billion dollars every time he blinks."

The ground shifts beneath my feet. *A billion dollars every time he blinks?* What does that even mean? I let out a nervous laugh, dismissing it, though there's a hint of disbelief in my tone. "I'm sure that's not true."

But deep down, as I stare at the glowing screen, a strange mix of disbelief and curiosity stirs in my chest. I try to ignore it, to tell myself that Ashvi's exaggerating, that she's just seeing him through the same rose-colored glasses I'd seen him through when I first met him. The chemistry, the laughter, the light-heartedness we shared—they don't make sense in the context of billion-dollar businesses and glossy magazine headlines.

No, this Isn't him, I think, *he's not like that. He's... well, he's real. He's grounded.*

Still, my mind can't help but wonder. Is this the life he was leading before? The one I don't know about? The life that feels so far out of reach?

I glance back at the article, the headline blurring slightly in my vision. *World's Sexiest Billionaire Heir.* The words keep repeating in my mind like a mantra.

My chest tightens.

I roll my eyes, trying to push away the thoughts. *Stop it. This isn't what matters.*

Yet, as I scroll back up to the picture of him, my heart does that strange thing it always does when I see his face. That little flutter of recognition. That *he's the one* feeling. He's more than just a man with money. He's someone who makes me feel like I'm worthy, like I belong. But what if this whole other world of his is something I'm not equipped to handle? Something so different from the life I've just escaped from?

I shove the phone back at Ashvi, rubbing my eyes with the heels of my hands. There's a heaviness in my chest now, a contradiction that I don't want to deal with.

"Oh, it's very true. Not only does he have a trust fund worth more than most first world countries, but he's invested in dozens of companies that are all Fortune 500 now."

"So? Who cares that he has money?"

"Ugh…because he's gorgeous and you should absolutely hit that."

Throwing a sweatshirt at her head, I laugh as she eats a mouthful of cotton as I set her phone on the bed.

"He's my boss now. You know how strict my mom is about that sort of stuff. And those kids need my help. So does Dean if everything about those kids is true."

"I thought you were going to try to find a job doing research, at least until you can get a new grant."

"I am, and I will, but they need me right now."

Warm arms wrap around my shoulders from behind, and I lean into my best friend. "Maybe you need them, too. All jokes aside, I want you to be careful."

"I'm not worried about Prescott," I fib.

"I'm not talking about your ex, Lila. I'm talking about your heart."

Unlike Ashvi, I'm not worried about falling for Dean. He has enough on his plate, as do I. It may take all my willpower, but my heart won't be the issue. It will be the desire to spend the night in his bed.

Thankfully, as I hear the patter of little feet down the hall, I know I have the best blockers on the planet. Kids are a very good deterrent.

The knot in my stomach tightens as Ashvi's words hang in the air. "Well, if you're not going to give the Dean train a go, can I climb aboard?"

I tell myself to stay cool, to laugh it off, but the flutter in my stomach tells me it's not that simple. I try to mask the little spark of something, but it's there, undeniable. I've spent the last couple of hours trying to ignore how much I *feel* when it comes to Dean, but here's Ashvi, my best friend, throwing out the possibility of her own interest in him, and suddenly, everything I thought I could ignore rushes to the surface.

I bite the inside of my cheek, keeping my gaze steady as I respond, pretending I don't feel that sharp sting of irritation.

"What happened to the Navy guy?" I ask, trying to shift the focus away from Dean and onto something, anything, that feels safer.

But Ashvi doesn't seem to catch on, or maybe she does and just doesn't care. Either way, I can feel her attention still lingering on the idea of Dean. I should be happy for her. Hell, she's my best friend. If she wants to go after him, that's her choice, but why does the thought of her even considering it make my chest tighten with a jealousy I'm not supposed to feel?

Because if I'm being honest, I can't help but *want* him. I can't help but want to be the one he notices, the one he cares about.

I close my eyes for a second, the back of my head hitting the pillow as I try to let the anxiety settle. I tell myself it's nothing. Just a fluke. I don't have any claim to Dean. He's a guy who was kind enough to help me out of my mess, and now he's probably just a guy who doesn't even remember my name when he's with someone else. But the thought of Ashvi going after him, of her being the one to get his attention, makes me irrationally annoyed.

Let's not even mention the fact that he's my *boss*. A long-standing rule for my mom's business that I know shouldn't be crossed.

I rub my temples, trying to clear the fogginess in my head. *Get it together*, I tell myself. *He's not your guy.*

The kids stand at the doorway watching me unpack and the little sponges are absorbing every word we say. Thankfully, Ashvi just shrugs and helps hang some of my clothes while I shove my underwear into the top dresser drawer as quickly as possible.

Not long later, Dean calls all five of us down for dinner. The kids are having a field day playing in my bedroom with the microscope I brought. Thankfully, I had some samples of foods stored on slides that they could view.

Ashvi and I have already finished off a glass of wine by the time she decides to head home, leaving me alone with Dean. Quietly, I gather all the dishes and nudge Oliver to help me at the sink.

Dean begins to stand, and I glare at him to sit back down and enjoy the beer he opened when he served dinner. Like a typical three-year-old, Evelyn is still pushing around the green beans on her plate.

Oliver and I make a game with the soapsuds and the utensils as we finish washing the dishes. I keep an eye on him as he stands on a barstool leaning over the sink, with the forks battling against the mixing spoons.

A rush of heat floods my back, and then I feel it— his hand, warm and firm, settling against my hip. The fingers flex once, a gentle press that sends a shock wave through my body. Every inch of my skin reacts like it's been lit on fire, the sparks crawling up my spine and down to my fingertips, leaving me breathless and dizzy. I swallow hard, my pulse thumping erratically. The air feels heavier now, charged with something raw, something electric. "You know there is a dishwasher," Dean's gravelly voice growls against my ear.

A sound similar to an agreement stumbles from my lips. He chuckles as he sets the additional plates in the open sink, and I instantly miss the loss of his touch as he steps away, sweeping Evelyn up into his arms. We'd discussed during the meal that tackling bath time after dinner would be best for a new routine.

Despite being wary about caring for the kids, Dean has great instincts. He even offered to do Evelyn's bath, something he'd done before when his sister visited with them. I'm not sure if it was nerves, but he disclosed the first time he took care of the kids, Oliver had just turned three and Evelyn was a few months old. His sister had dropped them off at his penthouse and ran off for a month before he and his parents could track her down.

My heart breaks every time I hear more about the children's upbringing.

Oliver and I finish up the dishes and make our way up to the bathroom, following the spurts of giggles, both male and female, mixing with the telltale sound of splashing water.

Dean's shirt is soaked through, the white cotton molded to him like a second skin. I have to force my tongue to stay in my mouth so he doesn't catch me ogling him.

"Hey, my man, ready for your turn?" he asks Oliver as Evelyn stands and reaches her arms out for him. Swapping places, I take the toddler out of the bath and wrap her in a bright pink towel.

Unlike his sister, Oliver speeds through his bath, the duo joining us in the bedroom as I tug the llama pajama pants onto Evelyn.

The couple of hours before their bedtime are spent in the playroom, and I notice Dean frowning at his phone as it continues to ping with notifications. At one point, he either mutes or turns it off and shoves it in his pocket with a deep frown etched on his face.

The kids fall asleep rapidly as Dean reads them a story, Evelyn slumbering across his lap while Oliver's head is tucked under Dean's arm. Without thinking, I grab my phone and snap a picture of the trio, ignoring more of Prescott's unread messages.

Downstairs, I pour myself another glass of wine and settle against the plush couch in the living room. Beyond the French doors is a screened-in deck running the expanse of the back of the house. I can't wait to spend time out there in the summer.

Snap out of it, Lila. I need to keep reminding myself that this is not a permanent situation. Just something to tide me over until I can get a new research grant and find a facility.

But watching the sunset over the bay leaves an ache in my chest. I've missed the town and people here and how, even though everyone knows your business, they are the biggest supporters.

"Hey." Dean settles onto the couch next to me with a glass of amber liquid. So lost in my own thoughts, I didn't even hear him descend the stairs and enter the room.

"Hi. Did you get the kids settled?"

"Yeah," he says, sipping his beverage. "Oliver asked when his mom was coming to see the new house."

I nearly spit my wine out. "Oh, Dean."

He turns toward me, and I see the pools of water lining his lower lids. "How do I explain to them their mom isn't ever coming back? How do I tell them that drugs meant more to their mom than they did? How do I navigate any of this?"

The nurturing part of me, the part that loved being a nanny when I was in high school and enjoyed babysitting my siblings, broke free. Reaching out, I grasp his hand and intertwine his fingers with mine.

"Dean, just one step at a time. That's the only thing you can do."

"I never wanted this…being a father. The fun uncle? The one that sneaks treats after bed and plays hooky from school? That's me. I'm not sure I can handle all this responsibility…but I want to try. I'm just…out of my element."

"I think just questioning whether you're capable of being a parent means you're already on the right path to being one. No one can be prepared to answer the sort of questions you'll face, Dean. Just answer honestly and help them understand that your sister had some flaws but loved them very much."

"Did she, though?"

"I can't answer that, but they adore you. You can do this, Dean, with or without my help." I squeeze his hand gently and start to pull my hand away, but Dean tightens his grip as he settles onto the couch.

I hate to admit how good his hand feels against mine. Despite his silver-spoon upbringing, Dean's hands are rough. My dad always said that was a clear sign of a hard worker.

The silence that grows between us isn't uncomfortable, but the mood is still heavy, like a weighted blanket that's not as cozy.

I twist on the couch, tucking one of my feet under my opposite knee. The selfish part of me doesn't release Dean's hand. I don't think I could if I tried.

"So, Ashvi had some interesting things to say about you."

Dean's body tenses before he turns his face toward me. "Oh, really?"

"Yeah, something about you being on a list of billionaire heirs."

"Mm-hmm, not just any list—world's sexiest."

He wags his eyebrows, and I find myself giggling.

"How much did you have to pay to rig that list in your favor?" I joke.

Leaning closer to me, Dean brushes his thumb back and forth across my hand. "You don't think I could have won it on my own? Don't you think I'm sexy?"

That silly song about being too sexy starts playing in the background of my mind as I lock eyes with Dean. Another giggle threatens to burst forth.

"I…" I begin just as Dean rotates his entire body to face mine, mimicking how I'm sitting. "I think I should head to bed."

"It's seven thirty."

"Well, maybe I'm tired."

"Or maybe I make you nervous."

"You don't," I reply, my voice cracking midway.

Somehow, Dean's closer now, his face mere inches away from mine. My fingers itch to reach out and touch the stubble along his jaw.

"I think you want me to kiss you."

Breathlessly, I reply, "Wrong again."

His eyes trace my movements as I lick my lips.

Suddenly, his mood shifts, and Dean moves back against the couch and takes a sip of his drink before reaching for the remote on the coffee table.

"Whatever you say, ghost girl."

Brusquely, I stand from the couch, my wine nearly spilling from my glass. "I think I'll spend the rest of the evening in the library. Thank you very much." My feet smack against the hardwoods as I move toward the front of the house, where I noticed a small library filled with books earlier. I make sure to grab the wine bottle on my way.

Just as I'm about to turn down the hall, Dean's deep voice calls out, "You know, I'm not going to kiss you until you ask me."

"Not going to happen."

Dean's laughter fills the living room as I walk away. I swear I hear him say, "It will."

"Arrogant bastard."

Chapter Seven

Dean

The mornings with Lila under my roof start with the scent of maple syrup and laughter. Not a bad combination.

I glance up from the financial report open on my laptop, the blue light from the screen casting a glow across the dark wood of my desk. I'm supposed to be focused on quarterly returns and partnership projections, but all I can hear is Evelyn's squeal from the kitchen.

"More pancake, Lila!"

Her tiny voice carries through the hallway, bouncing off the walls of this new house like it's always belonged here. I shut the laptop. Screw projections. For five minutes, I want to see what this house looks like with a little light in it.

I step out of the office barefoot, scratching at the stubble on my jaw. The hardwood is cool beneath my feet as I pad down the stairs toward the kitchen. The scent hits me before I reach the doorway—coffee, cinnamon, and something so warm it makes my chest ache.

She's got Evelyn balanced on one hip, her brown hair wild with sleep. Remnants of syrup cause some hair to stick to her cheek. Lila is talking to her in a soft, animated voice while flipping pancakes one-handed.

"Do you think butterflies like pancakes?" Lila asks, clearly mid-conversation. "Maybe they prefer nectar, but who can resist maple syrup?"

Evelyn giggles and says something unintelligible around her thumb. Lila kisses the top of her head like it's the most natural thing in the world. Like she's always been here.

And something in me settles. Softens.

She hasn't been here long—five days, maybe six—but the difference is impossible to ignore. The house is cleaner, sure, but not in a sterile way. It's lived-in. Dinosaur figurines are on the mantel, a crayon drawing of our family (stick figures with very large heads) is taped to the fridge, and the faint sound of beach music plays from her phone on the windowsill.

She fits here. God help me, she fits here too well.

Oliver comes bounding in from the living room, his footfalls heavy and loud like always. He wields a plastic sword in one hand and a bowl of dry cereal in the other. "Lila! Lila! I saved the deck from the lava monster."

"Again?" she teases, setting Evelyn into her high chair with practiced ease. "That monster never learns."

"I know!" he shouts, triumphant.

I lean in the doorway, arms crossed, letting the moment play out.

She's got on an old T-shirt I saw folded in the laundry room, soft and worn in with a faded baseball logo on the front. Her hair's tied up in a loose bun, and she's got pancake batter on her cheekbone. I have never seen anyone more effortlessly beautiful.

She catches me watching and freezes for a second, her cheeks pinking as she turns to flip the next pancake.

"Morning," I offer casually even though my chest is anything but.

She glances at me over her shoulder, giving a small smile. "Good morning."

Evelyn kicks her feet in the high chair, syrup already smeared across the tray. "Lila made Mickey Mouse pancakes," she declares with a sticky grin.

I walk forward, ruffling Oliver's hair as I pass, and glance down at the plate she slides across the counter. Sure enough, there's a pancake with two smaller pancakes as ears.

"Creative," I say, raising a brow. "Trying to outshine me already?"

She smirks, a flash of mischief in her eyes. "Just trying to keep morale up in the ranks, boss."

After breakfast, the house settles into a quiet rhythm. Oliver pulls out his LEGOS and builds a fortress on the living room floor while Evelyn curls into the corner of the couch with a stack of board books Lila picked out from the library.

Lila moves through the space like she belongs in it. She hums when she folds the laundry, plays hide-and-seek while brushing crumbs from the floor, and somehow remembers Evelyn's favorite snack and Oliver's least favorite color.

I try to keep to my office, really, I do. But every time I look up from my screen, I find myself listening for her voice. For her laughter. For the sound of her reading out loud.

I catch glimpses through the doorway. Lila sits cross-legged on the floor next to Oliver, helping him sort the blue blocks from the green. She listens with her whole body, leaning in, offering encouragement with a simple touch to his back or a proud smile.

My chest tightens watching it—that quiet, unspoken connection.

It isn't just that she's good with the kids. It's that she sees them. Really sees them. She makes Evelyn feel brave, and Oliver feel like the smartest kid in the world. She makes me…feel something I haven't let myself feel in a long damn time. Safe.

Around midday, I hear her laugh through the back door. I step out onto the deck with a fresh cup of coffee and watch from the top step as she races across the lawn with Evelyn tucked under one arm like a football. Oliver trails them, giggling and shrieking.

Lila collapses onto the blanket they'd spread beneath the oak tree earlier. Evelyn crawls up her chest to nuzzle under her chin.

And that dangerous warmth in my chest blooms again.

It takes every ounce of discipline I have not to go to her. Not to kiss the sun off her cheeks and brush the grass from her hair and ask if she's felt it too, this pull. This ache that doesn't feel like infatuation. It feels like coming home. But I don't. Because she deserves time. She deserves space. She deserves to choose this life without me pushing her toward it.

So I sit with my coffee. And I watch her fall into place in our world.

By the time late afternoon drapes soft golden light across the backyard, the house has quieted into a kind of hush that feels sacred. Evelyn's finally down for her nap with one chubby fist curled around her plush fox and the other pressed against her cheek. Oliver's on the couch with a book about knights and dragons, eyelids already fluttering shut despite insisting he wasn't tired.

And Lila?

Lila's in the kitchen, standing at the sink with her back to me, sleeves pushed up, wrists wet, humming along softly to some indie folk song playing low on the speaker.

I should be in my office. A contract waits for my signature, a dozen emails need a response, and the quarterly report won't read itself. Instead, I find myself leaning against the doorframe like some smitten fool, just watching her rinse out plastic cups and stack them neatly on the drying rack.

She moves with ease now. The way she sways on her toes and wipes down the counter with a flick of her wrist is all muscle memory. Habit. Like she's always belonged here. Like this house remembers how to breathe again because she walked in and opened every damn window.

I step into the kitchen quietly, not wanting to startle her, but she turns just as I reach for a dish towel.

"You stalking me again?" she asks with no edge in her voice, only warmth. Amusement. Maybe even something softer, hidden in the corner of her smile.

I grab a bowl from the drying rack and start towel-drying it, letting the silence stretch for a beat before answering. "Just here to help."

Her brows rise. "Really? Dean Harrington drying dishes? Should I be worried about the structural integrity of the universe?"

I laugh, and it comes easier than I expect. "Don't let the billionaire title fool you. I know how to load a dishwasher, and I make a mean mac and cheese."

She hums thoughtfully. "I'll believe the mac and cheese when I taste it."

I nudge her gently with my elbow as we work side by side. Not touching, not really. Just close enough that I can smell her faint floral shampoo and see the little splash of flour still dusted near her collarbone.

"How's the first couple of days been?" I ask after a moment, keeping my tone casual. "You settling in okay?"

She leans her hip against the counter, drying her hands slowly on a towel. "Yeah. I mean… yeah. It's a lot but in a good way. The kids are amazing. This house is starting to feel less like a guest room and more like a home."

I nod, trying not to show how much that means to me. That she's letting it happen. Letting us in.

"And you?" she adds, her voice quiet now. "Is this working for you?"

The question catches me off guard. Not because I haven't thought about it but because I have. Constantly. And not just in terms of logistics. But in ways I haven't let myself say aloud.

"You're great with them," I say. "Better than I even hoped for. Evelyn asks for you the second she wakes up. Oliver doesn't stop talking about your science facts."

She chuckles, but a hint of a blush rises on her cheeks. "I think they just like that I don't mind getting messy with them."

"Maybe," I say. "But it's more than that. You see them."

Lila's lips part like she's about to deflect the compliment, but I don't let her. I set the bowl down and turn toward her fully.

"You see them for who they are, not just who they're supposed to be. That matters."

She's still for a long moment, eyes locked with mine. There's something in her gaze, something raw and vulnerable and aching with the weight of old wounds. And I want to ask. I want to know what put that look in her eyes. But I also know it's too soon.

So instead, I reach for the dish towel again, giving her the space she doesn't ask for but clearly needs.

She takes a steady breath. "I never thought I'd want to do this, you know? The kid stuff. The routines. The chaos. I did enough of it growing up. But… there's something about your kids. Something about this place."

She doesn't finish the thought. She doesn't have to.

The air thickens between us, charged and warm, humming with things left unsaid. And I swear, if I took one step closer, I could see whether that look in her eyes is just exhaustion or if she feels this attraction growing between us too.

But I don't.

Instead, I offer her the smallest smile and reach up to flick a bit of batter from her cheek.

"You missed a spot."

She blinks, startled, then lets out a soft laugh. "Pancake battle scar."

I should step back. I don't. And neither does she.

We stand there, close enough to count the faint freckles on her nose, her gaze flicking to my mouth for a fraction of a second too long. But then the baby monitor crackles to life with Evelyn's soft, sleepy murmurs, and the spell breaks.

Lila steps back, brushing her hands on her jeans. "Duty calls."

"Yeah," I say even though part of me wants to keep her right here. Just a little longer.

She turns toward the hallway, pausing just long enough to look over her shoulder. "Thanks for the help, Dean."

Anytime, I almost say.

But she's already gone, the faint scent of sugar and soap lingering in her wake.

And me? I'm still standing in the kitchen, gripping a dish towel, heart pounding like I've just stepped off a ledge.

The house is finally quiet. It's the kind of silence you only get after bedtime with kids—the echo of laughter still clinging to the walls, dishes stacked in the sink, and the hum of the dishwasher the only sound breaking through the calm.

I should be down the hall. Technically, I'm still logged into an investor meeting I bailed on twenty minutes ago. But I made my excuses, closed the laptop, and came downstairs instead.

And there she is.

Lila.

Sitting at the kitchen table in an oversized navy blue sweatshirt, she has her sleeves pushed up and her hair falls loose around her face. She's got a mug of tea tucked under her chin and her laptop open in front of her, brows slightly furrowed as she types.

I lean against the doorway and watch her for a second, unnoticed. A small crease appears between her eyebrows when she's concentrating. She bites her lip when she's rereading something. Every now and then, she glances at her notes with a soft sigh, then goes right back to it.

Even when she's working, she's calming to be around. I walk over and pull out the chair across from her. She looks up, startled.

"Sorry," I murmur. "Didn't mean to interrupt the scientific breakthrough."

She huffs a soft laugh, closing her laptop halfway. "Hardly. I'm just reviewing a proposal I put together last year, thinking I could recycle part of it for another request."

I raise a brow. "Anything I can help with?"

She tilts her head, curious. "Do you know much about immunoglobulin E antibody-mediated food responses?"

"Not a damn thing."

She laughs again, and God, that sound burrows somewhere deep in my chest.

"But I do know a thing or two about putting together a pitch. If you want someone to bounce it off."

"I might take you up on that," she says, fingers sliding over the rim of her mug. "It's just... hard to focus sometimes. Hard to make it all fit."

She doesn't say what exactly she's trying to fit together, but I know. Work. This new life. It's a lot.

So I nod and don't press. "How about I grab my laptop and work here with you?"

Her eyes widen slightly, surprised. "You want to work... at the kitchen table?"

I grin. "I'm not so high-and-mighty that I can't trade a leather chair for a little wood. Besides, the view's better down here."

She ducks her head at that, cheeks turning pink. But she doesn't tell me to stop. Doesn't tell me to go.

Instead, she nods.

I dash into my office to grab my laptop, then return to settle across from her. We fall into a rhythm for a few minutes—keys clacking, mugs refilling, companionable silence stretching like a blanket over us both.

At one point, Lila pulls her knees up into the chair, leaning forward over her notes. A strand of hair falls over her cheek, and I have to physically restrain myself from brushing it back.

She catches me staring.

"What?" she asks, but it's soft, not accusatory.

I shake my head. "Just… you're really good at this."

"At what?"

"This whole… being here. With the kids. With me." I shrug a little. "It's like you've been here forever."

Something flickers in her expression—hope, fear, maybe a mix of both. She opens her mouth, then closes it again. I let it sit. I don't need her to say anything she's not ready to say.

She changes the subject. "Oliver asked if you and I are getting married."

I laugh, leaning back in my chair. "He did?"

She nods, smiling now. "I told him I didn't think so."

My stomach twists a little, but not in the way I expected. Not with regret. Just with that strange ache of wanting something you can't quite name.

"What would you say if I told you he wasn't the only one wondering that?"

She blinks at me, the smile fading into something more serious.

"I'd say… fools rush in."

"Every man hath a fool in his sleeve," I quote.

Another quiet stretch.

She closes her laptop, pushes it aside, and folds her arms on the table. "Do you miss it?"

"What?"

"Your old life. The money. The jet-setting. The power."

I consider the question. "I miss the simplicity of having a plan and knowing where I was going next. But I don't miss the cost of it. I don't miss feeling like I was building something and still had nothing real to come home to."

Her gaze softens. "You built something with them, Dean. Even before I showed up."

"Yeah," I say, voice rough. "But it didn't start to feel right until you came through that door."

She blushes again, looking away, but her smile says it all.

We don't stay at the table much longer. It's late. The tea's gone cold. She stretches and yawns, mumbling something about needing sleep. I walk her to the bottom of the stairs, and both of us pause, not quite ready to say good night.

"Thanks for the company," she murmurs, turning to go.

"Anytime," I reply.

And I mean it. Because the longer she's here, the more I realize I don't want a life that doesn't include her in it. Even if, for now, it's just quiet nights and shared glances across the kitchen table.

Chapter Eight

Dean

It's been just over a week of living under the same roof as Lila. I thought being surrounded by two young children would be the hardest thing I'd encounter over the last seven days, but instead, I find my growing desire for Lila makes each passing second nearly unbearable.

Despite a few nightmares from Oliver and Evelyn, the kids seem to have transitioned to their new situation as best as expected. So much so that Oliver moved into his bedroom at his own request. I've set up an appointment with a therapist in town to help the kids, but mainly, it's for me. The grief over my sister gets me late into the night, and I find myself tossing and turning. I can usually function on a few short hours of sleep, but a week straight isn't cutting it.

I've drowned myself in work to keep my thoughts about Gen and Lila at bay. I'm a silent partner in a few businesses, yet I'm very hands-on with others, especially when technology is involved. But I know running on empty will only last so long.

Today, I have a meeting as a shareholder in my favorite security firm as they try to navigate a possible acquisition. The two tech guys who started the business had once lived in a homeless shelter in Miami. I met them during one of the charity events I sponsor on behalf of my family to help runaway teens become entrepreneurs. Out of all the businesses I've seen flourish because of that charity, this one is my favorite. I was on the fence about the acquisition by a much larger tech firm but was willing to hear out both parties.

But it also means that my week of putting my life together after gaining guardianship of the little squirts is over. Now I need to figure out how to juggle my past life with my new one. Thank goodness for Lila, who plans to take the kids to the park today. She wants them to start making friends with kids in town who could potentially be their classmates. Oliver has about three months until he starts kindergarten, and Evelyn starts her new preschool class just a few weeks before that.

Quietly sneaking out of the kids' room, I'm not surprised to find the first floor barren. After her first week, I expect Lila to take advantage of whatever downtime she can get.

Back in my room, I shower, then pull on one of my suits for the first time since I left for Scotland. Was I required to wear the suits? Absolutely not. But it makes me feel like an important part of the businesses I work with. And frankly, I've always loved wearing a custom-made getup.

Approaching the kitchen, the smell of coffee greets me, and I nearly collide with Lila as she exits the pantry.

"Oomph," she says as I offer, "Sorry."

"Oh…um…you're wearing a suit," she says breathlessly, clutching her floral bathrobe around her chest.

"Yeah, I have a couple of meetings today."

She cocks her head to the side. "Here?"

"Yep. Virtual."

"Well, you look nice."

"Thanks."

The silence festers, and I can sense her awkwardness. Trying to spare her more discomfort, I reach into the cabinets for a mug and pour myself a cup of coffee.

"I was going to make myself some eggs. Would you like some?" I ask, turning around and finding her eyes darting up from my hips to my face. I smirk, knowing I've caught her ogling my ass. I spend enough hours working out to appreciate her attention. This also reminds me that I need to set up a gym in the house. Maybe in one of the additional spare bedrooms.

"Eggs sound good. Thanks. Want me to start some sausage or bacon?" Lila leans into the fridge, rummaging around for the breakfast items.

"We should have some bacon I bought. I hate sausage."

Bowing around the door, she looks at me with pinched lips. "Are you just saying that because people refer to men's dicks as sausages, and you're an uber male who prefers women?"

"That's sweet of you to call me an uber male," I add, chuckling as she rolls her eyes. "But no, I've hated sausage since I was a kid. One of my old nannies served it with everything, and I mean everything. She treated it like a protein for every meal of the day. Sometimes even the smell makes me nauseous."

"That's…strange."

"Tell me about it."

Handing me the carton of eggs, I start cracking them on the side of the mixing bowl.

"Will you eat it on pizza?"

"Nope."

"What a travesty. I love a meat lover's pizza."

"I bet you do."

"Oh my gosh," she says, hip checking me. "Can you not make everything so sexual all the time?"

"Can't help it. It's a gift."

We work seamlessly in the kitchen, putting together breakfast for ourselves and the kids for when they decide to wake up. Lila suggests getting them on a schedule on weekdays in the mornings. That way, their transition to school will be easier.

Her ease at being a nanny blows my mind. Despite whatever reticence she feels toward the position, she's simply amazing.

Once breakfast is plated and the toast pops out of the toaster, Lila and I scarf down our food just as the pitter-patter of feet descends the stairs.

She offers to take care of them while I head to the office to work on some projects. I have a few things to do before my meetings. One of which includes learning Lila's ex-fiancé's name and what he possibly could have done to screw things up with her. From what I know about my nanny, she would have only run if he did something truly horrific.

Pulling up Ashvi's number—because of course I made it a priority to get info on Lila's best friend for safety reasons—I type out a message, hoping she'll spill the details on Lila's ex.

It's not long before she replies with a name and nothing else: Prescott Hoolihan.

I recognize the last name immediately. The Hoolihans are notorious political figures with bad attitudes and even worse secrets. There had been rumors circling for years that they dealt in the black market for their own personal goods. I can't imagine Lila being wrapped up in that family. She didn't have a cagey bone in her body.

My investigation ends abruptly when Talon calls to tell me that Rory just got out of her regular doctor's appointment and she's dilated. The baby could come at any time now. I can hear the nerves in my best friend's voice, but Talon is the best man I know, and he'll be an amazing father.

Meetings fall into consecutive video conferences, and before I know it, my growling stomach alerts me that it's well past lunchtime. For someone who only turns a small profit on my investments, I feel like an hourly employee who's worked too many hours of overtime and has nothing to show for it.

When I scan the fridge's contents, nothing jumps out at me. With a glance at my watch, I decide to head into town and check out a restaurant to grab something to eat. Maybe if I'm lucky, I'll run into Lila and the kids at the park. I'm not sure when they headed out exactly, but I can't imagine they've been gone long.

I've finally convinced Lila to drive the SUV I ordered and return her rental. It was missing from the garage as I start my Lamborghini.

The drive into town is a peaceful twenty minutes. Farms and fields pass by in a blur, and I wonder if any of them belong to Lila's family. I need to take Claire up on her standing reservation for dinner.

With an idea in mind, I make a quick call just as I pull into a parking spot along the street in front of a hamburger joint located on one of the town's alley streets. I step out of the car, and the smell of barbecued meat makes my stomach cramp in anticipation.

Taking a chance, I order four burgers and enough fries to feed an entire hockey team, then make my way toward the park two blocks down the street.

As I walk, I let the scent of the salty air calm my nerves. The town lends itself to a movie set. The faded brick buildings, weathered shutters, and bright flowers in window boxes are idyllic. I can visualize Lila growing up here, and I know I've made a good choice in bringing the kids here. It's a far better life than wondering if their mom will come home or if food will be on the table at night. I love my sister, but she had clearly lost her way.

My breath hitches as I reach the park and witness the families milling about.

Fuck, my sister could have had this. I could have had this.

I take a deep breath and move closer to the mulch-covered, fence-lined area containing multiple plastic and wood playsets. That emptiness in my chest, the one that I suppressed as I got older, bubbles up to the surface. My parents never took us to the park as kids. It's not that we were home much outside of boarding school, but they didn't even have a swing set installed in our massive estate. Their idea of playing with us was taking us on the vacations they planned for themselves.

I find an unoccupied bench and set down the bag of food and drinks. Even though the chilly air is still crisp, the sun warms my skin in a way I haven't felt in a while. Even in Miami, I rarely took the time to soak in the sun.

Slipping my jacket off my shoulders, I glance around the park. I look for Oliver and Evelyn, ignoring the appreciative glances from a few moms as they stare in my direction.

When I don't see them, I move closer to one of the larger playsets, the yellow swirling slide catching my eye. As a kid, that is undeniably something I'd want to try.

As I approach, I see a group of four older boys, around the age of ten, squaring off against Lila, who's shielding Oliver and Evelyn as they stand at the entrance to the slide.

"Let me make this very clear. You push any kid out of the way one more time, and I will make sure that you're not allowed back at this park… ever."

"You can't do that," one little kid touts with puckered, defiant lips.

"I can, and I will. There are eight different slides in this park. If you're that impatient to wait for your turn, why don't you try out one of them instead?"

Watching the scene unfold, I'm not surprised the older kids huff and walk off the play set toward another. Lila waits patiently for Oliver and Evelyn to go down before she takes the steps downward. Oliver and Evelyn waste no time climbing the stairs to go down the slide a few more times.

"Hey," I say when Lila spots me.

"Hi. I didn't expect to see you here today," she says as she unscrews the cap of her water bottle.

"What just happened up there?"

"Oh, you know, just trying to teach some kids manners. Their parents aren't even here monitoring them."

"Should they be?" I ask naively.

"Always. Anything could happen at a playground. What if one of their kids fell and broke a bone? Or worse… you know… someone comes and takes them." Lila shivers as she sips from her water bottle and recaps it.

I didn't want to push that it's a silly playground in a small town. I know she has her reasons, and the longer I ponder, the more I can't imagine not watching the kids and something happening to them.

"Besides, the one that kept pushing the kids out of the way? I went to school with his mom, and let me tell you, the apple clearly didn't fall far from the tree."

"That so?" I ask, curiously wanting to know more about things she experienced growing up. When she simply shrugs, I say, "Come on, I brought lunch."

Lila thanks me and gestures for the kids to join us. Evelyn seems the most excited to get a sandwich of her own instead of sharing one with her brother.

As we finish, a group of four women approaches us, each of them carrying the same air of fake confidence. The way they walk, those exaggerated struts, the concerned head tilts, and eyes full of judgment all wrapped up in those perfectly painted-on smiles. I know this look all too well.

The woman in front, a boxy-blonde with an oversized fake leather bag, gives Lila a cold, calculating sneer. She tosses her hair back dramatically as if she's trying out for a Pantene commercial instead of preparing to sink her claws in. I can feel the tension rise in the air, thick and charged with something that makes my jaw tighten.

"Lila Wright, I heard you were back in town. Still working as a nanny, I see. Just like in high school. Jessica here"—she nods toward the woman sporting unfortunate chunky highlights that are more orange than blonde—"she heard that your fiancé ended things, and that's why you're back. Can't say I'm surprised. You never really could keep a guy, could you?"

As the woman's cruel words hit the air, something inside me snaps. Her laugh—sharp and mocking, like the cackle of a hyena—pierces through the quiet space, and a wave of disgust washes over me. I can feel my jaw tightening, my hands instinctively curling into fists at my sides. Who the hell does she think she is, talking to Lila like that? The venom in her voice, laced with judgment, makes my protective instincts flare up, and a raw anger surges through me.

I watch her, my gaze cold and unblinking, as she tries to tear down Lila with her petty comments. I want nothing more than to step in and wipe that smug look off her face, humiliate her in front of everyone. But then my eyes flicker to Lila, looking for any sign that she's okay— her expression, her body language, anything. I gauge her reaction to see if she can handle this on her own or if I should step in and make this woman regret ever opening her mouth.

But Lila? She's holding herself together, though I can see the tension in her posture. It makes my blood boil even more. How dare this woman use Lila's past as a weapon, especially when she doesn't know anything about her?

Just as I'm about to speak, the ringleader takes a step closer to Lila with venom in her eyes. "Don't ever try to discipline my kid. He can push around whoever he wants."

Noticing a chill in the air, I immediately wedge myself between the two women, which, unfortunately, draws the attention of the lead viper.

"I don't think we've met. I'm Ashley Campbell," the vile woman says, holding her hand out in a flirtatious greeting as her eyes travel up and down my body.

I glare at her hand, then move my gaze to meet her eyes, raising my eyebrows at her boldness.

"I've just moved to town, and those two kids your son was pushing? They're mine." My sharp tone carries the weight of an unspoken warning. My expression is hard, eyes colder than I mean for them to be. "I suggest it doesn't happen again."

Turning toward my group, I advise we pack up and head back to the house, ignoring the chatter going on around us. Vaguely, one of the women comments about who I am, clearly recognizing me from the numerous gossip rags floating around. My love life and the recent death of my sister have been a topic of discussion far longer than I expected. Yet it all focuses on me and not how my parents are coping. You know, the owners of a billion-dollar yacht business that serves clients like royalty.

I slip on my jacket as Lila collects the trash from lunch. Gathering Oliver's and Evelyn's hands, I nod for Lila to direct us to where she parked the SUV.

"I'm guessing that you and that group have a history?"

Lila's gaze drops to the ground as she shrugs. "I was an easy target. A girl who would rather spend hours in a science lab testing theories or learning calculus paints a bull's-eye dead center."

"Doesn't seem like that's the full story."

"She was head cheerleader and didn't take too kindly to the fact that I was her boyfriend's chemistry tutor. He dumped her right before junior prom and asked me instead. I said no, of course, but the damage was done. Honestly, though, she had it out for me since Ashvi was my best friend. And that in and of itself is an entirely different story that Ashvi can tell you one day." Lila stops at the black vehicle and unlocks the doors, gesturing for the two kids to hop inside the back.

As Lila finishes buckling the kids into the back seat, I approach, my boots crunching softly against the gravel. Something about the way she moves around them, so natural and instinctive, pulls me in like gravity every time. I can see how much she cares for them, the way she touches their heads gently before shutting the door like she's anchoring them to the world with every little motion. And it hits me how good she is at this, how much she's already giving.

I open the driver's side door for her, but before she climbs in, I reach out and stop her with a gentle touch on her arm. Her body stills under my hand, and I feel the slight hitch in her breath as she turns to face me. My heart is in my throat for a different reason now because I need her to truly know this.

I tuck a strand of hair behind her ear, my thumb grazing her flushed cheek, the soft heat of her skin grounding me. I watch the way she reacts to my touch. Her eyes flicker with something between surprise and vulnerability, and I can't help but feel the need to make sure she hears me and feels what I'm saying.

"You're worth a thousand of those women, Lila," I say, my voice low and firm, the words coming more easily than I expected. "They're jealous. They're catty and superficial, and they've never let go of that high school mentality because it's the only time in their lives they've felt like they had power. People like that… they're miserable. And because of that, they'll try to dull your sparkle. They'll try to steal your sunshine. But they can't. You're too bright for them."

Her breath catches, and I see her eyes well with something—maybe it's disbelief, or maybe it's hope. I can't tell, but the way she looks at me, so raw and open, knocks the air out of my chest. I feel the weight of what I said and what I'm offering. This isn't just some casual compliment. I mean every word with everything I have.

She doesn't say anything for a moment. Just stands there, staring at me. And at that moment, I realize I've stepped too far. I've shown her too much. I see it in the way her lips part, and her eyes widen. It's like I've cracked open a door between us, and I'm afraid that things will change if I step through it. Things will become real.

But then she surprises me. "I didn't ask for any of this," she says, her soft voice unsure but steady. "I never wanted to be anyone's target. I never wanted to be anything more than… me."

I swallow, nodding, not knowing what to say in response. Because she's right. She never asked for this. She never asked to be here in this mess. But she's here now, and I can't help but want to protect her, to shield her from all the things that make her feel small. The last thing I want is for her to think she's not worthy of the space she takes up.

I break the silence first, stepping back just enough to give her space. "You've got nothing to prove to them or anyone else. Just yourself."

She looks at me, then, and something is different about how she meets my gaze. Something tentative but trusting. Like she's letting me in, just a little. And for the first time since meeting her, I realize how much I'm willing to give her. How much I want to offer her.

But she doesn't have to take it if she's not ready. I'll wait.

She smiles softly. It's the kind of smile that makes everything feel lighter, like maybe we're both on the edge of something we're not sure we want to jump into, but it's something we're willing to explore together.

"What are your plans for the rest of the afternoon?" I ask, knowing that I have something in store for later.

"I was going to do some reading with the kids and help Evelyn with her letter sounds."

"Okay, I'll follow you back," I say as she hops into the driver's seat. "Oh, and don't worry about dinner. We have plans."

"We do?" she asks, her eyebrows lifting. Dinner had become Lila's thing. If science falls through, she absolutely has a calling as a chef.

"Yep." I walk away with a new smile on my face, relishing in the feel of leaving Lila perplexed. I could watch the way her lips purse all day even though it constantly leaves me wanting to kiss her.

Chapter Nine

Lila

It's not often that people slip something by me. Even in the eleventh grade, I found out about the surprise birthday party Ashvi was throwing me because I overheard her speaking with my mom. It isn't that I don't like surprises. It's just rare that they happen.

So far, they're three for three, though, if I consider the surprise regarding my ex included.

After the park, the kids had taken a much-needed nap, which left me about two hours of free time that I used to scribble away in my notebook about chemical reagents and mixtures that I could test the next time I found a lab with available supplies. This morning, I started reaching out to the colleges within an hour's drive to see if I could rent lab space. It isn't unheard of, but it's also not common within the science fields. If I can snag a grant before the end of summer, I may be able to purchase my own supplies, though buying from the school will make things easier.

Dean had popped into the kitchen while I was jotting down notes and calculations like a madwoman while sitting at the kitchen table as the kids snoozed. He'd given me that smile I was growing far too fond of before apologizing for interrupting and immediately exiting. I don't know what he had to be sorry about. It was his house after all. But I appreciated that he understood I needed the quiet. I may have watched his backside as he swept out of the room, marveling at the genetic masterpiece.

Gosh, I love science.

Even as I sit in the passenger seat of the oversized SUV, my mind doesn't stop racing with the possibilities of the new findings I'd read about in a science publication this morning from a friend in Michigan.

"You okay?" a gentle voice asks from beside me, and I nearly jump in my seat when I feel the pad of a finger brush across the back of my hand resting on my thigh.

"Sorry, just lost in my own little world," I explain as we barrel down the one-lane road heading toward my parents' house. Dean let it slip that we were heading there for dinner tonight when I saw my mom's name flash across his cell phone as we got in the car.

"Everything okay?"

"Yes. When my ideas start flowing, sometimes it's hard to shut them off. It used to irritate my parents when we'd be out somewhere, and I doodled in my notebook."

"I'm sure they're awfully proud of you."

Shrugging, I turn away from Dean and look out the front windshield. "I suppose all parents are proud of their kids in some aspect. They can't be too pleased I'm jobless right now, though."

"I doubt that makes any difference to them."

The silence stretches for a bit, and between the equations and theories slicing and swooshing in my mind, a thought pops free, and I open my mouth without thinking. "You know. You don't talk about your parents much. They must be just as proud of you for all your accomplishments."

Dean's easy demeanor slips away, and I immediately regret my question. He hardens in a way that hints he's closing off. Despite how wary I had been to return home after my breakup, it was never because of my family. Dean has heard all about them at various times since I've lived in his home. But those conversations only left me wondering about Dean's parents and sister. The latter, he still seems to be grieving, so I keep her questions off the table, but his parents are nothing more than a mystery to me.

"I doubt my parents, if you can even call them that, give a rat's ass—" He immediately checks the back seat to apologize for the curse word, but his stiff chest deflates when he sees both kids wearing headphones and watching a movie on the headrest screens. "As I was saying, they don't care about me or what I do. Some people seek out a fancy watch, designer handbag, or overpriced shoes to accessorize with. My parents? They chose children as their ultimate decoration."

"That's…"

"I mean, what better way to show your money and power than leaving your legacy with heirs? Too bad it's all blowing up in their face now."

Dean chuckles devilishly, and I'm left wondering if there is some underlying secret in the Harrington family. Since living with him, I've done my fair share of research regarding the elite Harringtons. Originally from Maine, they had a flourishing yacht business, and they moved their headquarters to Miami in the seventies. The list of their clientele left me speechless. Kings, queens, and sheiks custom order these enormous boats. I wonder if it was for their enjoyment or simply to be one of the few who owned a Harrington original.

Pictures of Dean's parents weren't hard to come by. It's clear they love every minute of their time with the rich. So much so that they have become celebrities themselves.

His sister, the main heiress and socialite, had taken her party-girl ways to the extreme. There were fewer pictures of her on the red carpet and more of her partying in nightclubs. Most were dated prior to five years ago, though. And I can only hope that she had been working to turn her life around when Oliver came into the picture.

I did my best to avoid searching Dean's name in particular. He made no effort to mask the fact that he was a playboy. It's in the way he flirts and carries himself. I doubt there is a single woman who could resist his charm. Myself included. That didn't mean multiple pictures didn't show up in articles of him at various charity events, a different woman on his arm each time. There was no need for me to feel jealousy though, even though she reared her ugly head. There's no disguising Dean's good looks. Even when he's not trying to look attractive, like now while he drives the vehicle, he oozes sex appeal. It's the way his hands grip and wrap around the steering wheel. The way the seat struggles to contain his large, muscular chest. The way his jaw ticks every time I shift in my seat. We women don't stand a chance.

But I'm sure as hell trying my hardest to resist him.

"What do you mean?" I ask as I gnaw at his words. He shifts his attention to me momentarily, cocking his eyebrow. "You said it's blowing up in their face now. What does that mean?"

"Is this the turn?" he asks, swiftly changing the subject.

When I nod, Dean turns the vehicle toward the worn gravel path I know all too well. The path isn't as tranquil as the one at Dean's house. No trees lining the path or flowers blossoming along the edge. Just acres upon acres of grass until we reach the front of the house.

Most family members park their vehicles around back near one of the many barns, but I direct Dean toward a small graveled area under a large oak tree.

The kids are already bouncing in their seats, ready to get out. Oliver's halfway through unstrapping his belts by the time I unbuckle myself.

"I'll come around," Dean growls as I reach for the door handle.

"Dean, that's silly."

"Don't argue," he says with narrowed eyes, staring at me until I pull my hand back.

Wordlessly, he exits the SUV and makes his way to my side. As he opens and holds out his hand to assist me, I'm struck by the realization that Prescott never once held the door for me. Not in the two years we dated and were engaged.

"Thanks," I mumble, hating how my heart leaps the moment our hands touch.

Together, we maneuver the kids out of their seats and walk toward the front door. To anyone looking at us, we probably appear as a unit. A family. Two parents with their two kids wedged between them. Part of that dream everyone is supposed to yearn for. For me, my dream has always been to use my knowledge to better the world. I thought Prescott changed my mind about shifting my focus, but as I glance at Dean out of the corner of my eye, I fathom that maybe he is the one changing my mind.

I smooth my hands along the sides of my pants, my nerves rolling like the stones in the driveway that crackle under my feet. The scent of my mom's daffodils lining the flower beds fill the air around us, reminding me of the warm days I'd spend outside with her, pulling weeds and planting bulbs.

"You don't have to look like you're being dragged to the barracks," Dean says with a smirk, his free hand shoved in the front pocket of his jeans and his other clasped with Evelyn's. He looks handsome in his jeans and blue-and-white button-down shirt, sleeves rolled up to his elbows in that effortless way.

And it's not until I'm in front of my parents' door, holding the hand of little Oliver, that I realize maybe I didn't warn Dean enough about the chaos he was about to find himself in.

"Dean… you still have time to turn around and go home. My family can be…a lot."

Ignoring my warning, Dean reaches out and presses the doorbell. Not that he needs to. I can already sense my mother standing on the other side of the door. The man has no idea how ill-prepared he is for tonight's dinner.

Mom opens the door wide and hugs Dean as if they've been friends forever. In my mom's defense, I want to wrap my arms around him too. Of course, it's for purely intimate reasons that I need to keep it in check if I'm going to continue living in his house. I will not be the one to break.

Dean and I quickly follow my mom inside the house, and the kids trail us like little shy mice. It's not until she gets down to their level and whispers something to them that they relax. Smiles grow on their lips, and their eyes sparkle with glee. My mom has a gift, truly, and it's the kid whisperer. It takes just a split second for Oliver and Evelyn to dash off ahead of us, skipping toward the kitchen.

Dean stares after them, mouth hanging slightly agape.

"Damn, how does she do that? It's the first time I've seen them smile like that since I took them to the State Fair a year ago."

"My mom has a gift. Would you like something to drink before I throw you to the wolves?" I ask, trying to mask the nervousness in my voice as I move down the hall.

"A beer if they have one."

We enter the open-air kitchen and living room space, and I'm not surprised to find my siblings all clamoring around the table, waiting patiently for Dean's arrival. They're treating him like he's my...

"He's not my boyfriend, guys. He's my boss. Calm down," I explain as I open the large fridge and reach inside for two beer bottles. I pop the top of one with ease, using the opener on the wall beside the fridge.

As I turn around, I notice my brothers haven't adjusted their stance toward Dean, but my sister eyes him appreciatively. I cannot blame her, but even with that acceptance, a little green monster sneers from inside me.

Taking a sip from my own bottle, I walk toward Dean and hand him the other. "Dean, these are my brothers Rowan, Crew, and Holt." The trio barely nods as I introduce them. I don't miss the clench of their fingers around their arms crossed against their chests. Rolling my eyes, I add, "And that's Hadley. She's Holt's twin. Everyone, this is Dean Harrington, and the two kids with Mom are Oliver and Evelyn."

"Nice to meet you," Dean says as he holds his hand out toward Hadley, clearly understanding that my brothers aren't going to return his greeting. "It must have been great growing up in such a large family."

Dean slips his hand free from Hadley's grasp, and she visibly pouts as Dean turns his eyes in my direction. His signature smirk is etched in place at my brothers' warm welcome instead of a furrowed brow I've seen him wear when he's confused.

"Anyone seen Dad?" I ask, trying to get one of my brothers to say literally anything. Their infuriating stares in our direction are becoming too much.

"He's outside. Strawberry harvest is coming up or have you forgotten already?" Rowan, the next to oldest brother, barks. He works on the farm with my father and was my closest friend growing up. Now, it seems the distance between us isn't just in age.

"I remember," I snap. I've spent enough years on the farm helping Dad with the harvest. Hell, it's the sole reason my first boyfriend dumped me, but also the reason I'm so passionate about my field of work. "I planned on bringing the kids to the farm this upcoming week so they could see everything that goes on and see some of the animals."

Thankfully, Mom chooses that moment to step over to the table, breaking the awkwardness.

"That sounds lovely, dear. Let me know which day of the week, and I can have something planned for them," she says warmly. The kids follow her lead and place a stack of napkins and a handful of utensils on the table.

"Maybe Wednesday? Tuesday is my day off, and Ashvi and I were going to drive into town."

"Sounds good to me. I'll have your father check the schedule."

Rowan's fists leave his arm and pound down on the table, startling Evelyn in the process. The three-year-old's lip begins to quiver, and Mom immediately moves her back toward the kitchen. Oliver follows dutifully. I can sense Dean's building fury toward the situation without even glancing his way. It rolls off him in waves.

"What the hell is your problem?" I bark, my hair flaring around my shoulders as I turn and give Rowen my full attention.

"I'm sorry. We're all supposed to believe this man needs help raising those two kids. Live-in help at that? Do you even know who he is, Lila? That man could hire the freaking *Supernanny* if he wanted to. But instead, he's here in our little Podunk town, paying you next to nothing to live with him and raise those kids. This entire thing seems fishy, and no one is saying anything."

"Rowan, that's not at all what's happening. And if you'd calm down, I'll—" I say just as the boisterous sounds of my dad's laughter fill the cavernous room. Even with Rowan's erroneous outburst, I can't help but mask my smile when my father enters the room.

"Ah, you must be the handsome Mr. Harrington my wife keeps talking about," he says as he approaches Dean and holds out his hand in greeting. The kind I had hoped my boss would have received from my siblings.

Dean pulls his stare away from my insufferable brother and holds out his hand in greeting to my dad. "Please, call me Dean."

"Everything working out with Lila and the kids?"

"Yes, she's great with them. I'm truly thankful for the help," Dean replies, smiling warmly.

Breaking their hold, my dad tugs me forward and wraps his arm around my shoulders in a one-armed hug. "Yeah, she gets that from Claire. Those girls could turn Chucky into an angel."

"I don't doubt that, sir."

"I'm sorry to interrupt, but you're telling me everyone is okay with this situation?" Rowan interjects. "No one else thinks this is weird?"

Narrowing my eyes at my brother, I nearly jerk away from my dad to give Rowan a piece of my mind. Instead, my dad pipes in. "No, it's no different from the thousands of other people your mother and her team have helped, or have you neglected to recall that this is just a job? One your sister is good at and is doing to help your mom out. Or have you forgotten that part?"

"No, sir," Rowan mumbles, cheeks reddening with each passing second.

"What is weird is your reaction to the situation, son."

"I'm just…looking after my sister, that's all," he says as his eyes drop down to the table, then flick over to me.

Just as I'm about to speak, Dean chimes in. "I think you're underestimating the strength and resilience of your sister. Just from the short time I've known her, she'd never do anything she didn't want to do. And I do think you owe her an apology for the ambush."

Would I? The thought twists like a blade in my chest. I spent two years in a relationship where I didn't even recognize the man I was about to marry. Not truly. Not the lies he spun or the secrets his family cloaked in polished smiles and bottomless glasses of champagne. I handed them my trust and my future, all for the sake of a dream I thought I couldn't reach on my own. And in return, I became a pawn in their carefully constructed game, a research trophy to parade in exchange for obedience. Even the little bit of research I've gathered since returning home left me bewildered. Web results with missing URLs. Pictures that led nowhere. All things Prescott's parents likely had taken down. I traded my freedom for ambition. And I didn't even see it happening until it was too late.

But then Dean's voice cuts through the fog in my head. Low, steady, unapologetically certain. His words aren't wrapped in pity but laced with belief in me.

And God, it disarms me.

His encouragement isn't flashy. It's quiet. Anchoring. Like he sees the pieces of me I'm still trying to glue back together and isn't afraid to hold them while I figure it out.

I feel it in the way he stands just close enough to make me feel protected but never caged. In the way he looks at me like I'm not broken. Like I'm more than just the girl who ran away in a wedding dress and a life that wasn't mine.

And at that moment, as his words settle into my bones, something inside me breathes again. Not fully. Not loudly. But it's a start. A reminder that maybe I'm not as lost as I think.

"Sorry, Lila," Rowan says behind gritted teeth. He'd never been one willing to offer up an apology, even as a young child. So this one is monumental to say the least.

Whirling back into the dining area like a cyclone, Mom carries a large bowl of pasta in one hand and another of sauce, setting them on the table, while the kids each carry in a basket of bread.

"Wonderful, everyone is here," she says, ignoring the conversation she had to have overheard. "Dinner is ready. Oliver and Evelyn, you can take the seats on either side of me if you'd like."

Dean watches on, breath held in as he waits for the kid's response. Up until today, the kids had been glued to his or my side. And specifically, at dinner, the kids notoriously inched their chairs as close to Dean's as the table would allow.

"Yes, please," Oliver says as Evelyn nods enthusiastically.

My mom guides the kids to the two seats, nudging my brothers out of the way with her hip in the process.

Once my mom sits, we join her. Dean opts to sit on the opposite side of the table from me, next to Evelyn. Dad takes up the helm of the table, smiling at Hadley as she speaks a mile a minute about a reality show she's been bingeing. I'm secretly thrilled that she's filling the silence and taking the attention away from me. As Mom passes a basket of bread to Dean, he winks in my direction before divvying up two pieces for Evelyn and himself.

Hadley seems to have broken the awkwardness in the room because dinner is filled with a whirlwind of conversations. Despite my brother's trying to interrogate Dean, he holds his own. And when asked what he does for a living, Rowan's eyes widened in surprise. Dean lists off so many businesses, charities, and grants he's a part of that he comes off like a walking Renaissance Man. Despite what Rowan thought earlier, I know Dean works hard, spending most of the day in his office and on the phone, but I'm left impressed with all the fields he invests in. Hell, the man knows so much about each area that he sounds more like a CEO than a shareholder.

"Wow," my dad says, shaking his head faintly. He shoves a forkful of spaghetti into his mouth.

Under the table, Hadley kicks me not-so-subtly on the ankle as she leans over her plate toward Dean.

"Are you single?" she asks, and both Mom and I admonish her immediately. "What? It's a simple question when you're getting to know someone. So, are you?"

"Yes, I'm single, though I did meet this woman a couple of weeks ago that I haven't stopped thinking about," he replies, those dark eyes of his twinkling from the light of the chandelier hanging over the table.

I immediately tuck my chin to my chest, letting my hair drape around my face like a shield.

"Oh, my." Hadley leans back in her chair and feverishly fans her face. "Did you contact her?"

"No, I never got her information, but I'm a big believer in Fate. So hopefully, things will work out for me in the end. I know without an ounce of doubt that I'm going to marry that girl one day."

I choke on the piece of bread I was chewing and make a quick excuse to leave the table and grab a glass of water from the kitchen. In my hurry, I don't miss Dean's deep chuckle at my exit.

By the time Mom serves us her homemade pecan pie, my family has thoroughly ensconced Dean in conversation, learning more about him and his family in an hour than I have over the past week. Even Rowan has started coming around to my boss.

Me? I'm left embarrassed and red-faced after my siblings took the opportunity to share stories of me growing up. Payback will be hell whenever any of them brings someone home.

We stay for another hour. Dean refrains from drinking a second beer when my dad offers and lets me indulge in a glass of wine with my mom. But as the sun dips below the trees, I know we're dangerously close to the kids' bedtime.

We bid a quick goodbye to my family as Evelyn nearly falls asleep in Dean's arms as he carries her out to the car. "I had fun tonight," he murmurs as he strains to latch Evelyn in her car seat. "Your family is great."

From across the vehicle where I'm helping Oliver get latched in, I send Dean a fiery glare.

"I don't think I'll be subjecting myself to that humiliation again anytime soon."

"Aw, it's just because they love you." Despite the sweetness in his words, I notice his timbre change as if he's suddenly recalling the passing of his sister.

"I'm sorry. You're right," I say, trying to ease the tension I created.

Like a game of ping-pong, Dean's mood switches back to being carefree. "Good, because your mom wants us to come back next week for family night."

I do little to mask my groan as I shut the door and make my way around the other side to my own seat, but of course, Dean beats me to it and grabs the door handle.

"Hey." His dark, steady gaze locks onto mine, rendering me useless. At moments like this, when everything slips away, I can see myself giving in to the attraction between Dean and me. It grows stronger every day, and what little bit of strength I have remaining seems to be fraying.

Licking my lips, I can barely utter my own, "Hey," and not have my voice scratch at the effort.

Dean reaches out and tucks my hair farthest from him behind my ear. Even as his arm reaches across my face, I can smell whatever cologne he wears. I'm a sucker for it. I wish I knew the brand so when I leave this job, I can spray my pillow and pretend it's him.

"Thank you for sharing them with me. I…just…yeah. Thank you."

Dean doesn't give me a chance to form a reply, not even a breath to gather the words that tangle somewhere between my chest and throat.

Instead, he's already opening the door, his hand firm and steady at the small of my back as he guides me inside like it's second nature to take care of me. Like touching me is a right he doesn't even have to think twice about. And I don't stop him.

I slide into the seat, the soft leather warm against my legs, and before I can reach for the buckle, he leans in close. Too close. His broad frame fills the doorway, stealing the air between us. One arm braces on the roof of the car, the other dips across my body, fingers brushing the hem of my shirt as he reaches for the seat belt. His scent—all clean soap, cedar, and something darker and headier—wraps around me like a secret I want to keep.

He fastens the belt with an audible click, his knuckles grazing my ribs, the heat of his skin seeping through cotton and reason. My breath hitches. Not enough to be obvious, but just enough for me to know this isn't just him being polite.

It's him noticing me. All of me.

And dammit, I notice him, too.

His face is inches from mine now, his mouth just a tilt away. Those piercing eyes flick to mine, and for a second, just a beat, it feels like the rest of the world fades away. Like he could kiss me right here in this quiet pocket of space between hesitation and temptation, and I wouldn't stop him. I'm supposed to be professional. Steady. A woman in control. But every time he touches me, every time he looks at me like that, that carefully built wall of resolve starts to wobble, brick by shaky brick.

Dean doesn't say a word as he slowly pulls back, his hand lingering for a second longer than necessary on the curve of my shoulder before he closes the door with a soft click. And I'm left there, heart thundering, pulse a slow and steady ache in places I swore I'd locked down.

In a moment, he's behind the wheel, flashing that smirk of his that I was beginning to grow extremely fond of as he starts the SUV. The grin was dangerous, but when he unleashes a full smile, I squirm in my seat as I realize how full-on hazardous the man is to my health.

Everything about Dean shouts at me to throw caution to the wind and give in to temptation.

I'm just not sure if I'm willing to take another risk.

Chapter Ten

Dean

The drive back to my house is quiet. Even the kids are so tuckered out they're not asking for endless baths or stories like usual. Lila stares out the window as the sky shifts from oranges and reds to navy. From the corner of my eye, I take her in, the way she sighs every so often, and how a small lock of hair keeps tickling her beneath her chin, and she tries to brush it away.

I was so close to kissing her when we left her family's home. Not just because I want to press my lips against hers more than my last breath but because she allowed me to be a part of something so sacred. Despite the less-than-warm welcome from her brothers, her mother, father, and sister took me in immediately. Her brothers eventually warmed up.

God, does she know how lucky she has it?

"Eyes on the road, Mr. Harrington," she demands with an edge of teasing as she catches me glancing at her. Apparently, I'm not as discreet as I think.

"Sorry."

"Can I ask you something?"

"Of course," I say, while internally I'm bracing myself for whatever flaw Lila will point out. With my own family, that's what I'm used to.

"Earlier, you thanked me for sharing my family with you. What…um…did you mean by that?"

Shrugging, I twist my hands on the steering wheel, the leather easing some of the ache in my fingers as I clench unknowingly.

"It's not worth reading too much into, Lila. I was simply thanking you for letting me be a part of your family tonight. Once we arrived, you could have told me to turn around, but you didn't."

"It was just dinner, and you're the one who set it up."

"Yeah, but it still breaks that boss/employee category we find ourselves in." Lila mumbles something under her breath, so I continue. "Before you, the only glimpse I had at seeing a semi-normal family was with my friend, Talon. And even his family is considerably fucked up by societal standards, except for his grandma GiGi. But when he married Rory, I got to see how a family could be. Her family is large like yours, and they have dysfunctional moments like we all do, but there is a lot of love there, too. The first time I met them, I knew that was what I wanted out of life. It was everything I never had."

"Dean," she says, reaching out to rest her hand on my arm. The warmth of her palm immediately soothes my racing pulse. It's not often I open up to people, but something about Lila has me telling her everything.

"It's okay. I know what I'm missing out on, but that doesn't mean I can't hope for it for the future, especially for those two," I add, my gaze flicking up to the rearview mirror to glance at the two kids barely able to keep their eyes open.

Soon, we're back at the house, the porch lights shining on either side of the door like little beacons in the night. Off in the distance, the white, green, and red lights from boats and docks shimmer their reflections on the bay. Any sort of tension I carried with me after dinner instantly melts away.

Just as I'm getting out of the vehicle, I feel my phone buzzing in my pocket. Grabbing the device, I read the name flashing on the screen as my heart pounds. It's the PI I have looking into the Hoolihans. He's doing me a favor after I invested in his daughter's company. Not that I needed quid pro quo. She had a solid business plan, and her idea is already creating waves in the tech world. But I'm not too prideful to call in a favor when it's needed.

"I need to take this," I say to Lila. "Can you grab the kids?"

"Of course."

I watch her lean into the car and undo the seat belt holding Evelyn in her seat. Oliver scrambles out of his and then rushes up the porch steps and into the house.

"Talk to me," I say without a smidgen of a greeting.

"Well, hello to you, too," Mike says as he chuckles like a man who's smoked one too many packs of cigarettes in his life.

"Yes, hello. What did you find?"

"Loads. This family has so many skeletons in their closets that they could open their own haunted house."

I dash into my office and close the door, not wanting Lila to hear my conversation. Over the past week, I've learned that she doesn't like people snooping in her business. Too bad for her, I always protect those I care about.

"More than what we already know?" The Hoolihans have a very public and sordid history in politics.

"The newspapers haven't even scratched the surface. It seems they have some heavy hitters in their back pocket keeping their reputation intact."

"What does this asshole want with Lila?"

My feet squeak against the hardwood floors that cover the outskirts of the room as I pace, the center only covered in a dainty cream, pink, and blue floral rug. I'd rather wear away the wood than the pretty accessory.

As Mike goes on about homicides, missing wives and mistresses, and one fatherly figure with a disgustingly peculiar taste for the underage, I catch myself grasping the back of my office chair. My stomach roils at the thought of Lila being caught up in their mess. She's so…innocent. So good.

"Do you know what they wanted with my Lila?"

"Yours?" he asks, catching the slip of my tongue.

"My employee… and wife one day. Hopefully."

The words come out quieter than I intend, but they slip out anyway, calm and certain. I hear Mike chuckle.

"That so?" he asks, not bothering to hide the amused disbelief in his voice.

I shrug even though he can't see, running a hand over the back of my neck, but my lips tip up just slightly. "Yeah. That's so."

Thinking about that day at the airport eases the clenching in my stomach. There'd been something about her, something more than just the chaos, the running mascara, or the wild way she filled up the space beside me like a storm I didn't know I'd been waiting for. Even then, before I knew her name or the weight she was carrying on her shoulders, I'd had this abstract, unshakable sense that she would change everything.

The more time I spend with her, the more I watch her with the kids, listen to her laughter drifting down the hallway, or find one of her mugs left on the counter like she's always been here, the more I understand the profound truth behind that gut feeling.

She hasn't just changed my life. She's become the best part of it.

And if she'll let me, if she'll take one look at all my flaws and still say yes, I plan to marry her one day.

Not because I need to save her. But because somewhere along the way, she started saving me.

"Does she know this?"

"She's in denial."

Mike's chortle echoes through the phone until a coughing fit takes over. It's a minute before he finally replies.

"I don't know the full details yet. I'm working on it. But it appears the marriage wasn't going to be for love. He is on his fourth at this point. Prescott's wives all mysteriously disappear."

"And no one has gone looking for them? I've never even heard about the other three. And what about the current one?"

"The current wife wants to be a first lady someday, so she's become a bit of a socialite in her own right. Seems she's a bit harder to get rid of. She was aware of Lila's existence, thinking it was nothing more than a fling for Prescott."

"But why Lila? Why the pomp and circumstance around their wedding? It wasn't a well-kept secret in their circle. What does she have that they want?"

"Her research. Lila's the patent holder for at least a dozen items regarding her recent research on food allergies, all funded under a lab they sponsor. They want the rights to all of it even though her contract states otherwise. We're talking about life-changing research, Dean."

"But what do they want with it?"

"They don't want the patents. They want them to disappear. Pharmaceuticals only make money when someone has to stay on meds for life. And what easier way than to convince someone of that than to become their power of attorney?"

"So what you're saying is they were going to get rid of the current wife, and he was going to marry Lila? Then…God, I don't want to think about it…and harm her in some way so that he becomes power of attorney, then takes over the patents himself. Then he pretty much allows any pharmaceutical companies to nullify the patent."

"That about sums it up."

My heart races as I sit and dip my forehead to the edge of the desk, trying to calm my erratic heart.

"But what about the current wife? She's still around."

"From the evidence I found, she's already on an extended vacation a.k.a. missing and has been since Lila ran off. The Hoolihans have quite a mess on their hands if this gets to the right kind of people. I've given all the evidence I've found over to the police, but you know how slow these things can take.

"Sorry for the bad news, my friend, but at least she's there with you. Prescott was seen leaving a club over the weekend, but if I see he's on the move, I'll give you a heads-up."

"Thanks, Mike."

I hang up the phone and toss it onto the desk, the weight of Mike's words anchoring deep in my chest. Prescott is still out there, still breathing the same air as Lila. And now that I know the lengths that bastard and his family went to in order to control her… hell, I can't sit still.

My fingers curl around the edge of the desk, knuckles going white as I stare out the round window that overlooks the backyard. The early light spills over the grass, golden and peaceful, but the tension in my body doesn't ease. If anything, it tightens, every muscle coiled with the need to do something. Anything.

She's inside right now with the kids, probably chasing Oliver with the toothbrush or convincing Evelyn that her stuffy is magic. And she doesn't know. Just one more weight added to her already heavy load.

Not anymore.

Not while she's under my roof. Not while I'm breathing.

I don't know what it is about her, this woman who walked into my life like a storm I didn't see coming, but I know with certainty that she's it. She's the one. The person who showed up just as everything else was falling apart and made it all feel steady again.

And I'll be damned if I let anything, or anyone, hurt her now.

She may not be mine in the way I want yet, but that doesn't matter. I'll protect her like she is. Like she's already everything.

Lila deserves more than just safety. She deserves a world where she doesn't have to look over her shoulder. Where she can laugh freely, sleep deeply, and love boldly. And I'll fight tooth and nail to give her that. I'll stand between her and every shadow that tries to creep in.

I rise from the chair, my jaw locked and mind already turning over the next moves. Extra cameras. A new security system. Whatever it takes. Because now that I know the truth, I won't stop. Not until Lila's safe. Not until she knows she's never alone again. Not as long as I'm here.

What a fucking mess.

A quiet rapt sounds on the door just before Lila peeks her head around the corner.

"Hey, everything okay?" she asks, but before I can answer, a tiny little nymph comes dashing into the room wearing her princess pajamas and crawls into my lap. Her damp hair falls into soft ringlets down her back. "Sorry. I came to tell you that they're ready for bed."

When I glance down at my niece, her big brown eyes stare up at me with all their innocence. My mind immediately flashes to a glimpse of her mother when she was young.

"You want Uncle Dean to tuck you into bed tonight?" Over the past few days, the kids have transitioned from Lila doing their bedtime routine to them asking for me. Lila says it's normal for them to want the reassurance that I'm still there after her newness has worn off.

She silently nods, little droplets of water from her hair dripping onto her arms, making her giggle. God, it's the best sound in the world.

"Alright then." I pull her into my arms as I stand. Though the conversation with the PI is fresh in my mind, I give my niece and nephew my undivided attention as I read through three bedtime stories.

After kissing them, and their stuffies, good night, I wait in the hall for Lila to say her own good nights to them.

The door to Oliver's room opens, and Lila steps out, slowly closing it behind her. As I'm about to speak, she holds a finger to her mouth and gestures for me to move farther down the hall, closer to her bedroom.

"You're so good with them," she says immediately, and my chest expands at her praise.

"It's…uh…easy being the uncle."

"You're more than that to them, Dean, and you know it."

I shrug, uncomfortable with the notion that I'm taking their mother's space. Lila lets me ruminate for a moment on her statement. Her eyes dart around the hallway where she hung a few pictures she found at the antique store in town.

"Um…I meant to double-check that everything was okay with that call. You seemed a bit worried."

I run my hand along the back of my neck, feeling the strain in my muscles. "Yeah, it's fine. Has your ex tried to contact you anymore?" She'd let it slip that he'd been messaging and calling her nonstop, even after she'd blocked his number. I finally got her a new phone, but with his family's connections, I know it won't take long for him to track her down. I was still curious as to why he hadn't shown up in town yet.

"Just in my email. The one I stopped using. Not to the phone."

"Good. You let me know if that changes."

Lila stares up at me, her big blue eyes searching mine as she bites her lip.

"Why?"

"Because I'm worried about your safety," I explain, stepping closer to her. The room closes around us, and only the small sconces on the wall provide a yellow glow.

"You know I'd never let anything happen to the kids."

While I know Lila would protect them with her life, I wonder if she would protect her own. She has to know that my biggest fear after the call is Prescott hurting her in some way—my beautiful ghost girl.

"Lila, I'm not only worried about the kids. I'm worried about you."

Her breath hitches as I lean closer, my hand brushing against the back of hers. The pull to draw her against me is stronger than ever before. She bites down on her lower lip at the moment of contact, and I can't tear my eyes away from her mouth and those luscious lips I yearn to taste.

"Why?" she whispers as if she truly can't comprehend that I want so much more from her.

The best parts of my day used to be when I would work on the projects I was passionate about or visit my best friend and his wife. But now? Now, it's getting back from a run to find Lila and the kids sitting at the breakfast table in the kitchen, munching on whatever delectable food she's prepared. Now, it's the end of the night, watching her treat my niece and nephew with the same kind of love as a mother. Now, it's the special smiles I get from her when I catch her eye. Now, it's the way my smallest finger traces the edge of hers.

"Because you're going to marry me one day," I say with an intensity that surprises even me.

Her breath hitches before she replies, "You keep saying that like if you repeat it enough, it will inevitably happen."

"It's called manifesting, sweetheart."

"You believe in that?"

"I believe in whatever I need to that gets me you."

"Dean, I..."

My name on her lips nearly knocks the breath from my chest. Soft and tentative, like she's tasting it, testing what it means now. What I might mean to her.

She steps toward me, her movement slow and uncertain, but something is determined in her gaze. And then her hand is on my chest, warm and open, pressing against my heart like she's grounding herself in me.

Her small palm is delicate, but its weight feels like everything. Like the moment before a storm breaks or the second before a kiss you know will change everything.

My heart stumbles in its rhythm, beating hard against her touch. She looks up at me, and I swear to God, I almost fall to my knees. Those big blue eyes... damn, I don't think I've ever seen anything more beautiful. They're shining with something soft and fierce all at once, like she's lit from the inside. Not with fear or pain but with something that feels a hell of a lot like want.

The connection between us intensifies, and I watch, fascinated, as Lila breaks our connection and glances down at my lips.

Fuck. I want nothing more than to kiss her right now, to feel the soft pillows of her lips against mine.

"Mommy!" A frantic cry rings out from one of the kids' rooms. Lila and I jump apart like teenagers caught by their parents.

"Do you want me to…?" she asks, hand on my arm offering comfort.

"No, no. I have it. You should go relax."

As the whimpers start pulling at the chain directly connected to my heart, I dash off to Evelyn's room without glancing backward at Lila.

I find the preschooler curled up in the center of her tiny bed, clutching her stuffed animal and crying in a way I've never witnessed. She inhales large gasps of air between each of her sobs.

"Oh, sweet girl." I pull her into my arms and vacate the spot where she just was.

"Mommy!" she continues to wail until she finally exerts all her energy and falls asleep in my arms like she used to when she was a baby.

My heart breaks all over again, knowing that my sister left these two precious children unable to fight her own demons any longer.

"Fuck, Gen," I whisper, leaning my head against the pale pink wall.

I'm unsure what else to say. That I need her, that her kids need her, that she left us too soon. But none of it changes the fact that she's gone, and now I'm left picking up her pieces and comforting her daughter when she screams out in the night for her mom.

And as much as it pains me, it will break my heart even more when Evelyn stops.

Chapter Eleven

Lila

One thing my mom always advocated for in her business is that the clients must give the nanny a day off during the week and an occasional evening, especially if they are live-in. I know taking the traditional day off isn't in the cards for me, but I'm not sad to be sitting in the old chemistry lab of the high school running some tests with microbes and petri dishes.

I'm still hoping to hear from one of the many universities I reached out to lease some space and equipment from them, or at the minimum, a new team I can work with, but until then, I'm stuck here at the high school using the old lab room that looks like it's been recently used as storage space.

The overhead light in the room flickers, whether from poor electricity or just lack of use, I can't tell, but I find myself sighing in frustration for the third time since I arrived an hour ago.

A light knock draws my attention toward the open doorway, where a woman with a school district badge pinned to her chest steps in, clipboard in hand and an easy smile on her face. "Hey there, Ms. Wright, just checking in to see how things are going. We're excited to have you here. Well, back here."

I blink at her, straightening a little. "It's… definitely a work in progress."

She chuckles. "Well, it already looks better than it did last week. You've clearly got a handle on the science side of things. Actually…" Her tone turns speculative, assessing. "There's a coordinator position opening up—district-wide. It's part-time, mostly curriculum oversight and teacher support. Flexible hours, pays decently, and honestly? Someone like you could really make a difference." She shrugs like it's no big deal, but her words land heavy.

I nod, unsure of what to say. That flutter starts in my chest again, part fear, part curiosity. Part that strange new hope that there's a way to have both. To be grounded and still reach. To stay without giving up who I am.

The woman grants me another warm smile, taps her pen against the clipboard, and says, "Just think about it," before disappearing down the hallway. She leaves me alone with the hum of old equipment and a dozen swirling thoughts as I return to the cluttered counter and pick up my notes with renewed focus.

Hovering over the ten petri dishes in front of me, I carefully drop the individual chemicals specified for each dish onto the appropriate half of the agar. This allows me to study a treated area against the control. My hope is that this new sample of Clostridium bacteria at different levels will prove an adequate solution to treat potential food allergies within the body before it even begins.

Happy with my progress, I cover the petri dishes, mark them, then place them in the incubator.

"Dammit," I growl. The lights flicker again just as I remove my gloves, scoot over to my laptop, and begin documenting what I've completed so far. With a glance at the clock in the corner of the screen, I notice I worked through lunch as my stomach rumbles.

Rolling my eyes, I realize I have another hour of documentation to write before I can end my day on a high note.

"Here you are," a rumbling voice says from across the room. My body jerks off the stool, and I nearly fall to the ground before I catch myself on the edge of the lab table.

"My God, Dean. You scared the crap out of me." My hand settles on my chest as I worked to catch my breath. My pulse races beneath my fingertips, and I wasn't quite certain if it is because of my sudden fright or because Dean was here in the room with me.

"Sorry," he says with a slight shrug. "You know, you're a very difficult person to track down."

A giggle escapes as I rearrange myself on the stool. "That's sort of the point. How did you find me exactly?" I inquire, though I already know the answer before he says it.

"Your mom. The kids wanted to see the horses, so I took them over there between my meetings. She offered to keep them for the afternoon."

"And that brings you here, why?" I ask as I continue pecking away on the keyboard.

The scent of sandalwood invades my senses, and I know without looking that Dean is close.

"I just wanted to see you and what you were working on. Is this the project you've been trying to get funding and a location for?"

"That would be the one."

He's closer now, leaning over the table, his fists on the charcoal gray top propping himself up. If I move just an inch to the right, I'm certain our thighs would brush. I'm too scared to take that chance.

With each day that passes, my resolve to stay away from Dean shrinks. The reasons having a fling with him would be a bad idea drift away and are replaced with all the reasons I should. The way he treats his niece and nephew as if they are his entire world. The way he turns his whole focus on you if you're speaking. The way he'd drop everything to help someone. He's the complete opposite of every billionaire I've had the displeasure of knowing up to this point. Everything about the man is hypnotic. And if he keeps working his magic, I'm going to succumb with a white flag high in the air.

"Tell me…" he says just as the lights flicker and then go out completely. "Is this what you've been working on all day?" The gruffness in his voice pulls my attention away from my computer. I find a ruddiness in his cheeks and his body stiff, the knuckles in his fist growing a blanche shade of white.

"I mean, yeah. It's the older part of the building, but the incubator is on a backup generator."

"Lila, you can't work like this," he barks.

With a sarcastic guffaw, I reply, "I don't have many options. And really, it's fine. Nothing you can do about it."

"Is that what you think?" He relaxes as he straightens. "You just say the word, sweetheart, and I could have a state-of-the-art facility built here in town by the end of the month."

"That's impossible." I shake my head to rid the thought of having a research facility all to myself. A place where no one would question my theories or patents. A place to make a difference.

"It's really not. It would please me a great deal to build this for you."

The temptation is robust, almost as much as the temptation to climb Dean like my own personal playground.

"No, Dean. I don't want you to spend your money on me. Plus, we'd have to follow a bunch of rules and regulations. Not even you can jump through the loopholes."

Reaching out, he tucks a strand of hair behind my ear that has escaped from the messy twist I put my hair up in. When our skin touches, that recently awoken garden of butterflies in my stomach takes flight. "Lila, I think you'd be very surprised to find out what I'd do for you."

All I want him to do right now is kiss me. I bet he tastes like mint from his toothpaste and something sweet like a dark chocolate. Dean looks at me almost expectantly, knowing the pull he has. The words settle on the tip of my tongue, but I can't seem to force them out.

"I, um… had a visitor today," I say, my fingers skimming the rim of the lab table. I try to sound nonchalant, but I can feel Dean's gaze flick over to me.

"Yeah?" he asks, tone easy. But when I look up, his eyes are already locked on mine.

I shrug like it's no big deal. "Someone from the school district. An administrator." I try to keep my tone light, but the words feel heavier than I expected.

Dean leans his hip against the table, brow raised. "Everything okay?"

"Yeah, fine. She just… offered me something. A part-time position." I pause, letting it sit between us for a second. "Science curriculum coordinator. For the entire district."

His expression doesn't change much, but I swear something flashes behind his eyes. Surprise? Concern? I'm not sure. I'm probably imagining it.

I keep going before I lose the nerve. "It caught me off guard. I didn't even know that was something I could do. I've always pictured myself in a lab or a research facility. Somewhere sterile and important. But today…" I shake my head, fingers tightening around the glass.

"What changed?" he asks quietly, voice pitched lower now, like he knows this is more than just a job conversation.

I glance toward the grimy window where the glass lost its brilliance decades before. My throat tightens. "I don't know. Maybe I'm just starting to realize that impact isn't always about publications or breakthroughs. Maybe it's about who's watching you. Who's learning from you. Maybe it's smaller… and somehow more important."

Dean doesn't move, but his gaze softens. "Sounds like she saw something in you."

"Maybe." I laugh, soft and unsure. "Or maybe she was just desperate. Maybe the old coordinator retired, and no one's filled the role since."

"I doubt that," he murmurs, his mouth twitching at the corners.

I chance a look at him, heart picking up speed. The way he's watching me—calm, steady, and a little too intense—makes my skin prickle in the best way.

Instead of wondering what staying here could mean, I say, "I'm almost done for today," and turn my head back to my laptop.

"That's fine. I'll wait."

"What for?" I ask, trying to ignore the screeching stool as he plants it beside mine.

"I want to take you to dinner, and I was hoping maybe you could show me some of your favorite places in town."

"Dinner? Just you and me? That's like a…"

"A date, yes."

"You want to take me on a date? I thought you just wanted to sleep with me," I say, embarrassment kissing my cheeks as the words fly from my lips before I can catch them.

"I want that too," he murmurs, voice low and steady, like a promise he has every intention of keeping. "But only when you're ready."

Dean takes a slow step closer, his gaze never leaving mine. There's no teasing in his eyes now. No clever smirk or easy charm. Just sincerity—raw and warm and steady.

"But more than that…" His voice dips, rough around the edges. "I want the rest of it. I want to take my future wife on a real date. Not because it's expected. Not because it's convenient. But because I want to learn everything about her.

"I want to know her favorite color. The dessert she orders when she thinks no one's watching. What makes her laugh until she can't breathe, and what breaks her heart wide open."

He's right in front of me now, close enough that I can feel his heat, the scent of him wrapping around me like a memory I haven't made yet but already miss.

"I want to know what she dreams about in the middle of the night," he continues, voice barely above a whisper. "What makes her tick, what sets her soul on fire. I want to know what she looks like in candlelight… the way her eyes shine when it's just the two of us at a quiet table, sharing something that feels like more than just a meal."

His hand lifts slowly like he's afraid to break the moment, and he brushes a stray piece of hair behind my ear.

"And I want her to know she doesn't have to give me everything all at once," he says softly like it's a secret just for me. "I'll wait. As long as it takes."

And somehow, with my heart thundering and his words pressed against the cracks of all the places I've kept guarded, I believe him.

I shouldn't. God, I shouldn't. But I do.

Because the way Dean looks at me like I'm not just someone passing through, not just a broken heart in recovery, is dangerous in a way that doesn't scare me. It seduces me. He's not asking for all of me right now, but with every word he speaks, with every gentle look, he's pulling pieces of me into his hands like he knows exactly how to hold them.

I drag in a shaky breath, blinking faster than I want to admit. He doesn't even realize it, but he's just obliterated another piece of my armor with that speech. And now I'm standing here in the ashes, heart exposed and too full, wondering how in the hell I thought I could survive this if it was only ever meant to be a fling.

Because this? This doesn't feel temporary.

What happens when a fling isn't enough? What happens when I realize I want the whole damn thing, dates and candlelight and the feel of his hand curled around mine on the porch swing years from now?

I power down my laptop, my fingers slightly trembling over the keys. There's no way in hell I'm finishing that online journal this afternoon—not with Dean still in the room, not with his words still echoing in my head, filling every quiet space inside me with hope and fear and this ache I can't shake.

"Alright, you win. But we go as friends," I say, blowing out a puff of air as I close the device and shove it into my bag.

Normally, I'd be furious with someone interfering with my time since I get so little of it right now, but when I turn to find Dean smiling like a kid on Christmas, all my anger slips away.

"Got it. Friends. I really didn't think you'd give in so easily."

"Whelp, I haven't eaten anything since this morning, and I…"

"What do you mean about not eating since this morning?" he demands.

"I… sometimes when I get so engrossed in what I'm working on, I forget to eat."

"How often does this happen?"

"More often than I care to admit. It's fine. It happens a lot when my team is focused on something. Well, what used to be my team."

Grabbing my hand, Dean yanks me from the room, down the hall, and out the side door of the school without a glance back at me until we approach the SUV.

"Get in," he spouts, his lips curling up as if he's in anguish.

I slip under his arm and into the passenger seat, figuring I can grab the expensive coupe he allowed me to drive this morning later. As he walks around the front of the vehicle, I take a second to admire the way the gray T-shirt hugs his broad shoulders, wide chest, and taut abdomen. Even his jeans are snug on his fucking amazing ass. I wonder what his boxer briefs look like beneath the denim.

I have to stop fantasizing about the man.

He slams the door shut, and I jump in my seat. Dean's playfulness slips away like the lines on the road as he pulls away from the school. I watch in fascination as his strong hands twist around the steering wheel. Even his knuckles are attractive.

Fuck, I need to get laid.

I make a mental note to myself to send Ashvi a message to see if she wants to go out soon. Slipping my hand into my bag, I reach for my phone only to jerk back against my seat as Dean takes the turn onto Main Street with the finesse of an F1 racer.

"Geez," I mumble, gripping the handle above the passenger door.

"Sorry," he replies, relaxing his grip and slowing the car's speed.

The road narrows a bit as it winds around the coastline, which has sandy beaches covered in driftwood.

"That used to be one of my favorite places to hang out as a kid after school," I point out. "There used to be a dock where I'd go fishing with my dad, but a hurricane took it out a few years back. The town never rebuilt it."

Dean doesn't say anything, probably sensing the melancholy in my voice. I miss those times with my dad. My parents always made it a point to spend individual time with each of their children when they could, and I treasured those times with my dad. In a house of seven, it was easy to get lost in the crowd.

Beside me, Dean clears his throat softly, his voice low but steady. "Everything still quiet on your end?"

I glance at him, my chest tightening just a little. "You mean Prescott?"

He nods, jaw ticking. "Just want to make sure he hasn't managed to get ahold of your new number."

"Um…" I say, fingers curling around the hem of my shirt. "Sort of. He's been calling and messaging my old phone, but I blocked his number. I'm almost afraid to check my email."

Dean's eyes lock on mine, warm but filled with an undercurrent of steel. "If anything changes or it gets worse, I want to be the first person you tell. Don't try to handle it alone, Lila. Let me take care of it. Of you."

The words land soft and sharp all at once, threading warmth through my ribs even as my throat tightens. He's not just offering help. He's offering protection. Reassurance. A place to land if everything goes sideways again.

And maybe for the first time, I don't feel like I have to carry it all by myself.

"Okay," I say on a heavy sigh as he parks the car.

"Why do you say it like that?" Dean asks, turning in his seat toward me.

"Because Prescott doesn't come across as someone to let go that easily. One time, he wasn't happy with our meal at this really expensive restaurant. Not only did he speak with the manager before we left, but he went so far as to have the entire restaurant shut down by the end of the week. It had been in their family for over a hundred years."

"God, I have no idea what I saw in him."

"Will you tell me if he reaches out again?"

"Dean, I would never put your kids in any danger."

"What about you? Seems like you're in a bit of danger yourself."

"He won't hurt me. He's probably still fuming about the canceled wedding."

Dean makes a noise deep in his throat as he exits the car. I dutifully wait for him to come over to my side because that is an argument I positively don't want to have again.

As he opens the door and I step out onto the pavement, Dean closes in. He's so close that the subtle salty seaside breeze mixes with his sandalwood scent. It's intoxicating.

"How much do you know about your ex and his family?"

"Um…" I shake my head slightly. "Not much other than they're investors and politicians. I'm not really big into gossip rags or anything. I mean, outside of finding out he is married, they keep things pretty close to their chest, if you know what I mean."

"Doesn't that seem suspicious to you?" he asks, my stomach clenching at the possibilities.

"Maybe, but…"

"Lila, there are things about them I want to tell you, need to tell you."

Pressing my hand against his chest, I allow my palm to settle against the soft cotton of his shirt, feeling the warmth of his skin seep through the material. "Not now, okay? I'm…not ready."

"When will you be? Because, sweetheart, I *will* tell you. Secrets are one thing I won't stand for."

"Can we just enjoy the night? I have a few places I want to show you," I explain, trying to distract him.

Despite my yearning to keep him close, Dean steps back, my hand falling back to my side, and shuts the door behind me.

"Later, then."

"Okay," I whisper.

"Where to first?"

"Let me tell you about this amazing bookstore in town. It's at the other end of the street. Where were you thinking of going for dinner?" I ask, glancing down at the small watch I wear on my wrist. A gift from my dad at my high school graduation. "The marina used to have an amazing restaurant, but I think it's fallen to the wayside over the past few years. A hurricane five years ago really took a toll on the town. Or so my mom said."

"Wherever is fine. I'll be honest, I didn't really research this too much. I just wanted to spend some time with you."

Stopping on the sidewalk, I turn to face him. "Why is that?"

"Believe it or not," he says just as a gust of wind tosses my hair across my face, causing the ends to stick to the corners of my mouth. He gently brushes them aside as he continues, "I like you, Lila. I like the way you're so ambitious. I like the way you take care of my kids as if they're your own. You do a much better job than I ever could, and it's going to suck if you decide to leave. And even though we're not alone much, most of all I like the calmness I feel around you."

"Wow," I mumble as his words wash over me. I feel like we barely know each other, yet we're so familiar at the same time.

My brain screams, "Abort! Abort!" but my heart flutters loudly, shouting, "Full steam ahead."

A quiet calm arises as we walk down the sidewalk. It's not awkward or uncomfortable. Truthfully, it feels more romantic than anything. As we walk, with Dean closest to the road, our hands feel like they brush against each other with each small swing. We're standing at least a foot apart, so I know it's only in my mind, but the energy between us builds with each step.

We pass the first side road, and I point out the direction for the marina and wildlife preserve, then the café and one of two bars in town. The Squeeze In has been around since the town was established and little has changed since then. There are barely any tables, but the bar spans the length of the place. Mom told me that one of the kids recently moved home and is taking it over after spending some time working with a bourbon distillery in Tennessee. Dean stops and leans toward one of the sea-mist-covered windows to get a better view, but I know from experience that the glass is almost entirely opaque.

"Looking for another venture?" I joke, knowing that Dean has his hands in more businesses than I can count, but he surprises me with a secretive grin and shrug.

We continue walking, Dean glancing at me every now and again as I go on about some of the businesses in town and a few that have left. There seems to be more empty shops than I remember, which leaves my heart clenching.

As we reach the last side road headed toward the beach, I point out the public beach access across from the 1920s Needle Palm Resort.

"Once it warms up, you should take the kids to the beach. The park rangers do a great job of keeping it clean. It's sort of our little hideaway here in Coral Bell Cove."

"Does it get busy with tourists in the summer?" Dean asks as a woman pushing a stroller walks in the opposite direction, eyeing Dean as if he were her favorite ice cream. I can't even blame her because he looks delicious with his slightly tousled hair and casual clothes.

"It can. Most locals head to the beach in the morning since tourists tend to go in the afternoon. But we have another special spot that only true Coral Bell Cove residents know about. Maybe I'll show you one day," I say flirtishly.

Dean picks up on it immediately and turns toward me, taking a step in my direction. "You'd do that for me, Lila? Share a piece of yourself?"

He's backed me up against the weathered brick of the building, leaning close enough that I can see the glimmers of gold in his brown eyes. Licking my lips, I murmur, "It's just a town beach."

"Yeah, but it's your town beach. And that makes it special."

I clear my throat, the words catching slightly as Dean steps back, putting space between us that feels far more like an abyss than a courtesy. His warmth still lingers on my skin, a phantom touch I'm not ready to lose. We probably look like strangers now, just two people casually standing on the sidewalk. But my body knows better. My heart certainly does.

I force a smile, voice quieter than I mean it to be. "The bookstore's just another block up."

My pulse pounds in my ears, and I can't stop the way my stomach flutters, nervous and hopeful. His words continue to echo in my chest, a mix of steady confidence and quiet affection that wraps around me like a promise I didn't even know I needed.

What does he see when he looks at me? I'm not polished or poised or remotely put together. I'm still unraveling pieces of myself and trying to remember who I was before everything with Prescott. Yet… Dean looks at me like I'm worth knowing. Worth staying for. Like maybe I'm not as broken as I feel.

And for the first time in what feels like forever, I let the thought in, just the edge of it, the possibility. Maybe I'm starting to fall for this man. And maybe that's the most terrifying, exhilarating truth of all.

Gesturing with his arm out wide, Dean says, "Lead the way."

Chapter Twelve

Dean

I'm making her nervous in the best possible way, and there isn't a single thing I can do to stop it. It's this impulse inside me to see how far I can push her to jump out of this box she's put herself in. Lila is this grand puzzle I'm dying to piece together.

The desire to reach out and grab her hand as we strolled down the main street was overwhelming. It felt like we were a couple as she waved at people we passed. Listening to her describe the stores still open and those that she remembered from her childhood leaves an ever-expanding hole in my gut. Even her wistful memories left me...wanting.

And jealous.

I expect us to continue walking down the street, so I'm shocked when Lila turns and crosses the street in the direction of a lighthouse. The old hinges of a gate squeak when we pass through and head to the entrance. A chalkboard sign indicates that A Page in Time is open in swirling cursive letters.

"I love this place," Lila gushes as a bell chimes when she pulls the door open.

When we step inside, it's easy to see why Lila mentioned the bookshop when we parked. There isn't a bare space not covered in books. Even the spiraling staircase off to the left, which I assume climbs to the top of the lighthouse, is stacked with books—old editions, if I'm not mistaken.

"Hi! Welcome to A Page in Time. Can I help you find anything?" a young woman asks from behind an antique desk with an equally as old typewriter set in the corner.

"Actually, I was hoping Bailey was in. Do you know when she'll be back?" Lila asks as I sidle up next to her, admiring the view out the window toward the bay.

"She just stepped out. Our dehumidifier is on the fritz so she ran to the hardware store to grab a mobile unit until the repairman can get out here. I suspect she'll be back shortly."

"Oh, that doesn't sound good. Isn't something like that expensive?" I ask, tugging my phone from my pocket, prepared to do some research. If this is a place Lila loves, I want to make sure it's taken care of.

Immediately, my search for dehumidifier repair or replacement comes up, and I know this could get costly real quick.

"Crew is home for the summer. Maybe I could have him take a look?"

The bell dings above the door as a soft voice says, "No luck with the repair guy. But I got...oh my gosh, Lila! You're home." She rushes toward Lila and envelops her in a hug to rival that of a long-lost sister. "I heard Ashvi say you were back, but I didn't believe it. But, oh my gosh, you're here." She hugs Lila again as the pretty blonde giggles.

"Sorry, this guy here has kept me busy," Lila points out with a tilt of her head in my direction.

"Oh, is this the fiancé I've heard so much about?" the elfish woman asks.

"God, no. This is Dean. I'm watching his kids. Dean, this is Bailey, and she owns this amazing bookstore."

We shake hands, and I don't miss the shimmer of curiosity in her eyes as she holds eye contact.

"I was telling Judy that Crew is home for the summer. Maybe he could look at the dehumidifier? He's always been good with that sort of stuff."

"No," Bailey says, her hair ballooning around her body as her head jerks toward Lila.

Lila's shoulders move toward her ears casually as she smiles. Clearly, there is a story between Bailey and Crew.

"If you'd like, I could make a few calls. It's sort of what I do."

"Repair things?" Bailey asks as I watch Lila out of the corner of my eye.

"No," I reply with a soft chuckle. "Put my money to good use."

"I still don't get it."

Lila chimes in, "He's a billionaire and owns like a ton of businesses. He probably has a handyman in his back pocket."

"Really?"

"Sort of," I say as I scroll through my contacts, but my eyes hang on my father's number. I may not have a handyman on retainer, but he sure does.

I step out of the main area, leaving the two women to catch up as I explore a back room with a bay window overlooking a garden. I think about Evelyn and how much she would love to play in the dirt and grow vegetables. That certainly wasn't something my parents allowed when I was young, and I assume my sister was the same way. Oliver always looks fearful when he comes inside after getting dirty in the backyard.

Taking a deep breath, I settle into one of the mid-century modern leather chairs that edge against the paned window and press the call button on my phone. Inside, I send a silent prayer that my father doesn't pick up despite my desire to help Lila's friend.

"Harrington," my father says abruptly as if I've inconvenienced him by calling. Of course, to him, I most likely have.

"It's Dean."

"Yes, I do have caller ID. What do you want? Money, a new yacht, an escort for an event?"

"No, Dad."

I wince immediately after I let the name slip.

"I told you not to call me that."

"Yes, I recall. It just slipped. Habit."

"Sounds like the same excuse your mother gives. Now, what do you want this time besides keeping our grandkids from us?"

Seems my parents are still upset I maintain guardianship over Oliver and Evelyn. Not sure why it matters all of a sudden when they could barely spare a minute with their own kids. My guess is they're desperate to maintain a familial heir for the company and I'm not on that ticket, nor do I want it. They want to mold and shape an innocent five-year-old instead.

"Look, I was just calling to see if you could spare the phone number for the company that installed the dehumidifiers in the Miami shop."

"Why? Planning a coup to take over the family business?"

"It's not my business as you've made sure I was aware many times, nor do I want it."

"Good. Making sure you didn't forget that fact."

"The number?" I repeat as I switch to speakerphone.

He reads off a series of numbers that I jot into the phone's notepad, then I turn the speaker back off. A strange conglomeration of fury and despair washes over me. A man I had once loved and respected treats me no better than the servants he has working beneath him.

By the time I stroll back to the main part of the bookstore, my temper has subsided a bit but not enough to wipe the worrying look off Lila's face. I'm not sure she realizes how attuned she is to my emotions. The way my mood affects hers. She does the same for me.

"Here," I cough and then repeat. "This is the number for a place my family used in Miami. Just tell them Dean Harrington gave you their info. I assure you they'll have you set up by the end of tomorrow."

"Wow," Bailey replies, her eyes wide with wonder as she snatches the paper from between my fingers. I sneak a glance down at Lila and smile tightly. She reciprocates and narrows her eyes, reminding me of my own nanny growing up, who would catch me in the midst of a lie.

The bell over the door chimes, and I peer over my shoulder to watch a young family enter the bookstore. The two smaller kids immediately smile and wave toward Lila.

At my raised eyebrow, Lila says, "They play with the kids at the park. Actually, the little boy invited Oliver and Evelyn to his birthday party this weekend. Sorry for the short notice. Kind of slipped my mind."

My knowing smirk turns into a full grin as I tell her to take my credit card and buy whatever gift she thinks is best. The same card I gave to her at the airport. She's tried to return it to me a dozen times already, but I continue to turn her down.

Bailey scoots over to the family here for a storytime session in ten minutes, but not before I overhear her tell Lila that she expects a girls' night with *all* the details.

I may be a man, but I know exactly what she's insinuating. It's too bad that Lila scurries away before anything between us can happen.

Leaving the shop, Lila and I walk back the way we came, our arms brushing every few steps. The days are growing longer, and the setting sun shimmers off the crashing waves of the coast. I get a good glimpse of the picturesque beach every time we pass an alleyway. It really is an adorable town. Weathered brick and wooden buildings that have stood the test of time line the streets, reminding me of a time when families took extended holidays together.

"You know, Coral Bell is great during the summer, but my favorite time is the winter. Christmas, specifically. The entire town gets all decked out in holiday garb. There is even a parade with floats and everything. It's...uh...how my parents first met."

"Really? That sounds like a movie," I tell her as we approach the quaint café.

She blasts that fluorescent smile up at me, and my heart stops beating. God, she's beautiful when she lets down her walls.

"It really does, doesn't it? You should hear my mom tell the story. Unlike my brothers, I never tire of hearing it."

The bell dangling above the café door jingles as I hold the door ajar for Lila to step inside, my broad shoulders barely giving her enough room to scoot by. The scent of warm, freshly baked bread wraps around me like a blanket, reminding me of the times I'd hide away in our family's kitchen, watching one of the staff prepare that day's meal.

As I follow Lila inside, the muffled hum of conversation, tinkling of forks against plates, and the flickering of tiny tealight candles in the middle of every table, umbrellaed by a single carnation, gives the café an intimate, homey quality. It is clear that Sweet Gum Café is a favorite in town, not just because of its well-used chairs and checkered tablecloths but because it also feels like a decadent slice of love.

It almost feels like a special rite of passage to eat here, and I know that Lila is the one to open that door. Every eye in the place turns in her direction once they notice our arrival. Dozens of hands go up in the air, welcoming her home and greeting her like an old friend. I can't help but grin as the blush rises on Lila's cheeks.

I catch a few knowing grins as I escort Lila to a booth toward the back of the restaurant. She slips across the vinyl bench easily, whereas I manipulate my large frame between the back of the seat and the table.

"Smells incredible in here," I say, offering her a soft smile. She reaches for the plastic-covered menus propped behind the napkin dispenser and slides one toward me, returning my grin.

"It always does. Even when they're closed, the smell lingers on the sidewalk outside."

"Seems like you'd want to keep this place a town secret," I say as I peruse the menu, my eyes instantly landing on a dish I haven't had in years. Heather, one of my parent's kitchen staff, used to make chicken piccata whenever I'd come home for a holiday from boarding school, knowing it was a favorite of mine. I've tried it at various Michelin-star restaurants, and nothing comes close to hers. But I'm willing to bet Sweet Gum Café knows what they're doing.

"As hard as we try, it's even more difficult not to share Aimee's dishes with the tourists. Because they're just that good. And that's been in her family for almost a hundred years. They had some hard times a few years back. Betsy, Aimee's grandmother, was diagnosed with stage four lung cancer. It was like she went to the doctor one day, and then she was gone."

"I'm so sorry."

Lila shrugs, but I don't miss the light sheen on her lower lids. "Her husband wasn't far behind, which left Aimee to pick up the pieces. Her parents weren't in the picture, and her grandparents raised her.

"So the entire town chipped in to get the café into shape while Aimee took some cooking classes at a college about an hour away. Ten years later, here we are, and Sweet Gum is thriving. In the summer, sometimes the wait is over an hour. People drive from all around to taste the local dishes."

Leaning across the table, Lila whispers as if she's offering me a secret code. "Aimee always leaves a few tables reserved for locals during the tourist seasons."

Chuckling, I lean back against the bench, hitching one arm along the top. "I like that story."

Lila beams under my praise, and I reach under the table to adjust myself in my pants. "And I like you," I add, to which Lila rolls her beautiful eyes. "So does everyone else, it seems." Subtly, I nod toward the group of men wearing dirt-covered gear, the telltale signs of a day of hard work. Since we walked into the place, their eyes haven't left my nanny. I can't even be mad, as I see her appeal plain-as-day.

From our seat in the back, I face toward the entrance, watching as the sun settles over the line of trees. Streetlamps flick on, dueling against the orange rays to decide who gets to illuminate the sidewalk.

Beneath the table, I'm brought back to the moment when I receive a stern kick to my shin, only to look up and find Lila's cheeks shifting to a color of red to match the tablecloth checks. She apologizes under her breath just as a harried server rushes to our table, offering her own apology.

"Sorry, folks, we're a little short-staffed…oh my gosh! Well, if it isn't Miss Lila Wright? I heard rumors you were back, but I thought, surely, she'd come pay me a visit," the woman exclaims jovially with a hand settled on her hip.

Lila dips her head before stepping out of the booth, wrapping her arms around the curvy woman. The woman's keen eyes latch onto me immediately and I feel the weight of their stare.

"And now, who might this be?" she demands, keeping a stern grip around Lila's waist.

"Sorry, Lisa. This is Dean Harrington. He and his niece and nephew just moved to town. Dean, this is Lisa."

"Nice to meet you," I reply, outstretching a hand for her to shake. Not even the jarred up and down movement can shake the thought of Oliver and Evelyn being called my niece and nephew. They feel more like my own than my own sister did.

"Likewise." Even lost in my thoughts, it's hard to miss her appreciative tone.

As Lila settles back into her seat, we both order a glass of sweet tea, and Lila requests an appetizer of the she-crab soup and Lynnhaven oysters. Two dishes she claims will change my life.

Seems like most things from this town possess that quality.

"So," she begins.

"So," I repeat, settling my arms on the table, bringing my body a few inches closer to her.

"Want to tell me about the phone call?"

Immediately, I tense, my fist reaching for the first thing it comes in contact with, the set of utensils wrapped in a napkin, and clench it for dear life. My neatly trimmed nails dig into the skin of my palm.

Through clenched teeth, I say, "I'd rather talk about you first."

"Okay," she replies with a smile, clearly trying to lighten the tense mood that's fallen over our table.

Thankfully, Lisa arrives with our drinks and promises to return shortly with our appetizers.

"I've read a few of your articles," I begin, and her eyebrows shoot up. "What made you choose to study food allergies? Did I get that right?"

"It's really embarrassing and sort of sad."

Lisa chooses that moment to drop off our appetizers at the table, then takes our order, quickly scurrying off to greet another set of guests. I gaze at Lila expectantly as she reaches for her spoon.

Scooping out some of her soup, Lila glances at me, then asks, "How old were you when you had your first kiss?"

That is *not* what I expected her to say.

"Ugh, eleven?" I respond in question, wondering where she's going with this.

She pauses, taking a few slurps of her soup, and I do the same, wondering if she'll change the subject again.

"I was twelve." Her chuckle is low with a condescending tone as she stares down at her bowl, spoon gripped in her hand. "You know, everyone says you always remember your first kiss, whether it be awkward or clumsy. It's a moment most girls cherish. Me? Well, I'd rather forget."

"Why?"

"Because the boy I kissed almost died as it was happening."

"What?" I shout, my voice echoing off the wallpaper-covered walls. Silence fills the room, and Lila's eyes dart around. "Sorry," I say to her just as voices start to rise again. "Please continue."

Her breathing changes to hurried and unsteady. "You know my family harvests strawberries. In the spring and summer, my siblings and I eat them all the time. I mean, they're delicious.

"Jacob Jeffries had been my crush since kindergarten. During the town's spring fair, he kissed me behind the cotton candy stand. I was in heaven. My crush actually gave me my first kiss, right?

"That's when things went downhill. And fast. In less than five minutes, Jacob's breathing went shallow until he could barely catch it at all.

"I rushed to find his parents, and then things got even more crazy. An ambulance came and rushed him to Norfolk General. He was barely hanging on, or so I was told.

"Apparently, he had a strawberry allergy that didn't present itself until then. I was so embarrassed and terrified. Since that moment, I knew I wanted to try to find a cure or fix of some sort for food allergies."

My fingers curl around the spoon, the metal digging against the rough skin of my palm as I think about the damage that the incident would have caused a twelve-year-old Lila.

"Wha…what happened to him?"

Lila's shoulders rise toward her ears, then drop as she releases a heavy breath. "I don't know. They moved away a year later. Mom mentioned that his lungs never recovered fully."

"I'm sorry, Lila. I can't imagine how it would feel to believe you knowingly harmed someone even though it was all clearly an accident."

"Definitely didn't feel like an accident at the time." She sits back against the bench and sighs. "Still doesn't. It took months for the guilt to subside a bit. I kept thinking, what if I'd actually killed him? All for a stupid kiss."

"I'm sorry, Lila. Truly."

"The worst part after I knew he survived was that I was terrified of doing anything with a boy ever again. Thank goodness for Ashvi. She's the one who pushed me to do something good with what happened and dared me to kiss the quarterback of the football team in high school."

My stomach bubbles in jealousy as I reach for an oyster.

"And…did you? Kiss him, I mean?"

"I never go back on a dare, Dean Harrington," she says, grabbing an oyster of her own. Her head tilts back, and I take a moment to admire her long, sleek neck.

"Hmm…" I say as her stare collides with mine.

Lisa deposits our main dishes, and we eat in comfortable silence, but my mind keeps looping back to her lingering question from earlier. I know Lila will drop it if I ask her to, but strangely, I want to tell her about the phone call from earlier. I want to tell her why I so badly want to give those kids the best upbringing I can. I want to give Lila all my trust.

"Something wrong?" she asks, as she nibbles on a breadstick that came with her salmon dish.

"No…nothing's wrong. Just thinking, that's all."

Gently cocking her head, Lila asks, "What about? The kids?"

"No, just wondering why this, being here with you, feels like something I shouldn't want or have."

She reaches out and swirls her finger across the condensation drips on her sweet tea glass.

"Do you still want it?" she asks, as if I didn't try to flirt with her whenever we are in the same room. Though I have toned it down so I wouldn't come on so strong. Lila's like a small bird just learning to stretch her wings again.

"I think about you too much. And not just you with the kids. I think about what you're doing when they go to bed. I think about what you do on your time off. I think about what you wear between your sheets at night. Just…you're one of my first thoughts in the morning and the last at night," I confess, wishing I could press the cool glass against my head without embarrassing myself. It's the most open I've been to a woman since my last relationship—a chaotic affair that I swore I wouldn't experience again.

Just as I'm about to brush my words aside and chalk it up to a moment of weakness, of vulnerability spilling out when I should've kept my mouth shut, Lila's voice breaks through, soft and trembling.

"I think about you, too."

My heart damn near stops. She's not looking at me, not quite, her gaze dropping to the floor like her shoes have suddenly become the most interesting thing in the room. She shakes her head, trying to catch her breath and her balance, like admitting even that much has taken something out of her.

"We work together, Dean. You're my boss, and the kids…" Her voice falters, trailing off into the silence stretching between us.

I scooch closer, not touching her, not yet. My hands curl into fists at my sides to keep from reaching for her.

"You were unexpected, Lila," I say, voice low and raw. "I never meant to fall for you."

Her eyes flick up, wide, disbelieving. "You have?" I can't help but shrug because what I had thought was simply like… has turned into something far more meaningful.

God, the way she says that, like she can't quite believe it, like no one's ever looked at her and wanted everything. Her cheeks bloom with color, a soft flush that crawls across her skin and makes my chest ache. She's standing so still, but her eyes… her eyes say everything. There's a softness there now, like maybe she's letting herself hope. Like maybe she wants to believe me.

"I didn't expect to," I admit, leaning closer across the table just enough that I can smell the vanilla in her hair. Lila mimics my movement, inclining I speak until there is barely any space between our faces. "But with the way my chest pounds whenever you're close by, I'm smart enough to know what that means."

Her lips part just slightly, and I swear to God, if I didn't think it would send her running, I'd kiss her right then and there. But I don't. I wait. Because she deserves to be the one who chooses.

Still, I don't miss the tiny smile tugging at the corner of her mouth or the flicker of something tender in her expression. A spark. A maybe.

And it's enough to keep me there, heart exposed, hoping like hell she'll catch it.

Lila's breathing changes—shallow, unsteady. Her eyes flick toward my mouth.

"I don't even know what to say to that," she confesses.

"I know. I'm not saying it to push you into anything. I just wanted you to know where I am with everything."

"I just need a little more time," she replies, the corner of her lip tilting upward as she mimics me.

"I know your ex hurt you badly, and you need to heal. I don't make billions rushing into things, Lila. I'm a patient man. I might spend every minute of every waking day imagining what it would be like to kiss you, hold you, taste you, have you. But it will only become a reality when *you* come to *me*."

The air between us is charged, filled with restraint. I'm sure that if she gave the go-ahead, not even the people in the restaurant or the table between us could stop me.

Wanting her is the easy part. Not acting on my desire is the part edging me toward my demise.

"I've never felt wanted like this," she says, just as Lisa sets down the billfold with the check. I slip a hundred inside without glancing at the total.

"I'm not going anywhere."

"What about when my time is up?"

"I'll still be here…waiting."

"Dean," she grumbles.

We leave the café just as the last bits of orange leave the sky. The air has cooled, and the stars are just beginning to make their presence known. One thing I've come to love about this town is the way the stars blanket the sky. The only other time I've experienced their marvel is in Ashfield, Tennessee, visiting Talon, or when I took a trip to Iceland a few years back.

We walk back to my car, remembering I'll need to drop Lila off at the school to get the SUV.

"Want to ride back with me, and I'll call someone to pick up the SUV?"

"Do people just do whatever you want all the time?" she probes.

"Usually," I reply as I press the button for the ignition, then turn to face her. "Everyone except you it seems."

Chapter Thirteen

Lila

Beneath us, the car hums quietly filled with heavy silence, but its not uncomfortable. Something unspoken bubbles with things left unsaid.

From my view in the passenger seat, I stare out the window at the passing oak trees. Blurs and streaks of shadows and the descending sun. Dean's muscular body is barely contained by the belt and driver's seat and his crisp, woodsy scent fills every cavity. I may never wash these clothes again if it means I can keep his scent with me when I leave.

We're headed back toward his house, passing my car at the school, and maybe toward something else, something we keep circling as if it might combust if we accept it head-on. I know I'm the one who continues to pull back, to keep that line in the sand deep and sure, but with each passing day, that line softens with the tide.

"Thanks for dinner," I say, my voice nothing more than a husky whisper.

Dean glances at me quickly, then turns his gaze back to the road. "Thanks for the tour."

The silence splices through the car again, but this time, I'm not the one to break the ice.

"You asked me earlier what happened on the call," he says, eyes locked on the road ahead. "It's not something easy to talk about, especially since I worked my ass off to keep it out of the news."

My body shifts toward his, curiosity taking over. I don't utter a word, just let him talk.

"My dad…he wasn't the kind of man myself or my sister missed. Or anyone missed really. He made a lot of money in the business and used it like a leash toward me and my sister. Any love from him was conditional. You had to earn it. Play the role."

My fingers toy with the hem of my shirt as I swallow. I know that kind of man—almost married one. They must have grown up reading the same manual.

"Growing up like that…" he says, his voice even but subdued, "you learn to disappear in plain sight. Be what they want. Be polished. Be silent. Be golden."

My heart thumps erratically in my chest, tightening it beyond measure.

"I tried to understand how he could treat us…well, me…with such utter disdain. It was never as bad for my sister. Then when I graduated from boarding school, I learned the truth."

He leaves the words hanging in the air, like a plump fruit hanging from a tree just out of reach.

"I'm the product of an illicit affair my mother had with my father's best friend."

The gasp tumbles from my lips before I can catch it.

"Mom confessed right after it happened, and he promised to keep it under wraps and stay with her so long as she made sure the business all went to him and cut ties with his friend. See, the yacht business comes from her side of the family, not his."

"And so, he…"

"He pretended I was his… at least to the public. Behind closed doors, he made sure I knew I was a second-class citizen. If it wasn't for Mom, I probably would have been shipped away forever."

"Dean," I murmur, my heart aching for the little boy who just wanted his father's love.

He muffles out a haunted laugh, and my nerves twitch in dread.

"That's not even the worst part. Once I found out who my biological father was, I learned he died in an airplane accident the year before. I never even got the chance to know the man.

"I once asked my mother to tell me about him, anything. My dad was standing just outside the door." Dean's fingers turn the palest shade of white as he grips the steering wheel. "Learned quickly not to make that mistake again.

"The entire thing blindsided me, left me feeling like a shadow in my own world. When I looked around, all I saw was a shell of a life. Big. Impressive. Empty."

A lump clawed its way up my throat.

"Whatever relationship I had with my father fell to the wayside. Now, he's nothing but a stranger and probably would have wished to stay that way until my sister died. They've been trying to gain custody of the kids even though Gen specifically requested me as guardian.

My guess is to make sure their actual future heirs fit into their world."

"What happened on the call today?"

"I called him Dad, and he snapped. As usual. Old habits die hard, you know? And then he threw a guilt trip about my mom wanting to see the kids.

"They don't know the first thing about raising kids. As far as I'm concerned, nannies and headmasters were our parents. What do they plan to do when Evelyn cries in the middle of the night or when Oliver asks for five more bedtime stories? Ignore them like they did to me?"

His jaw unclenches slightly. And that tiny shift wrecks me in a way I didn't expect. My heart cracks quietly, completely.

"They don't want the kids for any other reason than Oliver will one day inherit the business. They want to shape him into whatever they had planned for Genevieve and me. But I...those kids need me. *Need* me, Lila."

"I know," I whisper just as we turn onto the driveway that had seemed so picturesque when I first arrived. Now, it seems as dark as Dean's confessions.

"Sorry for letting it all out like that. You didn't sign up to nanny an adult, too."

"Sometimes it's nice to let it all out. Lord knows Ashvi has listened to me vent more times than I can count."

The car idles inside the garage, headlights beaming on the wall as Dean puts the car in park. With the press of a button, he turns the car off, but neither of us makes a move to leave the vehicle.

Looking straight ahead, Dean asks, "Do you miss anything about your ex?"

My eyes trace the strong lines of his profile as I contemplate how to answer. Do I go with the answer I've given everyone else, or do I go with the truth?

"I do." His eyes cut over to mine, his body shifting slightly in the seat. I peer down at our hands, resting close but not touching on the center console. My skin prickles with the desire to reach out and confess something real. But the words stick somewhere between embarrassment and wanting.

"I don't know how to say this," I admit in no louder than a whisper.

I can feel his gaze on me, steady and unwavering, as he speaks. His words linger in the air between us.

"It won't change what I think or feel for you," Dean says, and my heart skips, my pulse stuttering in my chest.

I lift my eyes to his, trying to process what he's just said, but all I can feel is a strange fluttering in my stomach. Nerves, disbelief, and something else too, something that might be hope.

His intense eyes are still on me like he's trying to decipher every thought that flickers across my face.

"How are you real?" I whisper, the question slipping from my mouth before I can stop it. His presence, his words, they feel too perfect to be true.

Dean's lips curl up at the edges, a slight smile that seems to melt the tension in the room. "I'm as real and as flawed as any man, sweetheart. But I thought I'd made it pretty clear by now that I'm completely captivated by you, Lila. From the moment I saw you running through that airport, I haven't been able to get you out of my head." He leans closer, and I feel it in my chest, the way his words wrap around me like a comforting embrace.

This isn't a fling to him. I can see that now. His gaze softens, sincerity pouring from him in waves. "None of this is a joke to me. Your feelings, your needs, your wants, and your desires—they matter, Lila. And I'm not taking any of them lightly."

My heart skips, the weight of his words pressing into me. No man has ever cared so deeply, so unapologetically, about me. Not like this. And it terrifies me, the way it stirs something in me I haven't allowed myself to feel in a long time. It's power, in the best possible sense. A power that makes me feel brave like I could take on the world if he's beside me.

I take a breath, steadying myself. "I… really like you too, Dean." The words come out quieter than I expected, but they're true, and they feel good to say.

"I'm trying, Dean. I'm trying so hard to work through my fears and doubts. Because being around you…" I falter, the words catching in my throat. "It's so easy and exhilarating and terrifying all at once. Yet it's comforting, too. But sometimes, my fear of messing up… it outweighs the possibility of something amazing. Something like this."

There's a long pause, where the silence between us thickens. Dean doesn't speak, doesn't try to fix it or fill it with words. He just listens. His eyes never leave mine, unwavering, and I feel every inch of his focus on me, on my words, on the vulnerability I've just laid bare.

And then, after what feels like an eternity, he speaks again. His voice is softer this time, as if he's trying to read me, to understand me. "What is it you miss about your ex?"

I freeze. My breath catches in my chest, and for a moment, everything about this moment feels delicate—

fragile, like I might shatter if I don't tread carefully. But even as the weight of his question presses down on me, I know it's a question I need to answer. For him. For me.

But more than that… it's a question that will push me toward whatever it is we're building between us. And for the first time, I want to let it. I want to see where this goes. I want to stop running from what feels so right.

The stillness stretches until I bravely reply, "It's not him so much as it's that I miss intimacy. I miss being in a relationship. I'm not sure if you can tell, but I don't think I'm a one-night-stand kind of girl."

"So, you miss sex?" His signature smirk I'm coming to love twists on the corner of his lips.

"Yes, but I also miss having a partner. Someone who has my back all the time. Someone to share my hopes and dreams with."

"And you had that with Prescott?"

My breath stops as I pause to consider his question. *Did I have that with Prescott?*

"I'm…I'm not even sure I was in love with him. I think I was in love with the thought of him, you know?"

Dean nods. "You never searched the guy on the internet?"

My hair brushes against my shoulders as I shake my head. "A bit, but nothing really came up. I wasn't brave enough to do a deep dive."

"Maybe do that tonight, yeah?"

I nod, knowing I probably should have done it a long time ago, especially when I confessed to Ashvi everything that happened. I wonder what an internet search of Dean would bring up. Probably hundreds of supermodels draped on his arm at events or lying half naked in a bikini on his boat.

Hesitantly, I inch my pinky closer to Dean's hand until just the tip of my finger brushes against the side of his.

"Dean," I sigh.

He juts out his pinky and wraps it around mine. The line in the sand blurs with every second.

"All good things are worth the wait, ghost girl. I don't expect anything from you. Not a decision. Not a concession. It may not appear that way, but I'm not afraid of working for something."

My chest twists, full and achy. I turn to him, heart pounding, our fingers still interlocked. I want to kiss him. I want to throw down the gauntlet I hitched over my shoulder all those weeks ago. I want to cross that line. God, I want to.

Instead, I lean forward, my lips just barely brushing across the roughness on his cheek. "Good night, Dean."

He returns my nod, a quiet smile touching the edge of his mouth as if he understands the courage it took me to take that leap. "Good night, Lila."

Opening the door, I step out, immediately missing the insignificant touch of his finger. My heart thuds like I've just launched myself off the nearest cliff, and I wasn't one hundred percent sure yet if I'd fly or fall.

Quickly, I make my way up the stairs to my room, ignoring the garage closing and Dean's feet echoing on the first floor. As I pass the mirror above my dresser, I pause and bring my hands up to cover the flushness in my cheeks.

"Oh, geez."

I know that my run up the stairs isn't what caused the redness, but the potency of the man I hurried away from. The man who seems less like my boss and more like someone I want more from.

From the corner of my eye, I spy a cream-colored envelope lying on my bed. I snatch it up quickly, the paper shaking in my hand as I read Dean's letter.

Lila,

Thank you for joining me today.

I know our dinner was probably in a small café, nothing fancy, but I know sitting across from you made it feel like the best table in the world.

You have a way of making things feel lighter, even when they're not. And I don't take that for granted. I don't take you for granted.

I'm glad you're here, not just for the kids, but for me too. I'm grateful you've stayed long enough to share the parts of me I don't usually let anyone see.

Sleep well tonight.

Dean

Well, fuck.

How did he even have this written before I agreed to dinner?

Immediately, I dial Ashvi's number, the phone nearly slipping due to my sweaty palms, and I'm relieved when she picks up after the first ring.

"Vi, I have a big…huge problem."

"What's that? You finally realize you've got a thing for Daddy Moneybags?"

"No…" I drone on, but mentally I'm screaming, *"Yes!"*

"Ah, so you *have* finally figured out that you have a crush on that insanely attractive man you work for?"

"Ashvi! This is not why I called," I scold, my fisted hand resting on my hip as if she can see.

"I know, but I just need to remind you that a man like that won't be single long. And despite whatever *thing* I have going on with my Navy man, your boss is at the top of my list."

Her comment shouldn't irritate me the way it does. I have no claim on Dean, and he should be able to date whomever he pleases. Except just the thought of Ashvi and Dean together causes my eye to twitch.

Staring in the mirror, I've never seen a worse version of myself.

"Vi..."

"Hold on. Can you take a picture with your phone? I want to see what shade of green you've turned so I can compare it to levels of jealousy."

"Oh my gosh, I hate you."

"No, you don't. I'm just helping my little baby bird spread her wings for the first time and realize that the huge hawk soaring close by isn't going to peck her eyes out. He wants to peck...something else."

"I swear, I cannot have a normal conversation with you." I chuckle, my body deflating as I sit on the bed and shift until my back is against the headboard.

"What fun would that be? We're best friends for a reason. If you can't be crazy with your bestie, then your friendship sucks."

"Agree."

"Now, why is it you called, my little baby bird?"

"Wow, are you actually going to let me talk now? What a turn of events."

Ashvi pauses for a moment, and I hear a cork popping free from a bottle of wine. What I wouldn't give for my own glass right now.

"Yes, you may proceed, but I will caution you that I'm pouring a glass of wine for myself and you. I know you're not here, so I shall drink it in your honor."

"You're too kind. Really."

"You know it, babe."

Filling my chest with air, I release it slowly and ask a question that has been running like a hamster on a wheel in my mind since I left Dean in the car. "Do you ever run an internet search on the guys you date?"

"Are you asking me in general, or specifically about someone?"

"Both?"

"Well, it depends on the guy. If I don't expect anything but a few dates and a good night in bed, then not really. But if I think something more is there, then absolutely. I mean, I don't want to find out I'm a side chick too late in the game…oh shit. Lila, that's not what I meant."

"It's okay. I was the side chick for two years and had no idea."

"In your defense, he was really good at hiding things. One day, I'd see an article about a wife, and the next second, it would be gone. Nothing ever showed up about you or the wedding…which was strange in its own right. They're a powerful family and all. I just assumed it was because he wanted to keep his private life private," she rambles.

Reaching out blindly, I grab the closest throw pillow and run my fingers through the strings of the tassels on each corner.

"You searched Prescott?"

"Oh, sweetie. You bet your ass I did, especially when you started pulling away, and I didn't hear from you for a year and a half. Do you know how long that is in friendship time? That's like a decade!"

"Why didn't you say anything?"

"Because you weren't ready to listen. Are you ready to now?"

"I don't know. Maybe?" I think back to the car ride and Dean insisting he wants to tell me things about my ex. It felt ominous then, but now it seems like an approaching black hole ready to pull me within its depths.

"That's good. I'm proud of you." I can hear her slurp the sweet beverage from her wineglass before it gently tinks back on the granite counters.

"You're not going to tell me?"

"I can be there with you if you decide to…but no. For all I'm concerned, Daddy Moneybags is willing to hold your hand through it all."

Visions of Dean gripping my hand flash in my mind, and I instantly feel my core tighten.

"Did you search him?"

"Um… yeah. You were going to live with a stranger for a summer. Of course, I did."

Biting my lips, I nod even though I know she can't see. I don't ask her for more, knowing that if she had thought he would cause trouble, she would have stepped in by now. Plus, my mom's company runs background checks on everyone.

"I missed you, Ashvi."

"Don't you do that. He'll get what's coming to him. Karma knows what she's doing."

The front door opening and then slamming shut echoes through the house, and I realize that any quiet time I had left is about to be quickly exterminated by two of the cutest kids I know.

"I need to go. Let's go out for drinks soon?" I ask as four little feet pound up the stairs, sounding like a herd of horses.

"You mean that?" Ashvi asks, her voice full of eagerness. The two of us never really got the chance to head to a bar and cut loose like most women in their twenties. I went away for college, and then Prescott happened.

"I do. But maybe local? I don't want to have to call a cab from an hour away."

"You got it. Let me know the next night you have free, and I will make time for my baby bird."

A giggle escapes just as two little heads pop around my door and peek inside. I quickly end the call with Ashvi, promising her my next available night, and sit up with my arms open wide.

"Hey, cuties. Have a great time with my mom today?" I ask them, ignoring the way Dean's shadow falls into the bedroom, his large frame leaning against the doorjamb.

His dark eyes dart over to the open letter resting on top of the duvet and then flick back to me before he smirks and exits farther down the hall.

If it weren't for the bouncing kids chattering around me and shouting about their day, I'd probably curl into my pillow and squeal like a teen who just found out her crush checked the yes box on her love note.

I am in so much trouble where Dean Harrington is concerned.

Chapter Fourteen

Dean

Two Days Later

The hotel room in the Knoxville Lodge owned by my best friend, Talon, is quiet in the way that luxurious, expensive places always are. Too quiet. Thick curtains covering the windows, walls meant to keep the world out. The most perfect, polished silence anyone could ask for.

And I loathe it.

I'm sitting against the upholstered headboard, the rustic lamp casting a pool of light across the folders I left resting on the nightstand. Notes I've read over three times and still can't recall what they're about. None of it is sticking. I keep eyeing the same sentence, rereading it and hoping it may click.

I'd left Coral Bell Cove in a hurry when Talon's wife went into labor. His voice rattled through the phone, full of worry, asking for my help. Talon was estranged from his family, so he didn't have anyone to turn to. He needed me there. So I drove straight here, eight hours of silence, my thoughts clouded with memories of my own life, of the kids, and Lila.

By the time I arrived, their daughter was just being born. I stood in the hallway of the hospital, the sound of her first cries echoing through the building, her tiny voice piercing the air like a beautiful melody. An overwhelming feeling swelled within me, but it wasn't just for Talon or the baby. No, it was because of something I hadn't fully realized yet. I missed Oliver and Evelyn, God, I missed them, but more than that, I missed Lila. I missed her presence in my life in a way that made everything else feel incomplete.

I had a flash as I stood there, looking at the new family formed in front of me. An image so clear and sudden that I froze. It was of Lila in that same hospital room, giving birth to our child. A son or a daughter, I didn't know which, but the vision felt so right, so undeniable. The idea of Lila holding our child in her arms didn't scare me in the least. It wasn't even just the physical act of it—no, it was the future that flashed before me. A future with her. A family. Something that suddenly felt like the most natural thing in the world.

I caught myself standing there, still as stone, my chest tightening with emotions I hadn't been prepared for. I hadn't let myself think about it, about what we might be, what we could be. But now, with the cries of a newborn in the background, I realized that I wanted it. I wanted to build something real. Something lasting. Something with her.

My mind pulled back to the present, but the weight of that thought clung to me, pressing deep into my chest. As I held the baby in my arms later that night, looking down at her tiny face, something shifted inside me. This wasn't just about Oliver and Evelyn anymore. It wasn't just about being a father figure to them.

It was about Lila.

She was the one I could imagine waking up next to every day. She was the one I could picture sharing all of this with. And the thought of it filled me with a calm certainty, like I'd been waiting for this moment my entire life.

It wasn't just a passing thought or a fleeting daydream. It was real. And when I thought about it, I knew without a doubt that I wanted that life with her. One day.

I could see it now, the life we'd build, the home we'd create, and yes, the family we'd have together. And that scared me. It scared me because it felt so right. But even more, it excited me in a way I didn't expect.

So as I held that baby in my arms, I made a promise to myself, to Lila, to the future that was slowly but surely becoming our own. I would protect her, care for her, and show her that this life, with me, could be everything she ever wanted.

And if she ever needed more time to see that, I'd give it to her. But I would wait for her because this was worth waiting for.

My phone sits beside me on the bed. Dark and unmoving. Taunting me.

It's not that I don't want to be here for my friend. I just don't want to be *here*. Under different circumstances, I wouldn't have left in the first place.

There is no way I could have expected that leaving the three people who have come to mean the most to me would be this hard. Before them, I would go anywhere at the drop of a hat. Like, say, Connecticut to find my lost sister. But now? Now, I can't imagine being anywhere else.

Yet here I am, wallowing in my misery alone in a hotel room. Talk about a change of pace for me.

Hesitantly, as if it were a snake ready to bite, I pick up the phone and stare at her name in the contacts. The name "Ghost Girl" shines brightly back at me from where I'd named it, like I needed to convince myself she was nothing more than a casual encounter.

She isn't.

I tap the screen, then quickly back out, blacking the screen again.

With a plop, I drop the phone back onto the bed and run a hand across my face. I'd never called her before. Nerves like that of a teenage boy rattle me to my bones. When I left two days ago in the early morning light, she'd come down into the kitchen to figure out what all the racket was. In a flourish, I headed to my car, but not before I told her I'd call to check in. I want to, even if for the kid's sake. But another part of me hesitates.

Lila's skittish. Guarded. I recognize the sense of self-protection because I'd worn it myself. I don't want to push or turn into another weight on her shoulders.

But, God, I miss her.

Her voice. The way she challenges me in her sharp, bright, witty way without even trying. The way she smiles whenever she gets a jab in toward me. The quiet strength she carries like a shield.

I miss being with her in my house…with my kids. I miss the insane way she always knows what everyone needs. Hell, I even miss the way she scrunches her nose when she's concentrating.

With a glance at the clock that reads 9:45 p.m. I pick up the phone again and hover over her contact information.

Fuck it.

I type something and hit send before I can talk myself out of it.

Dean:

> **Hey. Don't want to interrupt your night. Just wanted to see what you were up to.**

A minute passes. Then two.

I murmur under my breath how stupid I was being as I rake my hand through my hair. She's had to watch the kids all day and work on that stupid grant that I've been trying to convince her to let me fund.

Ghost Girl:

> **Hi, Dean. You're not interrupting anything. I could use a brain break.**

The pulling in my chest unravels.

Dean:

> **I love this lodge, but I miss home already.**

I hope she catches onto my underlying meaning— that it's her I'm missing.

Ghost Girl:

> We wish you were home too. It's been quiet, like the kind where it makes you wonder if something is missing…or a child is silently destroying something.

Dean:

> Were they?

Ghost Girl:

> I can confirm it was not the latter.

Annoyed by her contact name, I quickly go in and edit to her real name.

Dean:

> I left you a note, did you find it?

Lila:

> I did and read it twice.
> I should probably be embarrassed that I told you that, huh?

I smile, knowing that the letter consisted of nothing more than a few sentences, telling her how amazing she was. Overstepping the boss bounds, definitely, but knowing that she needed to hear from someone not family that she's incredible is worth every inch.

Lila:

> Did you mean it?

Dean:

Of course. You know I never say (or write) anything I don't mean.

Lila:

Thank you.

Dean:

You're welcome. And I hope you realize I wasn't just referring to your job. I mean you as a person. You're incredible.

Three dots light up on the screen, dissipate, then reveal themselves again. My palms start sweating, nearly dropping the phone onto my lap.

Lila:

You're so honest. And kind. And I haven't had a lot of that these past couple of years.

Dean:

I meant every word. How are the kids?

Lila:

<image>

I stare at the two cherubic faces squished up against Lila's hips on her bed, both of their stuffies wedged beneath their arms.

They miss you too. Evelyn woke up asking for her mom.

Fuck, that's my worst nightmare when I'm away, that she'll think I left them the same way their mom had.

Dean:

> <image>
> I went and saw Scarlett today. They get to go home tomorrow.

Lila:

> She's beautiful. Mom still doing okay?

Dean:

> Rory is one of the strongest women I know.
> Especially because she willingly puts up with Talon's grumpy ass.

Lila:

> Haha, I know someone similar. I want

The conversation pauses, and I wonder if she's settling farther into the sheets.

> Sorry. I wanted to know if you would take the kids to a birthday party this weekend. You said you'd be back?

Dean:

> Of course. You deserve a day off. I'll be back by tomorrow.

Lila:

> Everyone will be happy to see you.

Dean:

> **Does that "everyone" include a gorgeous blonde who ran through an airport in a wedding dress?**

I laugh under my breath. The knot I hadn't realized was tangled in my chest eases a bit.

Lila:

> **I'll let you decide.**

Saucy little minx.

Dean:

> **I'll let you get some sleep. I just needed to hear from you.**

Lila:

> **I'm glad you messaged. Sleep well.**

I set the phone down beside me, my mood levels better than it had been before I reached out.

The following day, I'm on the road before dawn breaks. I messaged a quick farewell to my friend and his new family, knowing that my baby gift would arrive around the same time they make it home. Because a baby can't do without a trust fund set up in their name, courtesy of their godfather.

One good thing about leaving before most people is I miss the stares and whispers. Despite it happening weeks ago, rumors still swirl around that damn magazine article naming me the **World's Sexiest Billionaire Heir**.

And it's not just the women confiding to various sources that they had snagged me, or my cheating ex, claimed we're still together. *Yeah, right.* It's the fact that people are starting to dig into my past. And if they go deep enough, the news about my real father and what really happened with the death of my sister will break.

I can't have either of those things come to light.

By the time I pull into the tree-lined driveway, the town is already starting to feel more confined—in a good way. More like a tight embrace that makes you feel like you're home.

I spot Lila's SUV in the garage bay, and I release a heavy breath as I pull my own vehicle inside.

The side door opens just as I step out of my car, and Lila emerges from the shadows of the mudroom. She's there in denim shorts and a soft green T-shirt, hair pulled back from her face, elongating her neck, and she's looking at me like she's been holding her breath since the moment I left. Like maybe she can finally exhale.

I don't say anything as I approach. No need to. My eyes say it all as I take her in from the tips of her pink-painted toenails to the wispy hairs on the top of her head.

Lila steps forward, down one stair, then the other, until we meet halfway.

"You're here early."

"I am."

"Did you leave in the middle of the night?" she asks, her voice low but steady.

"Something like that."

She smiles, that half smile she graces me with when she thinks I'm not looking. Without thinking, I reach for her hand, desperately needing some physical connection to her. Christ, her skin is soft and warm, so smooth against my callused palms. Years of doing anything I can to get my hands dirty and out of an office will do that.

I'm ready to loosen my grip on the off chance that she pulls away. But she doesn't. She glances down and then intertwines our fingers like they belong there. I take a small step forward until our feet are almost touching. Lila smells like clean linen and citrus—sunshine and science.

Neither of us pulls away, and my chest tightens with anticipation as her pink tongue reaches out to touch her lips.

"How is everyone? The baby is adorable."

"They're good. Happy. Shit, it's the most I've seen Talon smile since their wedding. And Rory? She was made to be a mom. I've never seen her look so…at peace."

"That's good to hear. The kids missed you."

"I missed them. And you. I kept thinking about you."

Lila's expression shifts, softening. "I thought about you, too."

Her words were quiet but no less impactful.

I want to kiss her. Pull her into my arms and destroy whatever barriers she's erected.

But I don't.

Not yet.

"About the party… there is a present in the back of the SUV, and both kids are excited for cupcakes."

"Thanks for getting that together. I'm not sure what to expect."

Her giggles reach my ears like a private symphony. "You and a crowd of sugar-rushed preschoolers. I kind of wish I was going now."

I kind of wish she was going, too. While I'm good with my niece and nephew, other kids can be a bit daunting.

"Plans?" I ask now that she has the rest of the day off.

"I'm meeting with Ashvi, but I'm not sure what we're doing tonight. Gossiping, I hope. I may stay at her place if that's okay?"

I quickly imagine her wearing those cutoff denim shorts and a cropped shirt exposing her abdomen and shoulder. Cowboy boots on her feet. I'd rather see them wrapped around my neck.

Coughing, I try to draw attention away from my growing erection.

"You can stay wherever you like."

"Okay." She takes a step back, pulling our hands apart. I miss her touch instantly. "Go find the rascals. They're waiting for you. I'll be here until you leave."

The kids are waiting, just like Lila had been, and I hold them close to me when they bound into my waiting arms.

Oliver rattles on about the party while Evelyn is more than content to rest her body against mine while in my arms. She's so much like me in that way. Genevieve was always the outspoken one. The one who never met a stranger.

I thought I knew the extent of chaos. I'd been to multiple celebrity events where a catfight broke out and concerts where the mosh pits engulfed the entire standing area. But nothing could have prepared me for Liam's (the playground friend) birthday party.

The Coral Bell Cove park is filled to the brim—kids running around adults, making their way in and out of the pavilion with frosting smeared on their faces. Plates litter the ground like polka dots. Balloons meet their demise on the concrete pad, a graveyard of their own making. Finally, someone cut off the stereo because I couldn't listen to *Kidz Bop* and *Baby Shark* again without losing all my brain cells.

I lean back against the fence surrounding the park, nursing a cup of red fruit juice that's starting to get warm. The sun is high, the sound of children's laughter drifting over the grass as they run and play, and I can't help but wish I had something stronger than juice in my hand. A splash of something a little more… adult.

Oliver is off with another little boy, pretending to sword fight with two Styrofoam pool noodles, their faces scrunched in concentration and the occasional battle cry that makes me smile. I watch them for a moment before turning my attention to Evelyn, who's sitting on a bench by herself, watching everyone but not quite joining in. Her little fingers are smeared with the icing from her cupcake, and she's methodically licking them clean, looking so deep in thought that I almost want to interrupt her.

But I don't. I love watching her like this, observing the world through her quiet, patient eyes. She's like Lila in so many ways, soft and still, yet always absorbing, always understanding more than she lets on.

And then the peace is shattered. I feel the shift before I see her. Ashley.

She's sauntering over, her designer sandals flapping against her feet as she moves with the kind of confidence that makes the air around her feel too warm. She's got that look on her face, the one that means she's about to stir up trouble. Her gaze locks on me for a moment, and I'm half expecting a smile, but it's more of a predatory smirk. She's up to something. I'm not sure what it is, but when she stops a few feet away, I can already tell it's going to be bad.

"Dean," she says in that low, teasing tone of hers, tilting her head slightly, the movement so practiced it's almost sickening. "Did you forget about me already?"

I don't answer right away, keeping my eyes on Oliver, still oblivious to the drama brewing around him. Evelyn glances over at Ashley for a moment, her cupcake held suspended mid-air as if she's already sensing the energy shift. But I'm not worried about the kids right now. I'm worried about Lila and how Ashley has made it her mission to get under her skin ever since she got here.

Ashley steps closer, her gaze lingering on my lips before flicking back to my eyes. She places her hand on the fence, leaning in, and I can almost feel her trying to fill the space between us with her presence.

"I don't see why you're wasting your time with Lila," she says, the words dripping with condescension. "You could have anyone, Dean. You don't need to settle for a nanny, do you?"

I freeze, feeling the familiar anger clawing its way up my throat. But I don't let it show.

Ashley continues, unaware of the effect her words are having. "I thought maybe you could use a break. Maybe… we could go for a drink? You know, blow off some steam?"

Her fingers lightly brush against my arm, and I feel a surge of irritation flood my chest. I'm not a saint, and a part of me has always been attracted to attention. But not like this. Not from someone like her. Not when I've already given my heart to someone else.

I straighten up, setting my cup aside, and lock eyes with her. "If you ever try that again," I say, my voice low, the warning clear, "I'll make sure you regret it."

Ashley's eyes flicker with surprise, but she quickly recovers, her smile stretching wider as if she's unsure whether she's actually intimidated. "What's the matter, Dean? You've never had someone who likes a challenge?"

I reply, voice firm, "If you can't see the difference between my interest in you and in Lila, maybe it's time you look a little harder. You won't like what you find."

She scoffs, clearly thrown off, but I don't let her get a word in. My gaze drifts around the park. I don't need to explain to Ashley that I'm already spoken for. She's smart enough to pick up on it.

Ashley stands there for a beat, her confidence wavering just enough before she turns and walks off, muttering something under her breath. She's not used to being put in her place.

Intruder gone, I watch as Evelyn continues to meticulously nip at her cupcake, her eyes always roaming. I need to ask Lila if there is a way I can nurture her watchfulness, instead of demeaning it like everyone had of mine.

As if she can feel my eyes on her, Evelyn sits up and returns my gaze.

"Uncle Dean," she calls out, holding up the de-iced cupcake. "Do you want the cake part? I don't have to eat it, do I?"

"You can skip it, Ev. But maybe don't let the birthday boy see you," I say, nodding my head in his direction where he's joined Oliver in the sword fight. "We may have a mutiny on our hands."

She nods as if she understands what the word mutiny means and goes back to licking away whatever icing on her cupcake she can find.

I'm smiling as I lift my phone from my back pocket. My background is now a picture of Lila and the kids that I snapped as she was helping them get ready for the party.

I haven't texted her since we left, but God, I miss her.

My feelings are ridiculous, considering I saw her just a couple of hours ago, but my mind hums in a way that hasn't quieted.

Dean:

Kid chaos in full effect. You've fed me to the wolves. I'm not sure I'll recover.

Lila:

I'm sure you'll survive.

Dean:

Rescuing me might be the only option at this point.

Lila:

Soldier on, my friend. It's only for another hour.

Dean:

I'll be buried with the balloons by that time.

Lila:

Be careful! They're likely to turn you into a piñata in that case.

Dean:

> **Have fun today, but not too much fun tonight.**

I can hear her rolling her eyes from here.

Lila:

> **Yes, Dad.**

I'm not sure she realized the effect her text would cause, my pants tightening from my cock stiffening. I wonder if she liked dirty talk in bed.

I'm still gripping my phone, barely registering the half-completed text on the screen as I hear the pitter-patter of little feet racing toward me. My mind is still wrapped up in the conversation from earlier, but the moment I look up and see Oliver barreling toward me, breathless and wild, something inside me shifts.

"Dad!" he yells, his eyes wide with excitement. "There is a pirate ship we get to hit with a bat."

My heart stutters in my chest. For a second, I can't breathe. The word "Dad" hangs in the air between us, louder than any noise coming from the party, reverberating deep in my soul. It feels like a punch, but in the most beautiful, gut-wrenching way.

I blink, trying to ground myself, but everything shifts.

What just happened? Did he just…?

His innocent face beams up at me, so filled with joy and excitement over some ridiculous childhood game, but I can't seem to shake the weight of what he just said. "Dad."

I don't even know how to explain what it does to me. It's like the entire world shifted at that moment. All the shit I've been running from, all the reasons I convinced myself I couldn't be a father, all the fear of screwing up—it suddenly doesn't matter. Because this kid just called me *Dad*, and it feels like it's been waiting to spill out for a lot longer than just today.

I force myself to focus, clearing my throat as I try to speak. But a part of me is still spinning because I never thought this would happen. Not like this. Not with someone like Oliver, someone who's not mine but who's been slowly crawling into my heart in ways I can't even put into words.

"Jesus, kid. Who in their right mind gives a bat to a bunch of four- and five-year-olds?" I say, my voice coming out rougher than I intended, a little strained, but the words fall flat compared to the riot of emotions tumbling through me.

Oliver doesn't seem to notice the shift. He's too wrapped up in his excitement, his voice a constant stream of energy. But I can feel it. That one word. *Dad.* It's like a promise, like it's just a matter of time before I settle into this role for good.

I just… never expected it to happen like this. Never expected to feel this way. It's like everything I've been building up in my life, the walls, the walls I put up so carefully, are starting to crack.

And I think I might finally be ready to let them fall.

Oliver cackles in my ear as I scoop him up and make my way toward Evelyn. She grabs my hand, and we head toward the pavilion in a trail of disasters waiting to happen.

Yet somehow in the middle of the birthday battlefield, I feel… fulfilled. Like maybe I don't have two lives anymore, just a single messy one.

And later, when the sun dips down, and the house grows quiet as the kids fall asleep, I think about Lila. Where my thoughts can take us to places she's scared of. If only she realized how safe she'd be with me.

How I'd never let anyone take advantage of her again. How I could love her. If only she'd let me.

Chapter Fifteen

Lila

I don't want to be here.

Currently, I'm wedged against the wall, half leaning on the high-top table, half sharing the stool with Ashvi. The lights and the music combined with the whiskey and sweat is far from the comforting smell of the coastline.

I could have done with a quiet evening. Maybe some wine, curled up on the couch with Ashvi while we caught up on everything that had happened since I'd left town. I would have happily listened to her chatter about her latest dating disaster or the new project she was working on. And I would have been perfectly content to let her show me everything she'd found on my ex, a curious distraction from the constant ache I've carried.

But apparently, Ashvi had other plans in mind.

The moment I stepped into her apartment, she'd practically shoved a dress into my hands, her eyes alight with excitement.

"Tonight, we're going out, Lila," she had said. "You're not hiding in your shell anymore."

And before I knew it, I found myself standing in front of her mirror, my reflection nearly unrecognizable. The dress—black, sleek, and entirely too revealing for my usual taste—hugged every curve, showing off parts of me I wasn't used to exposing.

Ashvi had worked her magic with the makeup, giving me bold eyes that made me feel like I was wearing someone else's face, and the waves in my hair styled in big bouncing curls, giving me an unfamiliar air of sophistication. I should have said no, I should've argued. But instead, I let her guide me, and as much as I hated to admit it, a part of me was intrigued. A part of me was excited to consider how Dean would look at me if he saw me in this version of myself. Would he even recognize me? Would he like it?

"Lila," she whines over her shoulder. "You promised you'd try to have a good time. Look, this place is filled with guys tonight."

Yes, it is. Guys we had gone to high school with, and some guys I can tell are here for the summer. I'm not interested in either. There's only one man on my mind, and Ashvi knows it.

"One drink? One. And then you can go back to being an antisocial scientist."

I nod and watch her gleefully jump from the stool and dance across the worn hardwood toward the bar. With her absence, I suddenly feel… visible.

Too much so. Gazes skirt across my chest and legs. Appreciative glances, sure, but violations all the same.

Whatever band plays on the jukebox fills the room with a steel guitar. A few couples brave the dance floor, doing a version of the two-step to the twangy beat.

The Horse Shoe isn't quite a dive, having been rebuilt about fifteen years ago after Durky's, the previous name, met its demise to a kitchen fire. Instead of wall-to-wall wood paneling, The Horse Shoe only commits to half a wall of paneling. Strings of twinkling lights twist around the beams crossing the expanse of the ceiling, and about one hundred horseshoes of various sizes are deemed artwork.

Ashvi returns from the bar with a sheepish grin and her shoulders hunched. My alarm bells set off.

Accepting the beer she hands off, I ask, "What?" narrowing my eyes.

She adjusts the brown leather belt strapped within the loops of her denim miniskirt like she's readying herself for battle. "Okay, so don't be mad, but I might have told someone new in town that you'd be here."

"Ashvi," I scold.

"Aw, Lila, it's just a drink," she exclaims, hoisting herself back on the stool beside me. "He's really nice, and he's the new veterinarian in town. Even has some rescue dogs. And he's wearing his sleeves rolled up to the elbow. You love it when guys do that."

I love when Dean does it.

"I'd also love it if my best friend didn't decide to start dictating my social life."

With a pleading look, she says, "You've been back for a while now and haven't even tried dating. And don't even dare throwing out that you just got out of a serious relationship. It was neither serious…nor really a relationship. Please, Lila. Give him a shot.

"He's sweet, Lila. Just give it a try. And if it's awful, we'll fake an emergency like a sprained ankle or severe diarrhea, and I'll drive us home. Pinky promise," she says, holding out her pinky to reiterate.

I'm starting to squabble just as a shadow falls over the table in the already dimly lit bar.

Ashvi is right. He is attractive. Tall, friendly smile, broad-shouldered, rolled sleeves. He's every girl's fantasy.

I need to prove that overstepping things with Dean would end in catastrophe. Maybe this is my chance. He could be my fantasy, too.

I give her a disdainful look as I grip her pinky with my own and shake it.

"Ashvi, good to see you again. Lila?" he says, placing his own beer on the high-top table and holding out his hand in greeting. At least he's drinking something with color in it and not a light beer.

I return his greeting. "Sorry, Ashvi didn't give me your name."

"Matthew."

"Nice to meet you."

Conversation flows with the usual first-date interrogations. Where we grew up. What we studied in school. Favorite sport. Yada, yada. The type of questions that left my mind wandering back to the house along the Back Bay channel.

I couldn't help but compare Matthew and Dean. How Dean's laugh was deep, caressing, while Matthew's seems intentional. The way Matthew leans into my space to speak more directly with me, whereas Dean silently demands all my space.

Just as the jukebox switches off and a band steps up onto the stage, my phone buzzes.

A text from Dean flashes on the screen.

Dean:

Kids asked for twelve stories tonight. The sugar from the party should have made them crash. But no, not these two. They said story time wasn't the same without you.

I agree.

Matthew is still talking. I catch bits and pieces of his golden doodle and a squirrel. Apparently, it's funny because Ashvi giggles beside me. I join in, having very little idea of what's going on.

Lila:

At The Horse Shoe. Ashvi said she wanted to dance tonight.

Three dots appear immediately.

Dean:

That sounds fun.

Lila:

It was a trick. She set me up on a blind date.

Dean:

She wants to see you happy.

Lila:

He's not for me.

You are, I want to tell him. Me and my freaking rules. I'm about to throw them all out the window. Besides Ashvi, because I tell her everything, who would know? And, God, I've been craving the taste of him. I bet his kisses are as demanding and possessive as he is.

Dean:

Let me know if you need an extraction. I can come up with something.

Lila:

I appreciate that. I'm sure I'll make it through the night. Who knows, maybe he'll sweep me off my feet while we're dancing.

Dean:

If your goal is to make me jealous, it won't work.

Lila:

? Really? You sure about that?

Dean:

Of course, I am.

I know he's right. Deep down, I can feel it—there's no competition. It's not just the way he looks at me, it's how he sees through me, how confident he is in himself, in us. It's that unwavering certainty that he knows exactly what he wants, and it just so happens to be me. I've never been one to fall easily for someone, but something about him, his quiet assurance, the way he makes me feel seen and valued makes it impossible not to like him even more. He doesn't hesitate, and his confidence makes me feel secure, even when I'm questioning everything else. He doesn't just make me feel safe. He makes me feel like I'm worth it. Worth all of him.

The night feels like it's floating by in a haze. The music, the laughter, and the constant buzzing of conversation all blend in a way that makes everything feel distant, almost surreal. By the time Matthew and I dance, I step on his toes far more times than I care to admit. Laughing each time as he gently corrects me, I manage to forget, just for a few minutes, why I didn't want to be here.

Matthew asks me if I'm enjoying myself, and I answer politely, not knowing how to express what I'm feeling. But I know it isn't anything more than a casual night out.

When the dance ends, Matthew gives me that polite, friendly smile, and I let him continue with his conversations. I'm not sure how I'm supposed to feel at this moment, with the weight of the past and the present swirling around me like an ominous storm. Ashvi, on the other hand, is glowing. I catch a glimpse of her smiling and dancing with someone new, and I know she's doing just fine. She's here to have fun, and I won't get in the way of that.

When the night winds down, I say my polite goodbyes. I don't linger long. I just give Ashvi a soft assurance that I'll be fine on my own before I slip into my car. As I drive away, the glow of the downtown grows distant in my rearview mirror. The lamplights linger until they're just a fleck in the sky.

The car's headlights cut through the night air, a sharp contrast to the calm stillness of the world around me. But tonight has been a moment of self-discovery. I'm not running anymore. I'm facing something, and though I'm not sure what it is yet, it feels like something is shifting inside me. And for once, it feels like the right kind of change.

I sit in my car with the headlights off for too long, just outside the garage bay. The house is dim, like it's readying itself for sleep, but the porch lights remain on. The upstairs window glows from the lamp I'd installed on a shelf in the hallway. I picture the kids asleep in their rooms. Safe from the world.

It's late. The sun having long since bid us farewell.

Ashvi messages me, apologizing profusely for blindsiding me with the date. And while Matthew turned out fine, I needed air. I needed to think. I needed time.

I needed Dean.

Somehow, my pull to him is stronger than the voice in my head telling me to keep my distance. Since we met on the plane all those weeks ago, the voice seems to have always been there, quiet but insistent. Don't make the same mistake. Don't lose yourself in a relationship again. Don't believe that he can't hurt you.

Dean makes it hard to listen. With each passing day, the voice grows fainter until it becomes barely a whisper.

I park my car in the garage and make my way into the house, hoping to find Dean in his usual spot on the couch in the sunroom, enjoying the cool night. When I don't see him there, I scurry up to the second floor to check on the kids.

Shucking off my sweat-covered clothes in my own room, I pull on a pair of leggings and an oversized T-shirt. I glance out the window while tossing my hair back into a ponytail and notice a dim light flickering off in the distance, right at the edge of the dock.

With a racing heart, I make my way down the stairs, slipping on a pair of sandals I left by the mudroom door before I go outside. By the time I creep through the fence and reach the dock, I'm not sure if it's my hurry to see him or the speed at which I nearly jumped down the flight of stairs that causes my breath to come out in quick puffs of air.

But Dean remains unmoving until the wood creaks underneath my feet.

"You came," he says quietly as he turns to look over his shoulder.

I nod. "I wanted to come home."

"Did your night of dancing and blind dates not lead up to the hype?" he asks as I sit on the edge of the wood beside him.

"No. It was fine. Just not the night I wanted."

His eyes search mine, only the reflection of the back deck lights glistening in their depths. He cocks his head like he's trying to be sure and not reading into something more.

"What are you doing out here tonight?" I ask, breaking the contact that was becoming too much to bear because I know Dean can see things I'm not ready to divulge.

"Fishing," he replies, holding up the rod gripped in his other hand. "Something Talon and I used to do at the lake near our boarding school."

"Oh. I didn't know billionaires knew how to fish. I thought you'd just have someone do the dirty work for you while you sit atop your luxury yacht."

Dean chuckles and rotates the handle of the reel one turn. "We do that, too. Want to join me?"

"That's okay. I'd rather just watch."

He dips his chin as if he understands my only reason for being out here is to be closer to him.

The earlier chill in the air is replaced by the warmth of being close to Dean.

"You make it hard to keep my walls up, you know."

"I'm not trying to," he begins, then pauses and settles the fishing rod in the PVC holder at the edge of the dock. "I don't want to play a part with you, Lila. I've done that enough in my life. I want something real. I want this with you to be real. I know you have your rules, and I respect them, but I can't deny wanting it all."

I'm not sure how to answer. How do I vocalize all the things I'm feeling? The inward battle of right and wrong is suddenly nothing more than a mess of smoke and mirrors.

I scoot closer to him an inch, and then an inch more until our thighs are touching. I lean in and rest my head against his shoulder and let myself exhale. His arm comes around me like an impulse. Like he's been waiting for me to give him an inch. I feel him kiss the top of my head—gentle, unhurried, careful.

"I'm sorry if tonight was difficult after everything," he mumbles.

"It was just the wrong place. I didn't want to be there. I wanted to be here."

"You can stay, you know. You don't have to find a new job and leave."

Dean's voice is quiet, but it vibrates against me, low and warm where his chest meets my shoulder. The words settle over me like a thick blanket, heavy and too tempting to ignore.

"How can I make a difference in the world if I don't?" I whisper. The lump forming in my throat almost chokes the words as they come out. I hate how small my voice sounds. How uncertain I feel. Like maybe I'm afraid of staying because I want to.

Dean doesn't move for a long beat, and I wonder if I've said too much, been too vulnerable. But then his voice returns, deeper this time, like a soft vow.

"You already have. You've made a difference in mine and those kids' world, Lila."

My heart stumbles over itself at his words. I press my lips together, trying to hold in the wave of emotion swelling in my chest.

"What if that's not enough?" I murmur, my biggest fear unfurling in the quiet like a secret I didn't mean to say aloud.

His response is immediate, quiet but fierce. "What if it is?"

He doesn't look at me, just lets the question linger in the space between us, as potent and full as the scent of bay water and sea grass hanging in the warm air. His arm tightens around me just a little more, like he knows I need to be grounded before I float too far into my own doubts.

The sound of the water gently lapping at the shore fills the silence. A bird calls out softly somewhere in the distance, the night wrapping around us like we've stepped into a dream. And maybe we have because this moment feels too fragile, too perfect to be real.

I yawn again, my tenth at least, but my body feels anything but tired. My limbs may ache from the long day, and my eyes may sting with the promise of sleep, but every nerve in my body is wide awake. Lit up. Buzzing. Because I'm sitting this close to Dean and his warmth pressed along my shoulder, his hand resting on my hip like it belongs there. And all I can think about is the pull I feel toward him. The way his nearness makes it hard to think straight.

I sit up, slowly, the absence of his touch like stepping out of a hot shower into cold air. My skin tightens, every inch of me aware of how close we still are, even though his arm has dropped away.

When I turn to look at him, my breath catches. He's silhouetted by the faint moonlight now, the silver outline tracing the sharp angles of his jaw, the strong slope of his shoulders, the dark waves of his tousled hair. He's always been handsome, painfully so in that sun-drenched, all-American kind of way. But like this, beneath the crescent moon, his expression unreadable and his eyes full of something deep and quiet, he looks like something ancient and powerful. Like he stepped out of a myth. A dark god forged from fire and earth, who knows how to hold a woman like she matters.

And I want him.

God help me, I want him more than I want to be safe, more than I want to be rational. I want to trace that sculpted chest with my fingers, feel his breath against my neck, let his lips wipe away every single one of my fears.

But I also know myself. I know what lines can't be crossed until I'm ready. And I'm not there yet.

"I wish you'd ask me to kiss you."

Dean's voice is rough silk, laced with something deeper. Something that clutches at the base of my spine and doesn't let go. His gaze roams my face, not with amusement or that teasing smirk I've come to know, but with a reverence that steals my breath. There's weight in the air now. A slow-burning intensity that simmers between us, quiet but undeniable. Like he's a man on the edge, gripping the frayed rope of his own restraint, holding back just for me.

It's heady, this sense that I have the power to undo him. That I could tilt the world on its axis with just one word. I've never felt so seen, so desired… so in control.

But then he looks away, his throat working as he swallows. "Not tonight."

The cool air suddenly feels colder against my cheeks, which flush with heat that's got nothing to do with the temperature.

I turn my head, pretending to look out at the darkness so he doesn't see the sting behind my quiet, "Oh."

I don't mean for the word to sound so small, but I can't help it. It's hard not to take his rejection personally, even when I know better. Even when everything about the way he's touching me says it's not rejection at all.

"Lila, look at me." His voice is softer now, but commanding. His hand lifts, warm and careful, fingers brushing beneath my chin as he coaxes my gaze back to his. "I want to kiss you more than I want to take my next breath."

The raw truth in his eyes nearly unravels me.

"But with you," he continues, his thumb grazing along my jaw, "I'm learning the beauty of restraint. I don't want you to wonder if I want you. I want you to *know*. I don't want to steal a kiss in the shadows and leave you questioning it in the morning. When we cross that line, it's going to be because you *ask* me to. Because you *want* to. And when you do, Lila…" He leans in slightly, his voice dropping into something intimate and full of promise, "I'll be ready. I'll be yours."

I don't know how to respond. How could I? My heart is pounding like it's trying to leap into his hands. I want to memorize every word. To fold them up and tuck them into the deepest, most wounded parts of me, the parts that have never been given this kind of patience. This kind of care.

God, who *is* this man?

I lean in on instinct, pressing my lips softly to his cheek. Right near the corner of his mouth. It's not a kiss— not really. But it's something. A promise of more.

His eyes fall closed at the contact, just for a second. And when they open again, I see it. That same devotion, that same longing still burning like a slow fire behind them.

"Good night, Dean," I whisper.

"Sleep well, Lila," he murmurs, the words brushing against my skin like a vow.

And as I turn and walk away, I can feel the weight of his gaze following me. Not possessive. Not demanding. Just…waiting.

Despite my sleepiness, I find myself tossing and turning during the night, the sheets nothing more than a tourniquet around my limbs. I should have told him to kiss me. It's what I want more than my next breath, but I can't bring myself to demand it.

Knowing the battle against sleep is a fight where I won't prevail, I slip out of the room and head down the stairs.

"Hey," Dean calls out as he walks into the kitchen wearing just a pair of boxer briefs. The higher pitch confirms that he is not expecting to find me in the same room at 3:00 a.m., especially not wearing a pale pink silk camisole and matching shorts. Thankfully, the glass in my hand doesn't shatter as I nearly drop it onto the granite counter.

"My God." I heave a lungful of air and lean forward, pressing my hands onto the edge of the counter.

Walking up behind me, Dean cages me in with his large, muscular arms. "What has you so spooked?"

His eyes widen as I turn around, my chest brushing against his arm until we stand face-to-face.

"Couldn't put some pants on?" I ask, my eyes darting up and down his bare chest.

"I didn't expect anyone else to be awake," he says with a smirk, knowing he's riling me up. "What brings you down here?"

Dean releases the counter, letting his hands drop down by my hips, his fingertip trailing along the edge of my shorts. Close, but not close enough.

"Wa – Water."

"I'm a little thirsty myself. Hungry, too." Dean's eyes blaze with desire as they stare back at mine.

"I think there are some leftovers in the fridge. Brownies, too," I whisper, and the sound goes straight between my legs.

Behind his briefs, Dean's cock hardens, brushing against my torso, not even trying to be inconspicuous about how much he wants me.

His fingers travel up the sides of my shorts and slip under the camisole. His rough fingers feel like a torch against my skin, and I hiss behind my teeth at the contact.

"Dean," I moan breathlessly.

"What if that's not what I'm hungry for?" he tells me as he steps forward, pressing his body against mine. I'm pretty sure my pussy is jealous at the contact. I do nothing to hide my sudden gasp.

Leaning forward, Dean presses his lips against my bare shoulder.

His free hand joins his other as he wraps them around my waist, his thumbs close enough to brush the underside of my breasts. It's a freaking miracle I'm able to hold myself back when every ounce of my body screams for me to take what I desperately want.

"What is it you want?" I murmur shakingly.

"I think you know exactly what I want. What I've wanted since I first saw you." Dean's voice is gravel and heat, his lips brushing my bare shoulder, his nose trailing up the soft curve of my neck like he's memorizing my scent. His fingers flex at my waist, holding back like he's tethered to some invisible line.

But I'm done pretending.

No more teetering on the edge. No more waiting for permission to want something or someone I've already chosen.

"Dean," I whisper, my voice low but firm. And when he pulls back, eyes searching mine, waiting for me to say something, anything, I rise to my toes, thread my fingers through the thick hair at his nape, and grip tight.

"I'm not asking." My voice is husky. Steady. "Fuck it. Fuck all of it. Kiss me, Dean. Touch me. Right now."

Something primal flashes in his eyes. A low groan rumbles from his chest, like the tension in him finally snaps, and then he's *on* me. His mouth crashes to mine in a searing, hungry kiss that scorches away any lingering doubt.

Our lips collide, all hot, demanding, and messy, and I honestly can't tell who moved first. All I know is that I *need* more.

Dean's hands grip my waist hard as he lifts me like I weigh nothing and sets me on the edge of the counter. The cold granite bites through the thin material of my shorts, but the press of his body between my thighs burns like wildfire.

"Fuck, baby," he rasps, grinding against me with a low growl. His hardness pushes against the very ache he's caused, and my legs wrap around him like instinct. Like muscle memory. Like I was *meant* to have him right here.

He pulls back a fraction, his breath ragged, his eyes wild. "You don't get to say things like that and not know what it does to me."

"I do," I say, pulling him closer with my legs. "That's exactly why I said it."

His mouth crashes into mine again, rougher this time, all teeth and desperation. And I kiss him back like I'm starving because I am. For him. For *us*. For every second of this tension that's been simmering for weeks, finally breaking into flame.

My lips part as his tongue begs for entrance. He explores my mouth as his hands reach up to cup my breasts. Dean pauses, just for a beat, before his hands move to my waist, gently shifting me closer to him. His eyes search mine, dark, heavy with want, but still searching for something. Permission. A flicker of doubt.

Slowly, gently, he gives me enough time to say, "No." His restraint is almost maddening, but I can see it in his eyes, the battle he's waging with himself. He's giving me a choice, letting me decide, still holding a piece of himself back.

But I don't want that space. Not now. Not here. I want every second of this. Every touch. Every word.

I don't need to say anything. We both know this is what we want. And as his body presses closer, I know I'm not backing away anymore. This is where I want to be.

When I lean farther into his touch, Dean moans as his thumbs brush the peaks of my nipples.

"I want to taste these. Can I, baby? Can I suck on your tits?"

"Mm-hmm," I utter, lifting my camisole to my neck.

My skin shimmers in the dull light coming from beneath the cabinets. The tips of my breasts a dusky pink against my pale skin. Dean squeezes one of the breasts while leaning forward and stroking his nose against the other.

"God, you're beautiful. These breasts?" he says as he cups both, his lips brushing against the soft skin of one. "They're so fucking gorgeous. Are they sensitive, baby?" I jerk as he pinches one of the nipples. "Can I make you come this way?"

"I…I don't know."

"Hmm. Challenge accepted."

Like a starved man brought to a world-class feast, Dean swirls his tongue around one point. It stiffens with each pass. I squirm on the countertop, rubbing my silk-covered pussy against his boxer-clad cock that perfectly aligns at our heights. My desire intensifies as he latches onto my nipple, sucking the peak into his mouth and gently brushing his teeth against the tip.

"Oh," I moan, and he quickly shifts to the other breast, giving it the same amount of devotion as the other.

My fingers curl tighter in his hair, holding on like it's the only thing binding me to earth. My body trembles, unraveling under his touch, the pressure mounting until it crests in a wave I couldn't hold back if I tried.

"That's it, baby," Dean murmurs against my skin, his voice low and rough. "Good girl. Let go for me."

His words fall like embers, each one lighting another fuse inside me. I cry out his name, the sound broken and breathless, my forehead dropping to his shoulder as I cling to him. Every inch of me pulses with aftershocks, my heartbeat echoing between my ribs like a drum.

He doesn't move away. Doesn't rush. Instead, his arms wrap tight around me, holding me through every quiver and quake, grounding me. He whispers against my temple, kisses scattered along my jaw and neck. Soft, reverent, addictive. His teeth graze the delicate skin beneath my ear, and I shiver again, a fresh ripple of heat curling in my belly.

When I finally lift my head, I find him watching me.

His eyes are nearly black with want, pupils blown so wide they eclipse the chocolate brown I've come to crave. His lips are kiss-swollen, red from mine. His hair, thick and tousled from my grip, falls over his forehead in a way that should be illegal. He looks utterly wrecked.

And it's because of me.

The thought sends another shiver through me. His chest rises and falls in deep, measured breaths, but I can see the restraint it takes. He's still hard beneath the thin fabric of his boxers, the sight enough to have my mouth go dry.

Dean lifts a hand, brushing hair back from my damp forehead before gently tugging my camisole into place. He cups my face in his palms, thumbs stroking over my cheekbones, tender and full of worship.

"You okay?" he asks, his voice hoarse.

More than okay. I feel worshipped.

I nod, unable to speak just yet, my body still humming with the afterglow. And as he leans in to press a kiss to my forehead, I already know I'm in trouble.

Because this wasn't just a release. This was falling.

"That was so hot, baby. I could watch you come a million times, but next time it's going to be in my bed and on my cock." His words cut through the quiet, that familiar blend of confidence and tease curling around me like a warm blanket. The edge of arrogance that once caught me off guard now feels like an anchor, something steady and unmistakably him.

My core throbs with the image, but before I can even formulate any response, a distraction in the form of a three-and-a-half-foot-tall child wanders into the kitchen rubbing his eyes. "Daddy? My tummy hurts."

"I'm sorry, kiddo. Let me get you a glass of water, and I'll come sit with you for a little bit, okay?" Dean tells Oliver, who nods and heads back toward the stairs.

Not giving me a chance to slide down from the counter, Dean steps back in, his broad frame surrounding me, one hand braced beside my thigh while the other hovers just inches from my waist. I feel caged, yet not in a bad way. More like bound to something real for the first time in a long time. His body heat sears through my skin, and the look in his eyes makes it clear he's not ready to let this moment slip away.

"Give this a chance, Lila," he says, voice low and full of something raw. "A real shot. What just happened tonight? That wasn't just passing time."

I know he's right. My body still trembles from the way he touched me, like I mattered. Like I was everything. And that's what terrifies me the most.

"I know," I breathe, my voice softer than I'd like. "It was… incredible. I just—" I pause, searching for words that don't make me sound like I'm trying to talk myself out of the one thing I want. "I've been guarded for so long, I don't know how not to be."

His hand brushes a few stray hairs away from my cheek, the tenderness in the gesture making my throat tighten. "You have every right to be, sweetheart," he murmurs. "Just… remember how good this can be."

I swallow hard. I want this—him. Not just the kisses and the electric touches that make me forget my own name. I want the connection, the emotion that settles deep in my chest like an anchor. I cross my arms out of habit, trying to hide the chill of the fabric against my flushed skin, only for his gaze to follow, dragging slowly across my chest.

I lift my chin and meet his eyes. "We take it slow," I say, stronger this time. "Not because I don't want you, because I do. Probably more than I should. But I need to feel like I'm walking into this with my eyes wide open. No regrets. No second-guessing."

The tension in his shoulders shifts, and something primal flickers in his gaze. And when his lips curl into a slow, satisfied grin, I know I've just rewritten the rules of this game, and we're both all in.

Dean silences me with a kiss once more, nibbling at my lower lip with his teeth.

"We can go as slow or as fast as you want, baby. Just don't overthink it. No need for regrets. Now, I'm going to go cuddle a kiddo for a while." Grabbing my glass of water from earlier, Dean downs the liquid and steps back from the counter.

My eyes dart down to the erection barely contained by the boxers.

"Guess I should go throw on some pants. I don't want to traumatize the poor kid."

I don't waste any time getting back to my room, though every ounce of my vagina begs me to head to Dean's room instead.

It's unfortunate that my brain tends to override what my body is already screaming for. I buzz with desire whenever Dean's close. It's like being next to a Tesla coil.

Maybe it's time to hang up my lab coat and let my body take control for a while.

Chapter Sixteen

Dean

I'd always loved living among the bustling streets of Miami. Between the barely clad women strolling along the beaches and the skyline casting its shadows from the scorching sun, I had been content in the big city. That was until my best friend moved to a small town, and I felt its charm like a second skin.

Neither of those compares to Coral Bell Cove. A beautiful conglomeration of my two favorite settings.

"Are we there yet?" Oliver asks from his booster seat in the back of the SUV. I wrangled the keys off the hook this morning and left Lila the keys for my car. The one she's terrified to even spare a glance at. I keep reminding her that it's just a car whenever she worries about driving it. If she were to get in an accident, she'd be the only thing I worried about.

"Almost. You were just here the other day. Excited to visit again?"

I quickly learned that the kids were obsessed with the horses and Ms. Claire. I was also a fan of Ms. Claire and obsessed with her daughter.

"Yes!" the duo shouts, and I laugh along with them as the breeze floats across me from the open window.

The farm is already humming when we pull in. A tractor crawls across a stretch of field in the distance, dust kicking up behind it in swirls. Horses graze lazily behind the fence behind the house, tails flicking, heads low.

"Horsie!" Evelyn cries out, her small hand banging against the window. She bounces in her seat with the little space she has available. I haven't seen her this excited since the birthday party.

I park near the barn where a slew of other cars resides and climb out, helping Oliver out of his seat and then Evelyn. The air smelled of hay and earth and the bit of dew from the summer morning. Peacefulness in a way I didn't anticipate.

Coming to the farm wasn't my original plan for the day, but after the moment with Lila last night, the thought crept in and rooted deep. I need to show her that this isn't just a passing attraction or a fleeting moment. What I feel for her runs far deeper than that, and I want her to see it, to feel it.

As I stand there, looking out at the barn and the sprawling grounds of the farm, I can't help but think about her. Her breathy sighs, the soft moans that still echo in my ears, the way she fits so perfectly against me, as though we were meant to be. I'm not a man who spends time reflecting on every little detail. Hell, most of the time, I'd rather just act than think too hard. But last night with Lila… it was different.

I should be thankful for the interruption, really. At the time, I wanted nothing more than to press her against that kitchen counter and finish what we started. But in hindsight, I realize the pause gave her the time she needed, the space to come to terms with whatever this is between us. And it gave me time to come to terms with it, too.

My feelings for her aren't something I can easily shake off. They're not something I can ignore or brush aside. And I don't want to. I want her to know that when I say I'm falling for her, I'm not doing it lightly. I've thought about this, about her, about us, and I know what I want. I want her by my side in every way.

When I left last night, I couldn't stop thinking about how perfect she had been. The way she looked at me, her eyes soft, her lips so kissable. And her body. God, her body was all I could focus on. I didn't just want her physically. I wanted to understand her and know her completely.

So I found myself gathering grants and opportunities for her, searching online for anything that could push her toward her goals. I figured that maybe this would be my way of showing her how much I care, even if she wasn't ready to hear the words yet. Maybe giving her the freedom she needed to breathe, the time she needed to think… maybe that would show her how serious I am. How serious I'm becoming about her.

I left the folder on the kitchen table, hoping she'll see it and understand that I'm not just looking to have her in my bed. I want to help her achieve everything she's been working for, and I want to stand by her side while she does it.

The kids immediately spot Claire by the fence, holding out an apple for the horses, and head her way. I spot Lila's brother near the barn, stacking crates into the back of a vintage truck. I've only met him at the family dinner, where he tried to play the protective brother role and put me in my place. Rowan Wright is a full-time farmer with a mug that doesn't give much away.

Like recognizes like.

"Morning," I call out as I cross the gravel.

He glances over his shoulder, squinting beneath the brim of his cowboy hat, and nods. "Morning."

Gesturing toward the horses, I try to break the ice by saying, "Oliver and Evelyn were promised horses. My orders were firm."

"Good bribe. Looks like Mom has it handled."

"Yeah, they're undeniably Team Ms. Claire. Want a hand?" I ask as he hefts another crate filled with strawberries into the truck.

Rowan pauses, then shrugs as he looks down at my work boots, scuffed from years of working on boats. "Sure, if you don't mind a few more scratches on those boots."

"I've had worse jobs. And despite what you may think, I didn't wear them just to stand around and look pretty."

"I'm not sure you want to know what I think," he murmurs as he closes the tailgate.

I follow Rowan toward the shed. The sun still hangs low, but the air heats, and the humidity rises quickly. Grabbing a few empty crates, I fall in step beside him.

We travel down the many paths lining the strawberry field until we happen upon another three-man group plucking strawberries and placing them in the crates. Rowan and I work in companionable silence for a few minutes, the kind where neither party is quite sure what to say.

Finally, Rowan breaks the silence. "Didn't expect to see you today."

"Wasn't planning on being here either," I admit.

"Lila still happy working for you?"

"She hasn't resigned yet, though I know she's been searching for jobs. But she never complains."

"And you? You're still being professional?" he asks, yanking a handful of plump berries and tossing them into the crate with the ease of someone who's been doing this for years.

I meet his gaze. "I know what I want. So does she. But I'm not rushing her. I have the kids to look after. The real life kind of baggage most women don't want to deal with."

"Lila's not most women."

Boy, isn't that the truth. She's one of the best women I know.

"This wouldn't be a fling for me," I confess.

Rowan responds with a long pause.

"She's been hurt."

"I know."

He nods, then he glances over at Oliver and Evelyn, now cackling wildly near the fence with Claire as she reaches out toward the horse's nose.

"She likes horses," he divulges. "When she was a teen, she'd come out here when we aggravated her too much. It didn't matter if it was day or night, rain or shine."

A smile grows on my lips. "I get it." I felt the same about being on a boat.

We worked together a few more minutes in silence, the air feeling lighter, like I've passed some sort of test. I've always been an overachiever.

"You know, Ashvi set her up on a surprise blind date the other night."

"Oh, shit. I bet that didn't go well. If Lila hates anything, it's a surprise."

"Noted," I say as I fill my second crate. "She didn't seem pleased when she came home."

"I bet not. Ashvi has always been the wilder of the two. She always wanted Lila to come out of her shell. Then when my sister left and pretty much cut everyone off, it hurt her."

"I don't know much about her time away, but I know she regrets it. Wishes she could take it all back."

"We and Ashvi just want her to be happy. She carries the weight of the world on her shoulders."

Secretly, I wonder if her family is part of why she desires to succeed in such a spectacular way. She frowns upon her mother's business yet pushes to follow in her footsteps. I understand wanting to make it on your own.

"You know, I think you've said more today than you said the first night we met," I point out.

"Asshole," Rowan replies as he gets up and shifts to another line of strawberries a few feet away. I follow just to live up to the nickname he's given me.

A few hours and several crates later, Rowan, myself, and his team have harvested what we could from the cordoned-off patch. He explains that they keep the far field open for families to pick strawberries on their own, which explains all the cars in the lot when I showed up.

"Business good here?" I ask, helping load the crates into the back of the pickup.

"Why? Looking for another investment?" he asks arrogantly.

"Been looking me up, Rowan? I'm so flattered."

"Don't kid yourself. Just looking out for my sister."

"Sure. And no, I'm not looking for another investment. I'm actually looking to cut back some. Just wanted to see how successful the farm is."

Slamming the tailgate harder than necessary, Rowan turns to face me. "We do just fine, Dean. Don't worry about us."

"Suit yourself. I didn't mean anything by it."

"Dean!" a little voice shouts as she barrels at full speed in my direction. Saved by the niece. "Ms. Claire says I can ride the horse if you walk with me! Can you? Will you? Please? I never get to ride the horses when we come."

"Sure, I can. Lead the way." I gesture for her to grab my hand and guide me toward the barn. I'm surprised when Rowan follows.

Claire greets me warmly as she ushers us into the barn and shows me the tan horse named Butterscotch that belongs to Lila. Rowan walks Evelyn and Oliver through the task of grooming the horse prior to riding, pointing out that the horse should be free of loose hair and dirt.

While the kids stand on a stool working the brush across the horse's body, Claire shows me the special spots around the nose that are Butterscotch's favorite spots. By the time the kids are done, the horse and I are best friends.

Rowan set up the saddle and bridle on Butterscotch and gently eases her from the stall out toward the corral.

Both kids energetically reach for my hand and tug me toward the exit, eager to get their ride on the horse.

"I want a horse, Uncle Dean," Evelyn exclaims as we broach the sunshine again. In the short time we were in the barn, the sun has risen high in the sky, and the temperatures have quickly followed.

"Maybe we can visit Ms. Claire's horses for a while. I'm sure Butterscotch would miss you if we got our own," I explain, trying to placate my niece as I release Oliver's hand and pull my T-shirt away from my chest.

The sweat is already beading on my skin and soaking through the thin cotton.

"Alright, who is going first?" Rowan asks now that Butterscotch has moved around the circle a few times.

I expect Evelyn to jump at the chance, but she tucks herself behind my leg and lets Oliver go first.

It's been a few years since I've spent the summer in Miami. I didn't consider that the humid heat in Virginia could be as strong. It sticks to you like a second layer of skin.

"God, it's hot."

"Oh, sweetie, this is nothing. Just wait until July hits," she proclaims as she retrieves a bottle of water from the fridge in the barn for me.

It's ice cold.

Plastic bottle clenched against my palm, I chug the cool contents at record speed.

"May I grab another?" I ask, just as a blustered breeze whips past Claire and me, sending dirt against our clothes and skin.

"Of course," she adds, dusting off her denim pants.

"I'll get it." Brushing past her, I head to the barn and open the fridge, taking a moment to let the cool air fan across my skin.

I tug my sweat-soaked shirt away from my skin before making the decision to remove it. I shove the material into the back pocket of my jeans and douse my head in the cool liquid.

"Ah, fuck. You read my mind," Rowan says as he steps into the barn, already yanking his shirt over his head. "The humidity is at like one hundred today."

"I'm from Miami, and it's hot even to me." Peeking out of the barn doors, I notice that Mason, Lila's dad, has stepped into the corral and is helping Oliver down from the horse. Evelyn is patiently waiting for her turn.

"You've got good kids, man."

"Thanks," I say with a grin. "I'm doing the best I can. I couldn't do it without your sister. She helped bring them out of their shell."

"Speaking of sisters, it seems she and her scheming friend are enjoying the show."

Brows furrowed, I search the confines of the corral but come up empty. That's when I see her and Ashvi in the shadows, parked on a bench beneath a large oak tree. Ashvi speaks in the animated way I've come to associate with her while Lila's eyes are locked on me. Making no effort to hide the fact that she's taking in her fill of me shirtless.

"Rowan," I call out as I head out of the barn toward the gate. "I'll be right back."

"Sounds good," he hollers in return as he begins walking Evelyn around the large enclosed circle. Once I step outside the metal fence, I pull my phone free to snap a few pictures.

"She's a natural." Turning I find Lila standing next to me, one of her bare legs propped up on the steel rod encased in a pair of well-worn cowboy boots.

Chuckling, I return my gaze to Evelyn. "Don't let her hear you say that. She's liable to get a pony for Christmas."

"My lips are sealed," Lila jokes.

The thought of her lips send me back to the night in the kitchen where she let me have her in ways I never expected…and wish to have again.

Fuck, she's all I've been thinking about.

"Ashvi up to no good again?" I ask as Lila's strawberry and vanilla scent swirls around me. My cock instantly stiffens.

"It's what she's best at. You'd think she'd feel bad about the blind date, but no…she wants to set me up on another one."

That news doesn't shock me. From what I've learned of Lila's best friend and the few times she's come to the house, when she has her mind set on something—she's going to make it happen come hell or high water.

"What if you went out on a date with me? A real one… not just as friends." I'm not sure where the idea came from, but now that it's rooted, I'm even more sure it's what I want.

"What?"

Lila's hand lands on my bare shoulder, scalding my skin. I'd thought the sun today was blistering, but it's nothing compared to the feeling of her uncovered contact.

My gaze collides with her, heat and desire flaming with each blink of my eye.

"Baby, if you don't remove your hand, I'm liable to take you right here in front of your family and my kids. And we don't want to traumatize them," I say through clenched teeth.

Quickly, she withdraws her hand as if I'd burned her and tucks it behind her back. My eyes flick down to find that her nipples have puckered through the white material of her shirt. Rowan walks past us, holding the horse's reins, eyes narrowed and flicked back and forth between the two of us.

A few farmhands walk by, carrying crates of their own, not paying us any mind.

I watch her cheeks redden as her chin tilts toward her chest. "Don't worry. I'm not one for sharing. Especially not where you're involved."

"Dean," she whines, her eyes darting around, looking everywhere but at me. Probably to make sure no one is listening.

She hasn't realized how persistent a billionaire can be apparently. "Lila, look at me," I demand, waiting patiently. The long wisps of her hair whirl in the breeze, brushing against my arm and chest, a few sticking to the sticky sweat on my skin.

Finally, she meets my eyes again, softening. "Go on an actual date with me. Tell Ashvi you're done with blind dates, and you have something else in mind."

"Out in the open?" she inquires, biting that plump bottom lip I yearn to taste again.

"Yes, out in public with an audience. Don't overthink it. It's really no different than last time."

The pause stretches, masking the neighs of the horses and squeals of the kids.

"Okay."

My eyebrows shoot up my forehead.

"I'm sorry, repeat that please," I urge, twisting to face her, crossing my arms against my chest like a shield. There is only so much devastation a man can take.

"I said, okay. I'd like to go on a date with you. A real one." Her eyes twinkle beneath dark lashes.

The breeze picks up more wisps of her hair and without thinking I reach out and tuck it behind her ear.

"What changed your mind?"

Lila leans closer, that invisible string between us drawing tighter with each passing second.

"Let's call it a change of heart."

Chapter Seventeen

Lila

The mornings always begin the same way now; the scrape of little feet on hardwood, a knock that never waits for permission, and Evelyn climbing under the covers beside me, radiating warmth and mischief.

I pretend to still be asleep, but Evelyn isn't fooled. A small elbow nudges my ribs.

"You said we could have pancakes today," she whispers, already bouncing slightly on the mattress.

I crack one eye open. "I said that three days ago. That promise is old."

Evelyn pouts, all chubby cheeks and preschool determination. "Old pancakes are still pancakes."

That gets a laugh out of me. I roll over and hug Evelyn into my side, her giggles shaking the bed, small and bright and filled with life. I didn't realize how much I missed this kind of honest and uncalculated affection until it became routine. It fills my ribs in a way science never has. It makes it hard to remember why I continue to fill out job applications and research grants.

But I do. I still fill them out despite how easy it feels to just let this all be enough. Despite the part of me that would love to stop trying to forge a path and just… be here. With them. With Dean. His presence has done something to me, something I didn't know I needed. The way he supports me without expecting anything in return, the way he gives me space to grow while still being there for me… It's like nothing I've ever experienced. It's even harder knowing I could give into his gracious request of finding my research himself. Too bad my pride stands in the way.

Even on days when I feel overwhelmed, like when he took the kids and me to the farm for horse riding, he always finds a way to keep pushing me forward. He's been so patient, giving me the time to write and apply for grants, even if he's got his own work to do. And I know it's not easy for him to keep everything balanced, but he does. I can see it in his eyes, the quiet pride he has in watching me get closer to the life I've been working toward. It's like he's rooting for me in the same way I root for myself.

I used to think I was only capable of loving something as structured and predictable as science, but now… now I'm not so sure. What Dean's offering, what this family is offering, has opened me up to possibilities I didn't even know I could want. And when he looks at me, like he actually sees me, it stirs something inside me. Something I don't know if I'm ready to name yet.

But I know this: everything I've ever wanted, everything I've worked for, feels that much more attainable when I have him here, cheering me on. When I can feel the support in his touch, in his words. He's more than just my boss. He's someone who believes in me, in a way I'm still learning to believe in myself.

Downstairs, I can already hear Oliver rummaging through the fridge, probably for orange juice or whatever he thinks he can sneak past me. At five, he's already decided he's a culinary genius. Dean is nowhere to be seen since he's usually up before dawn getting started on whatever venture he plans on tackling for the day.

Padding into the kitchen with my hair a nest and socks mismatched, I catch Oliver standing on a chair, peering into the top shelf of the pantry. He glances over his shoulder with a grin.

"You said pancakes," he says smugly.

"Two against one, it seems," I mutter, grabbing the mixing bowl.

By the time Dean finally shuffles into the kitchen, yawning and tugging his tie loose from the confines of its collar, the kitchen smells like vanilla and maple syrup. I have flour on my cheek, Evelyn has smeared chocolate chips across her mouth like war paint, and Oliver has taken it upon himself to flip pancakes with a form to rival any grandmother.

Dean leans against the doorframe. Watching us. Watching me.

An ache-filled kind of silence settles between us. His eyes linger a beat too long when I laugh. When I reach up to grab the cinnamon from the shelf, his gaze drops, subtle but intense. It's the kind of nothing that I feel down in my bones.

We haven't really talked about what happened. Not really.

The kiss that turned into more. The storm brewing inside me as his hands found every part of me I thought I'd buried. That night that confirmed nothing we did would be a mistake.

He brushes my fingers as he hands me a mug of coffee. They linger. Intentional and brief. But it sparks heat low in my belly that I haven't let myself acknowledge in years. He hasn't mentioned anything else about our pending date that I've agreed to, but with every passing glance, my anticipation grows.

The kids move around the kitchen like comets, wild and luminous, burning with energy. Evelyn sings to a caterpillar she's named Pickle. Oliver dares himself to jump off a tree stump into a kiddy pool we set up. I sit on the deck steps, sipping coffee that's now lukewarm. Dean drops beside me with a groan, stretching his legs out in front of him.

"You do realize you created tiny pancake tyrants, right?"

"You didn't complain when you had three helpings."

"That was self-preservation."

His arm brushes mine. Neither of us moves away. We sit in comfortable silence. The wind stirs the tall grass, carrying the scent of wildflowers and cut wood. Evelyn shrieks with joy. Oliver whoops after her. Somewhere in the distance, a bird sings as the sun warms my cheeks.

"You look happy here," Dean says quietly.

I glance at him. His expression is closed off, but unassuming. There's no agenda in his eyes. Just truth.

"I am," I say, barely above a whisper. Then, after a pause I don't expect, I say, "Which is terrifying."

He chuckles softly. "Because it means you might want to stay?"

I don't answer. I don't need to.

Another silence settles—thicker this time, fuller. He shifts closer.

"I don't want to scare you," he says, voice low. "I know this wasn't the plan. But I don't want to go back to how things were. Not before you."

My throat tightens. I stare at the dandelions pushing up through the cracks in the driveway.

"I just need to know if I'm imagining this *thing* between us. The real thing," he adds, softer still.

I meet his eyes. There's fear there, the kind that send my heart racing. Hope, too.

My voice comes out small, honest. "You're not."

And that's the scariest part of all.

Later that evening, after the kids are asleep and the sky has shifted to the darkest shade of navy, I find myself in the laundry room folding towels. I can't sleep. I can't read. So I do what's familiar—routine. Soft cotton, rhythmic motions. Domesticity as a distraction.

Dean appears in the doorway, barefoot, wearing a thousand-dollar rumpled T-shirt.

"Did you need something?" I ask.

He shakes his head. "No. Just… didn't want to go to bed yet."

I hand him a towel. Our fingers touch, and the air thickens. Electricity sparks between us. I nearly drop the terry cloth into his hand in fear of it catching fire.

He's watching me like he did that first night, like I'm something he wants but isn't sure he's allowed to reach for again.

"Lila," he murmurs.

My name sounds different in his voice, reverent, almost as if he's cherishing it. He takes a step closer. Then another, closing the distance between us. There's a question in his eyes, and for a moment, I feel that familiar hesitation rise in me—the urge to retreat and protect myself. But I don't. I don't step back. Instead, I take a small, deliberate step toward him, closing the gap.

His breath hitches slightly, and I can see the flicker of surprise in his gaze. I'm not pulling away, not hesitating. I'm choosing this, choosing him.

He slowly leans in as though he's waiting for me to pull back, to change my mind. But I don't. I let my body move closer to his, my heart pounding with the rawness of what I'm about to do. I meet him halfway, finally. His lips brush mine. Soft, then firmer. Confident. Familiar. This isn't like last time—rushed, frantic, fueled by storm and adrenaline. This kiss is patient. Intentional. Every movement says I'm here if you are.

My hands find the hem of his shirt. His fingers ghost up my arms, then settle on my waist. We move in tandem, breath mingling, bodies aligning like we've done this a hundred times. Like we've been waiting to get it right.

He lifts me onto the marble counter, and I gasp, the chill biting into the backs of my thighs. He grins against my mouth, pressing kisses to the corner of my lips, then trailing them across my jaw and down my neck. His hands explore with purpose, firm on my hips, gentle on my thighs, until I wrap my legs around his waist, holding him to me.

His clothes slide away like silk, discarded in the hush of the laundry room. The low thrum of the dryer is a heartbeat behind us, and every shift of his hands, every graze of his mouth over my collarbone, over my shoulder, sends my pulse spiraling.

I run my fingers through his hair, tugging lightly, reveling in the soft sounds he makes when I scrape my nails down his back. His breath is ragged now, his restraint fraying.

His hands slip beneath the waistband of my shorts, teasing the elastic of my panties. My breath hitches, wanting, no craving, more. To feel the rough calluses of his fingers against my slit. He knows what he's doing to me.

His name tumbles from my lips as I try to shift my body to get him closer to where I want. Where I need.

Dean's eyes are dark, his voice low and full of promise. "You've been driving me crazy all day."

I swallow hard. "I didn't mean to."

His smile is slow and entirely unapologetic. "You've been stealing my T-shirts, Lila."

I open my mouth to respond, but it's useless. Because he's already crowding me, his hands settling on my waist like he owns the space between us. As if he's been waiting for this exact moment to make good on all the tension simmering beneath the surface.

"You smell like dryer sheets and temptation," he murmurs against my throat, pressing kisses to the skin just beneath my jaw. I shiver when his hands slip around my pants, sliding slowly, so slowly, around my thighs.

"Dean…"

He drops to his knees.

I gasp, my hands gripping the edge of the counter for balance, for sanity, for anything to keep me grounded while he parts my legs with his shoulders and kisses the inside of my thigh like it's sacred. His strong hands tug me forward until I'm practically hovering over the edge.

The air is thick with heat and something heavier—need. His palms glide up the curve of my hips, holding me steady as his mouth replaces his hands.

I forget how to breathe as his tongue explores my pussy, mapping a journey of its own. I've never had someone work my body the way he can. Dean kisses and licks my body like he needs it to survive.

The world tilts on its axis as sensation crashes over me in slow, delicious waves. My fingers knot in his hair, and I'm gone, utterly undone by the way he worships me without ever saying a word.

"Dean," I whisper, voice broken, raw.

He doesn't stop. He never rushes. Every movement is controlled, deliberate, coaxing pleasure from me like it's his mission. And it has to be because by the time my body threatens to buckle, he's there, strong arms lifting me back onto the counter like I weigh nothing at all.

I can't speak. I can only hold onto him, shaking and breathless, as he presses a kiss to my temple and murmurs, "God, I love the way you come apart for me."

I laugh, but it's a soft, shaky thing. "I think you've officially ruined laundry for me."

He grins. "Good. Then next time, you'll have no choice but to do it with me."

And judging by the way my heart races when he kisses me again—hot and sweet and all-consuming—I know I'll never fold another towel without remembering this moment.

But then he stills.

Dean presses his forehead to mine, breathing hard. His hands are still on me, but they're no longer moving.

His voice is a low growl, full of want and intent. I chance a peek at his straining cock and know he's suffering and filled with so much restraint.

"Lila, as much as I want to keep going, and make no mistake, I do, I need you to know something."

I blink up at him, still dazed from the kiss, from the feel of him.

He gently tucks a loose strand of hair behind my ear, his thumb brushing along my jaw. "I want more than this. I want to take you to dinner, walk with you through town hand in hand, let you introduce me to everyone and say, 'This is Dean. He's mine.'"

His voice softens, roughened by emotion. "You deserve more than a quick, heated fumble in a laundry room. You deserve every bit of romance and respect I can give. So I'm stopping this for now because you mean too damn much to me."

My breath catches. His words are like a bucket of ice and a shot of whiskey all at once—jarring but warm and heady, too. He's giving me the power again, the choice. But at this moment, with my heart galloping and skin still buzzing from his touch, I already know the answer.

Still, I nod slowly, pressing a lingering kiss to his lips, one that's tender, grateful, full of promise.

He grins, brushing another kiss to my temple before helping me down from the counter and gathering my shorts with gentle hands.

As I dress again, his eyes linger, not with lust, but something deeper. Something that makes my stomach flutter and my knees threaten to give out.

The following morning smells like cinnamon and bacon. I wander down in leggings and an old tee, rubbing sleep from my eyes.

There's a note on the counter in Dean's handwriting:

Took the kids to the farm. Helping your brother with the harvest. Didn't want to wake you. Figured you'd appreciate pancakes without demands for seconds. Oh, and I tossed the sausage. No reason to have that stuff in my fridge.

My heart flips.

There's a text from Mom with pictures of Dean and the kids. Oliver grins like he's just won the lottery as he sits perched on a tractor, hands in the air like he's flying. Evelyn, her hair wild and cheeks flushed, holds out a carrot the size of her face to a gentle chestnut horse, her expression full of wonder and courage.

Pure and honest happiness.

But it's the background that holds my focus. The one constant in each photo—Dean.

He's not distracted by his phone or trying to take a call while half listening to the kids. He's there. Present. His hand rests protectively on Evelyn's back in one frame. His head tilts back in laughter beside Oliver in another. He's smiling in every single one, and not the polite kind reserved for photo ops or polite strangers.

No, this is real. And it hits me square in the chest.

Dean could be anywhere. Tucked away in some pristine office overlooking a boardroom or buried in spreadsheets and phone calls. He has every excuse in the world to be too busy, too preoccupied, too important.

But he chooses them. Every time.

That kind of undistracted and unwavering devotion is its own kind of aphrodisiac. It's not the muscles or the money that undo me, though he has both in spades. It's this. A man who isn't afraid to get a little dirt on his designer boots if it means making his niece laugh. A man who values bedtime stories and breakfast pancakes over power plays and investor meetings.

Where wealth and status define some men, Dean redefines what it means to be rich. And he proves it to me, to those kids, every single day.

And that… that's the sexiest thing I've ever seen.

Then a message from Dean chimes in.

Dean:

They're muddy, loud, and in heaven.

Lila:

So your parenting plan is manual labor and livestock?

Dean:

Works every time.

Lila:

You're dangerously charming when you're confident.

Dean:

Only when you're watching.

I smile too long at my phone. The kind of smile that seeps into your bones and lingers in the corners of your day. The kind of smile that improves the rest of your day.

With a destination in mind, I pack a cooler with watermelon, sunscreen, and a jug of sweet tea and head home toward Otter Creek Farms.

Once I step free of the car, the air hums with summer. A wet kind of heat that sticks to your skin.

Evelyn tackles me at the barn entrance, covered in sticky fingerprints and joy.

"LILA! I named the goat Waffles!"

"Excellent choice," I say, hoisting her up.

Around the barn, Rowan and Dean work shirtless under the sun. My brain flatlines as I take in Dean's taut abdomen—the mounds and valleys I traced with my fingers the night before.

"You always show up after they've hit peak destruction," Rowan calls.

"Total coincidence," I lie.

Dean wipes his brow and saunters over. He steals a slice of watermelon from the cooler I'm opening and grins. The lazy kind of smile that reeks of secrets.

"You didn't have to bring supplies," he says, voice low as he leans into me.

"I know. I wanted to."

We sit beneath a shady oak watching our small world unfurl. The kids chase chickens. Rowan cracks bad jokes. It's messy, chaotic, sun-warmed bliss.

As the sun dips, the kids collapse on blankets. The days fun drifting away with the sunlight. Oliver snores from his king's bed on the corner of the blanket and Evelyn sucks her thumb, curled into my side.

Dean watches us, eyes soft, smile slow and Rowan takes that as his queue to do his final barn check for the night. Leaving us.

"You fit here," he says simply.

I meet his gaze. "So do you."

He shifts closer, his hand settling on the small of my back. We don't need a label, not yet. We need space to keep choosing this, again and again.

He presses a kiss to my temple. My breath catches, and something inside me finally exhales.

The following morning, I surprise the kids with a clear terrarium box holding a butterfly chrysalis I'd picked up from the wildlife center in town. It's tucked safely in the corner, secured with a small twig and a mesh cover.

Evelyn gasps like I've handed her a unicorn. Oliver, ever the investigator, immediately asks a dozen questions.

We set it on the kitchen windowsill, just where the morning sun hits.

"It's a painted lady butterfly," I explain. "If we take care of this one and she turns into a butterfly, then I can see about fostering another one after."

Oliver nods solemnly like I've entrusted him with sacred knowledge.

Evelyn cups her hands around the side, eyes wide. "I'm gonna name her Maple."

Dean kisses the top of my head as he passes behind me, coffee in hand. "You've officially raised the bar. How do I top a magical butterfly transformation?"

I smile. "You keep making pancakes."

We all gather around the windowsill at least a dozen times that day. The kids argue over who spotted it twitch first. Evelyn sings to it. Oliver draws pictures of it with superhero wings in crayon. And I stand behind them, heart so full it aches.

Because love doesn't always come in fireworks or declarations. Sometimes it comes in pancakes, and caterpillars, and quiet, steady mornings where no one has to earn their place.

And for the first time, I don't just feel like I belong. I believe it.

Chapter Eighteen

Dean

don't know why I'm nervous.

I've closed billion-dollar deals with one signature. I've taken private calls from world leaders and argued policy with people whose names sit heavy in Forbes. But none of that compares to standing outside Lila's bedroom door, palms slightly damp, trying not to look like a man on the edge of losing it over a woman in a dress.

Because tonight… tonight is different.

Tonight, I'm taking her out. Not as a nanny, not as the woman who tucks my niece and nephew into bed, or the one who leaves her laptop open at the kitchen table with notes scribbled on napkins. But as mine. A date. A real one.

I knock once, then again. The door opens, and my heart forgets how to function.

She's wearing this soft pink dress that flares out just enough at the hem to be feminine and elegant but hugs her waist like it was stitched with her in mind. Her hair is pinned back on one side, curling over her bare shoulder, and those eyes, hell, those eyes, search my face like she's trying to read my mind.

If she could, she'd know every thought is some version of you're stunning. I'm done for. And I'm going to mess this up if I say something dumb.

"You clean up well," she teases, her voice light and maybe a little shy.

"You're breathtaking," I say, before I can stop myself.

Her smile falters, just for a second. "Dean."

"I mean it." I reach for her hand. "Come on, before I forget where we're going."

We head down the stairs quietly, the house already still with the kids tucked in at her mom's for the night. I unlock the car and open the door for her, watching the way her dress rides up a fraction when she climbs inside.

Focus. You've waited this long. Don't blow it.

The restaurant sits nestled in an old brick hotel, all art-deco charm and faded grandeur. The kind of place locals whisper about when they say "fancy." The lobby still boasts the original tiled floor and velvet-backed chairs that sag with time. But the dining room, soft lighting, white linen, the smell of roasted garlic and butter, feels like we've stepped into a different world.

She runs her fingers along the edge of the menu, biting her lip in thought. I can't stop staring.

"What?" she asks, her brow lifting.

"You're not even trying, are you?" I murmur.

"Trying what?"

"To be irresistible."

A flush rises in her cheeks, and she ducks her head. "You're going to make it impossible to concentrate on the food."

I grin. "That's kind of the plan."

When the server returns, we both order seafood—because when the ocean's practically at your feet, anything else feels like a crime. She picks the crab-stuffed flounder, her eyes lighting up at the words "garlic herb butter." I go for the blackened grouper, mostly because I know it'll come with those roasted potatoes in the same butter sauce she won't be able to resist stealing off my plate.

"Careful," I murmur, handing the server the menu once she's made her choice. "Garlic butter has been known to drive men mad. Don't say I didn't warn you."

She smirks over the rim of her water glass. "Are you saying you're easy, Dean Harrington?"

I lean in a little closer, resting my forearms on the table. "I'm saying I'm a man of simple tastes. Butter. Warm bread. A woman in a slinky dress who knows how to use her smile as a weapon."

She flushes, but it's the kind that makes her shoulders relax instead of tense. She rolls her eyes with a laugh and mutters something about "predictable men," but her gaze lingers on my mouth for a beat longer than necessary. I catch it, file it away like a prize.

The food arrives, steaming and golden and unfairly mouthwatering. Lila lets out a low moan at the first bite of her flounder, and I nearly choke on my wine.

"Jesus," I mutter under my breath. "You keep making noises like that and they're going to ask us to take it to go." She chuckles and unfortunately refrains from more of the audible enjoyment of her meal.

After dessert, something decadent with chocolate and espresso that Lila moans over like it's a religious experience, I pay the bill and take her hand again.

"Where are we going?" she asks as we step back out into the warm night air.

"You'll see."

The town theater is showing a black-and-white movie from the '50s. Romance. Laughter. Not a superhero in sight. We sit in the back row, our shoulders brushing, her perfume clinging to my skin like temptation.

Halfway through the film, she turns to say something, and I kiss her.

It's soft, gentle. Her lips part just slightly, and then we're falling into something deeper. Something real.

She pulls back first, her eyes searching mine. "Dean."

"I know." I press my forehead to hers. "I know. I just needed to do that once."

Her hand rests on my thigh for the rest of the film. No more words needed. The credits roll, slow and elegant across the screen, and Lila's hand slips into mine without a word.

The theater hums with soft chatter and laughter as people shuffle toward the doors, but for a moment, we stay seated. Her thumb brushes over mine, and I glance sideways to find her already watching me.

There's something in her eyes I can't quite name. Not hesitation, not exactly. It's softer than that. Maybe wonder. Or maybe that same ache I feel pressing against my ribs like it's been there for years, just waiting for her.

"You hungry?" I ask as we step out onto the sidewalk. The night wraps around us, warm and still, the town glowing under strings of lights hung between lamp posts and storefronts.

Her lips curve. "I just had a chocolate mousse that changed my life."

"So… that's a yes?"

She laughs, and God, I'd drive across state lines just to hear that sound again. "Maybe a little."

"Come on," I say, lacing our fingers together again. "There's a place two blocks over. I hear it's the best ice cream in town. Open late. It's practically law that we stop."

She pretends to groan but lets me tug her along, her shoulder brushing mine with every other step.

It's not crowded when we get there. Just two teenagers behind the counter arguing over what song to play next and the hum of an old chest freezer working overtime.

She picks lemon sorbet. I go for cookie dough. We take our cones to a bench outside, where the breeze carries the scent of salt and sea grass from the nearby dunes.

Lila swings one leg over the other and leans back, eyes on the stars above us.

"I forgot how quiet it is here at night," she says softly. "Like the world finally exhales."

I watch the way the wind toys with her hair. "You like that?"

She nods. "In Boston and Hartford, everything buzzes. Lights, traffic, ambition. You forget to listen to your own thoughts."

"And what are yours saying now?" I ask, keeping my tone light, but my gaze steady on her face.

She licks her sorbet, then shrugs one shoulder. "They're still sorting themselves out."

We sit in silence for a minute, my fingertips rubbing back and forth across her bare shoulder. It's not uncomfortable. Just thoughtful.

"I used to think I needed the noise," she says after a while. "The chaos of labs and grant deadlines. The constant forward motion. Like if I ever stopped moving, I'd… disappear."

"You're not disappearing now."

"No." Her eyes meet mine. "I think I'm finally learning how to stand on my own."

I shift, letting my knee rest against hers. "You don't have to choose one version of yourself, Lila. You don't have to be just the scientist or just the nanny or just the girl who kisses her boss in the back row of a movie theater."

That earns a quiet laugh. "You say that like it's simple."

"I don't think anything about you is simple." I grin. "But that's kind of the point."

She finishes her cone, wiping her fingers on a napkin, then looks over at me, eyes serious now.

"You make it easy to believe in the good things," she says. "Even when I've spent years preparing for them to fall apart."

My heart stutters. "That's all I want. To be something good. For you."

She reaches over, her fingers threading through mine again. "You already are."

We stay like that until the cones are long gone, until the teenagers inside lock the door and turn off the neon sign.

Then I stand and offer her my hand again. "Walk with me?"

She takes it. No hesitation this time.

We wander toward the beach, shoes in hand as we reach the sand. The moon glimmers on the water, silver threads woven through inky black. I roll up my pants and wade in a few inches, the surf cold enough to bite.

Lila stays on the edge, the hem of her dress fluttering around her knees. I walk back toward her, salt air curling between us, and slide my arms around her waist.

She steps in closer, her palms on my chest. "You're sandy."

"You're beautiful."

She rolls her eyes, but her smile is soft.

We don't kiss again. Not yet. We just stand there, pressed close, her cheek against my collarbone, my hands steady at her back. The ocean breathes around us. And for the first time in a long time, I don't feel like I'm rushing toward something or trying to escape it.

I'm just... here. With her. And that's everything.

The silence in the car isn't awkward. It's heavy. Buzzing. Thick with everything we didn't say back in that theater.

Her hand brushes mine on the center console and I swear it scorches. She doesn't pull away. Doesn't speak either. Just leans her head back against the seat, her eyes trained out the window like the quiet night might somehow offer her answers neither of us are brave enough to ask yet.

But I see the way her knees shift toward me. The way she bites her bottom lip when I glance over. And God help me; I'm hanging on by a thread.

I grip the wheel tighter.

"You okay?" I ask, my voice a little hoarse.

She turns, eyes shining in the soft glow from the dash lights. "Yeah. Just… thinking."

"About?"

She hesitates. "How different tonight felt. Good different."

My chest tightens. "Yeah. It did."

The road narrows as we pull into the neighborhood, the tires crunching softly on gravel. Lila tucks her hair behind her ear, and my gaze drops to the curve of her neck, her collarbone. I wonder what she'd do if I leaned in right now and kissed her there—slow and soft and reverent. If she'd melt into me like she did earlier. If she'd whisper my name like a plea.

Or a promise.

When I park in the driveway, neither of us moves. We just sit, suspended at this moment like we're both afraid to break it.

"I should probably…" she starts but doesn't finish.

I reach across and gently run the backs of my fingers down her arm. "You don't have to."

She turns to me slowly. "Dean."

I lift her hand, press a kiss to her knuckles. "I know. I'm not asking for anything. I just don't want this night to end."

A pause. Then, softly, "Me either."

I open her door and help her out, our fingers lacing together like we've done this a hundred times. Like our hands were made to find one another in the dark.

Inside, the house is quiet. Still. The kind of still that makes everything louder—our footsteps, our breaths, the thunder of my pulse in my ears.

I lead her into the kitchen, flick on a soft light. She leans back against the counter, her eyes never leaving mine. I take a step closer. Then another.

The tension, the restraint—it snaps.

She's in my arms before I can talk myself out of it. Her hands in my hair. My mouth claiming hers like I've been starved for weeks. Because I have. For her. For this. For the way she sighs into me like I'm the only air she's ever needed.

She tastes like dessert and hope. Like everything I've been craving since she stepped into my life. My hands find her hips, pulling her flush against me, and I swear I feel her breath catch when our bodies align. Her fingers slip into my hair, tugging just enough to make me groan.

"Dean," she whispers, voice shaky. "We should… I mean…"

"I know." My lips brush her jaw, her neck, the delicate shell of her ear. "We don't have to do anything. Not unless you want to."

She pulls back enough to meet my gaze, cheeks flushed, chest heaving. "That's the problem. I want to."

I rest my forehead against hers, breathing through the tension clawing up my spine. "Then let's want slowly. Let's want right. No hiding. No regrets."

Lila nods, her lips brushing mine in agreement. "Okay."

But her hands don't get the memo.

They slide under the hem of my shirt, fingertips skating over my ribs like she's memorizing the shape of me. My own palms are greedy, exploring the curve of her back, the dip of her waist, the soft fabric of her dress clinging to skin I want to worship.

"Dean," she breathes, and it's a prayer I want to answer.

I kiss her again, softer this time, like a promise. Like a man who's learning how to wait. Because I will. For her, I'd wait forever.

But right now? Right now, I get to hold her.

The house is dark and quiet, the kind of quiet that hums beneath your skin. Lila shifts beside me under the covers, the sheets rustling as she curls closer, her bare legs tangling with mine.

She smells like vanilla, strawberry, and my T-shirt. Like home.

We've been pretending to sleep for a while now, but neither of us has moved to break the illusion. Until now.

Her fingers trail a slow, lazy line across my chest, down the ridges of my stomach. My breath hitches, just a little, but I don't stop her this time. I can't.

Because the truth is, I've been on the edge since we walked through the door. Since she laughed in the car. Since she kissed me like she couldn't wait another second.

She shifts again, this time with purpose. Her mouth finds the curve of my neck, and her lips part in a kiss that has every nerve in my body firing. It's tentative in the best kind of way. All the tension of the night bringing us to this moment. I brace a hand behind her back, but she's already moving—sliding down the bed, blanket slipping with her like it's being seduced too.

"Lila," I murmur, a warning and a plea wrapped in one rough breath.

She doesn't answer. Just presses one more kiss to my skin, lower this time. Her hands trace down my abs, stopping at the waistband of my boxers.

Everything inside me coils tight. I'm not sure what she's up to, but whatever decision she's recently made, I'm not arguing against it.

I lift my head to look at her—only to find her eyes already on mine. Steady. Confident. Like she knows exactly what she's doing.

"You sure?" I ask, because I need to hear it from her. Because as much as I want her—God, do I want her—I want her wanting this more.

Her smile is soft. Wicked. Certain, then she lowers her mouth onto the ridge of my cock, and I forget how to think. Her mouth is warm, moist, and utter perfection. The urge to fist her hair is strong but I hold back, not wanting to scare her. I fist the sheets, my head falls back, and all I can do is feel.

The slow drag of her lips. The heat of her breath. The sound—soft and wet and reverent—as she makes me lose my mind, one breath at a time.

She takes her time. Drives me insane with how gentle she starts, like she wants to learn me, edge by edge, and burn every reaction into memory. And hell, if I don't want to give her every single one.

I groan her name—half praise, half surrender.

She doesn't stop. Doesn't rush. She's relentless in the most beautiful, devastating way.

When I finally come, it's with a curse and her name tangled on my lips, my hand in her hair, my entire body wrecked beneath her mouth.

She crawls back up, her smile smug and glorious.

"You okay?" she whispers, brushing her thumb over my cheekbone.

I catch her hand in mine and press a kiss to her wrist. "I will be. In about a week."

She laughs. I swear it's the sweetest damn sound I've ever heard.

And when she settles into my arms again, head resting on my chest like we've always belonged like this—I know I'm completely gone for her.

Chapter Nineteen

Dean

he first scent of rain hits me like memory—wet dirt and tension, the kind that coils in your chest before a fight you know is coming. The sky is swollen with gray, the sun barely visible behind thick storm clouds rolling low over the hills. I should be inside, reviewing legal paperwork, calling my lawyer again. But I can't take my eyes off Lila.

She's standing just outside the deck, curls pulled up haphazardly, a smear of dirt across her cheek, her tank top clinging to her skin from the heat. Evelyn is clinging to her leg, giggling about a caterpillar. Oliver is yelling something about feather armor. And Lila? She laughs. Loud and full and unbothered.

It guts me a little.

Because in another world, she would be mine already. Not just here. Not just helping. But *mine* in all the ways I haven't let myself hope for. And in this world, the one where my father is preparing to drag me through court to prove I'm unfit to raise these kids, she might still leave.

She doesn't know about the court date yet.

I reach for the phone in my back pocket, the screen lighting up before I can even unlock it. One text from my lawyer.

Attorney:
Your father has been in touch.

That hollow pressure in my chest flares again. Now in just a few weeks I have to prove I'm enough. To prove I've changed. That I'm not him.

I look back at Lila. She's crouched now, drawing a smiley face in the dirt for Evelyn. Her laugh floats up again, light and warm. The knot in my chest twists. I've never needed someone like this.

Not even before the kids.

Not even before everything fell apart.

Back in the kitchen, the storm finally breaks. Rain lashes the windows, thunder rattles the cabinets, and the sky goes dark with fury. I watch as the trio try to escape the rain, Lila attempting to stay behind the kids and stay somewhat dry but failing miserably. I rush to the laundry room, grabbing whatever towels I can from the cabinet, and scurry toward the mudroom. They're soaked through to their skin when they get back inside.

I try to make dinner, something easy enough for a bachelor billionaire, but the text burns in my mind. I don't even realize I've stopped chopping vegetables until Lila touches my arm.

"Dean?" she asks quietly.

I meet her eyes, and the strength there almost levels me. "My father contacted my lawyer."

She exhales hard. "God."

"He's filed a motion to modify the guardianship."

A beat of silence. She doesn't flinch. Doesn't panic. Just steps in close and places her hand flat on my chest, grounding me with that simple touch.

"Then you fight," she says. "And this town is not letting you do it alone."

God, I want to believe in that. In her.

The call comes the next day, just as the sun gives way to the stars. My father speaking up before I can even greet him, dripping disdain in every punctuated word. My lawyer transfers into the call, tense and tight-lipped. I don't look at Lila—I don't have to. She's there beside me, spine straight.

"I'm doing what's best for the children," my father says, his voice cold and practiced. "You're too emotional. Too unstable. Too close to the damage you've caused." It's just like him to equate me with Genevieve's death, as if I was directly related to it.

"You mean the damage *you* caused? You only want the kids to make perfect little puppets for the press," I say, teeth gritted.

He sneers. "You're nothing but a scared little boy trying to play house. You'll never be perfect for them."

And then Lila steps in. Right in front of me.

"They don't need a perfect man," she says, voice even. "They need someone who shows up. Someone who loves them. And they already have that."

My father's voice thins. "And who the hell are you to speak on this?"

"I'm the woman who's been raising them with him. Who sees how much they trust him. Who's earned their love the right way."

He doesn't respond. He just ends the call like the punctuation of a slammed door.

I don't say anything. I just sink onto the couch and drop my head into my hands. And Lila? She doesn't offer comfort. She sits beside me and doesn't leave.

After the kids are asleep, we sit by the fireplace in the dark. Neither of us talks. Not at first. The storm outside mirrors the one still boiling inside me.

Her hand is a warm reprieve as she touches my knee.

"I hate that he can still get to you," she says softly.

I sigh. "He's always gotten to me. That's the problem."

She turns toward me fully. Her legs brush mine. Her voice drops. "You're not him."

"I know. But that doesn't mean I don't wonder—why nothing I've ever done, or do, is good enough. It's not like I can change my mother's mistake. It wasn't my fault that all I ever wanted growing up was his approval… his love."

Her hand slides over mine warm and steady. "You've done more than enough. You're *doing* it. Every day."

I look up. Her eyes shimmer from the firelight, wide and open and so damn *present*. I'm not used to people staying like this. Not when things get hard. Not when I'm cracked open.

And maybe it's the way her hand tightens in mine. Maybe it's the way her body leans into me like she belongs there. Or maybe I'm just done pretending I don't want her in every way a man can want a woman.

"Lila," I say, voice low.

She doesn't speak, doesn't have to. She leans in and presses her lips against mine. Not a tease. Not a maybe. A kiss that demands an answer.

I give her one.

Her lips part, and that first taste of her tongue punches the air from my lungs. It's soft—unexpectedly soft—but it hits with the weight of every long look, every accidental touch, every silent what-if we've been avoiding since the first day she moved in. It's like the first kiss in the kitchen all over again.

I pull her closer, the slide of her mouth making it impossible to breathe right. Her hands cup my jaw, thumbs brushing just under my ears. There's no rush. No fire yet. Just a slow build, a deep ache of something long denied.

But it's there.

God, it's there.

The want, the heat, the simmering pressure of holding back too long.

My hands find her hips, her waist, her lower back. She lets out a sound—half sigh, half groan—and melts into me. Her body aligns perfectly against mine, like we've done this a thousand times before, like we *should've* done this a thousand times before.

Her mouth moves to my neck, soft, exploratory. I grip the back of her shirt to keep myself anchored, but it's not enough.

"You drive me crazy," I whisper, forehead pressed to hers.

Her lips curve. "The good kind of crazy?"

"Always," I murmur, voice thick. "I'm so fucking crazy for you."

In one motion, I stand, taking her with me, and her legs wrap instinctively around my waist. She lets out a soft gasp, clinging tighter, her hands in my too long hair, tugging just enough to make me unable to hold back as I seal my lips with hers.

We crash through the hallway to my bedroom like we're escaping something. Or maybe heading straight into it. Frames rattle. A small lamp falls onto the floor from where it's placed precariously on a console table.

She kisses me like she needs this to breathe, and I kiss her like she's the only thing that's ever made sense.

When we reach the bed, I set her down gently, but her fingers tug at my shirt before I can pull away. I help her strip it off, and her hands trace my chest like she's memorizing it for science, cataloging muscle and scars as if I'm her newest research project. The way my heart stutters when she touches certain spots should be documented.

I yank her shirt over her head next and pause, just for a second. Because she's beautiful. Not just in the obvious way. But in the way she watches me watch her. In the way she trusts me to *look*.

She arches slightly under my gaze. "Are you just going to stand there?"

"Yes," I say, hoarse. "Unless you tell me to touch," I add, reminding her of the previous challenge.

She reaches for my hand and places it directly over her breast. Her heart is beating so fast I can feel it against my palm.

"There," she says. "Now stop hesitating."

I touch and kiss and explore every inch of skin she gives me. Her breath catches as her body arches, and when I take her nipple in my mouth, she moans so softly it nearly breaks me in half. It's nearly impossible to ignore the growing erection behind my zipper.

She rolls her hips into mine, desperate and wanton. And *God*, the way she moves—like she's done waiting, too.

When I slide my fingers beneath the waistband of her shorts and pull them down, she lifts her hips without hesitation. Beginning at her ankles, I trail my fingers and lips toward the apex between her thighs. With a quick swipe of my fingers between her legs I can't hold back the devious grin that grows on my lips. She's wet already, soaked through, and the knowledge that I did this to her sends a shock straight through my cock.

I lean in again, dragging my mouth down her stomach, kissing each hip bone before dipping lower. She spreads her legs like an invitation—a dare.

And I accept both.

Slipping off her panties, the pale lace tossed somewhere behind me, I taste her like I've been starved. Her desire both sweet and salty, an addiction I can see myself growing fond of. Within minutes she falls apart under my tongue, my name a garbled mess crying out from her throat.

Control slipping, I undo my pants and slide them down my legs, my boxers and socks quickly following. My cock stands at attention, pointing directly toward its target as Lila sits up and tugs at the hem of my T-shirt, pulling it over my head.

"My God, you're gorgeous," she mumbles, her fingers trailing across the ripples of my abdomen. I bite back the moan.

"Grab the headboard," I command. Lila jerks in surprise, but her eyes flutter in excitement.

She scoots back on the bed toward the pillows. Her hand fumbling for a wooden slat, her other one tangled in my hair as I climb onto the mattress, following with my lips sealed against her folds. I work her slowly, steadily, until she's panting my name like it's a benediction and rocking her hips against my mouth.

"Dean," she gasps. "Please. Don't stop. Don't…"

She breaks on a cry, thighs trembling on either side of my head, breath hitched, back arched toward heaven. I don't stop until she pushes me away, spent and shaking. My cock a painful reminder that he wants the same attention.

I kiss the inside of her thigh, then crawl up her body.

"You okay?" I whisper against her lips, letting her taste herself. I nearly growl when Lila moans at the nibble.

She nods, eyes still hazy as she accepts my kiss. "More than okay."

"How do you want me, sweetheart? I'd love to feel you, all of you, but only if you're okay with that. I'm clean and get tested regularly. Whatever you want," I say through clenched teeth, barely holding myself together. I can't help but reach between my legs and stroke my dick. Lila knocks my hand away and replaces it with her own.

Fuck, I'm going to come before I get to slip inside her pussy.

"I'm clean. After everything with my ex, I… I needed to be sure. And I'm on the pill… I want to feel you too, Dean. Please."

I brace myself above her, her slim hand guiding me toward her slit, our bodies aligned. "I want you to keep holding the headboard."

She blinks up at me. "Why?"

"Because I want you to feel everything," I say, my voice low and tight. "And I want to *see* you lose control."

The flush in her cheeks deepens, but she doesn't argue. She reaches up and grabs the wood. And I sink into her in one slow, deep thrust. She cries out, her legs wrapping around me, pulling me deeper.

I have to stop myself from moving too fast. I want to savor this. The slide of her body against mine. The way she holds that headboard like it's the only thing anchoring her in a sea of yearning. The way she looks at me like she's finally letting go.

I thrust again. And again. Inch by agonizing inch. Slow and deep and firm until I'm seated fully inside her tight pussy. And it's fucking perfection.

I try to restrain myself, make it good and romantic for her, but my cock has a mind of its own, and my thrusts grow wilder, rowdier.

Her breath stutters. Her mouth opens. She tries to speak, maybe a curse, maybe a plea, but I swallow the sound with my mouth. Our tongues dance in a tango that mimics our bodies.

We build like the summer storms. Rumbling. Pressurized. Frightening in its intensity. Her muscles tighten around me. Her thighs squeeze. Her chest pushes upward. Her voice, God, her voice breaks into little gasps.

"Don't stop," she breathes. "Oh my…"

"Never," I whisper. "Fuck, baby. You feel so good."

Pulling out, I flip her around, jerking her hips in the air so I can get deeper. So she can feel me all over her body for the next day. I want to mark her.

I watch her hands claw and grip at the bedding as I plunge my shaft into her repeatedly. Lila's hips move in tandem, rocking back in time with mine.

We're our own symphony building toward our crescendo.

Feeling her walls clench around my cock, I flip her around again, wanting to see her face as she reaches her orgasm. Without asking, she reaches for those damn wooden slats of the headboard.

When we come, it's not silent. It's not soft. It's not careful. It's a surrender. And she's the fucking captain.

Her body clenches around mine, and I bury my face in her neck as the release rips through both of us. She holds the slats like it's salvation.

And I hold her.

She's still trembling under me when I finally collapse onto the bed beside her, my breath ragged, her skin damp and flushed. Her fingers slide from the wood, dropping to the sheets like she's too tired to move.

Outside, the storm has begun to quiet. Raindrops soften against the windows, thunder a distant grumble now. But inside me? It's still chaos. The kind that stirs when you realize you're halfway in love and unprepared for what comes next.

I turn my head and look at her. Lila's lips are parted, her chest rising and falling like she just ran a mile, her waves splayed across my pillow. She's breathtaking.

And she's still here.

That matters more than I know how to explain.

"I should feel ridiculous," she whispers after a minute, her voice still breathy. "I'm pretty sure I screamed. I hope I didn't wake the kids."

"You did, and they're fine," I say with a smile, my fingers brushing along her arm. "It was the best sound I've ever heard."

She laughs softly, then goes quiet again.

For a long moment, we lie there. Nothing but the storm and the sound of our breathing. Her head shifts to rest on my chest, and I wrap my arm around her waist like it's instinct.

"This wasn't just sex," I say vulnerably. Not a question. Not a plea. Just a fact I need spoken aloud.

"No," she says, even quieter. "It wasn't."

I close my eyes, trying to breathe around the sudden weight in my chest. Because as terrifying as it is, I already know…

I want more. I want to wake up with her tangled in my sheets. I want her barefoot in the kitchen with a toddler on her hip and pancake batter on her shirt. I want what my best friend has. I want every ordinary, messy, beautiful day with her.

"You okay?" she asks after a long silence.

I nod once. Then again. "Yeah. Just… trying to hold on to this."

She shifts onto her side, her hand sliding up to my chest, right over my heart. "It's not going anywhere."

But something in her voice tells me she doesn't fully believe it.

And neither do I. Because we haven't said the big things yet. Haven't touched the sharp edges of what this all means.

I roll to face her, sliding my hand along her jaw, cupping her face. "I don't do this, Lila. I don't let people in. Not like this."

She swallows. "I know."

"I didn't plan on you. I didn't even know I could want something this real again. But I do. I want you. And not just in the jokingly 'you'll be my wife someday' but for real in all the ways that matter."

Her thumb brushes against my jaw. "You have me," she whispers. "But—"

That word stops me.

But.

I brace for it.

"But I'm still scared," she admits. "Scared of losing myself again. Of building a life around someone else's world only to have it ripped out from under me."

"I don't want you to build your life around me," I say gently. "I want you to build it *with* me. Your own life. Your own dreams. But maybe, if you let me, I can be a part of it."

Her eyes shimmer. "You already are."

And that's when I know—I love her. Not because she fits into my life. But because she makes me want to be a better man inside it.

The morning smells like clean air and wet grass; the sky washed clear after the storm. Pale sunlight filters through the blinds, striping the sheets in gold. I wake slowly, the weight of something warm and soft pressed against my side.

Lila.

Her leg is draped over mine. One arm flung across my chest like she's claiming me even in her sleep. Her hair's a mess of waves across the pillow, and her lips are parted in a way that makes my chest ache and my body stir, even now.

But I don't move. I just watch her breathe.

And for a man who once built walls so thick no one could see over them, I've never felt more exposed.

She shifts slightly, murmuring something that sounds like my name. Her palm presses firmly against my chest as if sensing that I'm already deep in my head.

"I'm still here," she mumbles, not even opening her eyes.

"I know," I whisper. "I'm not sure I deserve that."

Her eyes blink open, sleepy but focused. "You deserve someone who sees you. All of you. Even the rough parts."

I nod, not trusting myself to speak.

After a few quiet minutes, she sits up and reaches for my T-shirt on the floor. I watch her stretch as she pulls it on, the hem hitting high on her thighs. It's a simple thing but packs a powerful punch to my chest. But it guts me all over again. I want this every morning. I want her to choose to stay.

I follow her into the kitchen, both of us barefoot and bleary. The kids are still asleep, the house wrapped in a rare kind of peace. I brew coffee while she digs through the pantry, humming quietly under her breath.

"I'll make breakfast," I offer.

She glances at me over her shoulder, one eyebrow raised. "You mean you'll reheat pancakes from yesterday."

"Reheating *is* a form of cooking," I deadpan.

She smirks and turns back to the cabinets.

God, I love that smirk.

We move around each other easily, bumping hips, passing mugs, brushing shoulders. Her fingers graze mine as she hands me the syrup, and I can't help the way I lean in, kissing the curve of her neck.

She shivers, just a little, that adorable ass of hers rubbing against my brief-covered cock.

"Still trouble," I murmur.

She grins. "You're the one who told me to hold the headboard."

My coffee nearly slips from my hand.

I clear my throat and turn to hide the grin threatening to split my face. "Worth it."

A knock on the front door startles us both. I glance at the clock. Too early for a lawyer. Too early for a neighbor. I open the door, and it's Rowan.

He holds up a bag of tools. "Tractor's acting up. Mom and Dad are gone this morning. Thought I'd rope you into fixing it since you claim to know how to fix boats. I have it on the trailer out front."

Lila appears beside me, wearing nothing but my T-shirt and her bare legs. Rowan's eyes flick from her to me and back, and a slow measured smile spreads across his face. I can't tell if he's happy or angry. I'm shooting for the former.

"Morning," he says, all innocent. "Hope I'm not interrupting anything."

"You are," I say flatly.

Lila elbows me in the ribs. "We were just finishing pancakes."

She disappears back inside, insisting I go help out her brother, and Rowan lets out a low growl. "So that's new."

"Don't," I mutter, grabbing my boots.

"I'm just saying, I hope you're being good to her. That's my sister. She's one of the good ones."

"I know," I say. "That's what scares me." After begrudgingly leaving Lila and the kids, I follow Rowan out to the driveway.

We work in comfortable silence for a while, tinkering under the hood while the sun rises higher and the scent of coffee wafts from the open kitchen window.

Finally, Rowan speaks again, voice quiet this time. "You in deep?"

I nod once. "Deeper than I planned."

"Does she know?"

"I think so."

He glances toward the house. "Then stop waiting for the next bad thing to happen. Everyone deserves some kind of happiness, even asshole billionaires hooking up with my sister."

I sit with that for a second.

Because happiness—*real*, bone-deep happiness— feels like a foreign language. One I've never been fluent in.

But Lila?

She makes me want to learn.

When we finish, I head back to the deck and find her sitting on the steps, watching the kids chase butterflies in the yard. Oliver yells something about being a butterfly hunter while Evelyn shrieks with laughter.

And Lila's holding a small clear container in her lap.

"What's that?" I ask as I get closer.

"Another chrysalis," she says, smiling. "Found it on the side of the porch railing yesterday. Figured the kids could watch it hatch."

I lower myself beside her, eyes on the tiny shell hanging from a stick inside the container. It's still. Motionless. Waiting.

"Looks dead," I murmur.

She grins. "Just looks that way. Inside, everything's changing."

That sits heavy in my chest. The weight of it. The *truth* of it.

"Like us?" I ask, voice quiet.

She doesn't look at me. Just watches the kids run wild through the grass. "Yeah. Like us."

I slide my arm around her and pull her close. She leans into me, warm and steady and *real*.

And for the first time since my father's call, since the court date, since the past came knocking, I don't feel like I'm bracing for impact.

I feel like I'm building something.

With her.

Chapter Twenty

Lila

omething about the air after a breakthrough makes everything feel sharper. Cleaner. Like the sky has rinsed Sthe world and left it raw and exposed.

That's exactly how I feel this morning. Raw. Exposed. Scrubbed down to the bone.

The sheets are still tangled around my legs when I blink awake, the memory from two nights ago cling to my skin like heat. Dean's hands, his mouth, the gravel in his voice when he told me to hold the headboard.

God. My whole body flushes.

I stretch beneath the sheets, sore in places I hadn't used in a while, and very aware of the hollow space beside me. The bed smells like him, cedarwood and firelight and something undeterminable but warm. Like safety, if safety had a heartbeat and broad shoulders.

But he's gone.

I prop myself up on one elbow, blinking against the pale sunlight slipping through the curtains. The room is quiet. Too quiet. No cartoons, no cereal bowls clinking, no sound of Evelyn dragging every stuffed animal in existence down the stairs. Just birdsongs and the soft ticking of the hallway clock.

Then I see it.

A note on the nightstand. His handwriting is steady, clean. Unfussy.

At the lawyer's. Your mom offered to watch the kids. Didn't want to wake you. Made coffee. – D

Coffee. Lawyer. Two words that snap me out of the dreamy haze and drop me right into the hard edge of reality.

The past few days weren't just about stolen kisses and thunderstorms. It was about his father calling, slinging threats like they were commandments, threatening custody and undermining everything Dean had worked for. And for what? Power? Control?

I sip from the steaming mug waiting in the kitchen. The bitter heat grounds me like it's trying to anchor my thoughts. But they still drift.

I didn't intend to step into their conversation. But I did. Every word is branded into my skull.

"You think moving to some farm town makes you a father?

"This isn't parenting. This is hiding. You're a disgrace to the family name.

"I'm going to make sure those kids end up with someone who understands responsibility."

And Dean's voice—calm at first, steady, and then shattered.

"You don't get to dictate my life. You forfeited that right the first time you put money above your family."

The silence that followed was louder than the thunder outside.

I press my hand to the cool surface of the countertop and take a breath. It hurts how much I feel for him. For the boy he was before the world hardened him. For the man he's become. The one who tucks notes beside the bed and brews coffee just the way I like it.

The one who still thinks he has something to prove.

I walk through the house slowly, toes brushing the new floorboards freshly scratched from toys, letting the quiet wrap around me like a memory I'm not ready to let go of.

The hallway still smells like rain and maple syrup, leftover from this morning's pancake chaos. A puzzle sits unfinished on the dining room table, Evelyn's butterfly puzzle, the one she insists on finishing all by herself, even though she demands my help every other piece. A pair of Oliver's mismatched socks lie abandoned halfway up the stairs, one inside out, the other crumpled in a way that tells me he took them off mid-chase.

I smile at the mess, at the lived-in feeling I used to avoid. This place isn't just a temporary address anymore. It's a heartbeat. A rhythm I've come to crave.

My phone buzzes in my hand. I glance down at the screen and freeze.

Dr. Rowley.

My thumb hesitates over the notification before I swipe to open the message.

Lila, we'd love to offer you the two-year research grant position. The lab at Chicago Biotech is thrilled at the possibility of working with you. Let us know soon and with any questions you may have.

My lungs don't seem to know what to do with air. I sink onto the edge of the couch, blinking at the email, reading it again and again as if the words might shift, soften, or vanish.

It's everything I said I wanted. Everything I spent years building toward. A prestigious lab, cutting-edge technology, a chance to make a name for myself in the field I've bled for.

But now…

I stare out the front window. The sun's low, casting long golden shadows across the lawn. I can hear the wind chimes tinkling softly from the back deck.

And just like that, the lab offer feels… less urgent.

I trace the edge of my phone, heartbeat tapping out a rhythm I don't recognize. This offer is a dream. But it's a dream I had before I knew what it felt like to be here. To be needed. To be seen.

Dean makes it so easy to believe in myself again, and not because he fills me with empty flattery. He sees the pieces of me I thought were too messy or too complicated to be loved and tells me I'm enough anyway. More than all those parts Prescott gaslit me into thinking were too much. They're enough for Dean.

He took the kids to the farm today, just so I could have a quiet house to write, apply for grants, and catch up on research. He left a cup of coffee beside my laptop, and a folder of possible opportunities to look into, each one annotated with little notes in his handwriting.

That's who he is. He doesn't just support me, he champions me. And that support? That attention? It makes me question everything I thought I knew. Because how do you walk away from a life that finally feels like it fits?

I don't make any decisions. Not tonight. Maybe not for a few days. But I tuck the phone away and press my palm to my chest, right over the place where my heart keeps whispering, stay.

But wanting something and believing you deserve it are two different battles. And I've only just begun fighting mine.

The screen door creaks open around noon, and all that peace and stillness shatters like a dropped dish.

"LILA!" Evelyn yells, a streak of dark hair and sticky fingers flying into my legs. "Did you know goats can SCREAM?"

I crouch to hold her, her little arms wrapping tight around my neck. "That sounds terrifying."

"Rowan said I'm part goat now!" she adds, like it's an honor. "Because I climbed a fence and yelled a lot."

I laugh, tears pricking unexpectedly at the edges of my eyes.

Oliver flops into the entryway behind her, shirt smudged with dirt, arms flung wide. "Rowan made me pull weeds. With my *hands*. Like an *animal*."

"Tragic," I say, ruffling his hair. "Shall I call Ms. Claire?" I ask referring to my mom.

He grunts already distracted by something else.

Dean appears behind them, holding a pie box and looking criminal in a wrinkled, light blue button-down shirt with sleeves rolled to the elbows and those stupid perfect forearms. His smile is hesitant, like he's waiting to see what version of me he's walking into.

"Hey," he says.

"Hey."

That's all. But it carries so much.

He steps close, not touching, but there's gravity in the air between us. A silent pull.

His knuckles graze mine when he hands over the pie box. Not an accident. Not anymore.

He leans in then, his hand coming up to cup my cheek, his thumb brushing just under my eye. His touch is reverent, tender.

"I've wanted to kiss you every second since I met you," he murmurs.

"So do it," I breathe.

And he does.

Not like other nights where we're hungry and aching and storm-driven. This kiss is slower. Still urgent, but deeper, sweeter. Like we're writing a promise we're not ready to say out loud yet.

When he pulls back, his forehead rests against mine.

"Your mom mentioned your replacement after the summer. I know you only signed up for the summer and despite every ounce of me wanting to force you to stay, I'm not going to ask. I know you have plans and dreams," he whispers. "But I hope you do."

My heart twists, splintering open a little more.

"I'm not going to promise I will," I whisper back. "But I hope I can."

Later that evening, the kids are full of post-farm energy and sugar, bouncing off the walls like two tiny tornadoes. I've just convinced Oliver to stop trying to catapult Evelyn off the couch when Dean reappears from the mudroom with a box in his hands.

"What's that?" I ask as I help Evelyn into her pajamas.

Dean grins, eyes flicking down to Evelyn and then back to me. "Something I found by the barn earlier. Thought it might distract them for more than five minutes."

He opens the box slowly. Inside, hanging from a stick, is a small, pale green chrysalis.

Evelyn gasps and reaches for it with sticky fingers.

"Gentle," I warn automatically.

She peers in with wide eyes. "Is it another butterfly?"

"A caterpillar that's turning into a butterfly," I say. "It's called metamorphosis."

Oliver makes a face. "That's a weird word."

"It means change," I say, kneeling next to them.

He eyes me suspiciously. "Like when you cry and then pretend you weren't crying?"

I blink. "Something like that."

Evelyn clutches the little box to her chest like it's made of gold. "Can I name her?"

Dean raises an eyebrow. "You're assuming it's a girl?"

"She's *sparkly*," Evelyn insists. "Her name is Pancake."

Oliver snorts and flops onto the rug. "Of course it is."

I laugh, but it hits me somewhere deep. This little box, this quiet family moment, this man who thought to bring home another chrysalis adding to our already growing butterfly foster family, for the kids and the woman he kissed like she was a secret he'd waited years to tell…this is the kind of life I didn't think I'd ever get to want.

And now it's here, unfolding in front of me like wings.

We set Pancake the Chrysalis on the windowsill in the dining room with the others, and the kids insist on saying good night to her before bed.

Dean watches me the whole time like he's memorizing my smile because it might be the last time he sees it. And that look, so intense, quiet, full of unsaid things, lingers with me as I tuck Evelyn into bed and read Oliver another chapter from his latest space book.

When they're finally asleep, I find him in the downstairs hallway, one hand pressed against the doorframe to his room—*our* room, maybe. I don't say anything. I just step into him, slow and sure, and wrap my arms around his waist. He lets out a breath like he's been holding it all day.

"I keep thinking I'm going to wake up and this will all be gone," he says into my hair.

I squeeze him tighter. "It won't be."

But neither of us says *forever*. Neither of us dares.

We lie on the couch, tangled under a knit blanket. My head rests on his shoulder, our fingers intertwined, the TV murmuring quietly in the background. We're still and we're not. My thoughts are racing. My heart feels too big for my chest.

"I used to think I wanted a life that made sense," I murmur.

He doesn't move. "And now?"

"Now I want one that feels like this."

His arm tightens around me. "Me, too."

And in the quiet of that moment, with the scent of candles and rain lingering in the walls, I finally let myself believe in the kind of love that stays.

The house has gone still again. The kids are down, the TV off. The silence that fills the space now is heavier than before—not lonely, but expectant. Like something important is about to happen, and neither of us is pretending to ignore it.

I head to the kitchen to wash out my wineglass. Dean follows a beat later, barefoot, his shoulder brushing mine as he passes me to grab a glass from the cabinet.

We're dancing in that space between comfort and need again—close, familiar, but edged with something far more dangerous.

My fingers fumble with the dish towel. "Still doesn't always feel real."

"What doesn't?"

"This. You. The kids. The ever-growing butterfly population." I glance at him, forcing a smile. "Sometimes I feel like I stepped into someone else's life."

He studies me with that same patient, unreadable expression he wears when Oliver is melting down or Evelyn won't let him brush her hair.

"But it *is* your life," he says softly.

"And what if I don't know how to live it right?"

Dean sets the glass down. His voice is even, but low. "You think you have to be perfect to deserve this?"

I look down at my hands. "I think I've spent so long being useful that I forgot how to be wanted."

He steps forward, one hand cupping my jaw, tilting my chin until I have no choice but to look at him.

"I want you."

The words hit harder than I expect. Not lustful. Not possessive. Just a truth, spoken like a vow.

"You have me," I whisper, leaning into his touch. "But I'm still learning how not to brush it off when something feels good."

His thumb brushes under my cheekbone. "Then I'll take it slow."

But when he kisses me, it's anything but slow.

It's soft at first—lips brushing, teasing—but there's heat under the surface, a hunger barely contained. His hands slide around my waist, pulling me closer. I feel him everywhere—chest to chest, breath to breath.

When I wrap my arms around his neck and kiss him deeper, he groans low in his throat, backing me up against the kitchen counter. I reach for the hem of his T-shirt and tug gently. He helps me pull it off, then rests his forehead against mine, chest rising and falling like he's holding himself back.

"Bedroom," I murmur.

He sweeps me up in his arms before I finish the word.

As he carries me, his eyes never leave mine with a look that steals my breath. Like he's afraid I'll vanish if he looks away. Like he's memorizing me.

The door shuts behind us, soft and final. He sets me down beside the bed but doesn't rush. His hands settle at my hips, warm and sure, and he just watches me for a moment. My heart is pounding, and I know he can feel it under his fingertips.

He leans in, kissing me again, deeper this time. His tongue traces the seam of my lips, and when I open for him, he groans into my mouth like he's been waiting years for this moment.

My shirt comes off first. Then his hands roam with careful patience, touching the places I used to keep hidden. I'm not self-conscious, not with him. He makes me feel like every inch of my body is worth worshipping.

When his mouth moves down my neck and across my collarbone, I clutch at his shoulders. The scrape of his stubble, the heat of his breath—it's all too much and not enough.

I whisper his name like it's a secret I've only just learned how to say.

"Dean…"

He lifts me, easing me down onto the bed with a devotion that makes my chest ache. Then he kneels above me, fingers teasing down the curve of my thigh, slow and maddening.

"You're shaking," he murmurs, brushing his lips over my ribs.

"I'm…" I swallow. "It's never been like this with anyone else. Just you."

He pauses. Looks up at me.

"What kind of 'this'?"

"Someone who sees me. Who makes me feel…" My voice cracks. "Safe. Wanted."

His mouth softens into something dangerously close to love.

"Good," he says, dragging his hand slowly up my side, "Because I want you so badly, it's tearing me apart."

He makes good on that promise, bit by bit, stripping away the last of my hesitation. My shorts. My underwear. My composure. Every touch is intentional. Every kiss demands a response I can't help but give.

By the time he moves over me, he's stripped bare, too. Not just physically, but emotionally. Every inch of his skin is etched with want, and his eyes hold nothing back.

When he presses into me, my whole body arches, demanding. The air leaves my lungs in a sharp, shaking breath.

"I want you to feel me tomorrow. Every step you take I want you to remember that you belong to me," he says softly, brushing a kiss against my cheek.

In the past, anger of being someone's possession would bubble like lava, but with Dean, the need inside me is so sharp, I need something to anchor me to him.

And God help me, I'd give him anything.

He thrusts inside me like a man haunted, like etching himself inside me. Deeper. Harder. Until I can't keep quiet.

His name leaves my lips again and again, tangled in breathless gasps and soft curses. The headboard rocks gently with every thrust, a steady rhythm I hold on to like a talisman.

I'm unraveling beneath him, in the best way, like he's pulling every broken thread and weaving me into something new.

His hand comes down beside my head, steadying both of us.

"I've never wanted anyone like this," he groans against my neck. "You wreck me."

I don't answer, I can't, but I tilt my hips and meet him, body to body, heartbeat to heartbeat, giving everything I have left.

And when I come apart, it's not just pleasure—it's a full release of my soul. Every wound, every doubt, every fear burns away under the heat of it.

He follows seconds later, collapsing onto me, breath ragged, body trembling. For a long time, neither of us speaks. He rolls onto his side, pulling me into his arms.

I press a kiss to his shoulder, curling into his warmth.

"Good night, Lila."

"Good night, Dean."

The morning creeps in quietly, golden light slipping past the curtains and stretching across the floor in long, lazy ribbons. For a few delicious seconds, I'm suspended in that half-wakeful place where everything still feels like a dream.

Then I feel him. Dean's arm draped across my waist, one leg tangled with mine, his breath warm against the back of my neck.

We're tucked together like we've always fit this way. And it does feel that way now—easy. Right. But that makes it all the more terrifying.

I shift slightly, enough to stir him. He murmurs something against my skin, pulls me tighter, and presses a kiss to my bare shoulder.

"I love waking up like this," he mumbles.

I smile into the pillow. "Naked?"

"Naked, wrapped around you, not entirely sure what day it is. Yeah."

I turn toward him, and his eyes, still sleep-heavy, find mine. He looks younger like this. Softer. Like the years of carrying everything for everyone haven't caught up to him yet.

"Do you still feel wrecked?" I tease gently, brushing my fingers over his chest.

He catches my hand and kisses my knuckles. "Completely ruined."

"Good," I whisper.

We stay curled up for a while longer, cocooned in the warmth of sheets and shared breath. His dick slips in and out of my sex in that lazy way that I'm starting to love until we both crest over the peak. But eventually, reality creeps in.

Pitter-patter steps down the hall.

Dean groans. "Our tiny alarm clocks."

Sure enough, Evelyn appears in the doorway, holding her stuffed lamb upside down by one paw, wild waves stuck to her cheeks.

"Waffle might be turning into a butterfly today," she announces like it's national news.

I glance at the clock. Barely seven.

Dean rolls over. "Let Waffle sleep in, baby. Like me."

Evelyn climbs onto the bed like a determined squirrel. "But *you* said I could see her wings. Maybe."

I grab the sweatshirt on the floor and pull it over my head, laughing as I head to the bathroom. "Give me one second and we'll check together."

Downstairs, Oliver's already at the table, eating a bowl of dry cereal like it personally insulted him. The kitchen is a mess—crumbs, boxes, a single sock on the counter—but I don't care. This kind of chaos feels good. Lived-in.

Evelyn races to the dining room windowsill, where Waffle still hangs motionless inside her little case.

"No wings yet," she sighs.

"She's not ready," I tell her, smoothing her hair. "Some things take time."

Dean appears with coffee in hand, still barefoot, wearing yesterday's jeans and the softest look I've ever seen on his face.

He hands me a mug and kisses my temple. "I think she's ready."

It takes me a second to realize he's not talking about the chrysalis.

My stomach flips.

The kids chatter on, voices overlapping like birdsong. Oliver declares he's going to build Pancake, Waffle, and Maple a habitat out of LEGOs. Evelyn insists butterflies need tiaras. But all I can feel are Dean's eyes on me—steady, quiet, hopeful.

And the truth hits me like an explosion. I want this. I want this messy, beautiful life. I want the tired mornings and sticky counters and conversations about butterfly royalty. But more than anything, I want the way he looks at me when I don't even know I'm being watched. The kind that you can just… feel.

Like I've already made a home without realizing it.

After a day out on the bay in the boat Dean had delivered a week ago, the kids are down again, finally, and the house has returned to that quiet I've learned to love. Not empty. Just settled. Lived in.

I step out onto the deck with my wineglass and a blanket, watching the fireflies flicker in the yard. The last orange smudge of sunset glows along the horizon, soft and warm and fading.

Behind me, the screen door creaks, and then Dean's there, barefoot again, whiskey in hand, his shirt slung over one shoulder.

"Thought I might find you out here," he says.

I tuck my knees under the blanket and gesture to the empty chair beside me. "Come sit."

He does, sinking down with a groan. We sit in silence for a while, our breaths syncing with the hum of summer night sounds.

"You okay?" he asks finally.

I nod. "I think so."

He tilts his head, eyes scanning my face like he knows exactly where my thoughts lie without even trying. "You don't have to decide anything yet. About staying. About us."

"I know," I say quietly, the words fragile but firm. "But I'm not sure I want to leave anymore."

That earns a small smile from Dean. Not surprise, just hope. Quiet and steady, like he's been waiting for me to catch up to what he already knows.

"I think…" I pause, the nerves tangling in my throat, sticky and stubborn. "I think I'm starting to believe that this life isn't borrowed. That it could actually be mine. That maybe I'm allowed to want something soft. Something safe."

His hand finds mine on the armrest. Warm, steady. Anchoring.

"You are," he says gently, voice laced with certainty. "And you don't owe anyone an apology for needing time. Not me. Not yourself."

I exhale slowly, watching the way our fingers intertwine. His thumb brushes the inside of my wrist like he's memorizing my pulse.

"But I also can't pretend that I don't still want to help people," I admit, turning my gaze toward the railing. The backyard glows in the last stretch of sunlight. "That I don't want to push the boundaries of science. Contribute something meaningful. I spent years chasing that dream, not because someone told me I should, but because it's part of who I am."

He says nothing, just listens.

"I want to stay," I whisper. "God, I do. I want to wake up to pancake mornings and bedtime cuddles and the way you look at me like I'm already yours. But I also want to make a difference in the world with what I know. I want both, Dean. And for the first time in my life, I'm starting to believe I might be allowed to have both."

His hand tightens around mine.

"You should have both," he murmurs. "Anyone who tells you otherwise doesn't deserve a seat in your life."

I look at him then, really look. The man who showed up not just for me but for every fractured part of my soul I thought was too tired, too tangled, too late to save. The man who would give me exactly what I wanted, without question, if I would allow him, but understanding enough to know I want to do it all on my own merit. And just like that, the tight knot in my chest loosens.

Because I'm not choosing one dream over the other. I'm just learning how to make room for both.

I squeeze his fingers. "It's just… I've always known what I wanted. A safe, steady path."

He nods. "I know that feeling."

"And now, for the first time, I don't want to run. But I don't know how to stay, either."

"You're already staying," he says, looking out over the water. "You're here now."

We sit in silence again, letting the night settle around us like a secret. And for the first time in a long time, I feel like I'm not just surviving anymore. Maybe I'm beginning.

Chapter Twenty-one

Dean

There's something about early summer mornings in a small town that reminds me of GiGi's old photographs, faded at the corners, a little too worn, and soft around the edges. The sky hangs low and honey-colored, the trees casting long shadows across the gravel drive. I stand barefoot on the front porch, coffee in hand, while the screen door creaks behind me like it knows I haven't slept.

Inside, the house is still. Peaceful in a way I never thought I'd earn.

Oliver and Evelyn are still out cold, their soft breathing filling the upstairs hall like music. It won't last. Oliver will be up soon asking for cereal, and Evelyn will want "pupcakes," which are her version of pancakes but with chocolate chips and the absolute demand of a three-year-old tyrant. But for now, I soak it in. The quiet. The stillness.

And the ache.

Because even in the beauty, the cracks are still there. I pull my phone from my pocket. One missed call. One text.

Dad:

> Let's talk like men. You're making a mistake.

The words turn my stomach before the coffee even has a chance. He doesn't say "hello" or "how are the kids." Just that. A warning disguised as concern.

But I know better.

My father has never known how to love without strings. Never offered anything that didn't come with expectations sharp enough to cut.

He thinks I'm playing house in the coastal town. That moving to Coral Bell Cove is a midlife crisis I'll grow out of. That I'm not capable of raising Gen's kids without someone like him and my mom calling the shots.

He's wrong.

I take another sip and set the mug down. Just as the first sleepy footsteps pad across the hallway inside.

Oliver appears in the doorway, hair sticking up on one side, Star Wars pajamas rumpled.

"Are we making pancakes?" he asks.

"Good morning to you too, buddy."

He leans against me, warm and floppy and all boy. "Evelyn says she gets the first one because she's littler."

"She also said her stuffed bunny is a doctor last night. You sure you want to let her make executive decisions?"

He grins. "Good point."

We're still laughing when Lila comes down the hall.

She's wearing one of my flannel shirts, oversized on her smaller frame, her hair twisted up in a knot that's already half-falling out. And just like every damn morning since she moved in, I have to pretend I'm not wrecked at the sight of her. Suddenly, I need to be closer to her and move back inside with the kids.

She moves around like she's always belonged here. Like it's hers. Like she's ours.

And I know I shouldn't be thinking like that. She's only supposed to be here for the summer—helping with the kids, finding herself again after a breakup that should never have happened to a woman like her. But every day, it's harder not to imagine what it'd be like if she stayed. And despite her words the night before, I know better than to get my hopes up.

"Morning," she says, grabbing a mug from the cabinet.

Oliver's already tugging on her sleeve. "Evelyn says she wants syrup on her pupcakes."

"Then Evelyn's going to have to say please," Lila replies with a smile, handing me the spatula. "You're on breakfast duty. I'm on coffee recovery."

It's simple. Domestic.

Dangerously close to everything I never thought I deserved.

By the time the kids are dressed and fed and cartwheeling through the yard, Lila's on the deck with a book she's not reading and I'm standing too close without an excuse.

"I got a call," I tell her, barely above a murmur.

She looks up, and her eyes soften. She knows. "Your father?"

I nod.

She doesn't say I told you so. Doesn't press. She just sets the book aside and listens.

"He thinks I've lost my mind," I add. "Thinks this is some… escape fantasy. That I'm endangering the kids by not living in a high-rise and sending them to boarding schools."

"And what do you think?" she asks.

I look out over the fields, the sunlight catching on Oliver's hair as he runs. Evelyn's giggling, her shoes kicked off in the grass, dancing with a butterfly she insists is named Bacon. Soon we're going to run out of breakfast foods to name the damn things.

"I think I've never been more certain about anything in my life."

Her smile is small but full of something that looks a lot like belief. "Then let him be wrong."

I want to kiss her.

I want to thank her for being the first person in years who doesn't look at me like I'm broken or reckless.

But before I can say anything else, my phone buzzes again.

This time, it's worse.

Attorney:

> **Guardianship petition officially filed. You'll be served this week. Hearing date TBD.**

My jaw tightens, and I close my eyes, counting to three.

When I open them, Lila is standing. She's already read the message over my shoulder, and her hand finds mine without hesitation.

"Whatever he throws at you, we'll handle it," she says. "You're not alone in this."

I want to believe her, but I've been alone so long, I'm not sure I remember how to let anyone carry the weight with me.

Still, I squeeze her hand back. Because I want to try.

By late afternoon, the sun hangs low and heavy in the sky, casting a golden sheen over the dock. The kids are knee-deep in a makeshift mud kitchen out back. Oliver's in charge of stirring with a stick, Evelyn is yelling about the need for "unicorn spice." Lila crouches next to them, laughing with that unguarded sound that makes my heart hitch every damn time.

I'm not sure how I got this lucky.

I lean against the deck post, arms crossed, soaking in the scene like a man about to lose it all. Because I know it's only a matter of time before the papers arrive. Before my father makes good on his threat and rips a hole straight through the life I've built here.

And I also know something else, something worse: the person who makes this feel like more than survival—the one who walked into my house with hesitant hands and a fierce heart—could walk out just as easily.

No matter what feelings are involved inside either one of us, I'd never ask her to give up her dream.

Lila looks up and catches me staring. Her smile falters, just slightly, like she knows what I'm thinking.

She makes her way over, wiping mud from her hands on her shorts. "You look like a man who's bracing for impact."

"Feels like it," I admit.

She stands next to me, our shoulders nearly touching. "You said your father never did this before. Never tried to take the kids when your sister would leave them with the nanny."

I nod. "He used guilt. Shame. He didn't need court documents. He used her."

She's quiet for a moment, processing.

"And now?"

"Now he's going to try to prove I'm unstable. That I walked away from the legacy. That I'm playing house in the middle of nowhere with a nanny and two kids I barely know how to raise."

Her head snaps toward me. "Is that what you think this is? Playing house?"

"No." My voice is rough. "But that's how he'll spin it. He'll look at you and see an easy target. A woman who moved in too fast, who doesn't have a permanent job, who—"

"Who loves your kids," she cuts in, eyes flaring. "Who puts them first every single day. Who walked away from a life she thought she wanted because it didn't feel like home anymore. You think I don't know what this is?"

I stare at her, stunned by the fire in her voice.

"You think I don't know what it means to be accused of being temporary?" she continues. "Because that's what people say about women who put their career first. We're flings. Fill-ins. The ones who show up in the middle of a storm and leave once the sky clears."

"You're not a fill-in," I say, stepping closer.

Her voice softens. "I don't want to be. But I need you to believe that I won't run if you don't push me."

I reach for her hand, curling my fingers around hers. "I don't want to push you. I just… I'm afraid of asking too much."

"Then don't ask," she says. "Just let me stay."

It's not a promise. Not yet. But it's a beginning.

And it's enough to get me through the next few hours, which is good.

Because when the black SUV pulls up the driveway, I know exactly who's behind the wheel. He doesn't bother knocking. He never has. I'm pretty sure he'd tear down the door if it were locked.

He walks in like he owns the damn air we're breathing. Same as always.

The silver in his hair is perfectly styled, not a strand out of place, like time itself wouldn't dare muss him up. He's tall and lean, but imposing in that sharp-edged way that makes people stand straighter when he enters a room. His bespoke suit fits like a second skin, every seam and stitch a reminder that his money doesn't just talk—it sneers. Arrogance drips off him in waves, subtle but suffocating.

He doesn't need to speak to make a point. His posture alone says it all. Chin slightly lifted, shoulders pulled back, eyes skating across the room like everything in it is beneath him.

Including me. Always me.

"I got your attorney's message about serving you," he says without preamble.

I square my shoulders, planting myself between him and the living room. "Then why are you here?"

He glances around, taking in the house details with thinly veiled disgust. "What I know is that you're hiding behind old barns and small-town clichés. That this"—he gestures broadly, like the house offends him—"isn't the life you were built for."

"I built this life," I bite back. "Every piece of it."

He scoffs. "And now you're dragging your sister's children through the mud of your rebellion."

That word sets me off—*rebellion*. Like choosing love over control is some kind of adolescent phase. As if my sister hadn't known what she was doing. Despite our ups and downs my sister knew how much I loved her kids. The same could not be said for how she felt about our parents. Most of the time Gen only pretended when she wanted something from them that I wouldn't give her.

Lila appears behind me, arms crossed, silent but steady.

He notices her and smiles like a snake. "And there she is. The nanny."

"She's not the nanny," I say through gritted teeth.

"Oh?" He tilts his head. "Then what is she?"

"I'm the woman who watches your son show up for those children every day," Lila says calmly. "And I'm not going to stand by while you try to paint him as anything less than the father he's become."

His eyes narrow. "You have no say in this."

"Then maybe I'm just here to watch you lose," she replies.

I feel a smile tug at my lips, even as the rage simmers beneath the surface.

My father doesn't back down. "You're a child playing adult, Dean. You're running a circus, not a household. You think a few pancakes and bedtime stories make you a parent?"

"No," I say. "But showing up every damn day does. And I'll keep showing up long after you're gone. And seriously, old man? What makes you think you get the Father of the Year award? All you want is someone to hand the business over to so it stays in the family. You couldn't care less about those kids."

He steps forward. "If you think a judge is going to side with you—"

"I don't care what a judge thinks." I interrupt. "I care what *my* kids see. I care what they feel. And they know who's been there. They know who tucks them in and kisses their scraped knees and listens when they cry."

His jaw tightens, lips thinning to a hard line. And I know I've finally hit the nerve I was aiming for. Good.

He spent years pretending his legacy could make up for what he never gave us. Empty words. Broken promises. A father only in name, never in presence. But I won't let him do the same to Oliver and Evelyn.

Not now. Not ever.

There's a beat of silence, heavy and brittle, and then he scoffs—a sharp, humorless sound that cuts through the air like a slap. Without another word, he spins on his heel and storms out, polished shoes striking the hardwood with clipped finality. The front door slams behind him, the sound echoing through the house long after he's gone.

It's fitting, really. There's a storm rolling in tonight.

And he just brought the thunder.

That night, steady rain taps the windows, a lullaby for a house full of tired hearts.

The kids are asleep. Lila and I sit on the couch, the fire flickering low, her head resting against my shoulder.

"I meant what I said earlier," she murmurs.

I kiss the top of her head. "So did I."

She pulls back just enough to look at me. Her eyes are wide, honest. "You're not alone in this."

"I know," I whisper.

And for the first time in weeks, I believe it.

It starts with silence. Not the heavy or uncomfortable kind, but the kind that only exists between two people who've been through something—who've stood side by side, stared down something ugly, and somehow still want to share a couch after it.

Outside, the rain has mellowed into a lazy tap against the windows, like the sky's just catching its breath.

Lila's curled into the corner of the couch, bare feet tucked under her, the hem of her sweater stretched over one knee. She looks soft and tired and heartbreakingly beautiful, like someone who's survived a long day and is still deciding whether to let herself relax.

She hasn't said much since my father left. Neither have I. But we're here. Together. That has to count for something.

"You okay?" I ask quietly, voice barely louder than the rain.

She glances over, her lips curving up into something between a smile and a sigh. "You've had a hell of a day, and you're asking if *I'm* okay?"

"I know how he is," I say. "You didn't sign up for that kind of drama."

She shrugs. "Maybe not. But I didn't walk away either."

That stops me. Because she could have. So many times, she could have packed up her things and gone. I wouldn't have blamed her. Hell, part of me was bracing for it.

Instead, she stood up to him. For me. For Oliver and Evelyn.

"You didn't have to defend me," I say, watching her carefully.

Her gaze flicks up. "Yes, I did."

And just like that, the distance between us evaporates.

I reach for her hand, our fingers finding each other like they've done it a thousand times. Maybe all those quiet mornings and late-night laughs have been adding up to this quiet pull between us.

"I've never had someone do that," I admit, my voice rougher than I mean it to be. "Stand in front of me instead of behind me."

She shifts closer, the couch cushion dipping beneath her weight. Her hand squeezes mine.

"You're not someone who needs rescuing, Dean. But you do need someone who sees you."

I swallow hard because her words feel like a hand around my heart.

"I see you," she adds, softer now.

I'm not sure what makes me move first—her eyes, the way they're shining in the low light, or the fact that I feel safe enough to want something for the first time in years. Need something.

But I do move. And she meets me halfway.

Our kiss isn't rushed. It's not fireworks or frantic hands. It's slow and deliberate. A conversation we've been having in pieces since the day we met. Her hands slide up into my hair, a spot I'm learning is her favorite. Mine find her waist, steady and careful. She tastes like tea and something sweeter underneath, something uniquely Lila.

I deepen the kiss just a little, testing the boundary. She doesn't pull away. If anything, she presses closer. I breathe her in. I could live in this moment.

Her sweater slides up under my hands as I trace the dip of her back, and she lets out a soft sound—half sigh, half need—that makes my pulse spike.

We stand together, still kissing, and I guide her back to my bedroom.

The room's dim, lit only by the lamp on the nightstand and the occasional flicker of lightning through the window.

I watch her as I peel off my shirt. Her eyes roam my chest, not like she's impressed, but like she's curious—hungry. She reaches out and traces a line over my shoulder, a tiny scar from years ago.

"You always carry everything, don't you?" she whispers.

"Not tonight."

We undress each other like we're unwrapping a secret—slow, reverent. When I finally slide her sweater off, revealing soft skin and flushed cheeks, I have to take a moment.

"Lila..." My voice breaks on her name.

She steps in, kissing me harder this time. Her hands are bolder now, finding the line of my jaw and the muscles in my back.

The air thickens with heat and something fragile. I want to consume her. I want to cradle her.

We collapse onto the bed in a tangle of sheets and limbs. Her skin is warm beneath mine, her mouth opening for me, her body arching in perfect rhythm to mine. And when I reach down, dragging my fingers along the inside of her thigh, she gasps and murmurs my name like a vow.

I pull back just enough to look her in the eyes. Her breath hitches as she reads my mind. But she obeys. Fingers wrap around the slats, and I see her eyes flutter closed, surrendering not just to me but to the moment, to everything we've built without saying a word.

I take my time. Every kiss. Every touch. Every slow, deep thrust is an unspoken promise. She doesn't have to wonder where she stands.

She's here with me.

When we finally fall over the edge together, it's not wild or messy. It's deep. Anchored. The kind of connection that leaves you breathless and brand new.

Afterward, she curls into me, her head on my chest, fingers tracing lazy circles on my skin.

Still coiled against me, her leg tangles with mine, her breathing slow and even, one of her hands rests on my stomach like she forgot to move it. Or didn't want to.

Her hair is wild. Her lips are parted. She looks like something holy.

And I... I don't know how to stop wanting her.

In the early morning light, that crisp golden hue, my hand drifts to her back, fingers tracing small, slow circles. She murmurs something against my skin but doesn't wake. And I let her stay like that because I'm not ready for the shift. For the moment she opens her eyes and remembers the thousand things waiting for both of us just beyond the edge of this room.

The legal battle.

Her need to save the world.

Whatever fear she's still holding on to that keeps her from fully falling.

I press my lips to the top of her head.

She stirs then, just enough to turn her face toward mine. Her eyes blink open slowly, soft and sleepy and a little bit wrecked.

We lay like that for a stretch of stillness before the sounds of the house begin to rise. Little feet on the stairs. The clatter of Oliver rummaging in the kitchen. Evelyn yelling about a missing stuffy.

And just like that, the spell breaks.

Lila sits up slowly, clutching the blanket to her chest, her hair falling over one shoulder. "We should probably get dressed before Evelyn walks in and asks why we're wrestling."

I chuckle, but it's laced with nerves.

Because everything feels more fragile now that the sun's up.

We move through the motions—coffee, socks, spilled cereal, and a dinosaur video playing too loud. But every time our eyes meet across the kitchen, something silent passes between us.

A question. A plea. A promise we haven't figured out how to keep. The moment hits me harder than I expect because I can see it clear as day. The kind of mother Lila would be. The kind of home we could build if my father silences his demands.

Later, when the kids are napping and the house quiets again, I find her on the deck, her legs pulled up under her, a cup of tea cooling beside her knee.

She doesn't look at me when I sit down next to her.

She doesn't have to.

"I should tell you something," she says quietly. "About a job."

My chest tightens.

"A job," I say.

She nods. "It's a lab in Chicago. A two-year project. I'd be leading it."

I stare out over the fields, throat dry.

"And do you want it?"

"I used to."

She finally looks at me, and the wind catches the ends of her hair, brushing them across her cheek.

"But something happened this summer," she says. "I found something I didn't know I was missing. And now, I don't know how to want the same things I used to."

I swallow hard, the lump forming in my throat bigger than I expect. "You don't owe me anything."

And God, I mean it. Every word. I'd give her the world if I could. Hand it to her on a silver platter with a bow that matched her eyes. Because Lila deserves everything. Every dream, every breakthrough, every moment of wonder she's ever chased. She's worked too damn hard and sacrificed too much to ever feel like she has to choose.

"I know," she says softly. "But I want to be honest. I want to want this… us… without wondering if I'm giving something up."

Her words aren't accusatory. There's no anger behind them. Just that steady, quiet truth that always cuts straight through me. She's trying so hard to do the right thing for herself, for me, for the kids. And I love her for it. Fiercely. Completely.

My voice drops lower, laced with something that sounds a hell of a lot like desperation. "I don't want to be the thing that holds you back."

Because it would kill me if I were. If loving me meant she lost a piece of herself, I wouldn't be able to live with that. I'd walk away before I ever let that happen.

"You're not," she whispers, fingers threading through mine. "But I need to know that I'm not just filling a space until it closes."

I squeeze her hand, my thumb brushing along the ridge of her knuckle. "You're not a placeholder, Lila. You're the reason I stopped feeling like something was missing."

I pause, letting that truth sink into the space between us.

"If you want that lab job, take it. I'll be cheering you on every step of the way. Hell, I'll drive you to the airport myself and set up a second home in Chicago if that's what it takes. But I won't let you forget that you're not in this alone. Not anymore. Whatever you want—career, family, a life filled with purpose—you can have it. All of it. And I'll be right beside you for every step, every stumble, every fucking triumph."

Her eyes glisten with something that looks a lot like hope.

And at that moment, I swear, there's nothing I wouldn't do to keep that hope alive in her. Nothing.

She leans into me then, her head on my shoulder, her breath warm against my neck.

"I'm not ready to say I'm giving it up," she whispers. "But I'm not ready to let it go either."

And somehow, that feels like everything. Because love doesn't always come wrapped in certainty.

Sometimes it comes in a butterfly that hasn't hatched yet. In hands that still shake. In a deck shared in silence. And that's just enough to keep hoping.

Chapter Twenty-two

Lila

It's one of those hot, high-summer mornings when the sun glints off everything too sharp. The humidity is thick enough to drink, and every breath I take tastes like honeysuckle and leftover thunderstorm. The cicadas' song fills the spaces between Oliver's distant laughter and Evelyn humming something tuneless in the screened-in deck.

I'm at the kitchen table folding laundry, sock after sock, towel after towel, when there's a knock.

Not loud. Not frantic. Just… steady. Measured enough that it puts something unfamiliar in my chest. The kind of feeling that says *this knock isn't here to borrow sugar.*

I toss the clean dish towel aside and move toward the door, every step slowing without permission. Worry that it may be Dean's father is at the forefront of my mind, quickly followed by an unpleasant visit from Prescott.

And when I open it—I stop breathing because I recognize the person on the other side immediately. It's her. Marin. Prescott's wife. Her eyes meet mine, and for a second, I swear the entire world holds still.

She's changed.

She's not the perfect, polished, porcelain woman I remember seeing in the magazine articles Ashvi showed me with bloodred lipstick and pearls clutched like armor. Today, she's all soft linen and flats. Her hair is dyed dark and tucked behind her ears like she gave up trying to style it, and her eyes… they aren't sharp anymore.

They're tired. Haunted.

That explains why no one has recognized her. Why I barely recognized her.

"I know I'm the last person you expected to see," she says. Her voice is too quiet for someone used to taking up all the oxygen in a room.

I don't answer right away, and my grip on the doorknob tightens.

She tucks a strand of hair behind her ear. Nervous. Marin Keating-Hoolihan looks nervous. "I just… Can we talk?"

Part of me wants to slam the door. Lock the past behind it, not that she has done anything wrong herself. It feels like I'm inviting Prescott back into my life.

But the rest of me, the part that survived her husband, the part that lived through the whispers and the sleepless nights and the questioning of my worth, sees something else in her eyes.

I step aside. "Come in."

She exhales like she's been underwater for days.

We sit at the table, the one coloring books and crayons strewed about and lemon tea rings on the wood. The laundry pile is still there. So is the sunlight and the sound of Evelyn laughing in the distance.

And somehow, that makes this feel real. Like she's not in control here. Like she came to me.

"I know you probably want to know what I'm doing here still married to Prescott," she says after a beat.

I just stare at her. "What *are* you doing here?"

She swallows. "I'm building a case."

My stomach drops.

"Against him."

The air rushes out of my lungs so fast I blink.

"Against your husband?"

"Soon-to-be ex-husband," she corrects.

I can't speak. I can barely move.

"While I've been in hiding, I started working with a lawyer. And a few other women. There are… God, there are a lot. And some of it's been happening for years. Mysterious deaths, murders, blackmail. Under everyone's noses." Her voice cracks. "Under mine."

The words hit like a punch to the gut. Sharp. Crushing. Unrelenting. My stomach turns, bile rising at the back of my throat as her voice continues to echo in my head. Murders. Blackmail. Deaths. And Prescott. *My* Prescott, or the version I'd convinced myself existed, had his hands in all of it. No wonder the Hoolihan family worked so hard to cover their tracks in the press.

The edges of the room begin to blur, the sounds dulling like cotton has been stuffed into my ears. The floor doesn't shift, but it feels like it should. Because everything beneath me suddenly feels unstable, like my foundation is cracking wide open.

"You disappeared." My voice is stiff, hollow. Like it's not even mine. "I know it was you who sent the text. Right?"

I don't even know what answer I'm hoping for. Maybe that she didn't. Maybe that this was all just a coincidence, a misunderstanding, a terrible dream.

But her response is a whisper, a confession weighted with guilt and fear. "I did. Because I needed to believe I could catch him in the act. I needed to see how far he would take it with you. How much do you know about his plans for you?"

I recall the conversation I had one early morning with Dean when he showed me all the evidence against Prescott that his PI had gathered. The plan to murder me and retain control of my patents, only to have them removed. I remember the anger I felt and how I took it out on Dean at first until my brother stepped in and set me straight. All of my anger and fear needed to be directed at Prescott.

But the fact that Marin knew all of this unleashes a new kind of emotion.

My throat burns. Not just with the rise of tears, but with shame. I swallow hard, trying to breathe, but my chest is tight, and my lungs feel compressed. Like the air itself is suffocating.

Dean warned me. The truth from home feels far more removed than hearing the truth from someone in Prescott's circle.

My fingers tremble as I press them to my mouth, as if that might stop the flood of panic crashing over me. I can barely speak, barely move.

And now? Now I finally see the truth and the scale of it. The way I was a pawn in something far darker than I ever imagined.

The worst part? I can't stop wondering what would've happened if I hadn't run. If Dean hadn't found me. If I'd stayed one more week. One more day.

Would I still be here?

Would I still be me?

I drop onto the nearest chair, knees buckling beneath the weight of realization. My palms are clammy. Cold. My heart's thudding too fast, like it's trying to outrun the truth I can't unhear.

"I didn't know," I murmur, voice barely audible. "I didn't know any of it until recently."

And now, for the first time, I understand just how much danger I've been in. Just how much he's been protecting me from. And I don't know if I'm more terrified of Prescott… or of the shame curling inside me for trusting the wrong person.

"I didn't come to make it okay. I came to say I'm sorry. I shouldn't have let him take it so far. But I'm not letting him do this to anyone else."

I look at her then. Really look. At the way her hands are shaking slightly. The way her voice, for all its practiced calm, keeps trembling around the edges.

And suddenly, I don't see the woman who betrayed me. I see the one who was used just like I was. Just differently.

"I used to think I was strong," I murmur. "Back when I had a plan. A lab. A career. But it wasn't until after I left him that I realized strength isn't about keeping your life neat."

"No," she says softly. "It's about surviving the mess and still waking up the next day."

I nod.

And for a long moment, we just sit there. Two women trying to carve something decent out of the wreckage. She tells me how she learned he had planned to murder her and take claim of her family's racing horse estate. Something only she was the last beneficiary and heir of.

She hands me a card when she stands to leave. "If you want to talk. Or testify. Tell your side of the story. You won't be alone in voicing his manipulations and emotional abuse. Or even just scream at someone who deserves it. You're not alone anymore. And no matter what, Prescott and his parents will pay for everything they've done to every person they've hurt. I'm going to make sure of it."

I don't take the card right away but then slip the cardstock from her fingers. She gives me a small smile. "If you watch the news at all, they're going to arrest him tomorrow. Should be some entertaining TV."

I watch her slip into her car and drive away on the gravel path disappearing among the trees. I still wonder how she found me.

And for the first time in a long time, I feel like I can breathe.

Later that night, I lie in Dean's bed and stare at the ceiling. I think about the way he holds Evelyn when she's scared. The way Oliver lights up when Dean shows up to help him build a lopsided LEGO city.

I think about the way he kissed me like I wasn't breakable. Like he didn't see my cracks as faults, but as spaces to fill with light.

And I wonder…maybe starting over doesn't mean forgetting everything that came before. Maybe it just means forgiving myself for what I let happen. And letting someone stay, even when it scares the hell out of me.

The house is quieter than usual. Evelyn is tucked into bed, one leg thrown over her stuffed fox, waves sticking to her cheeks. Oliver asked for one more story but fell asleep three pages in. I lingered longer than I needed to, brushing his hair back from his forehead, watching his chest rise and fall like the steady rhythm of something safe.

When I finally pad into the living room, Dean's there.

He's on the couch, legs stretched out, wearing an old hoodie and gym shorts. He looks up when I walk in, and the soft, uncertain expression on his face guts me. It's like he knows something shifted today, and he's waiting to see if it has cracked or healed.

"Hey," he murmurs.

"Hey."

I sink into the opposite end of the couch, tucking one leg under me.

He watches me for a second too long, then asks, "You okay?"

I nod. "Marin came by today. Prescott's wife."

His jaw tightens instantly. "Here? What did she want?"

"To apologize."

That gets a blink. "You're kidding."

"She's building a case against him. And everyone who helped cover up everything he and his family have ever done."

He exhales and rubs a hand down his jaw. "That's… a lot."

"It was."

I tell him everything. The way Marin looked small, tired, but honest. The way she didn't try to defend why she let it go so far. How tomorrow should make for some interesting news with the Hoolihan arrests.

He listens quietly, patiently. Like he always does when the world inside me is too loud.

When I finish, he nods slowly. "How do you feel?"

"Lighter. And also like I've been holding my breath for two years."

He shifts closer. Not all the way. Just enough that our knees brush.

"You can let it out now," he murmurs.

My eyes sting again. I blink fast.

"I'm scared," I whisper. "Of what it means if I stop being angry. If I stop protecting myself."

He reaches over and threads our fingers together.

"You're allowed to stop waiting for the other shoe to drop and start living, Lila."

I shake my head. "It's not that simple. Since I ran, I've constantly been looking over my shoulder."

"No, it's not that simple," he agrees. "But it's worth it."

The air thickens between us. His thumb moves across my knuckles slowly, like he's memorizing the shape of me.

"You don't have to run anymore," he adds.

That undoes me. Completely.

I shift, curling into his side, letting his warmth soak into my skin. My head rests on his shoulder, and his arm wraps around me like it belongs there. We sit like that for a long time.

And for the first time since my life cracked apart, I think maybe love isn't supposed to fix the broken things.

Maybe it just gives you a soft place to land while you heal.

The following morning, I try my hardest to ignore the urge to check the news. Deciding a shower is my best bet, I slip out of the comfort of Dean's arms. The steady pattering of the water against the tile soothes me. Steam curls through the air, clinging to the bathroom mirror and sliding down the glass shower door like rain on a windowpane. I tilt my head back, let the hot water trail down my spine, and close my eyes. My muscles, still pleasantly sore from the night before, begin to unwind.

It's early, too early, technically, but after tossing and turning half the night thinking about Dean and Prescott, sleep had become impossible.

I run my hands over my arms, chasing away the goose bumps that have more to do with memory than temperature. Dean's hands. Dean's mouth. The way he looks at me like I'm something he'll never stop craving.

I'm lost in the moment when the door opens.

I freeze mid-rinse, heart skittering in my chest. But it's only Dean, sleep-mussed and shirtless wearing nothing but joggers that hang dangerously low on his hips. He doesn't even flinch at the sight of me through the steam-covered glass.

"Morning," he mumbles, his voice low and gravelly from sleep.

I should be mortified. Embarrassed. Something. But I'm not. Instead, I stare. Not even pretending not to.

Because Dean is beautiful. Disarmingly so. His hair is a mess, sticking up in all directions. His abs flex as he moves toward the sink. There's a slight crease between his brows, like he hasn't fully woken up, and the way his eyes flick to mine in the mirror lights my entire body up with awareness.

He gets to work on his morning routine. Spits mint foam into the sink, rinses, and then turns to face me, arms folded loosely across his chest.

"Well, this is a hell of a way to start the day," he says, eyes raking over the foggy outline of my body behind the glass. "If I'd known there was going to be a view like this, I would've set an alarm."

I laugh, breathless and a little giddy, and reach for the soap, grateful for the cover even if the glass is too clouded for him to see much.

"You could knock, you know."

"I live here," he counters with a grin. "Besides, we're way past knocking, don't you think?"

That makes me blush, heat blooming in my cheeks that has nothing to do with the shower.

Dean walks over slowly, stopping just short of the door. "Want company?"

I arch a brow. "Dean."

"Kidding." He holds up his hands in mock surrender. "Mostly."

"You're terrible."

"You like it."

And dammit—I do.

Something about this moment feels more intimate than anything else we've shared. He could've looked away. Could've made a joke and left. Instead, he brushes a knuckle across the foggy glass, right where my shoulder is, and lingers there.

"You staying in there all morning?" he asks.

"Tempting."

"Well, if you get cold, I'm making pancakes."

He winks, and I bite back a smile.

A few minutes later, I shut off the water and step out, towel wrapped around me, hair dripping. The house is quiet, strangely so. The kids must still be asleep, probably worn out from the farm yesterday. That buys us the rare luxury of time.

I check my phone quickly and immediately read the headline about the Hoolihans being arrested under multiple charges of homicide and embezzlement. Whomever Marin hired didn't hold back with the charges. I only wish it was worse for them after everything they've put people through.

Closing the screen I sigh, wondering what all this means for me. If the fear of retaliation will fizzle away or if it will haunt me until my last breath.

By the time I get to the kitchen, the smell of coffee and frying batter hits me in the best way. Dean stands at the stove, spatula in hand, shirt still absent, his back flexing as he flips a pancake with practiced ease. Music hums from the phone resting on the windowsill—something low and sultry. Etta James, maybe.

He turns as I enter, eyes roaming lazily over me in his T-shirt and a pair of borrowed sleep shorts. His smile softens.

"Perfect timing. First batch is done."

"I could get used to this."

He hands me a steaming mug of coffee, his fingers brushing mine in that way that makes it hard to focus on anything but touch. Then he leans in and kisses me, a simple press of lips that somehow carries the weight of everything we've left unsaid.

As I reach for a plate, his hand circles my wrist.

"Dance with me."

I blink. "Now?"

He pulls me close, setting the plate aside. "Right now."

And maybe it's the music. Maybe it's the steam still clinging to my skin or the way his eyes soften when they look at me like I'm something fragile and rare, but I say yes.

His hand slides to my waist, the other holding mine gently, thumb brushing back and forth. We sway, slow and easy. The world melts away until it's just the two of us in the soft morning light, dancing barefoot in the kitchen like it's the only thing that's ever mattered.

Dean leans down, his breath warm against my ear. "You know… I've never wanted anything the way I want this."

My chest tightens. "Dancing?"

"This. Us. All of it."

I rest my head against his shoulder, letting myself fall into the rhythm of the music. Into the quiet certainty of his arms. Dean's hand slides around my waist, pulling me closer until barely a whisper is between us. The kitchen is quiet except for the soft hum of the radio. I can't remember the last time I danced like this. Maybe never. At least not in a kitchen with a man like Dean, barefoot, sleepy-eyed, and smiling at me like I'm his entire world.

His palm presses gently against the small of my back, fingers flexing like he's memorizing the shape of me. "You know," he murmurs, eyes locked with mine, "you've got a bad habit of making this place feel like home."

I swallow hard, heart thumping with a rhythm that has nothing to do with the song. "It's the pancakes," I joke weakly, but my voice cracks at the edges.

He chuckles, deep and low. "It's everything. It's you."

I don't know how to respond to that. Not without giving myself away. So I lean my head against his chest again and let the music carry us. It's slow and sweet, the kind of moment I didn't realize I was desperate for until I was standing in the middle of it. The sunlight slips in through the windows, casting golden beams across the floor like something out of a dream.

We keep swaying, and it's the most intimate thing I've ever experienced. More than sex. More than whispered promises. This is real. Uncomplicated. Safe.

Eventually, the music fades into another song, something more upbeat, but neither of us moves to break the spell. His hand stays at my waist. Mine stays on his chest, feeling the steady beat of his heart beneath my palm.

"You should probably finish breakfast," I murmur.

Dean lifts an eyebrow. "You saying you're not going to let me twirl you around the kitchen like a 1950s housewife?"

I laugh, but the sound is breathless. "Only if you wear a frilly apron."

His grin is boyish and mischievous. "Deal."

He spins me once, and I stumble slightly, laughing harder now. When I land against his chest again, his hands hold me a little tighter, his mouth dropping to my ear.

"You're everything I didn't know I needed, Lila."

I press my lips to his jaw, a featherlight kiss. "Right back at you, Dean."

And I realize I can't live my life waiting for the unknown. I need to live in the here and now, with the man who's quickly stolen my heart.

Chapter Twenty-three

Dean

Something about the scent of smoke and sugar always hits me right in the chest. How it clings to your shirt, seeps into your skin, or reminds me of long, humid summer nights, sticky popsicle fingers, and second chances around a firepit. Today, it smells like hope.

The town barbecue is already in full swing by the time we pull into the gravel lot beside the community pavilion. Someone's blasting Garth Brooks over the loudspeakers, the kids sprint barefoot across the grass, and the unmistakable sound of water balloons bursting sets off a ripple of shrieks and giggles.

Oliver is out of his booster seat before the SUV fully stops. Thank goodness for childproof locks. "Race you to the tug-of-war!" he yells when he's finally set free, darting across the lawn with the kind of reckless speed only a five-year-old can get away with.

Evelyn climbs out slower, blinking behind her pink sunglasses like she's taking stock of everything—the cotton candy machine, the bouncy castle, and the rows of picnic tables shaded by strings of lights. "Lila?" she says, holding up her arms.

Lila scoops her up without hesitation, tucking Evelyn against her hip like she was made for it. "Think they'll have lemonade?"

"Yellow lemonade," Evelyn insists. "Not pink."

I shut the truck door and catch Lila's eye over the roof. Her mouth curls in a soft smile, the kind that knocks all the air from my lungs. She's wearing a pale green sundress that hits just above her knees, her waves tied back with a scarf Evelyn picked out. She looks relaxed, sun-kissed, and more at home here than I probably ever have.

God help me, I think I'm in love with this woman.

Not the kind of love that's shiny and new and promises the moon without ever delivering. This is something steadier. Something that makes your knees shake for an entirely different reason. Once you realize someone fits like that, like they were meant to exist in your kitchen, your yard, and your life, you also realize how devastating it would be to lose them.

Lila meets my gaze again as she sets Evelyn down and grabs her bag from the passenger seat. "You okay?"

"Yeah," I say, clearing my throat. "Just… happy you're here."

She smiles again, softer this time, and links her fingers with mine. "Come on. Let me show you where to find the world's driest burgers."

I chuckle and press a kiss to her knuckles. "I've been told you haven't lived until you've had one of Dicky Smick's hockey-puck specials."

The truth is, I don't care what they're serving. I'm just glad we're here together, all of us. For the first time in a long time, it feels like we're not holding our breath.

The grill smokes steadily beside me as I flip patties and hand out paper plates like it's my calling. Every dad in town stops by with some comment about my transition from city money to country calluses. I take the jokes in stride because honestly, it's accurate. Three years ago, I was living it up, jet-setting across the world.

But now?

Now I know exactly how much to bribe Oliver with to eat coleslaw. I know Lila likes her coffee strong with two sugars, and only if she's had at least five minutes of silence. I know Evelyn's favorite dress, which lullaby calms her down fastest, and how Lila's shoulders relax when she's reading with her feet curled under her.

So yeah, I'm still learning how to be "local." But I'm also learning how to be theirs.

Dicky grins at me over the lid of the grill. "You've got that look, Dean."

"What look?" I ask the man I met just ten minutes ago.

"The one you only get when someone's crawled under your ribs and made a home there."

I laugh it off. But he's not wrong.

When I glance over my shoulder, Lila is crouched near the dessert table, helping Evelyn balance a lemon bar on a paper plate. Lila reaches out and grips the edge of the plate just before it topples over. Oliver is nearby, covered in face paint and powdered sugar, declaring war on the water balloon brigade.

She doesn't see me watching her, not at first.

Her hair is caught in a braid she must've twisted together since we arrived. The ends are curled softly where the heat from the day caught hold. Her sundress is a shade of pale green that makes her skin look sun-kissed and glowy.

And damn if that image doesn't settle right into my chest like it belongs there.

I make my way across the field, past the cornhole boards, and into the soft shade of the pavilion. It's cooler here, quieter too, enough that I can hear Evelyn's bubbly chatter and Lila's low laughter.

"Daddy!" Evelyn spots me and immediately reaches her sticky hands into the air. She'd recently taken up the moniker after hearing her brother call me Dad a few times. Lila watched me break down that night, both out of fear that they're forgetting their mother and complete joy that they see me as their parent.

I scoop her up, holding her against my side, and steal a glance at Lila. "How's the sugar patrol holding up?"

She grins. "Just bribed them with watermelon instead of cupcakes. I'd say I'm winning."

She's winning more than she knows. The kids are calmer around her. Lighter. Happier. Hell, I am too.

I set Evelyn down beside her again and lean in, dropping my voice low. "You're incredible with them."

Lila ducks her head but not before I catch the flush on her cheeks. "They're easy to love."

I'm about to sit down when a scream tears through the air. Sharp. Panicked. Young. The kind of sound that stills an entire crowd.

Heads whip toward the play area. A woman stumbles to her feet, a plate of deviled eggs crashing to the grass. She shouts something, a name, I think, but it's lost in the scramble.

Lila's already moving.

I blink, momentarily stunned at how fast she reacts. She darts toward a boy no older than Oliver, curled near the edge of the sandbox, clutching his throat. His face is blotchy and swollen. His lips are already tinged a scary shade of blue.

"EpiPen!" Lila shouts, dropping to her knees beside him. "Does anyone have an EpiPen?"

The boy's mother fumbles through a diaper bag with shaking hands. "He has one! He has one!"

I rush forward, heart thudding. The whole park is still now, quiet except for the sharp gasps of a little boy who can't get air. My stomach churns. Lila rips the pen from the mother's hands the second she finds it. No hesitation. No second-guessing.

"Hold him steady," she instructs, then plunges the needle into his thigh.

The boy jerks, but she's already murmuring calm reassurances, her hand smoothing over his hair, her breathing steady and sure.

My own breath catches. Because this, this woman is doing what no one else in this field full of parents and picnic baskets could do.

She's saving him.

Within seconds, his breathing starts to ease. The swelling doesn't disappear, but it stops getting worse. The crowd collectively exhales, but Lila doesn't move. She stays crouched beside him, hand in his, whispering soft things only he can hear. His mom is sobbing now, clutching both of them.

Paramedics arrive minutes later, summoned by someone in the crowd. Lila points out the small square of peanut brittle clutched in the boy's hand to them. Something he had clearly snuck when his mother wasn't looking.

They take over, and Lila steps back, chest heaving like she's run a marathon. She turns toward me. And I see it, the tremble in her hands, the shadow in her eyes. The past bleeding into the present.

I step up beside her. "Lila…"

She shakes her head once, hard. "I'm okay. I just…" Her voice cracks. "He's gonna be okay."

"You were amazing." My voice is hoarse and thick. "You saved his life."

Her throat works as she swallows. "It was all too familiar."

I don't ask. I already know. She once told me how the one rite of passage changed both of their lives. It's what drove her to science. What made her the kind of woman who doesn't just study things, she fights them. But now I understand the weight of that fight.

I touch her elbow gently. "Come sit. Just for a second."

She lets me guide her to a shaded bench behind the dessert table, Evelyn still lingering nearby with wide eyes and a half-eaten lemon bar.

"You did everything right," I tell her. "Every single step. I've never seen anything like that."

Lila lets out a shaky breath. "It brought it all back."

Her voice is quiet, but her eyes blaze with something fierce. "That boy… he didn't even know to check what he was eating. He just saw something sweet and took a bite. No one told him what peanuts could do to him."

"And now they will," I say, sliding my hand into hers. "Because of you."

She exhales slowly, letting her shoulders drop slightly. "It makes me think… maybe the lab isn't the only way. Maybe research isn't the only way to save lives."

I squeeze her hand. "What are you saying?"

Her gaze lifts to mine, steady now. "That maybe I could do more good in a classroom. That if kids learned young—if we educated them, made it real instead of abstract—maybe fewer would end up like that boy."

"And like your friend," I add gently.

She nods, eyes shining. "Yeah. Like him."

We fall quiet for a minute, watching as the boy is loaded into the ambulance, his mom sobbing with relief. The crowd is already breaking apart, drifting back to food and music and pretend normal.

But something's shifted in her. In me too.

Lila sits a little straighter.

"Do you think," she begins, voice tentative, "that it would be enough? Teaching, I mean. Running a program instead of being in a lab."

I don't hesitate. "If it's where your heart is, it's more than enough. It's everything. But you can do both. The job is part-time, remember."

She looks at me then, eyes wide and glassy and so damn beautiful I almost forget we're in the middle of a park.

"I believe in you," I say simply. "Whatever you decide. Lab, classroom, writing textbooks in a cabin somewhere, I'm proud of you. And I'll be right there, cheering you on."

Her lips part on a soft breath. "Dean…"

"Don't say anything yet," I murmur. "Just think about it. Let the moment settle."

She does. And then she leans in, resting her head on my shoulder as Evelyn climbs into her lap, already asking for another lemon bar.

The town goes on around us and is filled with laughter, music, and summer air, but for once, we're still. And I know, without question, that whatever future Lila chooses, it's going to be bright. Because she is.

The scent of charcoal and sweet corn clings to my shirt as I wrangle Oliver into his booster seat, his cheeks flushed from too much sun and too many cupcakes. Evelyn's giggling, sticky with lemonade and frosting, kicking her feet like the sugar rush hasn't quite worn off yet. Lila's a few steps behind us, hovering near the dessert table where the remnants of pies and brownies have been reduced to crumbs. She's smiling when someone says goodbye, but it doesn't reach her eyes. Not like it usually does.

She hasn't said much since the ambulance left. Since she knelt on the ground with a stranger's little boy in her arms, pressing an epinephrine pen into his thigh with the kind of practiced calm that shouldn't belong to someone her age. A calm born from experience. From pain.

I open the passenger door for her, resting a hand lightly on the small of her back as she climbs in. She doesn't lean into the touch like she usually does. She doesn't even look up.

The drive is quiet.

Oliver is out cold before we hit the main road, his head tilted at an impossible angle, mouth open. Evelyn's eyes flutter closed soon after, a faint hum of a lullaby drifting from her lips as if she's still in some dreamland made of bounce houses and sparklers.

Lila, though… she's wide awake. Her fingers twist the hem of her sundress over and over, the fabric wrinkled and damp in her grip. Her gaze stays pinned to the window, but I don't think she's looking at the passing trees.

I want to say something. To break the silence. But I don't.

She needs space to think. I've learned Lila is the kind of woman who feels things deeply but privately. Her mind is probably still replaying every second. How the boy's face had swollen, how he could barely breathe, how fast she had to act.

She saved that boy's life. Yet I know her well enough now to know she's not feeling triumphant. She's haunted.

When I pull into the driveway, the house is shadowed under a veil of soft dusk, the porch light flickering to life as I shut off the engine. I look over, expecting Lila to reach for the door handle, but she doesn't move.

"Hey," I say gently. "We're home."

She blinks slowly like she's coming up for air, nodding, but she still doesn't say anything. I get out, carefully lift a sleeping Evelyn from her seat, and press a kiss to her forehead. She murmurs something against my chest, curling into me like a kitten.

Lila finally steps out of the car. She closes the door with more care than necessary, like she's afraid the sound might shatter something inside her. The light spills across her face, and that's when I see it. Her eyes aren't just tired; they're unsettled. She's somewhere else entirely.

I pause halfway up the steps, glancing over my shoulder.

She's standing by the passenger side, one hand resting on the roof of the car, her eyes cast toward the night sky like she's looking for a sign.

I want to ask what she's thinking. If she's okay. If she's proud of what she did today because she should be.

"This isn't pretend for me, Lila," I say quietly.

"I know," she says. "It isn't for me either. That's what makes this so hard. My mind is all jumbled, and I'm so confused after today."

She doesn't cry. Neither do I.

But when she steps away and heads for the door, it feels like something is unraveling anyway. The front door clicks shut behind her, and the silence that follows is sharp. Too biting.

I stay in the hallway for a minute, her unsaid words echoing in my head like footsteps in an empty room.

I'm scared… but I'm coming back.

But tonight? Tonight feels different.

This time, she isn't walking away from me. She's walking toward something—clarity, maybe, healing, answers. And I want that for her. Hell, I want everything for her.

Moving toward the front porch, I watch the taillights of the SUV narrow into little red dots in the night, taking my heart along with them.

I step back into the house and turn off the porch light. The air smells like rain again, heavy and thick.

There's a storm coming. But whether it's real or metaphorical, I can't be sure anymore.

Padding up the stairs, I pause at the kids' doors. Evelyn is curled into a ball, one hand tucked under her cheek, her tutu crumpled at the foot of the bed. Oliver's still clutching his stuffy, one leg flung out over the blanket like he's trying to conquer the mattress in his sleep.

They're safe. They're okay. And Lila helped keep it that way today.

I walk into the kitchen, fill a glass with water, and lean against the counter as I debate drinking it or pouring over my head to wake myself up from this dream.

There's a faint crease in the curtain from where Lila tugged it back earlier this morning. A folded dish towel that still smells like the lavender soap she uses. All these little pieces of her are scattered through my home like breadcrumbs.

She's already part of this life. She just doesn't see it yet.

I want her to chase her dreams. I do. But I also want her to know she doesn't have to chase them alone.

The following morning, the house is too quiet. Oliver usually wakes me up before the sun, bouncing around with some catastrophic request involving cereal and dinosaurs. Evelyn, three and clingy in the best way, normally demands snuggles and cartoons before I've even had coffee.

But today? It's just me.

No smell of Lila's vanilla shampoo drifting through the hall. No humming while she folds laundry or cuts fruit for the kids. Just silence. And every creak of the floorboards sounds like an echo of her not being here.

The kids feel it, too. Evelyn curls into my chest, clutching her stuffed fox and lamb. Oliver's quieter than usual, pushing around his breakfast with a frown.

"Where's Lila?" he finally asks.

"She needed a break," I say gently. "Just for a little bit."

"Did she get tired of us?"

God.

"No, buddy. Never." I run a hand through his messy hair. "Sometimes grown-ups need space to figure things out. But it doesn't mean we don't love the people we need space from."

He nods, but I can tell he doesn't understand. Hell, I barely understand it myself.

I'm at Otter Creek Farm by noon, helping Rowan patch a fence near the back pasture. It's not that he doesn't have the men on hand to do the work. I think he somehow sensed that I needed to leave the house. Maybe it was Lila's doing.

The sun beats down relentlessly, and the sweat stings my eyes, but I welcome the physical distraction. The cows are loud, the barn smells like hay and heat, and I'm grateful for both. It beats standing in that empty kitchen pretending I don't notice how everything's still where she left it—her water glass, the folded throw blanket, and a rubber band from Evelyn's braid still resting on the table.

"She tell you where she's staying?" Rowan asks, tightening the drill bit on his impact driver.

I nod. "Ashvi's place."

"She okay?"

"I don't know."

He gives me a long, measuring look. "And you?"

I want to lie and say I'm fine, that this is just a blip. That she'll come home once she clears her head. But I can't. Instead, I wipe my hands on my jeans and sit on the edge of the truck bed.

"I keep thinking," I say slowly, "if I'm just good enough, she'll stay. But it's hard to compete with someone's dreams, especially hers. She's a freaking life-saving scientist."

Rowan leans his arms against the tool rack but doesn't interrupt.

"I've done everything right. I built the house. I hired help. I show up every damn day. I learned to braid Evelyn's hair and sit through Oliver's rants about dinosaur evolution. I try so damn hard to be steady. To be… safe."

Rowan nods once, slow. "And?"

"She's still halfway out the door."

We sit in silence, the wind stirring dust around our boots.

Then he says, "You can be everything good in the world, man, but you can't make someone believe they can have it. That's their job."

The words hit harder than I want to admit.

Back at the house, I move through the motions—dinner, baths, bedtime—but it's all muscle memory. I read *Where the Wild Things Are* with Evelyn curled against me, her thumb in her mouth, and Oliver pretending he's not sleepy even as he nods off mid-sentence.

Lila's name doesn't come up again.

But when I go downstairs, I catch sight of her sweater draped over the back of the couch. I press it to my face and inhale. It still smells like her.

I have no idea how to move forward without her.

Chapter Twenty-four

Lila

The stars are out by the time I slip my shoes on and step onto Ashvi's porch. The night smells like honeysuckle and warm asphalt, and my headache has dulled to a manageable throb for the first time all day. My body still feels like it's carrying the weight of too many truths. And one giant mistake.

I stare out at the street, wondering if he's home. Wondering if Evelyn has asked for me. Wondering if Oliver picked out a new rock for his collection and left it on the windowsill for me to find.

The guilt claws up my throat again. Because everything Ashvi said when I showed up last night was right.

I left. And I didn't just leave a man I care about—I left two small hearts who didn't understand why.

My phone's still on the counter inside, unanswered. I've turned it over more times than I can count, waiting for his name to pop up. But it doesn't.

He's probably angry. Maybe he's heartbroken. He's unquestionably realizing that he deserves someone braver than me.

I wrap my arms around myself, breathing deep, and I whisper into the night, "I'm sorry."

And I hope—God, I hope—that somehow, that's enough.

The silence tonight is different. It isn't peaceful—it's thick and pressing. It wraps around me like a wet blanket, too heavy, too warm, suffocating. I keep thinking if I just breathe deeper, it'll lift. That my chest won't feel like it's shrinking every time I think about Dean's face when I walked away.

I left. I keep saying it like it's a fact, like repeating it might numb the truth. But it doesn't.

I left, and now I'm sitting on my best friend's deck in someone else's borrowed pajama pants, sipping on tea I don't want, staring at a sky that used to feel full of possibility and now it feels like it's holding its breath.

What did I think would happen? That Dean would chase me? That he'd show up at Ashvi's door with Evelyn on his hip and Oliver holding a drawing that said *We miss you, Lila* in crayon?

God, I'm such an idiot.

He has enough on his plate without chasing the woman who couldn't even look him in the eye when she said goodbye. And that's the thing—I didn't. Not really. I didn't say goodbye. Not the kind that means something. Because I didn't want it to be goodbye.

I just wanted space. Clarity. One moment of silence away from the warmth of those kids, the way Evelyn curls into my side when she's tired, the way Oliver saves his best rocks for me and tells me secrets he won't even tell Dean. I wanted to feel like me again—just Lila. Not the Lila who makes pancakes and kisses bruises and falls asleep in a man's arms with her heart too full.

I wanted space to remember who I was before all this.

But instead, all I've done is sit in it. The silence. The distance. And now it's not helping. It's hurting. Because this isn't what I want. What I want is messy. Complicated. Full of children and dirt and love so big it scares me. What I want is Dean and I might have just broken him.

The screen door creaks behind me, and Ashvi steps out, barefoot and holding two mugs.

"Still thinking?" she asks, handing me a fresh cup that smells like cinnamon and apology.

"I don't know how to stop."

She sinks into the deck chair beside me. "You were scared. That's not a sin."

"I didn't say goodbye."

She hums into her mug. "That might be."

We sit in silence for a minute, the kind that only happens between best friends and feels safe even when everything else is unraveling.

"You know," she says after a while, "for a woman who spends all her time studying cause and effect, you're really bad at letting yourself *feel*."

That makes me laugh, but it comes out wet and broken.

"I thought leaving would make me feel free again," I admit. "Like maybe I'd get my edge back."

"Did it?"

I shake my head. "It made me feel like I lost everything I didn't even realize I'd been building."

She watches me over the rim of her mug. "So what now?"

"I don't know."

"You love him?"

I nod.

"And the kids?"

My chest tightens. "More than I should."

"There's no such thing."

I look down at my hands, the chipped polish on my fingernails, and how my skin still smells faintly of their shampoo.

"I just don't know if he wants me anymore," I whisper, the words raw in my throat. "If I've already broken too much for him to want the rest. All I've done since he's known me is go back and forth in relationship ping-pong."

Ashvi doesn't look at me with pity, thank God. She just exhales, long and steady, like she's been holding it in the whole time.

"That man?" she says, eyes sharp with knowing. "He's probably out in that field right now, shirt half off, covered in sweat and pacing like a lunatic, kicking himself for letting you go."

A laugh bubbles up despite the ache in my chest. "That's oddly specific."

She grins. "He told Rowan he's just trying to be good enough. Said if he's patient, if he stays steady, maybe you'll come back to him."

The fragile parts of me tremble at that. Because Dean was always good enough. He didn't need to prove a thing. I was the one clawing at perfection, measuring myself against some invisible scale of womanhood that said I had to be one thing or the other.

Brilliant or nurturing. Independent or loving. Career-driven or family-focused.

But maybe… I don't have to choose. Maybe I can be both.

Women all over the world are doing it—building empires, raising babies, loving deeply, and chasing dreams. I've just been so afraid of losing myself in someone else's life again that I forgot I get to write this one. I get to choose how it looks.

Dean never asked me to shrink myself. He never asked me to give anything up. I did that all on my own out of fear. And when I handed him my worst, my jagged pieces, he didn't flinch.

He held them with devotion.

And it could be that's the thing. Love isn't just soft and romantic, it's resilient. Maybe I don't have to compartmentalize myself to fit neatly into someone else's world. Because Dean didn't ask me to fit. He just made space.

It's time I stop running and stop trying to be less. Because I can be brilliant and soft. Strong and supported. Fierce and deeply loved. And Dean? He'll still be there, holding steady, just like he always promised he would.

Chapter Twenty-five

Dean

I'm rinsing off the cutting board, humming under my breath while the smell of garlic and tomato sauce lingers in the air. The kind of scent that clings to your skin and clothes and makes the house feel like a home. My mind drifts toward bedtime routines—bathwater, tiny pajamas, and storybooks read twice just because Evelyn insists the ending sounds better the second time.

Then I hear it. A sharp and high-pitched scream. But it's not the kind that spikes your adrenaline, not the kind that means someone's bleeding or hurt. It's pure joy shouted at the top of small lungs.

Then I hear her name.

"LILA!"

I drop the dish towel. My heart doesn't just race—it sprints. I'm halfway across the kitchen before I realize I've moved, drawn by instinct more than anything else. The screen door creaks as I shove it open.

And there she is.

Lila. Standing in the middle of the backyard, sunlight haloing around her, both of my kids wrapped around her legs like they might never let go again.

Oliver's talking a mile a minute, hand flailing, face split in a grin that could light the whole damn town. Evelyn clutches Lila's leg like a lifeline, little fingers digging into the fabric of her dress, her cheek pressed against Lila's thigh.

My knees go weak. She came back. I didn't expect her to.

I thought… God, I thought that was it. That she'd disappeared into the fog of my past, just another person I couldn't hold on to. My true ghost girl. But she's here. And everything inside me fractures under the weight of relief.

I don't breathe until she looks up and sees me. Our eyes lock across the yard. There's a tremble in her lips, something uncertain and fragile.

"I want to stay if that's still okay," she says, voice barely more than a whisper.

My chest tightens. I swallow hard past the lump in my throat and nod.

"It's more than okay."

It's everything. It's every prayer I never admitted I whispered at night. Every silent hope I buried beneath layers of guarded silence and responsibilities I didn't think I deserved to ask for more than.

Lila's back. And she's looking at me like she missed me, too.

Dinner is quiet in the way only families can be. Clinking spoons, soft giggles, and whispered conversations between two kids who haven't quite figured out how to keep secrets from their dad. Evelyn's pinky is looped around Lila's as they share a plate of garlic bread. Oliver is showing her the new drawing he made, a fire-breathing goat who also happens to be a ninja. She hums in appreciation like she never left, like there wasn't a whole night where her side of the house was cold and silent.

Lila moves around the kitchen like it's muscle memory. She doesn't ask where things are and doesn't fumble. She just moves. Sliding plates in front of Evelyn. Tucking Oliver's napkin under his chin even though he's old enough to hate it. Brushing crumbs from the table with the side of her palm.

And every time she looks up, her eyes catch mine. Neither of us says a word. Not yet.

Because how do you begin again when everything you've ever wanted just walked back in through the front door? You don't want to shatter it by moving too fast or asking for more than she's ready to give.

So I let the silence stretch, warm and full. Because the kids are glowing. Because I'm terrified that if I speak, the spell will break. Because I've never been this thankful to just sit and watch someone exist in my world again.

After dinner, Evelyn insists Lila read the bedtime story. There's no negotiation. No other option. She climbs into Lila's lap and opens the book like it's the most natural thing in the world. Oliver grumbles but joins her, scooting in close, his little head resting on Lila's shoulder.

And I stand in the doorway, arms crossed over my chest, breath held, watching how she wraps herself around them like she's never been anywhere else.

When the story ends, she tucks Evelyn in, then ushers Oliver to his room. One kiss to each forehead. One whispered promise I can't quite hear. And then the rooms go still. The kind of stillness that makes you feel everything more acutely.

I wait for her on the screened back deck.

Two glasses of wine. One tiny candle flickering on the railing. The summer air is thick with heat and the hum of cicadas. Somewhere far off, a dog barks. A boat cuts through the water. Life goes on.

And then she's there.

She steps outside barefoot; her arms wrapped around herself like maybe she's holding in more than just warmth.

Before I even think about the waiting wineglass or the hundred things I want to say, I move toward her. Lila stands like she's not sure if she belongs, arms crossed tightly over her middle, chin dipped down, those big blue eyes cautiously watching me like she expects me to shatter.

I reach out, gently curling my fingers around her wrists and coaxing her arms away from her body, from that guarded stance that tells me she's been holding herself together with sheer will. She lets me. And the second I pull her against me, she melts. Just folds right into my chest like she never left.

My arms wrap around her, strong but careful, like she's something precious I've only just been given permission to hold again. She buries her face against me, and I feel her inhale deep, like she's trying to memorize the smell of me, the feel of this, of us.

We stay like this—still, quiet, wrapped in something that feels more like a lifeline than a hug. Her hands fist in the back of my shirt, and I press my lips to the top of her head, breathing her in. This isn't just comfort. It's a need we've both been starving for. A moment we've been aching to return to.

And I'll hold her for as long as she lets me. Because she came back. Because she's here.

"I missed you," I say, nodding toward the wine as I reluctantly release her and grab the glass.

Her fingers brush mine as she takes it. That simple touch almost undoes me.

"I missed everything," she says. "You. Them. This."

I want to say a hundred things. I want to ask where she went even though I know, why she left, what changed. But instead, I study her face. The shadows under her eyes. The tight line of her shoulders. The part of her mouth that lifts just slightly like she's holding something back.

"I love you, Lila," I say, the words steady and sure. "I've been in love with you since the second week you were here. Maybe before. I just didn't know what to call it."

She freezes.

Her eyes shimmer in the low light. "Say it again."

I set down my glass and reach for her, tilting her chin so she's looking directly into me.

"I love you."

She kisses me. And it's not slow or cautious. It's not careful. It's the kind of kiss that says she's sorry. The kind that says she missed me too much to admit. The kind that erases every moment she was gone.

Her breath shudders out of her. "I love you, too."

She sets down her glass and then kisses me like she means it. Like she never wants to stop. Like this deck, and this moment, and this life could be enough.

Like we could be enough. We don't make it to the bed right away. Instead, we're a tangle of limbs on the hallway wall, halfway between the kitchen and my room, where she halts with her back pressed to the drywall, her breath shaky and her eyes impossibly wide. I kiss her again, slower this time, savoring it. Her lips part for me like they remember the shape of this, and it's something she never wanted to forget.

"I thought I lost you," I whisper against her mouth.

"You didn't," she breathes. "You just… scared me. This scared me."

I close my eyes, forehead against hers. "I know."

The apology is unspoken, tucked between the lines of our breath, our touch. We're both tired of explaining ourselves in words. For now, our hands do the talking.

Lila slides her fingers into the waistband of my jeans, and I grip her thighs to lift her against the wall. Her legs wrap around me like muscle memory, her back arching as she grinds against me with quiet desperation.

She clings to me like she's trying to anchor herself, like I'm her only tether to the ground. Just like she is for me.

Inside the bedroom, the room that hasn't felt full since she walked out, the air changes. Softer. Slower. Her breath catches as I lay her on the bed. Her hair fans across my pillow like she never left it. She's watching me with a look that's part hunger, part hesitation.

I pause, kneeling beside her. Letting her see that I'm here, waiting. Not pushing.

"I need you to say it, Lila."

She nods slowly, eyes never leaving mine. "I want this."

Relief cracks through me like thunder. I lean down and kiss her collarbone, her pulse fluttering against my lips. Every inch of her skin feels sacred now, mapped in memory and stitched together by longing.

I trail kisses down her chest, slow enough to make her sigh, soft enough to make her tremble. Her hands roam over my shoulders, nails digging in when I find the sensitive dip of her waist, her thighs opening beneath me with silent invitation.

When I finally slip inside her, it's not just heat or pleasure or lust.

It's home.

Her breath stutters, and I still, letting us both feel it—really feel it. How we fit. How this was never just physical.

She cups my face, her thumbs stroking over my jaw. "I'm right here."

And then we move. Together. Every thrust is a question and an answer. Every moan, every gasp, every whispered name is a vow we haven't dared say out loud.

She clings to me, body trembling, mouth pressed to my shoulder as I push her higher and higher. Her breath hitches, and she breaks. I follow seconds later, letting go in a way I haven't let myself in years.

After, we stay tangled in each other, skin slick, hearts thudding in sync.

"I love you," I murmur against her damp temple. "Even if you'd chosen to leave. Even if all I had left was a memory of you. I would've loved you anyway."

She presses her forehead to my chest. "You never asked me to stay. Not really."

I tilt her face up gently. "Because I wanted you to choose it. For you. Not because I needed you or the kids needed you or the town whispered that you were already half ours."

"And I do," she says quietly. "Choose it. Choose you."

Something inside me softens and releases. Like a grip I didn't realize I was holding finally loosens.

"I'm going to screw this up," I admit. "I'll mess up pancakes. I'll get grumpy when the dryer eats my socks. I'll probably talk business at inappropriate times."

She laughs, the sound curling into my chest and blooming there.

"I'll screw up, too," she whispers. "I'll forget to set timers. I'll hog the covers. I'll be late picking up Oliver from soccer because I get caught up looking at butterfly migration patterns or new studies on food allergies."

"I can live with that."

She kisses me again, soft and slow. "Then maybe we'll be okay."

"We'll be more than okay."

We lie there in silence, the kind that feels earned, not empty. Her fingers trace lazy circles on my chest. My arm is tight around her—like if I let go, she might vanish again.

But she doesn't. She's here. And now, so am I.

The sun's almost up by the time I finally close my eyes.

Lila's curled into my side, her hair fanned across my chest, one leg slung over mine like she never left. And even with the ache in my muscles and the adrenaline still humming through my veins, I can't bring myself to move. Not yet.

Because this moment is one I thought I'd never get again. She came back. She chose us. And I'm not sure I'll ever stop being stunned by that.

I run a hand slowly down her back, tracing the curve of her spine, memorizing every inch of her like it's the first time.

I think about the first morning she was here, stumbling into my kitchen barefoot and guarded, trying to pretend she wasn't just barely holding herself together. And now?

Now, she's folded against me like she belongs here. I press a kiss to the top of her head and let myself fall asleep.

When I wake again, it's to the sound of footsteps pounding down the hallway and the distinct crash of something ceramic shattering in the kitchen.

I sit up fast, heart racing, only to find Lila groaning beside me. She stretches, blinking against the light pouring through the windows, and mumbles, "If that's the coffee pot again, I'm gonna cry."

We stumble out of bed together like two hungover teenagers, limbs tangled in sheets and grins. In the kitchen, Oliver stands next to the counter, barefoot and wide-eyed, a bowl in shards at his feet.

"I was trying to make cereal for Evelyn," he says, already defensive. "You didn't wake up."

I glance at Lila. She steps forward, crouches down beside him, and smiles. "Next time, wake us up, bud. You don't have to do it all yourself."

He nods, still a little embarrassed. Lila brushes his hair back and kisses the top of his head. It's such a natural, instinctive gesture that it does something dangerous to my chest. Something permanent.

After Lila checks him over for any cuts, I grab the broom and clean up the mess while she pours cereal into two new bowls.

By late morning, the house has returned to its usual rhythm of sweet chaos. Lila folds the never-ending laundry on the couch, Evelyn dances around the living room in a tutu over her pajamas, and Oliver constructs something elaborate and clearly unstable with LEGO bricks that keep clicking against the hardwood floor.

I'm standing in the hallway just watching them, arms crossed, trying not to get too ahead of myself. But it's hard not to. The image in front of me is everything I've ever wanted and never thought I could have.

And right at this moment, it's mine.

"Dean?" Lila's voice pulls me out of my thoughts.

"Hmm?"

She's holding up one of my T-shirts. Her eyes meet mine, cautious but warm. "Is it okay if I keep stealing these?"

I walk over, take it from her hands, and pull it over her head right then and there. She laughs as her arms poke through the sleeves, and I kiss her forehead.

"You can have anything that's mine."

Her smile falters slightly, just for a second. "Even your last name?"

It's a joke. I know that. But the way she says it makes something shift inside me. A seed, maybe. One I wouldn't mind letting grow.

That afternoon, after naps and snacks and a rousing game of "find the missing stuffed dinosaur," Lila and I sit out on the deck with iced tea and silence. The kids are in the yard, chasing bubbles and giggling like it's the only job they've ever had.

It's warm out. Lazy summer heat. And the kind of quiet that feels earned.

"I have something to ask you," she says finally, voice soft.

I brace myself. "Okay."

"I think I want to say yes to the local offer. The science coordinator position for the entire school district." She mentioned it weeks ago while still conducting research at the high school laboratory.

"Yeah?" I ask, voice hoarse.

She nods. "Yeah."

I don't say anything. I just reach for her hand, link our fingers together, and bring it to my lips.

She leans her head against my shoulder. "It's not just for you. Or the kids. I need you to know that."

"I do."

"It's for me. Because for the first time in years, I feel like I can breathe."

I close my eyes and hold her hand a little tighter. "That's all I ever wanted for you."

She turns and presses a kiss to my cheek. "Then let's build something here. Not perfect. But ours."

I nod, not trusting my voice.

Because I don't need perfect. I just need her.

Chapter Twenty-six

Lila

The courthouse is colder than I expected.

Not just in temperature—though the air-conditioning hums with that sterile, too-clean chill that settles in your bones—but in atmosphere. The kind that prickles down your spine and makes your skin feel too tight for your body. I walk slowly down the hallway, the sound of my heels muffled by the thick carpet, the weight of what I'm about to do pressing into my shoulders.

I don't text him. Don't call. I don't need to.

If I told him I was coming, he'd probably try to talk me out of it. Not because he doesn't want me there, but because he'd think he was protecting me. Dean always wants to carry the burden on his own. Always has. But not today.

Today, I carry it with him.

The courtroom smells like dust and waxed tile, like too many people have sat in these seats with their futures held in the balance. I slip in just as the hearing is beginning. The door clicks shut behind me, and for a second, no one notices. Then Dean turns.

Our eyes lock.

He looks tired yet not broken. He never lets himself fall apart in public, but there are tight lines around his mouth and a tension in the set of his shoulders I haven't seen before. He's sitting beside his attorney, his hands resting flat on the table in front of him, like he's ready for a fight he doesn't want to have.

When he sees me, his lips part slightly in surprise. Or maybe even relief.

But it's the softening of his gaze that undoes me. No smile. No nod. Just that look, the one that says, *You came.*

I take a seat in the first row behind him, back straight, heart racing. I don't ask permission. I don't need it. I've earned my place here.

The proceedings start like any other. Formal, procedural, wrapped in so much legal jargon that it feels like a different language. The judge is a sharp-eyed woman with a tidy gray bun and no visible patience for nonsense. She barely glances up as the petitioner's attorney begins.

Dean's father sits across from us, perfectly composed in a tailored suit that probably cost more than my car. His lawyer is polished, her voice confident and cool.

"Your Honor, we believe that Mr. Dean Harrington's current lifestyle poses an unreasonable risk to the long-term development of the minors in question. While we respect his devotion, he lacks the resources, experience, and community support structure to raise these children alone. We also question Ms. Genevieve Harrington's state of mind when she signed the will, leaving her children in the guardianship of Mr. Dean Harrington."

She goes on, layering her argument with phrases like *lack of availability* and *emotional immaturity.* At one point, she even pulls out a printed article from two years ago, something tabloid-like that speculates about Dean's business dealings and his playboy lifestyle.

I want to scream.

Because I've seen him sit up all night with a sick child curled against his chest. I've seen him kiss scraped knees and burn his fingers making pancakes shaped like dinosaurs. I've seen him be *more* than enough.

I clench my hands in my lap. Don't move. Don't blink. Just wait.

When it's Dean's turn to speak, he rises slowly. His lawyer doesn't need to prompt him. He's not a man who performs. He's a man who tells the truth.

"I didn't ask for any of this," he says quietly. "But that doesn't make me less of a father."

His voice is low and steady. There's a rawness to it like he's pulled every word from deep inside. "I'm not perfect. God knows I've made mistakes. But those kids? They're my life. They were my sister's life. They are my every morning, every night, every in-between moment. And I will fight like hell to keep them safe."

There's a silence in the room when he finishes. A stillness that feels almost sacred.

He sits again, not looking back.

And then, I stand.

"Ma'am?" the judge asks, lifting one brow in a mixture of curiosity and warning.

I clear my throat. "My name is Lila Wright. I'm not family. I'm not here on behalf of the petitioner or the defense, but I work for CBC Nanny Services that Mr. Harrington hired. I've been living with Dean and the children for the past few months. I've seen the reality behind the accusations."

The judge hesitates, then nods once. "You may proceed."

I walk to the front, my heart thudding so loudly I'm sure everyone can hear it. But when I start speaking, my voice doesn't shake.

"Oliver and Evelyn are happy," I say. "They are loved. They are safe and well-transitioned. Not because of money. Not because of location or structure or anything else the petitioner has claimed is lacking. But because of Dean."

I glance over at him. His jaw is tight. His eyes are locked on mine.

"I have watched that man give every piece of himself to those children. He makes sure Evelyn's night-light doesn't flicker because she's scared of the dark. He plays baseball in the backyard with Oliver even when he's dead tired from work. He shows up for them—*every* single day. And if this court is trying to determine what kind of parent he is, then let me be clear: he's the kind every child deserves."

When I sit back down, I feel Dean watching me, but I don't turn. I just breathe. And I wait.

The judge calls for a recess. When she returns, her verdict is swift. The petition is denied.

Dean's father storms out before the gavel even falls. His lawyer doesn't meet anyone's eyes. The judge offers a tight nod, and then it's done. Just like that, it's over.

But what settles over the room isn't relief. Not yet. It's the weight of *finally.*

Dean rises slowly. His attorney claps him on the back, and papers shuffle around them. But all he does is look at me. And then he's in front of me, his arms pulling me close, his hand cupping the back of my head like he's afraid I might vanish.

He doesn't say thank you. He doesn't need to. His silence says it all.

The courthouse doors close behind us with a definitive thud, sealing away the tension and uncertainty that had filled the room moments before. The sun outside is blinding, a stark contrast to the dim interior we've just left. I blink against the light as the reality of what transpired slowly settles in.

Dean walks beside me, his hand finding mine with a familiarity that sends a comforting warmth through me. Neither of us speaks; words feel inadequate to capture the whirlwind of emotions swirling within us. Relief, gratitude, and a lingering apprehension intertwine, creating a tapestry of feelings.

We reach his sports car, and he opens the passenger door for me, his gaze meeting mine with an intensity that makes my breath hitch. "Thank you," he says, his voice low and earnest.

I shake my head, a soft smile playing on my lips. "You don't have to thank me. I was exactly where I needed to be. My mom dropped me off after grabbing the kids. You should know she and my dad both wanted to be here."

He nods, closing the door gently before walking around to the driver's side. As he starts the engine, a comfortable silence envelops us, the kind that speaks volumes without uttering a single word.

The drive back to his house is quiet. The hum of the engine and the rhythmic passing of trees are the only sounds accompanying us. I steal glances at him, noting that his jaw is no longer clenched and the tension in his shoulders has eased. He's still processing, but there's a newfound lightness to him.

Upon arriving, the familiar sight of the house brings a sense of calm. The kids are at their favorite place, the farm, and the house is momentarily still. We enter and Dean heads straight to the kitchen, pulling out two glasses and pouring us each a drink.

He hands me a glass, our fingers brushing briefly, sending a jolt of electricity up my arm. We sit at the kitchen island, the sunlight streaming through the windows casting a gilded glow over everything.

"I was terrified," he admits, breaking the silence. "The thought of losing them… it was unbearable."

I reach across the counter, placing my hand over his. "But you didn't. You fought for them, and you won. They know how much you love them."

He nods, his eyes meeting mine. "I couldn't have done it without you."

I squeeze his hand gently. "You were never alone in this." I don't even have to tell him that the entire town signed a petition for Dean to keep the kids. I had a backup plan.

We sit in silence for a moment, sipping our drinks as the weight of the day's events gradually lift. The front door opening signals the kids' return, their laughter and chatter filling the house.

Evelyn runs into the kitchen, her eyes lighting up when she sees me. "Lila!" she exclaims, throwing her arms around me.

I hug her tightly, my heart swelling with love. "Hey, sweetheart. How was the day with Ms. Claire?"

"Good! We painted butterflies!" she says excitedly, pulling away to show me her paint-splattered hands, then immediately hugging my mom.

Oliver enters next, a shy smile on his face. "Hi, Lila."

"Hi, Oliver," I reply, ruffling his hair affectionately. "Did you have a good day?"

He nods, his eyes flicking to his father. "Dad, is everything okay?"

I cover my smile with my hand. Hearing the kids call him dad never fails to send my heart galloping, just like I know it does for Dean.

Dean kneels, pulling both kids into a hug. "Everything's perfect," he says, his voice thick with emotion. "We're all together, and that's all that matters."

The kids beam, their innocence and joy a balm to the day's earlier stress. We spend the rest of the afternoon in the backyard, the sun casting long shadows as it begins its descent. The children play, their laughter echoing, while Dean and I sit on the deck, watching them with contentment.

As evening falls, we prepare dinner together, the kitchen filled with the comforting aromas of home-cooked food. The kids chatter about their day, their stories animated and full of wonder.

After dinner, we settle in the living room, the soft glow of the fireplace casting a warm light. Evelyn curls up in my lap, her eyes heavy with sleep, while Oliver leans against his father, a book open in his hands.

Dean reads aloud, his voice steady and soothing, the words weaving a tapestry of imagination and dreams. I watch him, my heart full, knowing that this is where I belong.

Later, after the kids are tucked into bed, we find ourselves back on the deck, the night air cool and crisp. The stars twinkle above, a silent witness to our shared peace.

The evening air is warm and thick with the scent of cut grass and grilled food. It clings to my skin in the most familiar way like childhood summers and everything good that ever came with them.

I'm sitting on the porch swing, legs tucked under me, a glass of wine balanced on one thigh, gazing out onto the bay, watching the water ebb and flow with the tide. Something is sacred about this slice of life. Something that feels like it should be wrapped in glass and protected.

I look over at Dean, and our eyes catch for just a moment. It's not long, but it's enough to send my heart skittering against my ribs like it's never learned rhythm. He still wants me. After everything. He sits beside me. The air between us is full of everything we haven't said yet.

"I meant it," I say after a long beat. "What I said in court."

He turns toward me slowly. "I know."

My eyes find his. "I didn't say it for show. Or because I wanted to be the hero. I said it because I believe it. Because I've seen it."

"I know," he says again, voice rough. "You didn't have to speak up. But you did."

Dean looks at me like I'm standing on the edge of something. Something wide and terrifying and beautiful.

And then I lean forward.

"I love you," I whisper, like it's the first time I've said it. It's not the first time I've said it to a man, but it's the first time it feels like enough.

He pulls me into him slowly, carefully, like I might vanish if he moves too fast.

"I love you too," he murmurs against my hair.

And for the first time in a long time, love doesn't feel like a risk. It feels like a promise.

I don't know how long we stay like that on the porch. The wine is forgotten beside us, the cicadas fading into the background. All I can hear is the sound of his breathing and the steady beat of his heart pressed against my cheek. For a moment, it feels like time has folded in on itself—like the heartbreak, the uncertainty, the empty spaces I left behind have been smoothed over.

But I know better. I've lived long enough to understand that love isn't the absence of pain. It's the decision to stay even when it hurts. To fight even when you're tired.

And I think—no, I know—that Dean's patience did just that.

"I meant what I said," he tells me, his voice barely above a whisper. "When I said I loved you. I meant it then. I mean it now. I'll mean it tomorrow."

I tilt my head just enough to look up at him. "You didn't hesitate."

"Didn't have to."

A beat of silence passes before I say, "I did. I hesitated. I left."

"And you came back."

Those words undo me. My throat bobs as I swallow, and my breath hitches in my chest. "I thought I had to choose between the life I planned and the life I wanted."

He slides a hand up to my cheek and brushes his thumb over my skin. "And now?"

"Now I know the life I want is here."

God help me, I don't think I've ever said words that struck deeper. I want him to scoop me into his arms and carry me through every room in this house—building a home in every corner of it. Instead, he presses a kiss to my forehead, trying to anchor the storm of feelings surging through me.

"You want to stay up?" he asks. "We can sit out here for a while."

I shake my head, eyes warm and tired. "No. I want to go to bed."

My heart thuds a little harder in my chest. He nods slowly and reaches for my hand.

We walk inside together. No words. Just the rhythm of our steps on old wood, the soft creak of the door, and the weight of everything we're trying to say without saying it yet.

In the bedroom, he watches as I slip out of my sundress. Not like it's a performance. More like I'm shedding the weight of the day. I grab one of Dean's old T-shirts from the dresser, the one I used to steal when I first moved in and pulls it over my head. It falls to my thighs, swallowing me up in something that feels like us.

Dean strips off his shirt and jeans, then climbs into bed beside me. The lights are off, the room bathed in moonlight filtering through the blinds. He reaches for my hand under the blanket, and I tangle my fingers with his.

"I was afraid," I say softly.

"I know."

"I didn't think I could trust myself to want something good."

"You can."

I turn to face him, our noses almost touching. "What if I mess it up again?"

He shakes his head. "Then we figure it out. Together."

And that's when I kiss him. Not like the sweet and tentative porch kiss. This one is deeper. Hungrier. My fingers slip into his hair, pulling him closer, and he groans against my lips because nothing has ever felt this right.

He pulls me into him, his hands tracing the curve of my waist through the fabric of my shirt. My breath catches when he presses me down gently against the mattress, his body settling over mine like we were made to fit this way.

I don't rush him. And he doesn't rush me. We take our time rediscovering each other in touches and whispered promises. This isn't just about heat. It's about healing. It's about belonging.

Later, when we're both wrapped in the quiet hum of each other's presence, my head resting on his chest, he runs his fingers through my hair and says, "I want more of this."

I hum. "What part?"

"All of it. Mornings. Bedtime stories. Arguments over grocery lists. I want every damn ordinary moment if it means I get to have them with you."

I press a kiss to his ribs. "Then we'll build that. Together."

I fall asleep holding his hand.

Chapter Twenty-seven

Lila

The email stares back at me like it knows every secret I've tried to bury.

The cursor blinks beside my message, a quiet pulse that mirrors the rhythm in my chest. I've typed the words at least six times now, maybe more, and deleted them just as quickly. Not because I don't know what I want. But because admitting it, putting it in writing, and pressing send… makes it real.

Fully funded. Prestigious. Career-defining.

The kind of opportunity that people fight their whole lives to get. The kind of dream that used to keep me up at night with excitement and hunger. That glittery version of success I used to chase like it could save me from myself.

And now?

Now it feels like an echo of someone I used to be. Especially with the news of the Hoolihans trial gaining worldwide coverage. Marin made sure the family would be locked away for a very long time. She hasn't needed my deposition so far, but I'm certain it's coming. And I'm ready. With Dean by my side, I'm prepared for anything.

I hover the mouse over the send button one last time, my other hand resting lightly on the kitchen counter where Evelyn's butterfly jar sits beside the toaster. I glance at the pale green chrysalis hanging from the twig, still and silent, holding its breath like me.

Maybe we're both about to break free.

With a soft exhale, I click.

Thank you for the opportunity, but I respectfully decline.

The moment the message disappears from my screen, something inside me exhales. Something deep and tight and aching. Like I've finally loosened the last knot tethering me to the life I thought I needed in order to be worthy.

My phone buzzes before I can even take a sip of my now-cold coffee. I don't have to check the screen to know who it is.

Ashvi:
So??

Lila:
I turned it down. Officially.

Ashvi:
HOLY SHIT.

You just broke up with a prestigious fellowship. How do you feel?

Lila:
Lighter.

Ashvi:

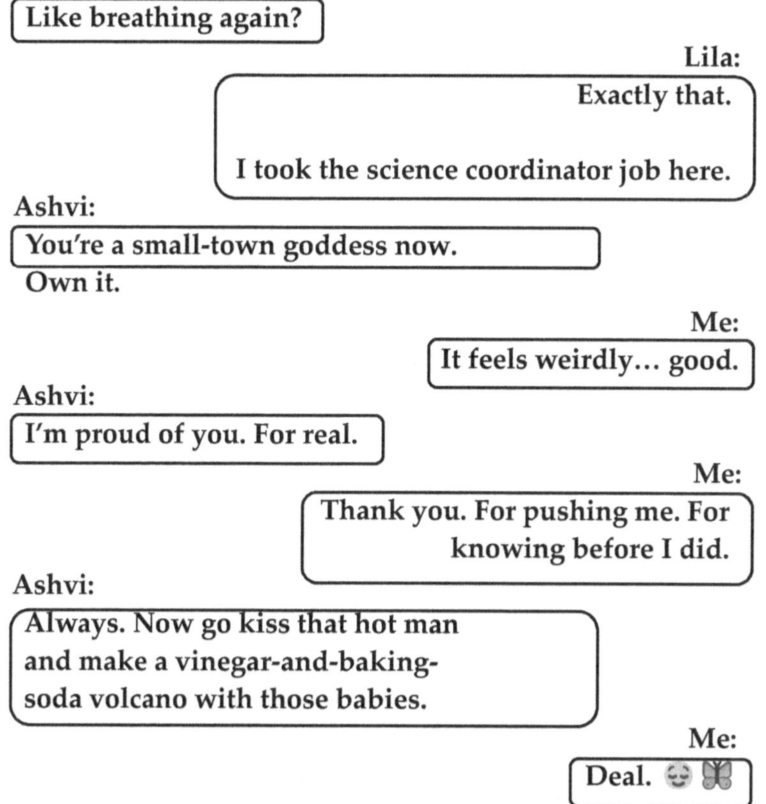

I smile and set my phone aside, letting the silence of the house settle around me like a soft quilt. It's the kind of quiet that only comes in the pause between big choices and bigger beginnings, the kind that feels like peace.

The butterfly jar on the windowsill catches my eye again.

But this time, something's different. The chrysalis is cracking.

I lean closer, holding my breath, and watch as the delicate shell begins to peel away. One wing, still crumpled and damp, pushes through the opening, followed by another.

"Evelyn!" I call, voice barely above a whisper but loud enough to send her little feet pounding through the hallway. "Come quick, sweetheart."

She barrels into the kitchen seconds later, curls bouncing, cheeks flushed. "Is it happening?!"

I nod, crouching to her level. "Just in time."

We sit on the floor together, shoulder to shoulder, watching in awe as the butterfly slowly emerges, stretching its wings wide under the filtered morning light. Monarch orange. Veined in black. Fragile and fierce.

"It's beautiful," she whispers, eyes wide.

"So are you," I whisper back, brushing a strand of hair behind her ear, swallowing the emotion that swells too fast to contain.

She looks up at me with that gap-toothed smile I swear could light a thousand rooms, and something inside me just settles. Clicks into place like it was always meant to be here.

"Can we let her go now?" she asks, eyes still on the butterfly.

"Not yet. Her wings need time to dry." I press a gentle kiss to the top of her head. "But soon."

Later that afternoon, I'm outside, barefoot on the back deck, watching Oliver and Evelyn chase each other through the grass with plastic swords and a jar of bubble solution that's already half empty. The sky is the most perfect blue, like it was painted just for us.

Dean steps outside, wiping his hands on a dish towel. His shirt clings to him in all the right places, hair a little damp, as if he just stepped out of the shower. He doesn't say anything, just watches me for a second. Like he's trying to figure out if I'm real or just another thing he's scared to lose.

"You look like someone who just conquered the world," he says finally, his voice low and warm.

I lift a shoulder. "Maybe I did."

He walks toward me, stops just shy of touching, like he's asking without words. I lean into him, fitting under his arm like I belong there. Because I do.

"You're quiet," he murmurs.

I hum. "I turned it down."

"The lab?"

I nod.

His silence stretches long, but not heavy. Just thoughtful. Then he lets out a slow breath. "Are you okay?"

"I am," I say truthfully. "I thought I'd feel lost without it. But instead… I feel found."

He looks down at me, something bright flickering in his eyes. "You don't need it to be extraordinary. You already are."

I press my forehead to his chest, breathing him in—cedar, summer, home. He tilts my chin up with one finger and then he kisses me. Soft and slow. Like a promise and a prayer all wrapped into one.

That evening, we gather around the quilt in the backyard. A picnic dinner spread between us, the kids catching butterflies and pretending they're wizards in a magical forest. Evelyn darts back to the deck, holding up the jar with the butterfly, now dry and ready.

"Can we let her go now?" she asks, eyes round and reverent.

I nod, standing beside her.

Dean moves to my other side, one hand resting gently on the small of my back. "Want to do the honors?" he asks softly.

Evelyn nods and opens the lid slowly, carefully. For a beat, nothing happens, then, with one delicate flutter, the butterfly takes flight, rising into the golden dusk like she knows exactly where she's going.

The kids cheer.

Dean leans in, whispering, "She found her wings."

"Yeah," I say, heart full to bursting. "She really did."

And I know we weren't just talking about the butterfly. We were talking about me.

The sun dips lower, casting orange hues across the backyard as the scent of grilled meat and sizzling corn wafts through the air. Oliver's and Evelyn's laughter rings out as they chase fireflies, their bare feet dancing across the grass. I sit on the quilt, a glass of sweet tea in hand, watching the scene unfold with a heart full of contentment.

Dean approaches, a soft smile playing on his lips. He settles beside me, his presence warm and grounding.

"You did something brave today," he says, his voice low and sincere.

I glance at him, the weight of the day's decision settling in.

He reaches out, his fingers intertwining with mine. "Are you sure about this? The job, staying here… me?"

I turn to face him fully, searching his eyes. "I'm sure. For the first time in a long time, I'm not running toward something that looks good on paper. I'm standing still, choosing what feels right in my bones."

He leans in, pressing a gentle kiss to my forehead. "That's all I've ever wanted—for you to choose it. Not because of me."

I smile, my heart swelling. "It's not because of you. It's because of me. And them. And the way this town, this house, this life makes me feel like the best version of myself."

We sit in comfortable silence, watching the children twirl and laugh. Realizing that this place, this man, these children didn't just fill the cracks. They made something entirely new. Something stronger. I'm not running anymore. I'm rooted. And as the wind shifts and a butterfly lifts into the sky, free and sure, I know the truth deep in my bones. This is not the end. This is where everything begins.

Epilogue

Dean

Ferris wheels and sticky fingers. Glow-in-the-dark bracelets wrapped around Evelyn's wrist like treasure. Oliver with cotton candy smeared across his face, grinning like he's just seen an actual member of *Paw Patrol.*

This is what summer looks like now.

The town fair lights up the skyline, all oversized bulbs and childhood wonder. It's loud and chaotic in that beautiful, small-town way where everyone knows everyone, and no one's ever really lost. Music drifts from the speakers above the games booths, a sugary pop tune echoing against the rustle of the midway. The scent of kettle corn, fried dough, and freshly squeezed lemonade weaves through the air like a memory you want to bottle and keep.

Lila stands a few feet ahead of me, holding two lemonades in her hands, her laugh catching in the air as Evelyn tugs her toward the carousel. Her hair's in a ponytail, her cheeks flushed from the heat, and I swear I've never seen anyone look more like home.

"Daddy, watch!" Oliver calls, hurling a baseball at the tin can pyramid with surprising strength for his size. He misses the first two throws, then knocks them all over with a loud clang on the third. A small stuffed bear lands in his hands a moment later. His grin is all pride and sugar.

He runs back with a balloon in one hand and the bear in the other. "Dad! Look what I won!" It still feels surreal for the kids to call me Dad and Lila Mom, but to them, that's what we are and I accept the title with such an honor I never knew I wanted.

I crouch down to take it. "You throw those baseballs like a champ."

He beams. Lila hands me a lemonade, and her fingers linger on mine. There's a moment, small, quiet, but it catches something deep inside me. The world slows for half a heartbeat.

I'm so in love with her. Madly. Entirely. Unequivocally.

We ride the Ferris wheel just before sunset. Oliver insists on going with Evelyn, and Ashvi dons her aunt honors and joins them, so Lila and I end up in the next car. The wind moves through her hair, and the whole world seems to pause as we rise above the fair.

The sky is streaked with orange and lavender, painting everything below in a warm, forgiving light. I glance over and catch her watching the horizon, one hand resting gently on the metal railing. There's a quiet peace in her expression, the kind that only comes after the storms have passed.

"Did you ever think this would be your life?" she asks, head leaning on my shoulder.

"No," I admit. "But I think I always hoped for it. Even when I didn't believe I deserved it."

She lifts her head and looks at me, eyes steady. "You deserve all of it. You always did."

I hesitate. My heart's hammering. The small velvet box in my pocket suddenly feels like it weighs ten pounds.

When we reach the top, I shift slightly, taking the box out of my pocket. Her brow furrows.

"Dean—"

"I've loved you since the first time you spoke about *Fast and the Furious* on the flight to Scotland. Since the night you held Evelyn while she cried. Since every skinned knee you mended and every time you stayed when it would've been easier to walk."

Her eyes are wide, shimmering.

I twist, careful on the tiny metal bench, and open the box.

"I want all of it. The chaos. The quiet. The peanut butter on the couch cushions and science experiments in the bathtub. I want to write you letters when you don't expect them and take you to any place in the world. I want you, Lila Wright. Every version. Will you marry me?"

Her hands fly to her mouth. She nods so fast, tears streaking down her cheeks. "Yes. Yes, of course."

I slide the ring on her finger just as the Ferris wheel dips back down into the multicolored light.

The second the Ferris wheel jolts to a stop and we climb out of the gondola, Lila's hand still tucked securely in mine, ring glinting like it belongs there, I swear my chest could split open from how hard my heart is pounding.

That was it. The moment. The question I've been aching to ask, and she said yes. A breathless, tearful, yes.

Lila barely has time to step down before Evelyn barrels through the crowd, pink-stained face beaming from adrenaline. Oliver follows close behind. Ashvi slows her walk behind him, observing them at a distance.

I glance at Lila just in time to see her face crack into the softest smile, one that settles deep in my bones. "We got engaged," she says, voice hushed but certain. "Your dad asked me to marry him."

Evelyn gasps so loudly a couple by the lemonade stand turns to look. "We're getting married?"

I kneel to her level, pressing a hand to her tiny shoulder. "Well, technically it's just me and Lila, baby girl. But you're a part of it, too. Always."

She squeals and throws herself into Lila's arms. "Can I wear a dress?"

"You can wear *two*." Lila laughs, spinning her in a little circle. God, I love them both more than I know how to say.

And then, like a freight train of glitter and noise, Ashvi finally catches up. She halts just feet away, eyes bouncing from Lila to the ring and back again.

"Wait. Wait. What?!" she shouts, hands flailing. "You got *engaged*?!"

Lila ducks her head, but there's no hiding her glow. "Yeah. It just… happened. At the top."

"I've been wrangling this duo, and you were out here getting *proposed to* on the Ferris wheel?!"

"She said yes," I add, uselessly.

Ashvi barrels into Lila with a squeal so loud I think I lose hearing in one ear. "You're getting married. *You're getting married!*"

Lila's laughing and holding Evelyn in one arm and hugging her best friend with the other, and I swear I could live in this moment forever. Pure chaos and absolute perfection.

But then Ashvi turns on me.

"You." She stabs a finger into my chest. "You better treat her like she hung the damn moon. She's not just the smart girl or the beautiful one. She's the whole freaking galaxy. And if you ever hurt her, I'll curse your Wi-Fi and hex your shampoo."

"I believe you," I say seriously even though a chuckle is working its way up. "And I plan on treating her like the marvel she is, every single day."

She nods once, satisfied, then turns back to Lila and grabs her hand, inspecting the ring. "Oh, this is so you. Understated, timeless, deceptively sparkly."

Lila rolls her eyes, but her voice is soft when she says, "I still can't believe it's real."

Ashvi brushes a tear from her cheek, smiling like a proud parent. "You deserve every second of this, Lil. I knew from that first week, when you panic called me because you were moving in with a stranger, you were already halfway gone. Oh my gosh, your family is going to flip!"

I glance at Lila, and her eyes meet mine across the space. There's no hesitation anymore. Just warmth. Certainty. And something deeper than all of it—love.

A love that takes root quietly and then blooms all at once.

Oliver squints at the oversized ring on Lila's finger. "Is that a real diamond?"

"Real as it gets," I say. "What do you think?"

He shrugs, but he's smiling. "Cool. Do I have to wear a penguin costume?"

"No. You can wear a cape if you want," Lila says, laughing.

We spend the next hour indulging every whim: a second round of cotton candy, another ride on the Tilt-A-Whirl, even the dunk tank where Rowan volunteers as the local hero. Evelyn throws her ball and misses by a mile, but Rowan plays along, and the entire booth cheers like she knocked him into the water herself. Rowan winks at her behind the splash, though I don't miss his narrowed eyes when they clock in on Lila's new accessory.

A pair of teenagers offer to snap a photo for us in front of the fair sign, and I say yes before I can overthink it. We pose with the kids, Lila between us, the flash capturing our joy in a frame I'll carry in my wallet for the rest of my life.

As we wander through the midway again, we pass a neighbor I barely know. She pauses, glancing between the kids and me, and then at Lila.

"Aren't you the nanny?" she asks, voice syrupy with judgment.

I don't even blink. I wrap my arm around Lila and kiss her temple. "She's my everything."

The woman blinks, startled. "Oh. Well… congratulations."

We keep walking.

The lights dance across the pavement. Evelyn squeals when she sees a cart selling glow-in-the-dark necklaces, and Oliver tugs at my hand, begging for one more ride.

I glance at Lila, and she just nods. "Go."

Later, when we're home, and the kids are in bed, she sits on the porch swing, one leg curled beneath her. I hand her a cup of tea and sit beside her. The mug warms her hands, and the sound of frogs and crickets fills the silence between us.

She turns toward me, her fingers brushing my jaw. "That was perfect."

"It was you," I say. "You make everything feel like that."

Her smile is soft. "I don't need a big wedding. Or a fancy plan. I just want what we already have."

I lace my fingers through hers. "We've got a lifetime to build it, any way we want."

She leans her head against my shoulder. We sit like that for a long while, the porch creaking gently under our weight, the stars blinking above us. The warmth of her pressed against my side is better than any blanket. The quiet peace of knowing she's mine now? That's the stuff no amount of money or legacy could buy.

"I used to think happy endings were only in books," she whispers.

"This doesn't feel like an ending," I say. "More like chapter one."

She laughs quietly. "Yeah. The real beginning."

Inside the house, one of Evelyn's drawings flutters slightly in the breeze from an open window. It's a crooked heart with all our names scrawled inside it. I catch sight of it and smile.

We sit in silence, but it's the kind that says everything. We found a way through the grief, through the ache. While what we made is not perfect, it's ours. Something worth holding on to.

Holding her hand beneath the fading twilight, I think back to that first flight when everything in my life was about boardrooms and bank accounts. I never thought family would be the thing that gave me purpose and not numbers or power. But then she sat across from me, and everything changed. Turns out, love didn't clip my wings. It gave me a reason to land.

Stay in Touch

Newsletter: http://bit.ly/2WokAjS
Author Page: www.facebook.com/authorreneeharless
Reader Group: http://bit.ly/31AGa3B
Instagram: www.instagram.com/renee_harless
Bookbub: www.bookbub.com/authors/renee-harless
Goodreads: http://bit.ly/2TDagOn
Amazon: http://bit.ly/2WsHhPq
Website: www.reneeharless.com

Acknowledgments

No book is ever written alone, and this one is no exception.

To my family—thank you for your endless love, patience, and encouragement. You've cheered me on through every chapter, celebrated every small win, and reminded me why I do this in the first place. I'm forever grateful for your belief in me, even on the days when I doubted myself.

To my incredible editors, Nicole McCurdy and Jenny Sims—thank you for your sharp eyes, thoughtful feedback, and unwavering support. You helped shape this story into something better than I ever imagined. Your passion for storytelling pushed me to dig deeper and write more boldly.

To my proofreader, Crystal Burnette your attention to detail helped bring clarity to the final pages. Thank you for making sure this book left my hands clean and confident.

To my amazing alpha reader, Patricia. Thank you for being the very first to falling in love with these characters alongside me. Your feedback was crucial in the early stages, it kept me motivated.

And finally, to the readers—thank you for welcoming my stories into your hearts. It means more than words can say.

About the Author

Renee Harless is a *USA TODAY* bestselling romance writer with an affinity for wine and a passion for telling a good story.

Renee Harless, her husband, and children live in Blue Ridge Mountains of Virginia. She studied Communication, specifically Public Relations, at Radford University.

Growing up, Renee always found a way to pursue her creativity. It began by watching endless runs of White Christmas- yes even in the summer – and learning every word and dance from the movie. She could still sing "Sister Sister" if requested. In high school, she joined the show choir and a community theatre group, The Troubadours. After marrying the man of her dreams and moving from her hometown she sought out a different artistic outlet – writing.

To say that Renee is a romance addict would be an understatement. When she isn't chasing her kids around the house, working her day job, or writing, she jumps head first into a romance novel.

www.ingramcontent.com/pod-product-compliance
Lightning Source LLC
Chambersburg PA
CBHW061046310726
48969CB00004B/1096